Eleven Hours to Murder

ALSO BY D.B. BORTON

THE CAT CALIBAN MYSTERIES

Eleven Hours to Murder

D.B. BORTON

JOFFE BOOKS

Joffe Books, London
www.joffebooks.com

First published in Great Britain in 2025

Cover art by Dee Dee Book Covers

ISBN: 978-1-80573-307-2

To Skip Smith,
who has kept my little financial boat afloat for decades
with patience and humor,
and in memory of
Maureen Wood,
stalwart feminist and Northside community activist

CHAPTER 1

Blood hammered my eardrums. Sweat tickled the back of my neck like a spider's caress. The soles of my feet vibrated. The light in the room shifted subtly as feathery clots of snow drifted silently past the window. My breath caught as I reached out a hand and pressed the button.

$2,863.27.

Damn.

I stared at the numbers on the page before me as they blurred and melted. I blinked.

I would not cry.

A dark hand descended into my field of vision and covered the page.

Startled, I looked up to see another hand moving toward me. Then I was unplugged and the sound rushed in — the rhythmic crash of drums coming up from the basement; a mellow, sinuous horn from overhead; a swell of organ from across the hall; and a rough voice fighting to be heard from a distance.

Another voice — closer, louder, insistent — coming from the man who was holding my earplug: Moses Fogg, retired cop, friend, tenant, and business partner in Fogg and Caliban Investigations. "Cat, I been trying to get your attention."

I pulled myself up from the sinkhole of my despair and remembered: the Battle of the Bands had come to the Catatonia Arms.

It had all started with Leon Jakes, the neighborhood's leading teen entrepreneur and a pal of ours. His latest project involved the rehab of a building on Hamilton Avenue, which ran through the middle of the business district in Northside and connected our neighborhood with Clifton to the south and College Hill to the north. The new owner intended to restore the site to its former glory days as a popular music venue. The Park Theater building had undergone many transformations since it had opened its doors in 1913, both before and after its brief ascension to national prominence for the quality of the bands and individual performers it booked as Northside Park. My tenant Kevin O'Neill, a fountain of fascinating trivia, had told me that in its longtime incarnation as the Alpha Theater, it had first specialized in adult films and later in more highbrow — but not necessarily less risqué — "art films." Most recently, it had served as a bakery. I assumed that Leon had been hired to help clean the sugar and confetti sprinkles off the floors and paint the walls, not to rewire the building or upgrade the plumbing. But in the process of cleaning the place out, someone had found a complete drum set in a storage closet and bestowed it on Leon. He was thrilled.

Our erstwhile paper girl, Hope Smith — now playing in a successful all-girl band — had offered to give him lessons on the drums. Unfortunately, there was no place in the Jakes house to set them up. Leon's three older brothers had colonized the basement with weights and exercise equipment they were unwilling to move out, even though they no longer lived at home. And when I recalled the basement of my former family home in the suburbs, I imagined the basement in the Jakes' modest house similarly crammed with the excess baggage of five family members. Leon's newly rebuilt storage shed was stuffed with the tools of his many trades, not to mention the god-awful greeting cards he peddled, and the overflow

3

rubbed elbows with two cars, one functional and one not, in the Jakes' garage.

That's how we came to be hosting a drum lesson in our basement.

In my previous career as a suburban housewife, I'd frequently been called upon to negotiate agreements between family members that could rival the Camp David Accords in complexity, not to mention emotional intensity, so this was one skill I'd carried over into my new career as landlady and private investigator. In fact, motherhood had prepared me well to run a small apartment building; though relations were generally amicable, there were minor eruptions within my new family at times and they weren't always predictable.

Moses, whose bike repair equipment took up more space in the basement than anything else, had been surprisingly receptive to the idea.

'Some folks been talking about starting up a little jazz band," he'd said, looking thoughtful. "If we had drums set up down there, we could maybe use it for a practice space."

You might not think that cops, even retired cops, would be musical. "I didn't know you played the drums," I'd said.

"Not me. I play the horn. George the one play the drums. No way Delia gonna let him set up the drums at his house."

So that was one tenant down. Melanie Carter and Alice Rosenberg, who lived in the apartment above Kevin's, had a reputation to uphold as patrons of the arts, since Mel was a potter as well as a martial artist. I worried that Al, an attorney for Legal Aid, would want a contract covering hours of practice, decibel levels, and so on, but they were buffered from basement noise by Kevin's apartment and inclined to be magnanimous.

"Sure," Al said. "Mel can lug their equipment for them when they go on tour. And provide security."

"How long do we think it will take for Leon to become bored with this?" Mel asked. "I need to be starting seeds down there in March. I don't need that much space, but I don't know what the racket will do to the seedlings."

I was pretty sure that my two cats, Sophie and Sadie, would have voted paws down on the proposal to disrupt their naps with loud, obnoxious noises, so I didn't consult them. Our two wild animals, on the other hand — Moses's beagle, Winnie, and her sidekick, my small, black feline hellraiser Sidney, were all in.

Kevin O'Neill, bartender and resident with the longest tenure at the Catatonia Arms, was the toughest sell, not only because he worked late and slept late, but also because he was on the ground floor. I took Leon with me to ask him.

He had not looked pleased. He frowned at me. "Why does it have to be drums? Why couldn't it be something softer and sweeter, like a flute? Why couldn't he take flute lessons?"

Leon shrugged. "Ain't nobody never g-g-give me no f-flute," he said reasonably. "'Sides, I like the d-drums."

In the end, Kevin had capitulated, though I suspected that he, like Mel, was hoping for a quick disillusionment on Leon's part. But Leon wasn't a quitter, as indicated by his long-term commitment to becoming a detective and his long-standing role as my operative.

As for me, my hair was already white and so short that I doubted it could be curled by a little drumming in the vicinity. My eardrums were another matter — hence the earplugs.

Today was Leon's first lesson. To drown it out, everyone was playing music but me. Until Moses had unplugged me, I had been cocooned in silence, alone with my misery.

Now Moses nodded at the papers on my desk. "How's it going?"

"I've added these goddamned numbers five times and gotten five different results. It's hopeless. I started early, but I'm already watching the deadline slip away."

"You ought to let your cousin Delbert teach you how to do your taxes on the computer. I'll bet he can set it up so all you have to do is type in the numbers and push a button. That's what I hear, anyway. No need to make yourself miserable, Cat. This is 1988. You ought to move with the times."

We both looked at the machine I was trying to ignore, even though it occupied most of the space on my desk. My cousin Delbert had tried to drag me into the digital age by purchasing and installing a shitload of equipment while my back was turned and I'd been working around it ever since.

"This from the guy who can't figure out his answering machine," I grumbled. "You're hardly an appropriate spokesperson for advanced electronics. Anyway, why were you trying to get my attention?"

"We got a client. That's what I came to tell you."

A rumble started up from the basement — a drum roll.

I looked down at the numbers littering my desk.

"A paying one?"

"Didn't say he wasn't."

The drums crescendoed, cymbals crashed.

I smiled.

Then a series of sonic booms erupted, and I winced. "Where are the animals?"

"I'm keeping them upstairs to save their hearing. The ones with taste are in my apartment, grooving to Dizzy and Charlie."

Those would be the older cats, Sadie and Sophie, who were probably curled up in a closet.

"Winnie and Sidney are hanging out at Al and Mel's. I guess they dig Janis Joplin."

"Well," I said, "every family needs a rebel."

CHAPTER 2

"Tell me something about our client." I had a death grip on the armrest in the pre-crash position I always assumed when Moses was piloting the Fairlane. He hurtled through the stop sign at Spring Grove with the casual confidence of an ex-cop who never expected to be arrested and I reflected that if we were going to be flattened by a semi, this would make a convenient spot, with the vast expanse of Spring Grove Cemetery to our left.

"His name's Matt Perle, but he mostly goes by Perley. He's a Vietnam vet, joined the force as soon as he got out of the service — Marines, I think. Took early retirement last year to help out with the family business, so I'm told."

"Which is?"

"Perle Electric — big electrical contractor. You see their signs on construction sites."

"Yeah, that sounds familiar. So, what does he want from us?"

"It's an old missing persons case. Wants us to find out what happened to his sixteen-year-old sister. She went missing in the summer of '69."

"Summer of '69? That's almost twenty years ago. How cold can a case get? Does he really think we can find her after all this time?"

"I think he knows what the odds are. If he doesn't, we'll tell him."

We slid through an orange light at Mitchell Avenue and headed for the Vine Street Hill Cemetery.

"Moses, you were already working Juvie in those days, weren't you? You remember what they were like. Hell, I remember what they were like, and it's a damn miracle my own daughter never went missing — at least, not past mealtime. Summer of '69? We're talking Woodstock, right? Around that time? If Franny's best friend had been willing to go with her, she would have gone for sure."

"Bella, too." He shook his head. "We just thanked our lucky stars she didn't have her driver's license yet."

"Did she have other siblings, this missing girl?"

"I don't know, but I think they're one of those big Catholic families, the Perles."

"Are the parents still alive?"

"Don't know."

He stopped for a light at Vine Street and I took a breath.

"So this girl — what's her name?"

"Leila. Leila Perle."

"So she just left the house one day and didn't come back?"

"Cat, you know as much as I do. We about to find out."

He careened into a U-turn, pulled up to the curb, and killed the engine.

"That's it there, across the street." He nodded at a big brick house with a large front yard and a lot of sidewalk to shovel.

I studied the house. It was one of those blocky brick houses from the teens or '20s with rows of windows on two floors and a dormer on the third, two chimneys, and a bay window visible at the side.

"If we don't think we can help him, we won't take his money, right?"

8

Moses was looking down at the car keys in his hand. "Cat, sometimes folks are satisfied knowing they did their best. We can go over the case, and even if we don't find anything new, we can maybe reassure him that everything that could be done was done. Could be that's all he's asking."

"So, you don't think we're going to find this missing girl after nineteen years?"

"I'm not optimistic."

Shortly afterward, we were seated in a living room old enough to be called a parlor, on a plaid couch that was not worn but well-used. Matt Perle sat on its twin opposite us, with a coffee table between us and floral armchairs on either side. The fabrics told me that Mrs. Perle, Matt's mother, was a practical woman. A Lego construction resembling a space station in one corner and a box overflowing with toys in another testified to the presence of children in the house, whether visiting or in residence, and Mrs. Perle had chosen upholstery fabrics that would hide spills, stains, and dirt. But were the heavy curtains closed for the same reason — to protect the fabric? The room was dim, lit only by a floor lamp a few yards away; the table lamps closest to us were off. Outside, the sun was blazing the way it often does in the aftermath of a snowstorm but you'd never know it from where we were sitting. A mantel clock ticked in the eerie silence. It could have been a house in mourning for a beloved child gone missing in the past months, not almost twenty years ago.

And yet, the space was filled with her presence. Above the mantel was a family portrait, a studio photograph showing a mother and father surrounded by six children, three girls and three boys. The two older boys looked to be in their teens, the oldest girl in her preteens, the other two girls under ten, and the toddler on his mother's lap, wearing a sailor suit and cap. But this was only the most prominent of the myriad of framed family photographs and snapshots covering the mantel and two end tables. Not that I could actually make out their subjects in this light.

Matt, a middle-aged man wearing a faded Reds baseball cap, turned his head to follow my gaze, squinting as if trying to see the photograph from my perspective. He wore jeans and a turtleneck that didn't conceal broad shoulders and a thick neck. The skin on his rather flat face looked weathered, as if he'd once spent time in the sun, but its pallor better matched the silent dimness of the house.

"Yeah," he said, "that's the full orchestra, so to speak. That's us."

"Orchestra?" I assumed he was joking but wanted to make sure.

"Well, yeah. Or more likely, a marching band, with my father as drum major. Our job was to follow him, respond to all his directions, and make him look good. But there was always a straggler or two — somebody with a different destination or no destination at all. We drove him crazy and most of the time, we weren't even trying."

He laid another photograph down on the coffee table so Moses and I could see it. "This is the last picture I have before Leila disappeared — I mean, the last one taken of all of us." Moses and I leaned forward to look. "It wasn't that easy to get all of us together at that point, not least because Leila wasn't speaking to half of us. But we took a family vacation up to Put-in-Bay that last Christmas and this was the result."

"May I?" I leaned over and switched on the nearest table lamp without waiting for permission. I thought he flinched slightly, but he said nothing.

The photo showed a family group seated at a table in a restaurant, a passing waiter caught turned in the direction of the camera as if he had been given a bit part in the family drama that was unfolding. The father glowered at the camera and the mother's smile didn't animate her face, as if she were playing by the rules of a game she had already walked out of. Both Matt and his older brother wore grimaces intended to pass as smiles. The older girl wore a faraway look on her face; she sat rigidly upright and stared at nothing. The next younger

10

girl wore a practiced expression of annoyance, boredom, and barely contained frustration that I recognized from my daughter Franny's teenage years, and it was this connection to Franny that encouraged me to conclude that she was our runaway, Leila. Her little sister wore an anxious frown, eyebrows colliding over eyes that had slued sideways to look at her sister. The youngest sibling frowned down at the tablecloth. No one had altered this photograph: no amount of retouching could transform this family into a happy one.

Matt smiled ruefully. "Probably tells you all you need to know about our family dynamic." He extended an index finger and placed it on each family member in turn. "My father Frank, who for two days has been watching his plans for a congenial family reunion going up in smoke. My mother Theresa, who's doing her best to pretend that it's not happening, and who is wondering whether it's time yet for her next tranquilizer. My brother Frank, Jr., who's irritated because he's stuck on an island and forced to play a part in the family hostilities when he'd rather be home working on his '57 Chevy. Me, Matt, who wants nothing more than to ditch this charade and go back to college to finish his senior year, at which point his life will belong to the Marines and his family won't have anything to say about it. My sister Mary, who is still toying with the idea of becoming a nun at this point and who is working on her out-of-body transportation skills. Like me, Mary is attracted to the idea of turning her life over to a higher power — one that outranks my father. My sister Leila, who is on strike against the injustices of the world as embodied by her parents, who are mean, authoritarian, stupid, square, crass, and heartless. My sister Katie, who takes Leila as her role model but hasn't yet acquired the willfulness and daring that entails. My little brother Timmy, the afterthought, doted on by everyone but too young to understand the emotional whirlwind surrounding him."

When we didn't comment, he went on quickly. "It's not that my father was an ogre, you understand, but everything was changing and he wasn't receptive to change. He would never have dared to challenge his own father the way we challenged him, especially Leila." He shrugged and gestured at Moses. "Well, you both know what I'm talking about. You were there. You especially, Moses. You probably spent most of your time in Juvie refereeing between kids and parents. Maybe you don't know what it's like to live with that at home, but it's exhausting."

"You sound like my wife," Moses said, shifting in his seat. "She always used to say she couldn't understand how I could work with kids all day and understand so little when it came to my own kids."

I had a shitload of experience in family skirmishes myself and could have said so, but I refrained. The old wounds still hurt sometimes, and besides, we weren't here to discuss my family problems.

Instead, I said, "Which of her siblings was Leila closest to?"

"I guess I'd say she was closest to Katie because they shared a room, but I'd also say that she wasn't particularly close to any of us that last summer. She was sixteen and thought she was grown up — too grown-up for Katie, who was only fourteen."

He seemed at this point to get derailed by memory, so I prompted him. "What happened that last summer?"

"She had started going to Northside Park on weekends during the school year that spring. You know what that was?"

Moses glanced at me and said, "We know something about it but why don't you tell us?"

I was taking notes in a small notebook, but Moses was relying on me and on his own memory developed over years of experience.

Matt shrugged. "I never went myself. It was kind of a gathering space for teenagers and a music venue all rolled into one. The guy that started it — I forget his name — really seemed committed to providing a safe space for teens, as well as a kind of midwestern mecca for the latest rock music. I gather that his lineup was impressive. And he didn't serve alcohol, since his target clientele was under twenty-one and he didn't need the hassle of constant police raids looking for underage drinkers. But as for the rest of it, I guess there was plenty of sex, drugs, and rock 'n' roll."

I was frowning. "How did she get there? Did she have a driver's license? Did she own a car at sixteen?" Both the size of the house and her family tie to Perle Electric told me she might have been given a car, but would a controlling father have encouraged that kind of independence? I didn't think so.

"She had a license, but no car," Matt said, nodding to acknowledge the reasonableness of the question. "She was saving up for one. Most of the time, she took the bus." He pointed. "It comes right down Mitchell here to Spring Grove, and right on into Northside, so it's an easy ride. But other times, she'd get a ride with someone, especially coming home, and especially after she started working at the Aquarius Coffeehouse, just down from Northside Park."

"When did that happen?" Moses asked.

"She started working weekends in May, then picked up more hours in June when school let out for the summer. My dad wanted us all to work — he didn't want us to rely on him for money — so he could hardly complain, even when she came home late and reeking of cigarette smoke. You might not think he'd notice that since he smoked himself, but it was hard to miss. I don't think he had a clear understanding of how many hours Leila was spending at Northside Park and how many at work and she was careful to muddy the distinction. At least, that's what I think. Most of what I'm telling you I got from my sisters and my mother later, except for what I observed during the week I spent at home after graduation and before my officer training started. I wasn't there that summer, you understand."

Moses leaned back and closed his eyes. "So, when you say 'sex, drugs, and rock 'n' roll'—"

"She got in with an older crowd. I guess she dumped her boyfriend. She spent a lot of time with musicians, and they were older than the teens in the audience. She was a musician herself, owned an acoustic guitar she took everywhere with her, like she was waiting for her big break, you know? She became kind of a groupie for some local bands, especially one called Wildfire — you heard of them? They never hit it really big, like the Allman Brothers, but I guess they were pretty successful for a while, and they were just breaking out that summer. They lived in a house in Clifton and apparently Leila spent some time there. That was one of the big revelations from the detective's report."

"This would be the police detective?" Moses asked.

He shook his head. "No, sorry, I haven't mentioned it yet. After Leila disappeared, maybe three weeks after, my father hired a private detective to look for her. I can give you his report. I never met him, but I read his report. Seemed pretty thorough to me." He looked at Moses. "Police detective was a guy named Jack Rausch — you know him? He'd retired by the time I joined the force, so he had plenty of experience when Leila disappeared, but he had his hands full."

Plenty of experience, I thought. Which is to say old. Like us.

Moses shook his head. "Don't know him, but I've heard of him."

"So, on the day Leila disappeared," I prompted him, "what happened?"

"Okay, right." He picked up a small piece of paper from the coffee table and frowned down at it. "So on Wednesday, August 13th, Leila went to work at the coffeehouse as usual, finished her shift at three in the afternoon, and walked out the door. We don't know where she went or who she saw between that time and Thursday night, when she got on a bus headed for Woodstock in Bethel, New York. We have a witness who talked to her on the bus, and she told him where she was going. After that, all we have are unconfirmed sightings. The detective wasn't able to find anyone who talked to her between Columbus, where the witness got off, and New

York — at least, nobody credible — and none of the local kids he found who attended the festival could remember seeing her there. Of course, most of them didn't know her and wouldn't have any reason to recognize her. And Hitchens — that's the private detective, Walter Hitchens — admitted that he didn't talk to every Cincinnati kid who attended the festival. He focused on kids who moved in the same circles — school, church, the Park, Aquarius. Nothing."

"How many people were at Woodstock?" I asked.

"Upwards of four hundred thousand. Some say five hundred thousand."

I resisted looking at Moses and he resisted looking at me. Needle in a haystack.

Matt was leaning over the coffee table now, offering us two more photographs.

"These are some closer shots of Leila. I thought you'd want them. My brother Timmy took them."

Moses laid them out on the coffee table in front of us. My breath caught.

Leila Perle was as pretty and as ordinary as any other sixteen-year-old. She was fresh-faced and bright-eyed, with a hunger for life and a hope for the future that no amount of acting would ever successfully conceal. One photograph looked down on her from a slight high angle as she sat at the kitchen table, looking up at the photographer in surprise but with a dawning humor, a smile just visible at the edges of her mouth. The other showed her in partial profile, bent over a guitar, mouth open as if singing, long strawberry-blonde tresses draped over the near shoulder. She was wearing makeup in this picture, which made her look older. Both photographs were slightly fuzzy and their colors faded.

I stopped my hand in the act of reaching out to touch her face. In my mind, I addressed her directly for the first time, but not the last: *Oh, honey, what happened to you?*

Finally, I spoke aloud. "How did the witness identify her — the man on the bus, I mean? Did she give him her name?"

Matt nodded. "She told him her name was Leila and she was wearing her necklace." He angled the kitchen table photograph toward himself, then back in our direction. "You can see it here. I gave it to her for her birthday and she wore it all the time."

The necklace was silver and spelled out "Leila" in script. The tiny dot over the *i* looked like a tiny diamond chip.

"She told him she was going to Woodstock and they chatted a little about music. Then he started reading and she looked out the window for the rest of the trip. He left the bus in Columbus. Hitchens checked him out. He was a medical student from Columbus with an internship at Cincinnati Children's Hospital going home for the weekend. Apparently, he went back and forth a lot, and he was just killing time at the station one night, drinking coffee and reading flyers, when he saw the one Hitchens had posted about Leila. Pretty damned miraculous Hitchens found him at all."

"Where was the bus headed?" I interjected. "You said Leila was headed for Bethel, New York, but the bus wouldn't take her all the way there, would it?"

Matt shook his head. "The bus was going to Cleveland. Leila could have taken it to Cleveland and then found an eastbound bus to take her to New York. Or she could have transferred in Columbus. We just don't know. Hitchens didn't find any witnesses who could confirm it either way."

"Sounds like Hitchens was thorough, like you said," Moses observed. "Is he still around for us to talk to?"

"Yes, I'll give him a call," Matt said, making a note.

"We'll also need contact information for your other siblings," I said. "I assume they'd all be willing to talk to us. You said Katie was probably closest to her?"

He held up a paper. "I have all that information here. I don't know if she'll talk to you, but I'm pretty sure the rest of them will. But, like I said, that summer Leila was putting distance between herself and her family, and there can be a big gap between fourteen and sixteen. So, their relationship was complicated, and Leila's disappearance devastated Katie. I mean, it really hit her hard. She kept insisting that Leila would never leave without telling her goodbye. She said that over and over. She wouldn't listen to the detective and she wouldn't listen to any of us. She idolized Leila, and after Leila disappeared, it was like — I don't know. It was like she wanted to live the life Leila would have lived if she was still around. I wasn't here at the time, but Frank and Mary both told me she got to be quite a handful for our parents. Anyway, I'm just telling you this to warn you that she's not a very reliable witness and she's still emotionally fragile."

"Okay, good to know," I said. I would reserve judgment the way I always did when one witness called another witness crazy.

"She might not even talk to you," he warned again. "She said afterward that she never should have talked to Hitchens because he didn't understand anything and he didn't believe her. She said — well, I won't say any more. You can judge for yourselves."

"Your parents—?" I let it hang.

"My father died of a stroke in 1972. Mother's not well, but we can go up and talk to her when we're done here."

I leaned forward. "What do *you* think happened to your sister?"

"I really don't know, Cat," he said, barely lifting his shoulders. "I guess I think the most likely thing is that she met somebody at Woodstock who said, 'Hey, come join our band.' And she went off with them to New York City or Chicago or Poughkeepsie or who knows where and never looked back. And maybe she got into a heavy drug scene and OD'ed or was killed in a car accident or lived on the streets until the cold got her." His eyes flicked to Moses. "I have a cop's perspective, you know. I know what happens to kids on the street."

"But you think if she were alive, you would've heard from her."

"I think so, but I just don't know." He spread his hands. "She'd be thirty-five now. Could she be raising kids

17

in suburban Milwaukee? She could be. That's the hell of it. I just don't know."

"Let me ask this," I said, setting my notebook down on the table. "Why now? Why have you decided to reopen the case?"

He scratched his forehead, causing the Reds cap to bob. "I saw the *Enquirer* article about the reopening of Northside Park, and that brought it all back. My mother saw it, too, and I could tell it made her sad. She has an inoperable heart condition — she's not well enough to have the surgery. So, we don't really know how much time she has left and I can tell that it bothers her to die without knowing what happened. She's grieved for a long time, but I think it would ease her pain just to know."

"What if it doesn't?" I asked. "What if knowing turns out to be worse?"

He shifted uncomfortably. "In that case, I might tell her that you didn't find out anything. I'll take the responsibility of deciding."

"You do realize that that's the likeliest outcome. After nineteen years, the chances that we'll find out anything are slim."

"I know that, Cat. I do. On the other hand, after nineteen years, some witnesses might be ready to talk. It's a crap shoot."

"Then why not ask Hitchens to reinvestigate? He knows more about the case than anybody."

"I just want a fresh pair of eyes. I'm not questioning the job Hitchens did; he did the best he could do at the time. But maybe you'll see something he didn't. And also, I trust Foggy here. He spent a lot of years in Juvie and that gives him more experience than anyone I know when it comes to tracking a missing teenager." He looked at Moses. "You'll do it, won't you?"

"We'll do what we can," Moses said solemnly.

We explained our fees and asked for a retainer. He wrote out a check and handed it to Moses, then said, "You told me that you didn't have any other cases right now."

We both nodded and Moses said, "That's right."

"You understand, we're kind of up against it. Look, I know how that sounds. We waited nineteen years and now we're in a hurry. It's just — my mother. We don't know how much time she has left." His voice quavered a little.

Moses hadn't put the check away, and now he held it suspended over the table. "Perley, tracing witnesses after nineteen years takes time. You know that. We may get lucky, we may not. Cat and I always do our best, and that's what we commit to. But if you'd rather hire somebody to work on deadline so that you can tell your mother you did all you could, you should find somebody willing to do that. No hard feelings."

Matt held up his palms, as if pushing the check away. "No, no, I want you guys to do it. It's just — well, if somebody came to you tomorrow with a new case, I'd be willing to pay extra for your full attention to this one. Sorry, I didn't mean to offend you."

"Understood. Your case will have our full attention."

Matt went to check on his mother and returned to say that she was asleep, so we agreed to talk to her another time and soon found ourselves back in the Fairlane, a box of files and papers on my lap.

"What's wrong with him?" I said.

"Who? Matt? Why do you ask?"

"He's gaunt, Moses — at least I think he is, for all I could tell in that dark room. He has the look of a stockier man who's lost weight. And he was wearing a ball cap. I couldn't even tell the color of his hair."

"Cat, lots of men wear ball caps in the house these days. He didn't look good, though — you right about that. Guess I reckoned his family troubles could be taking their toll. Could be that's the real reason he retired — to take care of his mother."

I was gazing out the window at the play of light and shadow on the snow. I decided to drop it.

"How many people did he say attended Woodstock?" I asked instead.

19

"Around four hundred thousand."

"Half male, half female, you think?"

Moses shook his head. "Harder for the girls to get past their parents."

"So, say a hundred and fifty thousand girls. How many of them do you think were skinny with long blonde hair?"

"Maybe a hundred and twenty thousand."

"That's what I thought."

CHAPTER 3

We stopped for lunch at Arnold's, where Kevin was working a day shift. He was too busy behind the bar to join us, but we promised to fill him in on the new case. As an early and enthusiastic supporter of my new career, he always received regular updates from me. As a fountain of useful information and useless trivia, he was often valuable to us. And now he had the added advantage of age: unlike Moses and me, he had been a teenager in 1969. The same was true of my other tenants, and one of them, Mel, showed up just as our lunch was served, and sat down. When she took off her coat, we could see from her brown-smeared tee and unbuttoned overshirt that she had been working in the studio, throwing pots, and some of them had landed on her chest. Kevin served her usual Guinness with a smile.

"He's in a good mood," Moses said. "Hasn't said a word about the drum lesson yesterday."

Mel watched Kevin's retreat. "It's February. Any day now, the Valentine's decorations will go up, and as long as we don't complain about them, he won't complain about the drum lessons."

"Easy for you to say," Moses grumbled. "You got younger eyes than me. When he puts that red cellophane over the lights, I swear I'm going to fall and break a hip."

I was watching Kevin, too. "He's not in love again, is he?"

"Not that I know of," Mel said. "I think Leon's drums and the loud music are making him relive his youth — you know, back when we all listened to loud rock and never gave a thought to hearing loss. I think he's feeling like a teenager again. He used to have a Jim Morrison poster on the back of his bedroom door as a teenager. I wouldn't be surprised to see another one go up."

I glanced at Moses for clarification, but he had just taken a bite of his Reuben.

Mel caught the look. "Jim Morrison was the lead singer for The Doors. You know, Cat — 'Light My Fire.' Surely you remember that one."

I pressed a palm to my forehead. "Oh, god, yes, do I ever. Franny had been playing it in her room for a week before I realized what the lyrics were saying. I thought if Fred figured it out, he'd break the record and the record player, too. She was only — what, twelve?"

"Yeah, but she was always in the vanguard, according to what you've told us about her."

Moses was frowning now. "You let her keep the record?"

I shrugged. "Barn door after the horse was out and all that. She already knew all the lyrics by heart. I couldn't prevent her from singing them. But she wasn't allowed to play it when her father was home. That little compromise made me her jailer, according to her. And according to her, I was, I think the word was, 'tripping' on my dictatorial power."

Moses's eyebrows rose over his bifocals. "She used the word 'dictatorial'?"

Mel's sandwich arrived. "Gotta hand it to her," she said. "That's a pretty sophisticated analysis." When I frowned, she added, "Not accurate, maybe. You were trying to protect her."

"Wouldn't've been no compromise in my house," Moses said. "I'm with Fred: break the record and confiscate the record player."

Mel and I exchanged a look. "Right, Mr. Juvie. That would've worked," I said.

"Tough love," Mel agreed, nodding. "Gets 'em every time."

Moses and I stopped at Kinko's on the way home and made a copy of the detective's report, then settled in at my kitchen table to read it. It was about ten pages long, with appendices listing all the witnesses he had interviewed and all the locations where Missing Teenager flyers had been posted. The former list identified the witnesses by name and their connection to Leila, as well as telephone numbers. The detective, Walt Hitchens, concluded that the only thing he could say for certain was that Leila Perle had taken the bus from Cincinnati to Columbus, about a hundred miles north, on the night of Thursday, August 14th, apparently bound for Woodstock. The last sighting had put her in the Columbus Greyhound station, but he had been unable to discover what had happened to her after that. He could not even confirm that she had arrived at the Woodstock Festival in Bethel, New York.

"That's pretty vague," I said. "How do you think he looked for evidence?"

Moses nodded at the page in his hand. "This is a report written for an anxious family, Cat. He's trying to avoid making them any more anxious than they already are. What I reckon he means is that he couldn't find any unidentified bodies of teenagers matching Leila's description between Columbus, Ohio, and Bethel, New York."

"Where did he look? NCIC? Was it even around back then?" I knew that the National Crime Information Center kept a database of so-called unidentified deceased persons, but I also knew that it was officially off-limits to lowly gumshoes like us. Only law enforcement agencies had access.

"I don't know if it was around or not. If it was, it would've been checked by the police detective working the missing persons case. That would've been standard operating procedure. Maybe that's what he's referring to."

"Think we could get into it?"

"Let me think about it. We can get into it somehow, just a question if we want to do it through legitimate means, or—"

"Go see Arnie." Arnie was a hacker we knew who had helped us on several cases. If it came to a choice between hiring Arnie and hitting the road in a VW van to visit all the police departments between here and Bethel, New York, I voted for Arnie.

"You said this was the report he wrote for the family. Does that mean you think there's a longer, more detailed report somewhere?"

He shook his head. "I doubt that. If we're lucky, he's got a good memory. If we're even luckier, he'll still have notes."

"Think that's possible, after nearly twenty years?"

"Anything's possible," he said.

Once we were ushered into Walt Hitchens's office the next day, my spirits lifted. Located in a shabby, three-story building on the fringe of downtown, the small office was crammed with file cabinets that matched the ones in the reception area, all of them scarred, rusted, dented, and elderly, as if recovered from the *Titanic* and purchased as a job lot in a used office furniture sale. There was another year's worth of filing piled on top of the desk and on the floor. In the middle of the desk, a large Persian cat sat immobile in the Sphinx position like a giant cream-colored paperweight and regarded us through slitted eyes. The young receptionist, whose scrutiny of a clothing catalog we'd interrupted, had knocked on the door, opened it, and spoken through her chewing gum.

"Moses Frog and Cab Calloway, Uncle Walt."

Moses corrected her, but she'd already turned back to her catalog and shut the door.

Hitchens, who had stood and started around his desk, opened his arms in an elaborate shrug and grinned at us. "Kids. Whatcha gonna do? My secretary retired at the end of last year and I haven't replaced her yet."

I surreptitiously raised my eyebrows at Moses: he was successful enough to afford a secretary. Moses's face remained impassive: *don't believe everything you hear*, it said.

24

Walter Hitchens was probably a little younger than we were — in his late fifties, maybe — and on the short side with untidy graying brown hair, wispy over his ears, a broad face to accommodate his broad smile, and a prominent nose. His tie was pulled loose over a long-sleeved white shirt, commodious to accommodate his paunch and rumpled. He shook hands enthusiastically.

"Want some coffee? We got a Mr. Coffee machine, so it's impossible to screw up."

We declined, but he persisted. "Sure? It's her best trick, making coffee, and she only spills it half the time."

His accent held traces of someplace else — maybe Philly? I was trying to imagine him inspiring confidence in a prominent business owner like Frank Perle, but maybe he was more prepossessing when not on his home turf. And anyway, I was hardly the person best suited to give him makeover advice. His price was probably right and I was equally unqualified to advise him on that score. He seemed genuinely glad to see us, and for our purposes, that was all that mattered.

He resumed his seat behind the desk and Moses sat in one of two vinyl-upholstered Danish modern knockoffs across from him. I approached the desk and slowly extended my hand to the cat.

Hitchens indicated the cat. "Mr. Fluffy."

At first, I thought the cat was going to decline our acquaintance, but then, slowly, he stretched his neck and sniffed my fingers with the air of a sommelier assessing a vintage, tilting his head to find the most advantageous angle. After thinking things over, he butted my hand gently and I gave him a pet before taking my seat next to Moses.

Hitchens was pointing a finger at us. "So, you two are gonna look for Leila Perle? Well, I wish you luck."

I smiled ruefully at him. "We appreciate that, we really do. We know what we're up against. Frankly, we were afraid you'd resent us and try to obstruct our investigation."

This is the kind of thing Moses would never say and it made him uncomfortable whenever I spoke this directly about things people preferred not to acknowledge. I felt him shift in his chair next to me.

Hitchens raised his palms. "No, no, no bad feelings here. Anything I can do to help. I don't blame the family for taking another stab at it. But the old man's dead now, right? Frank Senior? So, who hired you?"

"I knew Matt, the second son, from work," Moses said.

He nodded. "You were a cop. Yeah, that makes sense."

Some cops are offended to be fingered so easily, but Moses wasn't one of them. Maybe it had something to do with the pride he took as a Black man who had earned respect in the community and made a successful career despite prejudice and discrimination. Or maybe he just didn't care. "I know I look like a cop and act like a cop," he'd said on more than one occasion. "Ain't no way I can pretend to be somebody else after all these years."

"I never met Matt," Hitchens was saying now. "He was off doing some kind of military training. Talked to him on the phone once and he seemed like a nice enough guy, but he didn't have anything for me. Caught up in his own life, you know. Not a lot of time for his kid sister. Well, hell, if I was headed for 'Nam in 1969, I wouldn't be thinking about anything else, either."

"We've read your report," Moses said, "and it was very helpful. We can tell how hard you worked on the case. But we figure there were things you left out of the report — maybe things you didn't want the family to hear. So, we wanted to get your perspective."

"And we also wondered if you still had any case notes or tapes from interviews — anything like that you might be willing to share," I put in, my eyes drifting toward the file cabinets.

"Yeah, sure, sure. I got all that here for you." He stood, lifted a box from the floor behind his desk and set it in front of him, to the annoyance of the cat, who stood and looked daggers at him. "Sorry, Fluff." From the printing on the side of the box, it had previously contained Seagram's 7. "You read all this, you'll know what I know — assuming you can read my scrawl." He gave us an apologetic smile. "Something you can't make out, just come ask me."

More than we'd hoped for. Moses and I exchanged a look. Moses retrieved the box and set it on the floor by his feet so that Hitchens could resume his seat.

"That's real generous of you, Mr. Hitchens," he said.

"Walt, please. And Fluff, of course."

"Okay, Walt. We look forward to going through it all. But I wonder, if you have a little time, if you'd be willing to talk informally about the case and about impressions you had and conclusions you may have drawn that might not be evident in the case notes."

"Yeah, sure. 'Course, it was a long time ago and my memory isn't as good as it used to be. I know you know what that's like."

I leaned forward. "What do you think happened to Leila Perle? I mean, what does your gut tell you?"

"Well, Cat, since you put it that way." He folded his hands in front of him on the desk. "I think the girl's dead, don't you? I don't know how or why or when or where. But she came from a good Catholic family that loved her and wanted her back. She thought the old man was an ogre, okay, but he wasn't any different from a lot of fathers, especially in those days, and he genuinely loved her, no matter how angry he was with her. Nineteen years is a long time to hold a grudge, and if she were alive, she'd be in her mid-thirties now. You can't tell me that she would never have contacted her family if she was still alive. I don't buy it. I mean, maybe if it was a case of physical abuse or sexual abuse, yeah, but I didn't turn up anything like that. So, I don't buy it."

He slumped back against his chair and draped his folded hands over his stomach in a more casual, thoughtful position. "Now, if you're asking me how she died, my gut doesn't have a strong opinion about that. Maybe she went off with somebody she met at Woodstock. Maybe she joined a band. Maybe she met up with somebody who was passing himself off as a promoter and he offered to make her career. Or maybe she never made it that far. She could've sat next to the wrong person on the bus — and I don't believe, by the way, that the wrong person was the intern from Columbus. Or maybe her bus ticket didn't get her that far and she started hitchhiking. Kids did in those days and she'd mentioned it to a couple of her pals, although it's hard to tell how seriously to take that. I just don't know. What I do know is you've got your work cut out for you."

"Fair enough," Moses said. "So, let me ask this: where would you start, if you were in our shoes?"

"I hate to say it, Moses, but if I were in your shoes, I'd start by re-interviewing all the witnesses, especially the kids. Well, I mean, the ones who were kids when I interviewed them in 1969. One of them must know where Leila was between the time she left work and the time she boarded the bus the next night. Bound to. She stayed with somebody. But the battle lines were pretty clearly drawn back in those days, and to most of them, I represented The Man." He made air quotes to emphasize the last words. "Specifically, I represented Leila's old man, of course, and there was no way they were going to rat her out. Some of them might have felt sorry for the family, but their loyalties were all on the other side. Most of them were perfectly pleasant, I don't mean to say that they weren't. But a wall is still a wall, and there was no way I was getting past that. I said that to Frank at the end — that he might get different results in six months or a year. But I guess he didn't take that advice?"

"Not as far as we know," Moses agreed.

Walt nodded. "Can't blame them. They'd face all that pain and disappointment all over again." He sat forward a little. "Got any idea why they're doing it now? Opening things up, I mean."

"Matt saw an article in the paper about the revival of Northside Park."

"The place where Leila used to hang out? Yeah, I saw that, too."

Mr. Fluffy, a.k.a. Fluff, had slowly made his way across the desk and let himself down onto Walt's lap. He began kneading Walt's belly with his forepaws. I deduced from his bulk that he was no lightweight and from the expression on Walt's face that his claws were sharp as scimitars. But Walt made no move to dislodge him.

"Matt also says his mother is terminally ill, doesn't have long to live. He mentioned 'closure.'"

Walt frowned. "Yeah, maybe, I guess. Except if you believe in the afterlife, the way Catholics do, don't you figure on seeing your dearly departed on the other side? She could get the whole story then from the horse's mouth. Except they've got this thing about purgatory, right? Maybe the old lady figures on spending a lot of time there. Either of you Catholic?"

We shook our heads.

"So, no help with the theological questions." He shrugged. "Okay."

The cat had curled up into a beach ball on his lap, a hump just visible over the desk. Given the size of Walt's belly, it must've been crowded there.

"We brought your list of the people you interviewed," I said, setting it on the desk in front of him. "Mind taking a look and telling us who you'd especially want to interview again, if you were us?"

He found a pair of reading glasses on the desk and fitted them over his ears in such a way as to explain the tufts of hair sticking out there. Cat Caliban, Ace Detective.

He scanned the page. "Well, I don't think the family can help much. I don't think they had a clue, not even the little sister."

"Katie?" I asked.

"Yeah, that's right, Katie. Not a fan of mine. Thought I was an imbecile and didn't bother to hide it. Had her own fantasy about the bond between her and Leila. Kept saying

Leila wouldn't have taken off without telling her. But Leila, by all accounts, was spreading her wings that summer and I doubt she would've told Katie half of what she got up to."

"What she got up to?" I repeated.

"Yeah, you know, hanging out with older kids and musicians, smoking—"

"Drugs?" Moses asked, frowning.

"Probably. There was a lot of it around. It's all in there." He nodded at the box of notes. Then he raised his head and looked at Moses.

"Hell, you probably remember as well as I do. Hard to turn something down if all your friends were indulging. Point is, Leila didn't spend much time at home that summer. She told her folks she was working, and sometimes she was, but not always. There was this band she liked and she used to go over to their house in Clifton — a dump, you know? Where all the band members were living and maybe a girlfriend or two. To hear them tell it, Leila wasn't a girlfriend, just a kid who hung around. But I'd talk to those guys again if I was you and if I could track them down. They never hit it really big, as far as I know, but they had some success, so I doubt they still live in Cincinnati. Musicians with ambitions don't, for the most part."

I was scanning my notes. "What was the name of the band?"

"Oh, hell, I don't remember. Forest Fire? Burning Bush? Not Earth, Wind, and Fire, I would've remembered that."

I put my finger on a list of bands that Leila had supposedly liked. "Wildfire?"

"That was it. And there was another band after that. What the hell was their name?"

"Rough and Reddy? Leapin' Leopold? Vibe Machine?"

"I think I meant the Leopold one. They were local."

"Boyfriends?"

He shrugged. "You'll see some boys' names on the list there. Some of them might have been boyfriends. There was a guy named Jeremy something."

I put my finger on a name. "Jeremy Fox?"

"That's him. I think they were just getting together when she disappeared. He didn't have much to tell me, except that she was dying to go to Woodstock. Everybody told me that."

"What about her best friend?"

"Who was that?" He ran a finger down the page. "Oh, I see her. It's Mary Grace, isn't it? I remember that the best friend had a name to inspire confidence in a Catholic mother — misplaced, in my opinion, because those are the ones who really go wild when they let loose. I don't think this particular one had done that yet, and I got the impression that Leila had kind of outgrown her. But she'd be worth talking to because I had the sense that she knew more than she was telling me and felt guilty about it. So, like I said, I don't think she was close enough to Leila to have really important information, but she knew something."

"How about the boss?" I prompted. "Martin Yeager?"

"At the coffee shop? Nah, you can talk to him, but I don't think he paid a lot of attention to what the girls got up to. Not like the Northside Park guy. What was his name? Willis?"

"I think it was Wiley, Chaz Wiley."

He looked up and took off his glasses, pointed with his index finger. "Yeah, yeah. And he had a girlfriend. I don't remember her name, but I thought she had more on the ball than anybody else I talked to. Wiley had me convinced that he needed to keep tabs on the kids as a matter of self-preservation, but it would've been a lot of kids to keep tabs on, and I'll bet she did more of that than he did. From what I hear, you might smell a little pot in the bathrooms sometimes, but that was all. No emergency runs to the hospital for bad acid trips or alcohol poisoning. Cops I talked to corroborated that — the place was pretty clean, they said. No underage drinking that they could see."

I was looking at a duplicate copy of the list. "Chaz's girlfriend, would that be Vicki Saylor?"

"Sounds right. Yeah, Vic, that was her. I'd definitely talk to her. She was always around and I don't think she missed much. She's one who might be willing to say more now than she did then."

"Anybody else? How about the friends from work?" I was thinking about Franny at that age and an older friend she made one summer when she was working as a camp counselor. This friend had finished her freshman year in college and Franny regarded her as the height of sophistication. We all got tired of hearing her quoted at the dinner table.

"What were their names?" He put the glasses back on and scanned the sheet.

"Joyce Ridgeway, Helen Margolies, Sally Hunt, Linda Monniter, and Gigi Beck."

"Yeah, they might be worth having another go at. One of them, the Beck girl, was the last one to see her before she showed up on the bus. She said she hadn't seen Leila since the Wednesday she disappeared, when she ended her shift at the coffeehouse. No wait, I take that back. One of the other girls saw Leila walk out the door but didn't speak to her. And the older woman — I forget which one that was — she had been working that shift with Leila, but she didn't see Leila leave. They all said Leila had talked about getting to Woodstock, but they didn't know how she was getting there, and they all said they hoped she hadn't hitchhiked. But they might not have been telling me all they knew, any one of them."

"You talked to them in person? Was this at the coffeehouse?"

"All except Beck and Ridgeway, I talked to in person." He tapped the page in front of him. "Ridgeway was in school at Bowling Green and Beck was at Ohio State, so I talked to them on the phone. Those two and the older brother Matt — those were phone interviews, and none of them seemed promising enough to make me think I'd get more if I paid them a visit in person."

"How about these other local kids you talked to who went to Woodstock? You ever get the sense that any of them knew more than they were telling?"

He laughed. "I think they all knew more than they were telling about what they got up to at Woodstock, but as far as what they knew about Leila? Not really. But I could be wrong. Kids can be really secretive, you know? Hell, maybe they all saw her skinny-dipping in the pond or rolling around in the mud with some twenty-two-year-old guitar player. They wouldn't have told me if they had. But maybe they'll tell you now."

"Tell us about the other sightings you mentioned in the report."

He nodded, thought, and pulled at his earlobe. "We put up flyers everywhere — a thousand flyers, at least. Good quality color images, you know? Frank Senior was footing the bill and he could afford it. Five-hundred-dollar reward for information, too. Train stations, bus stations, service plazas along the route, rest stops, some truck stops, you name it."

"You did this all yourself?"

He made a dismissive gesture. "Nah, through connections. They put up my flyers when I have 'em, I put up theirs. Calls came in from all over. Mildred fielded them — she was my secretary, the one who just retired. Man, she was in her element on a missing persons case! She could smell a scam artist a mile away." He tapped his nose. "We'd decided not to mention the necklace on the flyer, so everybody that called, Mildred asked them about jewelry. If they couldn't describe the necklace, that was usually it — no follow-up call from me. Some of the scammers made something up, like a peace symbol on a chain or love beads, and you had to give them points for trying."

"That's how we knew the intern was genuine, by the way. He described the necklace exactly, down to the little diamond chip over the *i*. When I met with him in person and showed him the picture, he recognized it. And, of course, the conversation sounded like Leila, who had told everybody she wanted to go to Woodstock."

"And you never suspected him of having anything to do with Leila's disappearance?"

He gave a snort of laughter. "Of course, I suspected him. Are you kidding? If my eighty-eight-year-old granny had called up to report a sighting of the girl on the flyer, I would've investigated her, no question. So, I investigated him — the intern, though he must be a fully licensed doctor by now. Didn't find anything suspicious. I'm not saying you shouldn't investigate him, you should. But if you get anything on him, I'll be shocked. He was a pediatric cancer specialist, for chrissakes." He cupped his hands and wiggled his fingers. "Had an office filled with fuzzy, cuddly little animals."

"Unlike you."

He shook his head. "I've only got the one, and nobody ever accused Mr. Fluffy of being cuddly."

He winced, and I deduced that Mr. Fluffy had punctuated this observation with a pawful of claws to the belly.

"And since you ask my advice, the box contains notes on all the phone calls we ever received in response to the flyer, including the handful of unconfirmed but possibly legitimate ones. You want to follow up on them, knock yourself out. But I wouldn't recommend it."

There was a single knock and the door opened. The receptionist's head appeared. "Max Wisencracker is here to see you, Uncle Walt," she mumbled through her gum.

We stood up and shook hands. A thud on the other side of the desk told us that Mr. Fluffy had been dislodged as Walt stood. Moses picked up the box and we left. The next client gave us a rueful smile as we departed. I wondered what his name really was.

CHAPTER 4

When Moses didn't start the car immediately, I said, "Is this the part where we stake out the building and then follow him to a ranch house in suburban Dayton where Leila is raising three girls with an insurance salesman?"

Moses snorted through his mustache. "You know we don't have that kind of luck, Cat."

"So, you believe him?"

"Mostly, I do."

"Yeah, I know, everybody lies about something. What do you think he's lying about? You think Mr. Fluffy isn't really named 'Mr. Fluffy'?"

"No reason to lie about that unless you gave him a better name."

"I believed him, too."

He slotted the key into the ignition. "You believed him 'cause he had Mr. Fluffy to vouch for him."

"So, what do we do next?"

"Well, we know we can find Wiley at Northside Park and Leon can introduce us. That's low-hanging fruit and we might as well take advantage. He might be able to save us time tracking down some of the other witnesses. I'll call and try to

35

set up a look at the original PD case file. You take the box Hitchens gave us and go through it tonight."

Today was Wednesday and tonight was Moses's weekly poker game with his cop buddies.

He started the car. I gripped the armrest as we took off. "One of the first things I want to do is track down the intern. Before we start scouring the NCIC for unidentified teenage bodies between here and New York in the past nineteen years, I want to satisfy myself that he's credible."

"That's a good plan."

"Yeah, but how do I go about it? You think the state licensing board will have a current address for him?"

"Best place to start. Sounds like he probably got licensed in Ohio."

"And if that doesn't work, I can try the OSU Alumni Association, I suppose, though I'll probably have to lie to get anything out of them. But I guess he'll be easier to track down than all those other witnesses."

"Listen here, Cat. You know what you ought to do?"

"Look through the Cincinnati phonebook?" This had been one of his favorite recommendations not so long ago.

Now he shook his head. "Old school. You ought to go down to the library and explain what you need to a reference librarian. Ask her to show you how to look folks up on the computer. It's time you learned how to use all that fancy equipment Del bought you."

"I paid for it," I grumbled.

"That's my point. You bought it and you ought to be using it. You need to take a class, but we don't have time right now. A reference librarian can show you the basics."

But before I could get into Walt's box that night, my daughter Franny stopped by to borrow some bedding. She and her boyfriend Jon Garfield, who went by "Garf," rented a house in Clifton with four other people, and they were expecting houseguests that weekend for a regional gathering of the peace coalition they belonged to. To Franny, the '60s weren't dead. She had extended her youth as long as possible by becoming a perpetual college student, currently majoring in social work at UC. You might think that by now, she'd have enough college credits to claim a degree, but she hadn't collected enough of them in one place and had changed her mind about her major enough times so that even with transfer credits, they didn't add up. She'd been at her current major for two years now — a record for her — so I was hopeful. She worked at a health food store and never gave up on her mission to transform me into a tofu-eating, clean-living vegetarian. But since she was out of the house now and not colonizing my refrigerator with expired soy milk and seitan, I just let her nutritional advice go in one ear and out the other. I figured every family needed a kid bent on saving the planet, and neither my stockbroker daughter, Sharon, nor my business executive son, Jason, was up to it.

I saw Franny checking the labels on the sheets for banned substances as I made her a cup of herbal tea.

Then Kevin arrived for his update on the case, and it occurred to me that Franny might be useful as a consultant on '60s counterculture. So, I told them what we knew about Leila Perle's disappearance in 1969. I could see that Franny, who had only been twelve at the time, identified with Leila. Franny also owned a guitar, thankfully no longer taking up space in my living room, which she played competently to accompany her tone-deaf singing of folk music and protest songs. Could she have been lured to her destruction by a fast-talking guy claiming to be a record producer when she was Leila's age? She was the most intelligent but most emotionally vulnerable of my children, and looking at her now, I had no doubt that the answer to that question was yes. After wearing her hair in an Afro in her late teens and early twenties, followed by a haircut even shorter than mine for a few years, she had grown her hair out again so that it fell just below her shoulders, and she looked very like her teenaged self and not unlike Leila Perle.

Upstairs, there was a burst of laughter from the poker game.

"Walt thinks she might've met somebody at Woodstock who talked her into joining their band or promised her a successful singing career?" Kevin's eyes glittered. He loved to exercise his vivid imagination on our cases and his solutions were usually the most fanciful and outrageous — though not, I should add in all fairness to Kevin, necessarily more outrageous than the truth. And anyway, with Kevin came treats, like the brownies that now sat on the coffee table, so I was willing to indulge him. I took a bite and gave him my full attention. "And this somebody might have abducted her and kept her as a sex slave ever since."

"Well, I doubt that. I guess it does happen, but—"

"No, no, it does happen. Take Ronnie Spector, for example."

"Who?"

"You know, Ronnie Spector. The Ronettes? You've heard of them."

As I was shaking my head, he burst into falsetto, closing his eyes and raising his hands.

Sadie, who was curled up on the couch between me and Franny, leapt to her paws and bolted from the room, Sophie right behind her.

He was singing multiple parts in multiple voices now, none of them concordant with a redheaded male bartender and sometime bouncer.

Sidney came running, adding his own voice to the performance. That's my boy — always running toward danger.

I was still watching Kevin with my mouth open when Franny joined in.

They sang, palms to cheeks, eyes closed, heads wagging. The poker players had gone silent.

I gripped Kevin's arm. "Okay, okay, I remember."

"You do?"

"I think so. Maybe. Sort of."

"Well, anyway, she lived with this famous record producer, Phil Spector, who you should have heard of but probably haven't. And eventually, once he got rid of his first wife, he married her. But he was a real weirdo, so I've heard, and he kept her imprisoned in this mansion in Beverly Hills or someplace and wouldn't let her sing or even leave the house or see her family or anything. That's what I heard. So, it is possible. Something like that could have happened to Leila."

Caught up in this story, I was tempted to ask whether this relationship had lasted for nineteen years and how it had ended, but I was afraid that if I followed that particular red herring, we'd never get back to the case.

"We all think — that is, Moses, Walt, and I — that some of the witnesses from the original investigation might be more forthcoming now, after nineteen years. I'm especially interested in talking to anybody from Cincinnati who might've attended Woodstock and might've seen Leila there, but I don't know how to go about finding them. Any ideas, Fran?"

"Geez, I don't know, Mom. Have you seen the pictures? Woodstock was, like, this total mob scene. There must've been thousands of people."

"Four hundred thousand, at least."

"Yeah, so, like, it would be maybe a chance in four hundred thousand that you would run into somebody you knew unless you came with them. But I can see why you want to try. I think you should put up signs in the right places — Crazy Ladies Bookstore, the Unitarian church, our health food store, the Highland Coffeehouse, maybe Bogart's. And because of the music connection, maybe talk to somebody at WEBN. I don't know if they'd announce it on the air, but I know a few people from the radio station went to Woodstock back in the day. I guess when Northside Park reopens, you could post it there, too."

"I just say I'm looking for information from anybody who went to Woodstock and give my phone number, or should I say what it's about? I want to motivate people and not frighten them away."

Franny looked doubtful. "You know, maybe you should try calling a meeting of people who went — kind of like a reunion — and ask them to bring pictures. Kevin can cater."

"Here?" I asked, looking around my crowded and messy living room.

"No, someplace public. Like maybe Crazy Ladies."

"That's a good idea," Kevin put in. "They have a community room available for meetings. I'll bet Maureen would let you use it."

The feminist bookstore in Northside was a hub for '80s countercultural activity.

"You could pass around Leila's picture" Franny said, nodding.

"Wouldn't I put it on the flyer?"

She looked thoughtful. "I guess I'd separate the two things, the missing flyer and the meeting announcement. If Leila's picture is on the meeting announcement, people will take one look and say, 'No, don't recognize her. No point in going to this meeting.' But you want people to come and reminisce, to, you know, jog their memories. Somebody might say, 'What about that woman who was dancing topless in the rain on top of that sound truck? Could that have been this Leila chick?' And then people would take another look and decide that it was."

"But Franny, you're acting like once a hippie, always a hippie," Kevin objected, now that he knew his own role in the scheme. "I'll bet most of those people sold out and joined the Establishment years ago. They're probably all bankers and lawyers and real estate agents and dentists by now."

Franny shrugged. "Some of them are. And some of them are helping refugees and demonstrating against the war in El Salvador with me and Garf. Some of them are working with Al at Legal Aid to provide free legal services to the poor. Some of them are helping the homeless and working in soup kitchens. Some of them are keeping the books for local nonprofits or donating their services to low-cost clinics or volunteering to provide free dental care in Third World countries. They haven't all sold out."

"Okay, but if they're as busy as all that—"

"We just put a notation at the bottom of the flyer that says, 'Refreshments provided by Kevin O'Neill.' That will bring them out."

That was true. Because of his position at Arnold's as bartender to the city, Kevin knew everybody and everybody knew Kevin, whether they were members of the Establishment or countercultural types.

On her way out the door, Franny paused and put a hand on my arm. "You know, Mom, you keep calling Leila a 'girl,' but she wasn't a girl, really, was she? She was sixteen."

I was baffled. "What should I call her?"

"A woman. She was old enough to be sexually active."

"She's still a girl to me," I said grumpily. I was sometimes willing to follow Franny's feminist directives and sometimes not.

When they left I started a To Do list, then dug into the box of case notes and tapes Walt had given us. Some of the notes were written in a tidy, legible feminine hand — presumably, the recently departed Mildred's — but these were, as predicted, inauspicious. Most of the notes were written in a nearly indecipherable scrawl in pocket-sized notebooks and would take some time to decrypt. But the entries were brief, for the most part. That made the tapes more enticing. I began by matching the labels on the tapes with Walt's list of interviewees and setting aside the ones I wanted to listen to first. I calculated that he had taped a third of the interviews; maybe the other two-thirds of his informants were paranoid about their FBI files. Well, I should say "sensitive." "Paranoid" would suggest that these people's fears were unreasonable, and I knew from a previous case that they weren't. But one of the missing tapes was his interview with Leila's little sister Katie, who had presumably been too young to have an FBI file.

Moses had loaned me his tape recorder. I put on the headphones and inserted the interview with Nandil Suresh, the intern who was purportedly the last person to have seen Leila, the only person who could confirm that she was on a bus headed for Woodstock.

Both the strong accent of the informant and the quality of the tape, which had perhaps never been good and only deteriorated over the years, made the interview challenging. But Suresh was clearly trying to be helpful and seemed patient with Walt's requests for repetition. His story was that he had sat next to a young woman on the bus from Cincinnati to Columbus on the evening of Thursday, August 14th. He was a medical student at Ohio State with an internship at Cincinnati Children's Hospital who went back and forth between his home in Columbus with his wife and two children and Cincinnati, where he rented an apartment close to the hospital.

"It was 10:30 at night, so quite dark outside and also inside the bus," he said. *"I turned on my light to read my medical journal, but as you must know, that gave me only a small circle of light. I could not see the young lady who sat next to me very well at all."*

He described how he could see that she was wearing something low-cut — a long dress, as he later realized — and her necklace glinted in the available light. She had long blonde hair.

"Had she been wearing any other jewelry — earrings or rings?" Walt asked.

"I believe she was wearing rings — silver rings. But if you asked me to describe them, I really could not do so. Nor could I tell you whether or not she wore earrings. She had long hair, you see, and it covered her ears."

Could he estimate her age? Walt wanted to know.

Suresh paused, as if giving this question due consideration. Finally, he said, *"I am not good with ages, you know. My pediatric cancer patients are all under thirteen, and my own children are five and seven. I can definitely say that this young lady was older than thirteen. But she was wearing makeup, and that makes it even more difficult to judge her age. She wasn't tall, but as she was seated, I really couldn't say how tall she was."*

Continuing, he described how they had struck up a conversation when Suresh dropped his pen and she retrieved it for him. He couldn't remember how it started, but thought he'd said something about being clumsy and she'd said that she was clumsy as well. To be polite, he'd asked if she was a college student returning to campus at OSU.

"She told me that she was on her way to the Woodstock Music Festival in New York. I had never heard of this festival, but she said that all the most important young rock musicians and folk singers would be there, and that it would celebrate peace and love and the Age of Aquarius. I asked her if The Beatles would be there, or The Rolling Stones. Those were the only rock groups I could name. She said that she thought they probably would be. Everybody would be there."

Then he'd asked if she was a famous folksinger herself, traveling incognito to Woodstock.

"'I confess that I've never heard of a famous singer named Leila,' I told her, 'but I don't know much about music, as I'm sure you can tell.' She laughed and said no, she was not famous."

Had she seemed excited?

Yes, she had definitely been excited. *"I had the impression that she was starting out on a grand adventure — that was how it seemed to me."*

Then he'd gone back to his journal article. What had she done? Nothing, as far as he knew.

"She turned her face away, so she was either staring out the window or napping. When the bus arrived at the Columbus station, I wished her a good trip and said that I hoped she'd enjoy the festival. She smiled and said, 'I will.'"

"So you last saw her on the bus? Was she getting off in Columbus?"

"I don't think so, but I can't be sure. Certainly, I got off the bus first, and I didn't look back to see if she was behind me."

Suresh said that he hoped nothing bad had happened to her, and his voice sounded a little throaty when he said it. *"She was so happy."*

The recording had stopped, so I pushed the rewind button and played it through again. It seemed straightforward enough. We were lucky to have anything at all. She could have sat next to somebody who'd ignored her the whole time and never spoken to her. A more detailed description would have been nice, but we could hardly expect it from a brief encounter on a dark bus at night.

I flipped through Walt's notebook until I found a date that matched the date on the tape. After studying the scrawled notes, I concluded that he had shown Suresh a photograph of Leila wearing her necklace and that Suresh had recognized the necklace. *Looks like her*, Walt had scrawled.

I next listened to the interview with Leila's best childhood friend, Mary Grace O'Shaughnessy. Mary Grace was clearly awed by the detective and frightened by the disappearance of her friend. She was sad as well, but that sadness had multiple causes, and it was difficult for her to separate the current loss from the gradual erosion of the friendship. There were flashes of other emotions as well — resentment that her friend had preferred new friends to Mary Grace and perhaps even a tinge of satisfaction that she had been proven right in predicting what Leila's behavior might lead to.

"She started hanging out at that music club and meeting older kids," Mary Grace said. *"I was worried about her. I know she was smoking, which was strictly forbidden by her dad. And then she got that job at the coffeehouse and she was out till all hours. She asked me once or twice to cover for her and, you know, say she'd been with me at my house or something. I agreed to do it once, and I was a nervous wreck, worrying that her mother would call and ask to speak to her. And what was I supposed to say? She's in the shower? Then Mrs. Perle would just have called back, and then what? So I said never again. And she seemed okay with that. She just said, 'Okay, that's cool. I'll think of something else.' But by then she wasn't coming around much or calling, anyway. I used to see her at choir practice, but she pretty much stopped coming when she started working full time at the coffeehouse. She told me she'd go back in the fall."*

"When was the last time you saw her?" Walt asked.

"It was on my birthday, August 6th. We have this, like, tradition of going out for lunch on our birthdays, and that's what we did. We

always take the bus downtown to Woolworth's and eat at the luncheon-ette there. Usually, we pig out on hamburgers and banana splits, but she didn't eat much. She just said she wasn't hungry, but then she lit a cigarette, and I thought that smoking was killing her appetite. I told her so, but she just laughed."

"Did she tell you she was going to Woodstock?"

"She said she was dying to go, and she'd get there if it was the last thing she did. I didn't see how she could manage it, and I told her so. But she said she'd figure out a way. She seemed really determined. But she told me it was a secret and made me swear not to tell anybody, so I didn't. I guessed that she had figured something out, though, because her mom didn't even call to ask about her until after Woodstock was over. Well, what could I do? I knew the festival had ended on Sunday 'cause I saw it on the news. I don't usually watch the news, but I was kind of fascinated by this big event she'd talked about and thought I might see Leila in the crowd, if she made it to the festival like she planned, which I never did. Anyway, when Mrs. Perle called on Tuesday to see if I was back from a choir trip Leila was supposed to be on, what could I say? I couldn't pretend that I'd been on a choir trip, because eventually, Mrs. Perle was bound to ask my mom about it. So, I had to tell her that I'd gone on the choir trip back in June and Leila hadn't gone."

I knew from reading Walt's report that Leila had given her mother a mimeo about a choir trip and had her sign the permission slip. Walt had noticed that the dates had been altered and asked Mrs. Perle about it. Leila had told her the original dates had been changed because the choir director had gotten sick. She hadn't questioned this explanation. So, nobody had wondered where Leila was until the Tuesday following Woodstock, August 19th.

"I'm worried that Leila might have tried to hitchhike home, especially if she'd maybe spent all her money by then. Lots of kids hitchhike, but it's dangerous."

I heard the voice of authority, presumably her parents', coming through.

"Do you have any other theories about what could have happened to Leila? Could she have just run away from home, for example?" Walt asked. He didn't try to influence her answer by asking if Leila hated her parents or her life.

By now, Mary Grace was crying; I could hear it in her voice. *"I don't think so, I really don't think Leila is that kind of person. I mean, she complained about her folks a lot, but lots of kids do that. They don't all run away. But maybe I'm wrong. I don't know her as well as I used to, I know that."*

After a slight pause, she whispered, *"Thanks,"* and I guessed he'd handed her a handkerchief. I hadn't been a detective for long, but I'd already learned the practicality of stocking up on handkerchiefs.

I strained to hear Mary Grace's next statement, which was barely above a whisper as well.

"She was still wearing her friendship ring, the Claddagh I gave her. The Irish kind, with the two hands and the heart."

Another pause filled with the sound of weeping. Then Mary Grace said, *"I was so angry with her. I was furious that she made me kind of like an accomplice. And then I was the one who had to tell her mom that she hadn't been on a choir trip at all."* This came out in a confessional burst of passion. Her voice was so thick with emotion and tears now that I was having a hard time understanding her. *"I didn't tell her about Woodstock, I didn't, but I guess they found out anyway."*

Walt said in a soothing voice, *"It wasn't fair to put you in that position. She shouldn't have done that to you."*

More sobbing followed and Walt didn't interrupt. When the noise died down, he said, in a gentle voice, *"Even though you've grown apart a little recently, you probably know Leila better than anyone. You're her best friend and you've known her most of her life. So, I'm really relying on you to help me understand her."*

I gave him points not only for making her feel important, but also for speaking about Leila in the present tense. Whatever his suspicions about Leila's fate, he wouldn't upset this fragile teenager by hinting at them.

"Tell me this. Do you think Leila is the kind of person who might go off with someone — maybe a boy she likes or a musician who wants her to join his band or somebody who offers to promote her music career?"

Her voice was clearer now. *"Gee, I guess she might do any of those things, especially if there was music involved. She can be kind of impulsive and she's obsessed with music. She has this little transistor radio that her dad gave her and she listens to it all the time. I think she spends most of her money on records. Some girls spend it on clothes and makeup, but I think Leila spends it on records. And of course, she was saving up to buy a car."*

"Does she have a lot of money to spend?"

"Well, she's been working, so I guess she does. She paid for our birthday lunch. But I never got the impression, you know, that she has that much more money than I do. I mean, the Perles are pretty well-off and they give a lot of money to the church, but Leila just gets an allowance like most of the kids I know. The money from her job goes to her car fund and records, like I said, and that music club she hangs out at."

"Northside Park." I assumed that Mary Grace nodded, because he went on. *"So, Leila is obsessed with music and I know she owns a guitar. Did she buy that with her own money, by the way?"*

"No, she got it for her birthday last year."

"Do you think she has serious ambitions to be a singer?"

"Oh, yes, she has a beautiful voice. And she taught herself to play. She sang in the school talent show last year and this year, and everybody thought she was good. My brother says she could be a professional someday." Then she added, *"I like to think of her at Woodstock, sitting around a campfire."* She interrupted herself, *"Oh, I know from TV that it rained a lot and got muddy, but not all the time. So I see her sitting around this campfire playing her guitar and singing with other people, and they're playing and singing, too."*

"Let's hope you're right," Walt said.

The interview was over.

47

CHAPTER 5

For Moses, Thursday mornings were always devoted to recovery and cleanup from the Wednesday night poker game, which gave me extra time to go through Walt's materials. By the time I headed out with Moses in the late afternoon for our meeting with Chaz Wiley at Northside Park, I had a legal pad full of notes and questions, along with a full set of partial paw prints from my boy Sidney, who had chased the pen around in a fit of boredom. I had listened to most of the interview tapes and could attest that Walt had been diligent. Reluctantly, I had decided that we needed a more legible copy of Walt's notes and had spent the better part of the morning typing them out. From an information standpoint, I had wished that Walt had been more expansive, but as an indifferent typist translating writing that was barely legible, I was relieved that he hadn't been. Moses had listened to interview tapes while he cleaned the kitchen.

I'd handed Moses a carbon copy and told him, "You owe me."

"I'll buy lunch," he said.

"For the next week."

He'd had a chance to read my own notes before we'd left and now asked, "What do we most want to know from this guy?"

"I'd appreciate a more adult perspective," I said. "He and the intern were the oldest people Walt interviewed, I think. It sounded like he knew her casually because she hung around the Park a lot. He claimed not to have known that she was going to Woodstock, although he knew that she wanted to. He says lots of the kids who hung around the Park talked about going to Woodstock, but very few of them actually went. He also says that she was a good musician with an excellent singing voice. Apparently, he let her play one night at the Park and he was surprised how talented she was. Like all the people who knew her best, he could imagine her running off with a music producer, promoter, or a band."

"All the people except Katie," Moses put in. "At least, that's how I read Walt's notes."

I nodded. "That's how I read them, too. But then Katie was adamant that Leila wouldn't have gone anywhere without telling her. So, I don't know how much weight we can give to her contradiction."

Moses was pulling up to the curb in front of Northside Park behind a delivery van with its back door open and "J & B Concessions" painted on the side. We could have walked to the old theater from the Catatonia Arms, but the sidewalks were still covered in ice. The two-story, red-brick building trimmed in white still had its original semicircular "Park Theater 1913" sign under its crenellated roof.

Leon was the first person I saw as we pushed open the door and entered the old theater lobby. He was a rangy teenager wearing a white painter's coverall and waving a dripping roller at us with a careless enthusiasm that left no doubt how he'd come by the paint spatters that covered him.

"Hey, M-miz Cat! Hey, Moses!"

"Hey, Leon. You're looking pretty professional." I nodded at the coverall.

He looked down at himself while the roller continued to drip — on the uncarpeted floor, on his sneaker. "Mr. Chaz, he g-give me this overall 'cause I been c-coming right from school to paint and he say he d-don't want to get in no trouble with my mother."

I had often felt similarly in the past and began to think that Chaz Wiley and I might get along famously.

Leon gestured at the wall he was painting. "It's g-going to be a picture here once I get f-finished. A m-m—"

He faltered, frowning in concentration, and after giving him a minute to recover the word, I suggested, "A mural?"

"Yes, m-ma'am, that's it, a mural." He pronounced the word with care. "And it's going to have r-rock 'n' roll people in it, like famous people, and they b-b-bands."

"Drummers, I guess," Moses said, and Leon grinned a little sheepishly.

Two men emerged from a door to the interior. The shorter of the two signed something on a clipboard and handed it to the other with a clap on the shoulder. He looked up, saw us, and headed in our direction. He was a good-looking man, with a slight build and a smile that showed white teeth beneath his mustache. Both his shaggy, shoulder-length brown hair and his mustache were liberally frosted with white, but the color could be premature because his age was difficult to guess. The laugh lines that raised his age above the twenties weren't visible until he was within handshake distance.

"This the boss?" Moses asked, shaking his hand.

"Of Leon?" the man said, turning to look at Leon. "No way. Leon is an independent contractor." To each of us in turn, he said, "Chaz. Good to meet you."

We didn't really need an introduction from Leon, of course. But Leon's reputation in the neighborhood gave him so much cachet that we took advantage when we could. I'd mentioned Leon when I'd called to make the appointment. It was kind of like getting the Godfather's blessing.

Chaz steered us through the door to the theater, saying, "Why don't we step into my office?"

I had realized from Walt's taped interview with him that he was a relatively soft-spoken man and maybe a little reserved.

50

He hadn't spun out his answers the way some informants had, although he'd seemed willing enough to answer follow-up questions.

His office appeared to be a large, rectangular folding table covered in papers, carpet and tile samples, posters, photographs, and miscellaneous plumbing doodads — a faucet, a sink trap. A director's chair and two folding chairs sat near the table and Moses and I took the folding chairs, leaving him the chair with his name on it.

Moses and I looked around the room with curiosity. I guess I had been expecting raised seating, but the floor was flat — a large expanse of wood so scarred and stained that some of its imperfections must have dated back to 1913. The walls were painted midnight blue. In the front of the room was a wide wooden platform, presumably the stage, where several people were busy at work. At the back of the stage, a man on a ladder adjusted a huge screen that hung suspended from the ceiling, taking direction from somebody who must have been stationed in the old projection booth above our heads.

"What's your capacity?" Moses asked.

"Nine hundred," Chaz said, "but don't tell the fire department."

Nine hundred was a lot of kids to keep track of, I thought. Aloud, I said, "Will there be seats like theater seats?"

He shook his head. "Just carpet, and some cushions scattered around." He gestured at one wall. "We'll put in a few banks of seats over there for the old-timers and people who can't sit on the floor. We still have some of the original theater seats, so we'll use them in recognition of the building's history."

He seemed to be waiting for us to open the conversation about Leila, so Moses said, "I think Cat told you that we're reopening the investigation into Leila Perle's disappearance."

He nodded. "What can I do to help?"

The man on the ladder at the front of the room shouted a question and Chaz gave him a thumbs-up.

When he turned back to us, I said, "Maybe you could start by just telling us about Leila and what she was like."

He thought for a minute and then said, "I didn't know her at all well, but she was around so much that I knew her name and a little bit about her. If you'd just met her, you probably would have said that she was like every other sixteen-year-old girl in those days — skinny, long hair, too much eye makeup, eager to please—"

Again, he caught something in my expression, because he interrupted himself. "Not her parents, probably, but none of them are eager to please their parents. I understand that better now that I live with teenagers myself. But most of them want to please other people, especially the girls."

"So, was she like every other sixteen-year-old girl in those days?" I prompted.

"She was and she wasn't. What most of them cared about the most was boys and their friends. The more mature ones had strong and often well-informed political views: they covered their backpacks in peace symbols or love beads and marched to end the war in Vietnam. What Leila cared about the most, as far as I could tell, was music. She was always plugged in." He cupped his hands over his ears to represent headphones. "She had this little transistor radio she carried around with her and she was always listening to music. It must've been powerful, too, that little radio, because she listened to stations from all over. Most of the kids listened to Jelly Pudding on WEBN — you know what that was, right? A local radio show aimed at a teen audience? Station owner let his son do it. So, most of what the kids knew about music they got from Michael Xanadu, who did a really good job of introducing them to new music. But Leila knew about bands and musicians that nobody in Cincinnati had ever heard of. I'll give you an example. I happened to mention to a group of kids that I had booked Santana for a gig in late June. This was before Woodstock, so nobody outside California had heard of him yet. But Leila had. 'Cool,' she said, 'I really dig that Latin beat he has. He's amazing!'"

"And Leila wanted to be a singer herself?"

"A lot of kids wanted to be singers or play in a band. I only heard her one time, but it seemed like she was always toting that guitar around, so I guess she did want to be a performer."

"When did you hear her?" Moses asked.

"What happened was we had a band from Dayton booked and they canceled because their lead singer got laryngitis. Okay, so we still had Bob Seger coming down from Detroit. Then that night — it was a Friday night, I remember — we had this incredible storm. I'm talking torrential rains and high wind. So anyway, one hour before the show, Bob Seger's manager calls to tell me the bus is stuck at a truck stop south of Toledo and can't be fixed. They've given up on the gig and are just trying to get home to Detroit. Then the local singer we had booked as the third act called to tell me she was sick. I'm pretty sure she just didn't want to go out in the storm, but I couldn't blame her."

A middle-aged man in jeans and a Perle Electric uniform shirt open over a Grateful Dead T-shirt approached. He had a female sidekick, similarly attired but with a pencil stuck behind one ear, who hung back. Stitched over his pocket was the name "Tom"; stitched over her pocket was the name "Kathy." "Sorry to interrupt," Tom said, looking at Chaz. "Want to show us exactly where you want that extra outlet, boss? Kath is mapping out the circuit."

Chaz shook his head. "Ask Stacy or one of the other light show guys. They'll show you where." As the electrician turned away, he said to us, "Where was I?"

"All your performers had just canceled," I supplied.

"Right. By then, there was a handful of musicians in the house from different bands and I proposed a jam session. I got five of them to agree. But meanwhile, we've got fifty kids sitting around waiting for the music to start. So, Vic said, 'Why don't you ask Leila to sing?' I go, 'Leila who?' And she says, 'You know. *Leila*.' So, then I asked Leila if she wanted to sing a few numbers while the musicians were setting up."

"Had she asked you before to let her sing?" Moses said.

"No, but after Vic suggested it, I remembered I'd heard that Marty let her sing at the Aquarius sometimes."

"That would be Martin Yeager, her boss?" I asked.

"Right. So, I let her sing. I only did it because the house was small. If word got around that anybody with a guitar could show up and talk their way onto the stage, I'd be mobbed. But damned if she wasn't good. I'd gone upstairs to talk to the light show guys, but when I came back downstairs, she was singing this one song she wrote, and when she finished, you could've heard a pin drop. Even the musicians on the stage had stopped to listen. I had to go down to the basement then and get some more pop, but I heard she sang an encore and one other song before the jam session started."

"You think she was good enough to be a professional?" Moses asked.

"I thought so, sure. I thought one of the bands might snap her up."

"But that didn't happen? Why not, do you think?"

"Well, it might have happened some time, but she disappeared not long after that. Plus, not many rock bands were looking for a female vocalist. They should have been, but they weren't. Janis Joplin and Grace Slick were the exceptions, not the rule. Vic said she was too young yet to sign on with a band, but I wouldn't know about that."

"Would that be Vicki Saylor, your girlfriend at the time?" I asked. "We're hoping to speak with her and hoped you might have an address."

He grinned. "Sure, I do. She's Vicki Wiley now." He glanced at his watch. "And she ought to be here any minute."

A woman with a full head of frizzy pale blonde hair popped out of a door down front, yelling, "Where's Vic?"

From behind us, a woman's voice shouted, "Here! Who's asking?"

I turned to see a tall brunette with a ponytail carrying a bulky shopping bag in her arms.

A young man appeared behind the frizzy blonde. "We're fighting over the tampon dispenser. God, how did my life get so glamorous?"

"Be there in a sec," the ponytail said, and added the shopping bag to the collection on the table. She planted a brief kiss on Chaz's head. "What's up?"

"Vic, these are the detectives who are reopening the Leila Perle case."

We introduced ourselves and shook hands.

"We'd love to talk to you when you have a minute," I told her.

She nodded. "I'd better go see what's up with the tampon dispenser first."

As she walked off, Chaz asked, "Anna with you?"

She raised her arm in a vague gesture but didn't turn. "In the lobby with Leon."

"Vic's the one to talk to about Leila," Chaz said. "She always knew more about the kids than I did. To tell you the truth, I never knew Leila's last name until that detective came around to ask about her. Then I forgot it until you called. I knew a lot of names in the old days, back when my memory was more functional than it is now, but they were all first names and nicknames. They were my customers, sure, but it wasn't like I was going to sell them insurance policies."

"You didn't know Leila's last name but you hired Perle Electric to do your electrical work here," Moses observed.

Chaz followed Moses's gaze to the stage, where the two electricians were conferring with two young men, all of them backlit by the glare from the enormous screens behind them. The woman electrician was kneeling on the stage, drawing and talking, and the others were studying her drawing. At first, Chaz didn't seem to understand the comment. Then his eyes opened wider. "Perle Electric — you're saying they're related to Leila? No shit! I didn't know that."

A smaller, younger version of Vic Wiley entered from the lobby and made her way toward us.

"Hey, Dad," she said. "I'm going down to the hardware store with Leon to buy more paint."

A lesser man might have objected that Leon wouldn't need more paint if he put more of it on the walls and less of it on the floor, his coveralls, and his shoes. An ordinary man would have asked how much this trip to the paint store was going to cost him.

Chaz Wiley just said, "Make sure Bill gives us our discount."

As she retreated, he turned back to us and grinned. "Kids," he said, shaking his head. But his voice was full of warmth.

CHAPTER 6

Vic reappeared with a mug in her hand and, dragging another director's chair away from the wall, unfolded it awkwardly with one hand and sat down next to Chaz. Her chair said "Boss Vic" on the back.

She was taller than Chaz by several inches. She had thick dark hair with auburn highlights pulled back into a ponytail that exposed an olive complexion on a makeup-free face, with a smattering of freckles.

"So, you two are looking for Leila? I thought she'd disappeared into the crowd at Woodstock and never resurfaced."

"Was a lotta that going around," Chaz remarked.

"Really?" I said, pen poised. "Like who?"

"He's just saying that," Vic said, giving Chaz a look. "Nobody else we knew."

"I told them that you were the person to talk to about Leila. You kept better tabs on the kids than I did. I didn't even know she was missing until that detective came around."

Vic had fished a packet of cigarettes out of her pocket and now she lit one. Chaz unearthed an ashtray from beneath a pile of papers and pushed it in her direction. Vic turned to us. "What do you want to know?"

"Did you know that Leila had gone to Woodstock?" I asked.

"I knew she wanted to go. In fact, I knew she wanted to go badly, so even though I didn't know how she was going to manage it, I guess I thought she might. I wouldn't have bet against her."

"So, she never mentioned taking the bus to New York?" Moses asked.

"God, no, I wouldn't have expected that."

"Why not?"

She took a thoughtful drag on her cigarette. "Well, I guess because I thought she'd find a ride with somebody from here who was going. But maybe in the end it was a last-minute thing — you know, like the money came through and all the cars were full already, something like that."

"Can you give us the names of some of the other kids she might have been close to in those days?" I asked. "Who did she usually sit with when she came here?"

Vic and Chaz looked at each other. "Oh, gosh," she said. "Who did she sit with? Well, let's see. For a while she was sitting with the Wildfire groupies — Blondie and Rainbow and that kid with the spiky red hair."

"Rainbow?" I echoed.

Vic made a wry face and flicked ash into the ashtray. "I assume she rechristened herself. Then later, Leila would sit with Destiny's crowd — the Black kid with the Afro out to here" — she raised her palms to illustrate — "and his girl-friend and the pale kid with green eyes and Coke-bottle lenses and the girl that never smiled and the twins with the glasses." She took a puff from her cigarette. "And that tall, bony girl, what was her name?"

"I thought Destiny was tall and bony," Chaz put in.

"Any of these kids got last names?" Moses said.

Vic laughed. "After twenty years, I can't even remember their first names — which, as you noticed, Cat — were mostly nicknames."

58

Chaz put an affectionate hand on her shoulder. "Babe, I can't believe you remembered that much after all this time."

I made a note and said, "Why did she sit with two different groups? You said first she sat with the Wildfire groupies and later with this other group. How come? She have a falling out with the Wildfire group?"

"Don't look at me," Chaz said, hands raised.

"I think she might've had a falling out with the band members," Vic said. "Just as well, if she did. She was too young to be hanging around them. Maybe they finally realized it." When we let that comment lie still for a minute, she added, as if in explanation, "They were takers, those guys. I didn't like to see the girls mooning over them."

"And what do you think they took from Leila?" I studied her face.

She seemed about to say something, then changed her mind. "They took her song," she said at last. "That's what they took. They took her song and made a goddamn fortune off it."

I wasn't keeping up, but Moses asked, "You mean the song she sang here one night?"

"Oh, yeah, babe, I was telling them about that night Leila sang." He looked uncomfortable. To us, he said, "Vic thinks they remade Leila's song into their first big hit."

"I don't think it, I know it." He started to object, but she talked over him. "You didn't hear it, not the whole thing. You were out front, dealing with refunds, and then you were running around. You only heard part of it. When Wildfire released their album early that next year and I heard the song they were calling 'Magdalena,' I couldn't believe it. It was Leila's song, the one she called 'Angelina.'" Ash exploded from her cigarette as she flicked it. "I couldn't believe it. I kept scanning the liner notes for Leila's name, but it wasn't there. Not a single goddamn mention."

"Hey! I just thought of something. I bet we have a recording." He turned to us. "In those days, we recorded all the music, so we have this amazing archive, which I need to transfer to CDs, but that's another story. We should have Leila's tape, right, babe? That should settle it."

She waited a beat too long before saying, "Sure, we ought to have it somewhere."

Moses started to speak, when Chaz interrupted him. "Wait a minute, wait a minute. I just thought of another thing. I can't believe I just remembered this. There was a guy asking about Leila a couple of months after she disappeared." He pounded his forehead with his fist. "The hell was his name? Older guy, looked totally out of place, but he used to come in sometimes. Anyway, he was from Nashville — had a mother in a nursing home in Roselawn. He used to come up and visit her regularly, and sometimes he would stop in at the club. You remember him, Vic?"

"Guy with a receding hairline? Used to wear dress slacks and polo shirts? No facial hair?"

"That's the guy. So, one day he asks me about Leila. He was there the night she sang — couldn't get back to Nashville because of the weather. Said he'd been thinking about her ever since and he had a band he wanted to match her up with. Did she have a contract or an agent? He was a music producer, he said, but wanted to fly under the radar at the club, for obvious reasons."

"You didn't tell me." Vic's voice was a little accusatory.

"I didn't? I thought I did. Maybe you were out of town. Anyway, what could I tell him? I hadn't seen Leila for a while, and then the detective had come around and said she was missing, and then we'd heard she'd gone to Woodstock before she disappeared. Seemed likely she'd been approached by another band or another agent, so this guy — the Nashville guy, I mean — went away empty-handed."

"We'd love to hear that tape," I said.

"Sure, I can dig it up. Will you remind me, babe?"

But Vic's attention was elsewhere, or nowhere, as she stared through a veil of smoke, as if at people and events from the distant past. Her forehead was creased.

Moses asked, "Were there other local bands Leila hung out with?"

At the same time, proving once again Moses's frequent accusation that I was myself a blunt instrument, I asked, "Vic, do you think Leila was romantically involved with any of the guys in the bands?"

She took a long drag on her cigarette, then answered Moses first. "There were a few other bands, sure. She sat with the Leopold crowd sometimes, and occasionally with the Amblers from Amberley and a band from Hyde Park called 'Mr. Hyde.' There was also this band from Covington that called themselves 'Zero to Sixty,' but they were breaking up that summer and stopped coming in."

I was impressed not only that she could name these bygone bands after almost two decades, but that she could do so with a straight face.

"As for the question about romantic involvement" — she put air quotes around the last two words, then stubbed out her cigarette — "yes, I suppose she was probably involved with some of the guys she was hanging out with. There was a lot of that going around. I didn't see myself as a chaperone. After all, Chaz and I weren't married at that point, so I was no poster girl for sexual restraint. But younger girls sleeping with older scumbags? I did object to that. So, would I have said anything to Leila about her romantic entanglements? I might have. But have you ever tried talking to a teenager about sex or tried giving them advice about their sexual partners?"

I nodded. "I have, as a matter of fact."

"Then you know how far I got."

I felt Moses shift beside me and knew he was grimacing. You wouldn't think a cop who had worked Juvie all those years and dealt with the fallout from so much unprotected sex would have been so averse to the subject.

After a short silence, Moses turned to Chaz, who was looking equally uncomfortable, and asked, "Do you have a mailing list from the old days?"

Grateful for the change of topic, Chaz sat forward. "We do, and you're welcome to it, but I don't know how much good it will do you. Most of the names are given names we wouldn't recognize, and most of those kids have left home by now. So even if their parents still live in the same place, it's going to take a lot of digging to get to the kids you want to talk to."

"If you can provide us with a copy of the list, with notes on any names you think might be relevant, we'd be obliged."

"And any contact information you have for the Wildfire band members," I put in.

"I think only two of them still live in town," Chaz said. "Adam Glass — he was their lead guitarist and front man — and Trace Wingfield, their keyboardist. But the others should be coming for a reunion to coincide with the Northside Park reopening in two weeks."

Startled, I spoke before thinking, "Two weeks?" My eyes swept the room.

Chaz laughed. "Don't worry, we'll get there."

I expected Vic to roll her eyes or tease him, but she had something else on her mind as we stood to go and didn't react.

When Moses shook hands with Chaz, he said, with some embarrassment, "Look, I know you've got a lot on your plate right now, but there's some urgency on the part of the family to get this case closed."

"Urgency after nineteen years?" Chaz looked doubtful.

"The mother's in poor health, not expected to live much longer," Moses said. "Reading about the reopening here upset her, we gather. They're talking about getting some closure for her before she goes."

Chaz looked around. "I'll do my best, Moses, but—"

A disembodied voice called, "Springsteen's agent is on the phone, Chaz."

I raised my eyebrows. Even I had heard of Bruce Springsteen. Was this what Chaz's staff was told to say whenever he needed to get rid of somebody? Or did he really have those kinds of contacts?

62

Chaz smiled ruefully. "We can't afford him, but I'll ask anyway for the Friends and Family rate." He shook hands with me and hurried off.

"You think she's dead, Leila, don't you?" Vic said. She scrutinized our faces.

"What do you think?" I countered.

She stood and folded her arms across her chest. "I think if she were alive, she would have sued the shit out of Adam Glass. Maybe not when she was sixteen, but when she was thirty? What jilted lover is going to stand by and let her ex reap the benefits of her creative talent? At sixteen, Leila was already showing an independent streak. That I do remember. Do we really think that whatever happened to her turned her into a doormat by thirty?"

Food for thought.

63

CHAPTER 7

"Yeah, but look here, Cat," Moses said on the way home. "We can't assume that Vic is right about the stolen song. After all, she wasn't the only one in the audience that night. Are we going to believe that nobody else spotted a similarity between this Wildfire song and a song Leila sang only twice? Vic may know something about music, but there were professional musicians in the house. Didn't even one of them come forward to comment on the likeness between this song on the new album and a song they heard sung the year before? And would the band take that risk?"

"They probably changed it enough to disguise it. And they also probably figured, with such a small audience that night and people's attention divided between the girl on the stage and the preparations for the jam session, the odds were in their favor. But I agree that we should investigate Vic's accusation with an open mind."

"And if we establish that Vic's accusation could be true, then what are we saying? That the band kidnapped and killed Leila to save their royalties? Before they'd even released the song and had royalties to save?"

"And their reputations as songwriters. But you're right. It would mean they were already planning to steal the song when Leila disappeared. Still, I think we need to investigate this whole stolen song accusation. And while we're at it, we need to figure out if there's any evidence for the plagiarism that would stand up in court. A notebook containing all of Leila's original songs dated and written in her handwriting would come in handy right now. That's one reason I want to go back to the Perle house and search Leila's room."

He frowned. "Cat, that room would have been searched by the original investigators. You think there could still be something there?"

"I've said it before and I'll say it again: nobody can search a teenager's room like a mother."

"You don't think Mrs. Perle searched it?"

I shrugged. "Probably. But it could have been too painful for her. Best to make sure."

"You hoping for love letters from the boy she ran off with?"

"Or a letter from an agent offering her a contract, or an offer from a band in Idaho to join up with them, or a threatening letter from Adam Glass, or a diary that tells us her plans — any of those would be welcome."

He had pulled into the parking lot at the Catatonia Arms and we were sitting there with the engine idling. "You think this Glass could've followed her from Cincinnati and killed her?"

"I wouldn't say 'anything's possible,' but that certainly is. It would be smarter not to kill her on his home turf."

He nodded. "You got a point there." He glanced at his watch. "You hungry? Want to split a pizza?"

I looked at him. "You can't have pizza. Last night was poker night."

"So?"

"So, you just spent the night drinking beer and eating potato chips and cheese doodles."

"So?" He was frowning at me. "Anyway, since when have you signed on with the health police?"

He was right, of course. It wasn't like me to question the poor nutritional choices of others. Maybe I had been spending too much time with my daughter Franny.

65

I shrugged. "Fine. It's your funeral."

He put the car in reverse and I gripped the armrest.

"If everybody lies about something, what were those two lying about — the Wileys?" I asked.

"He doesn't want us to think he knew Leila all that well. I suppose that makes sense, given the kind of crowds Northside Park drew. He wouldn't have much reason to single her out, I don't guess, not even from the hardcore fans."

"Except that she knew more about music than most of the others. That made an impression on him. And he knew — and remembered — that she had been singing at the Aquarius."

"That's true. So, let's say he's stretching the truth there — he knew her better than he lets on."

"We have to consider all Leila's possible boyfriends, right? Statistically speaking, women are most likely to be killed by their husbands and boyfriends."

He sighed. Despite a long career in policing, he was still a romantic at heart. "You're right. And I suppose she could have been involved with Wiley, though he and Vic seem pretty attached to each other. 'Sides, he was what? Mid- to late twenties? Pushing thirty? Would've seemed ancient to a teenager."

We hurtled through a red light at Knowlton's Corner and careened into a left turn. I braced my feet against the floor. The oncoming driver, paralyzed with terror, didn't think to hit the horn until we were halfway down the block.

When I recovered my breath, I said, "He's not the only one who could be holding back. I think Vic knows something she's not telling us."

"Yeah, but she told us a lot. She told us that Leila was probably involved with at least one of the Wildfire band members."

"Which gives us even more reason to investigate them because it gives them more than one reason to want her out of the way, one personal and one professional."

I caught his grimace and wondered whether he was reacting to my observation or to the slow-moving panel truck in front of us.

"I don't know, Cat," he said. "Those were the days of free love. I don't know how threatened the average band member felt by a discarded girlfriend, if that's what you're thinking. I can't see the average male rocker seriously worried by threats to expose his sexual extracurricular activities. Was a time they cultivated that kind of reputation. Maybe they still do."

"You could be right. I still want to have a little chat with Wildfire." We pulled into the parking lot at LaRosa's and I commenced the decompression protocol. Then I sat still, collecting my thoughts.

"Moses, I'm more convinced than ever that we need to do what we can to confirm that sighting of Leila on the bus. All this time spent on Leila's Cincinnati connections is probably wasted if she was alone on the bus in Columbus."

He nodded. "No mention of a transistor radio in the witness statement."

I cupped my ears. "Chaz said she was always plugged in. No way the witness wouldn't have noticed earphones."

"Nothing else to do on the bus," he agreed. "She wasn't a reader and she wasn't reading. So where was the radio?"

"And another thing that bugs me — something she said about Woodstock."

"About The Beatles and the Stones? Yeah, I wondered about that, too."

"Leila was too knowledgeable to believe that they were going to show up at Woodstock. She would have known the lineup."

"Unless it was fluid, still changing up to the day the festival started."

"Was it?"

He shook his head. "Don't ask me, Cat. I wasn't paying attention."

"I guess she could have just been trying to impress him, telling him that The Beatles and Rolling Stones were playing, if she figured out that those were the only bands he'd heard of."

"No, I agree with you. It doesn't sit right."

That night, while Moses practiced his horn, I took my third glass of wine and my fifth slice of pizza to the office to commune with my tax forms. I didn't expect that inebriation would improve my calculations, but I hoped that it would blunt the edge on my anxiety. And in fact, I began filling in blanks with reckless abandon, skipping all those bothersome recalculations. Sidney, who loves pizza, followed me into the office and batted around a pizza crust, then left a small trail of tomato-colored partials across the "Form 1040" heading. I added a few tomato-colored smears myself when I tried to shoo him away.

I was in quite a cheerful mood when Chaz Wiley called to tell me that he had a copy of the mailing list for me if I wanted to pick it up the next morning.

"Unfortunately, I didn't find the tape of Leila's performance," he said. "There's a gap in the collection that covers the summer of '69."

"You mean they've gone missing? Or have they been stolen?" I asked.

"Don't know," he admitted. "I seem to remember that we missed some tapes at the time, and this must've been one of them. I thought at first that somebody just wanted a tape of their favorite band and helped themselves. But because there were several tapes missing and they were labeled with some of the most prominent performers, it seemed more likely that someone was planning to sell bootleg tapes and make money off them. We had Grand Funk Railroad, The Kinks, Arlo Guthrie, Iggy Pop, and Bob Seger during that time, and sometimes bands would try out new material here, because they weren't risking much if it didn't work, and that would make our tapes more valuable. We kept our ears to the ground, but we never heard of anything on the black market like these tapes. After we discovered the theft, we started storing the tapes in a locked cabinet that was bolted to the floor, so we never had any more problems, except for once when

68

somebody stole a tape right off the recorder when nobody was looking. Anyway, sorry we don't have the recording for you, but I don't see how it could help you trace Leila."

"No, probably not," I agreed. But I was disappointed. It was as if I'd caught a glimpse of Leila in the distance, and then just as she was turning around, she'd vanished.

The next morning, I took my lists of names to the public library downtown, stopping off at the Wileys' house in Clifton to pick up the old Northside Park mailing list. A helpful librarian named Janet found our key witness, Nandil Suresh, in a physicians' directory for Columbus. He was affiliated with Children's Hospital and the Wexner Center for Pediatric Research. Seeing his credentials in an official publication sobered me and shook my doubts about his credibility.

After that, Janet introduced me to their computers and to a square-shaped black plastic pancake she called a "floppy disc" or "floppy" that contained the entire Cincinnati telephone directory. At first, I doubted that this approach would save me much time, but once I got the hang of it, I had to concede that it did, especially because my alphabetizing skills were down there in the basement with my typing and math skills and I didn't have to flip back and forth through tissue paper pages. I went home with a list of forty-seven numbers to call. These did not include a considerable number of women I couldn't find, who had likely changed their names since 1969.

In working with Walt's list of names, I had to admit admiration for the detailed quality of his notes. He may have been behind on his filing, but he had stuff to file. In thinking back over my cases so far, I realized that all of my case reports would fit in a single file and I resolved to do better. As soon as I finished my taxes, I would try to add to my case notes from memory.

Meanwhile, any optimism I had felt about the names I had found faded quickly as I realized that the women were likely to be more valuable witnesses than the men. I also reminded myself that many of these numbers were numbers for parents and not for the kids who would have known Leila. Add in the number of duplicate names for John Smiths and D. Andersons and I began to wonder what I had actually accomplished.

I was sitting at the kitchen table with the list in front of me when Moses walked in. I had managed to reach Matt Perle and arranged to see Leila's room in the late afternoon. Other than that, I had made exactly three phone calls and left two messages — one with a minion from Dr. Suresh's office and one on an answering machine. Not everybody had an answering machine, I now realized, and I don't know why it took me so long to realize it, since I didn't have an answering machine myself. As for the messages I had left, I doubted that I would have called me back.

"It's hopeless, Moses. I don't even know how to talk to an answering machine. And if the person who picks up the message doesn't know Leila from Adam, there's no incentive to call me back and tell me so. Which means I can't cross them off my list." I lifted the page and let it drop. It caught the edge of the table and slid to the floor. I regarded it lugubriously. "What we need is—"

"A Mildred," he finished for me. "Well, why don't you call Walt and see if you can get her number? She's been retired for a month, maybe she's bored and ready to take on some contract work."

I felt my shoulders lift. "Really? You think she would? You think Matt would pay for it?"

"No shame in admitting that we called in a specialist. Let's ask her to do what she does best and conduct the preliminary interviews. Walt trusts her instincts, so we should, too. She can tell us who we should interview in person." He had picked up the list from the floor and was looking it over. "She can also ask about these folks you don't have contact numbers for when she talks to the others. I'll bet she can fill in a few blanks."

By mid-afternoon, we were seated in a small but comfortable living room across from a petite woman with wavy gray hair and sharp dark eyes behind bifocals. She wore a sensible skirt, a floral-print blouse with a Peter Pan collar, a cashmere cardigan, and flats. She looked just the way a Mildred ought to look, which is to say like somebody's grandmother and not like somebody's operative. She asked intelligent questions as we filled her in on the case and made intelligent comments. She had an impressive memory for the details of the case — better than my memory of my own recent cases, I had to admit.

When we stood to go, I thanked her sincerely for her willingness to help us out. "Walt spoke so highly of you. We feel fortunate to have you on our team."

"To tell you the truth," she said, "I'm glad to have the opportunity to revisit this one. I always hated failures, especially the ones that involved missing kids. And I was good then, that's true, but I wasn't yet in my prime. I'd like to take another crack at it."

From this I gathered that she had screened witnesses other than respondents to the missing flyer.

"If any of them were involved with Leila, I'll find out." She gave me a firm handshake and winked at me.

CHAPTER 8

At the Perle house, we were admitted by Matt's older brother Frank, a middle-aged man with a receding hairline and a care-worn face. "Matt asked me to apologize for him," he said. "He can't make it — something came up."

I felt perhaps unreasonably annoyed that the person pressuring us the most to speed up the investigation couldn't be bothered to show up, and Moses, sensing my reaction, said hurriedly, "That's okay. We've already talked to him, anyway."

"Mary and Timmy are both here," Frank said, ushering us into the living room. "Matt said you wanted to talk to all of us."

Still irritated, I said, "Katie couldn't make it?"

Frank and Mary exchanged a look, while Timmy, a man who had clearly outgrown his childhood name, looked uncomfortable.

Mary said, "Katie can be hard to pin down. I think Matt told you how difficult Leila's disappearance was for her."

Frank frowned. "That doesn't mean you shouldn't con-tact her. You'd think she'd cooperate if she was really con-cerned about finding out what happened to her sister." There was anger in his voice.

"Of course not," Mary said — just stating an opinion, not attempting to smooth ruffled feathers. "We're just warning you that she can be difficult."

Mary and Tim — I could not think of him as "Timmy" — had the same wide forehead, high cheekbones, and rounded chin as their brothers, but they must have taken after their mother as well. They had Leila's thick strawberry-blonde hair and Leila's complexion. I could tell this, I noted, because there were more lights lit in the living room than on our previous visit. A sound from upstairs made Tim jump to his feet, but Mary put a restraining hand on his arm. "Sarah's with her. She's fine."

It crossed my mind that Mrs. Perle's children seemed to care a great deal for her, and once again, I rejected the idea that Leila would have refused all contact with her family for the past nineteen years if she was still alive.

Still peevish, I said, "It's too bad Matt's not here. There was a question I wanted to ask him about the necklace."

"The necklace?" Frank frowned.

"You can ask us," Mary offered. "Maybe one of us will be able to answer it."

"I just wanted to ask where he got it."

Frank was still frowning. "Where he got it? Why would you want to know that?"

It was Mary who answered. "They want to know if it was unique. They want to be sure that the girl on the bus was really Leila, our Leila, and not another girl with the same necklace."

"Another Leila?" Frank said.

"I think he ordered it from an ad he found in the back of a magazine," Mary said. "I don't remember which one — *Sports Illustrated*, maybe? But I guess you could choose from lots of names. I don't think it was very expensive. He was a college student on a tight budget."

"There was a girl named Leila in my seventh-grade homeroom," Tim said. "And wasn't there another Leila at Leila's summer camp for a couple of years? Katie would know."

"It was one of my *Popular Mechanics* magazines," Frank put in. "That's where Matt saw the ad. But didn't the man on the bus identify Leila from her picture?"

"We're just double checking," I said.

"The doctor sat next to her on a dark bus at night," Mary said. "And he was probably sympathetic and eager to help." She turned to me. "I think you're right to double check."

We asked them to talk about Leila and about the summer she went missing. Frank took the lead, portraying his younger sister as a rebel misled by bad company. It was clear that he was angry at her, and Mary didn't try to talk him out of his feelings. She may have been the oldest female sibling, but she had rejected the role of family peacemaker. In fact, it became clear that she had dodged the role for much of her life; Leila had proved to be a difficult teenager, and Mary hadn't interceded for her with their parents.

"I was an early childhood education major at Mount St. Joseph at the time, and I had zero interest in teenage angst and drama. I think we all avoided family time in those days. But I don't want to give you the impression that we were any more dysfunctional than the average family because I don't think we were." She shrugged. "We were going through a bad patch, but don't all families do that?"

I glanced at Tim and the eye contact made him uncomfortable.

"Leila was a brick," he said. "She was always so supportive of me, like in fourth grade when I was being bullied on the bus. She talked Mom into signing me up for karate classes, and then she told me to change into my uniform before I got on the bus. It could have gone the wrong way, I guess, but it didn't. Leila told me that bullies were essentially cowards, and it turned out she was right. I really missed her those last couple years when she wasn't around so much, and when she was around, she was — I guess now they'd call it 'emotionally unavailable.' She told me she was sorry she hadn't spent much time with me, and she promised to do better." He swallowed, and his voice was hoarse. "Then she was gone."

"What do you think happened to her?" Moses said after a short silence. He looked around at the three siblings.

Mary said, "I guess we all assume she's dead. But I don't know how or why. I'd really like to know that, Moses."

"I think she met the wrong guy," Frank said. "That's what I think. She was only sixteen, for Christ's sake, and she thought she was grown up. She wanted to assert her independence."

"When you say, 'wrong guy,'" Moses said, "are you talking about a romantic entanglement or something more professional, like a band member or a music producer or an agent, somebody like that?"

"Could have been any of those," Frank said.

"Likely older?"

Frank looked at Mary and she nodded. "Probably. I think she'd decided that most of the boys her age were too immature, and I guess that made her easy prey for someone who presented himself as older, more experienced, more knowledgeable, and more sophisticated. I have three boys myself and they can be challenging. I've sometimes wished I had a daughter. But then I think of Leila and how vulnerable she was, and I thank God I don't have a daughter to raise."

Moses shifted his gaze to Tim. "Tim, any theories?"

But Tim just shrugged and shook his head. "I really don't have any idea what happened to her. But like Mary, I do really want to know. I know it could be bad, and then maybe I'll wish I didn't know, but not knowing is hard. It feels like we owe it to Leila to find out."

"So, should we have a talk with your mother?" I said. "We were going to talk to her last time, but she was asleep and Matt didn't want to disturb her."

Nobody spoke and everybody looked uncomfortable.

"Matt hasn't told your mother about us," Moses guessed.

"He didn't want to upset her unnecessarily," Mary said. "And he wanted to see what you found out first. If it was too painful, he didn't want to have to tell her."

"Makes sense," Moses said. "And I doubt she could tell us anything."

Mary looked relieved. "Honestly, I don't think she could. She was going through a lot in those days anyway, when Leila disappeared. The business was going through a rough patch, which kept our father in a foul temper. Plus, he and Leila were constantly fighting. He was drinking more than usual. I'd broken up with a boyfriend she liked, and Frank was talking about moving to Chicago. She was actually on tranquilizers for a while."

"Did things get worse when Leila disappeared?"

"No, they got better," Frank said. "The crisis brought us together. Dad stopped drinking and I stopped talking about moving away. We supported each other."

I could tell from their expressions that nobody disputed this account.

"We'd like to see Leila's room," Moses said. "Even if it's changed, we'd like to see it."

I had thought that Frank might challenge us, but he just said, "Tim, why don't you take them up? I'll check on Mother."

As we mounted the stairs, I said to Tim in a low voice, "Do we need to be quiet?"

"No, you don't have to. We told her some friends were coming over."

He led us up the stairs and opened a door off the upstairs hall, then stepped back. What I expected was a sparsely furnished room abandoned by two teenagers and reclaimed for guest or storage space. What I saw looked like a museum exhibit depicting a teenage living space from the early '70s. There were still stuffed animals on the beds and posters on the wall that had achieved the status of "vintage." To be honest, it was a bit creepy.

The room was large and contained two matching four-poster beds, as well as matching dressers, desks, and night-stands. The door across from us opened onto a bathroom, and closets had been added on either side of the hall door. I assumed that Leila's side of the room was the one with the record player on a small stand. On Katie's side, the desk was positioned in front of a window. Leila's walls were decorated with posters: the Monterey Pop Festival, the Jimi Hendrix Experience, and Janis Joplin. Katie's walls featured a colorful *Sergeant Pepper's Lonely Hearts Club Band* poster over the bed, but the rest of her wall decorations were small paintings or reproductions of paintings, including an amateurish dog portrait. On Leila's side, the music theme continued in a bulletin board above the desk crammed with photographs of musicians and singers, most of whom I didn't recognize. Leila's records were overflowing two milk crates on the floor. On the wall near Katie's desk was a tidier bulletin board covered, for the most part, in drawings.

I went over to look. "Are these Katie's?"

"Yeah," Tim said. "She's pretty good, don't you think? Leila was always the musical one and Katie was the artistic one."

The drawings were good. Some were caricatures, some more realistic, and some were impressionistic — just a few lines, as if the essence of the subject had been distilled. Several were group portraits of different bands and some of these were caricatures. In fact, most of the drawings were portraits. A handful featured musicians and singers.

"Did Katie go to Northside Park as well?"

"Not as much as Leila, I don't think. I'm not sure she even went before Leila disappeared. I think she knew that it would have ticked Leila off. But she went a few times afterward."

Conducting her own investigation? I speculated.

"I'll start on the closet," Moses said. "Why don't you take the desk?"

The desk proved interesting, but not particularly relevant to our investigation. On top were a *Webster's Dictionary* and several spiral-bound notebooks containing class notes. I made a note to ask about Leila's address book and maybe a loose-leaf binder for school, since these were items that a police investigator might have taken and since I hadn't found them in Walt's box of case notes. The main desk drawer showed the same chaotic abundance that characterized Leila's record collection: pencils, pens, erasers, scissors, screwdriver, stapler, markers, stray stamps, several notepads, single earring, pop top, rubber bands, pet collar, rabies vaccination tag, dried-up ink pad, several coins, paperclips, and a ruler. I removed the drawer and looked behind it, then lifted it to look underneath. Nothing. But as I was replacing it, I saw a name scrawled in pencil on the side of the drawer in the back: Billy Collins.

Tim was sitting on the edge of Katie's bed, apparently lost in thought.

"Billy Collins," I said. "Does that name mean anything to you?"

He shook his head and I made a note in my notebook. The second desk drawer was devoted to school work, mostly graded assignments, from algebra to English essays to history quizzes and a labeled diagram of the eye — but no binder. The third desk drawer was crammed with clippings. These appeared to come from a variety of sources, from the *Cincinnati Enquirer* to *Rolling Stone Magazine* to *Seventeen*. All reported music news — band tours, band breakups, new albums, interviews with musicians and singers, and a handful of ads for guitars. There were also reviews of albums and performances. In a manila folder at the bottom was a collection of letters which appeared to be responses to fan mail that Leila had sent and which often featured signatures, few of which I could read and even fewer of which I could identify.

After checking the drawers for other names and concealed documents, I turned my attention to Leila's bulletin board. Some of the images were clearly publicity stills sent in response to Leila's fan letters. Others were clippings from magazines. The most interesting thing about the bulletin board was the wide range of musicians represented. I could identify The Beatles, The Rolling Stones, Peter, Paul, and Mary, The Supremes, and The Temptations. I could also identify two of Franny's favorites — Joan Baez and Bob Dylan, singing together.

I'd have to ask Moses if he recognized any of the others, but I could still hear him moving around in the closet. I guessed that he was going through all the pockets, looking for anything the original investigators might have missed.

I was putting off going through the record collection. Instead, I turned to the dresser hopefully. But I found no secret stashes of love letters or risqué photographs or birth control pills. Okay, I didn't really expect to find birth control pills because she would have taken them with her. Even if she had broken up with the guy she got them for, would she have stopped taking them, especially if she was headed to a music festival? Unlikely, I thought. There wasn't anything else to find, not even sexy underwear.

On top of the dresser — a surface well-dusted, I noticed — were a jewelry box and an oval-shaped mirrored tray with a small collection of bottles of scent. I studied the latter, then picked up the bottle that had the least amount left. Tim's back was to me when I sprayed a little bit on my wrist, but his reaction was immediate. He turned around, an expression of shock on his face.

"What—?" he began, then spotted the bottle in my hand. He swallowed. "It smells like Leila. It smells so much like Leila." His voice was choked.

I held up the bottle. "Heaven Sent by Helena Rubinstein. Did she always wear it?"

He reached out and I handed it to him. He sniffed the bottle. "She wore it all the time, I think especially after she started working at the coffeehouse, when she came home smelling like cigarette smoke. Katie was always bugging her about that. God, it makes me miss her so much! You wouldn't think a smell could be so . . ."

Having hit the jackpot on my first try, I didn't bother sampling the other bottles. I'd found the one most associated with Leila.

"May I borrow this?" I didn't know what I was going to do with it, but it gave me an intimate connection with the missing girl.

I picked up the jewelry box and took it to the bed. "Can you look through this and see if you notice anything particular that's missing?" I saw his look of dismay when I opened the lid to reveal how full it was.

He gave me a sheepish look that hadn't fully recovered from the strong emotion evoked by the perfume. "I really don't notice women's jewelry all that much," he said apologetically. "You should probably ask Mary. I mean, I know that Leila always wore the necklace and also Mary Grace's friendship ring, that's all I can tell you."

If he was right, then Leila hadn't just worn the friendship ring for her birthday lunch with Mary Grace. Suresh, the bus witness, had thought she was wearing rings but hadn't been able to describe them.

"Did she wear other rings?"

"Maybe? Sometimes? The friendship ring she wore all the time, I know that."

I was poking around in an earring compartment. "She had pierced ears?"

He shrugged, but I hadn't really expected an answer. My son Jason would not have been able to answer that question about either of his sisters.

The nightstand was practically empty. It contained a box of Kleenex, a few bottles of nail polish, a pencil stub, and a piece of scrap paper containing some figures. From the look of them, I guessed that Leila had been adding numbers, perhaps calculating the cost of her trip to Woodstock. I declined to check her arithmetic.

"Were Leila's fingernails painted the last time you saw her?" I asked Tim.

Again, he shrugged. "Sorry. I guess I'm just not that observant."

"It's not important," I assured him. "She had plenty of time to paint her nails between the last time you saw her and the time she boarded the bus." I couldn't decide whether she would have wanted to freshen her nail polish or remove it for a more natural hippie look.

Scrutiny of the underside and sides of the dresser drawers found nothing. Jimmy Collins had rated a single mention on Leila's furniture.

Moses backed out of the closet, shaking his head in my direction, and wandered over to look at the bulletin board. He ran his fingers over it, grinning. "'Pears she liked all kinds of music. Here's Odetta, and Richie Havens, and Carlos Santana. Here's Aretha Franklin in between Patsy Cline and Janis Joplin."

Tim had come over to look at the board with us. "She did like all kinds of music. Somewhere here there should be . . ." His index finger hovered over the collection of images. "Yeah, here it is. Billie Holiday. She was a big fan. That's why she had such a hard time saving for a car. She couldn't resist spending money on new recordings."

"She had a transistor radio, isn't that right?" I asked. "Did she buy it for herself? Do you know what happened to it?"

"No idea what happened to it. She would've had it with her when she disappeared. She never left it behind. My dad gave it to her. He did a lot of business with Japanese trading companies — mostly buying conduit for big construction jobs. So every year at Christmas when other companies sent fruit baskets and hams, the Japanese sent advanced electronics. Leila was always wired for sound."

Moses and I sat down on the floor and began going through the records one by one, pulling them out and examining the album covers for any secret papers. But there weren't any.

I sighed and tried reminding myself that Mildred had taken on the most tedious work and I should be grateful.

Moses stood and stretched his back, then helped me up. "We're missing something, Cat. I don't know what it is, but we're missing something." He reached up and removed the Monterey Pop poster from the wall to look behind it. My gaze swept the room and landed on a Perle Electric ball cap hanging from one corner of the dresser mirror. I felt a small jolt in my head as if someone had flipped a switch.

I went to the desk drawer, rummaged, and brought out the screwdriver. To Tim, I said, "Do all the Perle kids know how to wire a plug?"

He nodded. Moses was watching me as I bent down to examine the wiring next to the record player stand.

Moses tapped my shoulder. "Not there, Cat." He went to the closet, slid open the door, and disappeared inside. We could hear him moving things around. "Hand me that screwdriver," he said.

Tim and I crowded in behind him to watch him unscrewing a vent in the far corner of the closet close to the floor. "I wondered why this was here." He removed the register and I handed him a small flashlight retrieved from my back pocket. He extricated a shoebox. Tim and I were helping him to his feet when Mary came in with Frank.

Frank's face went ashen. He put a hand on the door frame to steady himself.

"My god! It smells like Leila in here," Mary said.

I showed her the Heaven Sent bottle.

She nodded. "That's it. Heaven Sent cologne and Breck shampoo."

Frank added, "At least, that's what she smelled like until she started working, and then she smelled like cigarette smoke."

Mary shook herself. "Find anything else?"

"We're about to answer that question," Moses said, taking the box to the bed, removing the lid, and turning it over to empty its contents out.

On the top of the pile, once buried at the bottom of the box, was a folded piece of paper headed, in a careful script, "Last Will and Testament of Leila Angela Perle."

CHAPTER 9

Mary was the first to speak. "What does a sixteen-year-old girl need with a will?"

"Look at the date," I said. "She wasn't sixteen, she was twelve. And she didn't need it, she just enjoyed the drama of making it. Didn't you ever do that when you were a kid — imagine your own death and your own funeral?"

Mary looked bewildered. "Why would I do that?" She turned to her brothers. "Did you?"

Tim was busy reading the will, but he shook his head. Frank, who was returning to his normal color, said, "All my fantasies ran to hot cars with a lot of chrome and busty babes wearing swimsuits or" — here he raised his hands to his chest, palm up — "those blouses that they tied up under their boobs to show their midriff."

"Imagining your own funeral — it's a girl thing," I said.

Mary was still frowning. "I guess all the fantasies I starred in featured me as a missionary in darkest Africa, feeding hungry babies and bringing the light of God to the heathen."

I was relieved to see humor in this self-portrait. She smiled ruefully. "As for imagining my own death, I really don't think I ever got as far as martyrdom."

"Anything we should know about in there, Tim?" Frank asked.

"Well, if she died, we were supposed to send a lock of hair each to three boys she liked, but the only one I recognize is Jeff Ringgold. Didn't he used to live a few doors down?"

"That's right," Mary said. "They must have moved away not long after she wrote that."

"How about this one?" Moses held up a small metal disk on a chain; the name etched on it was *Paul*.

That took me back. It had been years since I'd thought of those plain metal name disks that preteens used to trade around to practice going steady.

The three siblings looked thoughtful.

"There was Paul Horst," Mary said doubtfully. "They belonged to our church and Paul was in Leila's grade at school, but I really don't remember her having a crush on him."

"If she did, maybe it only lasted two days," Tim contributed unexpectedly. "That happened sometimes. Kids would trade disks on an impulse because everybody wanted to have a girlfriend or boyfriend, but that didn't mean you really liked the person. A day later, you could be wondering what you were thinking."

"Now that sounds like Leila," Mary said. "She had terrible taste in boys."

"You're sure it wasn't Paul McCartney?" I said, and even Moses looked startled.

"Where would Leila have met Paul McCartney?" Frank asked.

"She wouldn't have. But in the throes of Beatlemania, some girls got disks made so they could pretend to be going steady with him. My daughter Franny was one of those girls."

"Well, whoever he was, I doubt that he was responsible for her disappearance," Frank said. "I don't think anyone was wearing those things by 1969. It was all love beads and peace rings."

Tim had folded up the will and now placed it to one side. "She left almost everything to Katie. Are we going to tell her?"

The two older siblings exchanged a look. "I guess, eventually," Mary said.

"A lot of these papers look like poems she got good grades on," Frank said. "And here's a copy of the school magazine with one of her poems in it."

"This packet is all letters from her friend Terry." Frank was shuffling through a pile of papers, some of them in pastel colors, and they released a faint, musty, floral scent. "They used to be a threesome — Leila, Mary Grace, and Terry — until Terry's family moved away. Looks like they'd kept in touch all those years, which is pretty remarkable, if you ask me. I can barely remember my best friend's name from second grade."

Tim was examining other papers. "Here's a guy who copied out the whole Elizabeth Barrett Browning sonnet — you know, 'How do I love thee? Let me count the ways.' You can tell he worked hard on it, too." Tim looked up. "God, did you know Leila had this many boyfriends?"

"Well, admirers," Mary amended.

"What about this one?" I turned it around to show them. It was four lines scrawled on a paper napkin. The handwriting was bold and assertive.

Tim read it aloud.

Sometimes Leila's eyes are a disguise,
And sometimes a revelation.
Sometimes they're dark and starless skies,
And sometimes a conflagration.

Frank blew out air. "That's in a whole different category, that is. You can't tell me that a fifteen- or sixteen-year-old boy wrote that." He pointed accusingly at the paper. "A man wrote that."

"I agree with you. Any idea who?"

"Somebody too old to be giving it to my sister."

"Somebody who likes to play with language," Mary put in. "A poet or songwriter, like Leila."

"This one's more recent, too, don't you think?" Tim said. "And it's written on a napkin. So probably she got it at Northside Park or the Aquarius. She could have met a songwriter in either of those places."

If the latter, I thought sourly, *it probably came from some jerk too cheap to leave her a tip.*

"According to the detective, she met lots of songwriters — or at least, lots of band members." Mary took the paper from me to study.

"Maybe he was in that band Wildfire she was so crazy about that summer," Frank said.

"Could be," Tim said. "But there were other bands, too. It could have been any of them. Katie might know."

"If we could ever talk to her, we might find out," I said, trying to suppress my annoyance.

"Maybe somebody will recognize the handwriting," Moses suggested, ignoring my complaint. "It's pretty distinctive."

"How about this guy?" He held up a Polaroid showing Leila sitting on the lap of a man in his twenties. She had her arm draped around his neck and both of them were laughing at the camera. The man was good-looking, with long dark hair and dark eyes and a long face punctuated with laugh creases. "Or this one?" The man in this picture, also in his twenties, was thinner than the first man and had long blond hair and a mustache. He and Leila were leaning companionably together, shoulder to shoulder, and both were grinning.

The three siblings leaned in close.

"I guess they're not blatantly sexual, either one of them," Mary said doubtfully.

"You ask me, a man that age has no business with a sixteen-year-old girl in his lap," Frank said.

"They were in her secret stash," Tim pointed out, "the one she was hiding from us. That ought to tell us something. Otherwise, they would be in one of her albums."

"She had sense enough to know that Dad would've hit the roof if he'd seen that lap picture." Frank folded his arms and leaned back, and it seemed to me that he was getting angrier and angrier with Leila the more he found out about her life in the months before she disappeared.

Another thought followed that one. *How would Matt react?* There was little chance now that Moses and I would witness his first unguarded response, and that annoyed me all over again. You might presume that Matt was in the clear on his sister's disappearance for any number of reasons, including the fact that he'd hired us to investigate, but it didn't do to make assumptions. Of course, we wouldn't see Katie's reaction, either.

Mary had picked up an old diary, and after hunting around on the bed, found a small rusted key that she fitted into the lock. She'd been going through it while we looked at pictures. Now she said, "I know it doesn't have anything to do with Leila's disappearance, but it's fascinating all the same. She must have been eight when she wrote this. Frank, you'll have to read her account of Thanksgiving dinner. It's hilarious!"

Then she closed the book abruptly, squeezed her eyes shut, and took in a deep breath. When she opened her eyes again, they were filled with tears. "It does have something to do with Leila's disappearance," she said softly. "All this" — she gestured at the objects on the bed — "it all brings her back to life and reminds me how much I miss her." Her gaze took in Moses and me. "At least you've given me some hope. You've already found something that the previous detective didn't."

"Well, I don't think he'd ever lived with teenagers." I was prepared to be magnanimous toward Walt, who had shared all his notes with us. "People who haven't mistakenly believe that they're less devious than the average master criminal."

"But if you really want to help," Moses put in, "you can all encourage Katie to talk to us. You all agree that she was the closest observer of your sister's behavior in the house, and especially that last summer. We need to talk to her."

They all agreed to help, and we left then, taking with us the napkin poem, the two Polaroids, and the bottle of Heaven

Sent. Moses had his eye on the clock, worried he'd be late for his first rehearsal. I confessed to him that I felt uncomfortable about raising anyone's hopes.

"I know what you mean, Cat. Be embarrassing if we didn't find anything new, but that doesn't mean we can find Leila."

"What bothers me most is not what we found but what we didn't find."

"Yeah, it bothers me, too. From what we hear, Leila was a songwriter herself."

"Yeah, so where are her songs?"

CHAPTER 10

Al stopped by for Happy Hour after a hard week of litigating and trying to bully her clients into doing the things that were in their best interest to do. Accompanied by his pint-sized amanuensis Maurice, Leon stopped by to deliver the valentines that we had ordered from him. Of course, we all had plenty of cards left over from last year and the years before that, but Leon seemed to think that we had at least a homeroom full of new recipients we would need to cover every year, and nobody seemed willing or able to talk him out of this assumption.

Kevin stopped by to warn us that the Valentine's decorations would be going up in the hallway that weekend.

"Just remember your agreement with Moses and leave one of the light bulbs uncovered," I said.

But he wasn't listening. He had noticed the collection of items from Leila's room on the kitchen table. He picked up the perfume bottle. "What's this?"

"Leila's perfume."

He burst into song. "*Sud-den-ly, you are all of the things that you want to be!*"

Al joined in. "*A little bit naughty but heavenly,*" they sang, "*in Heaven Se-e-ent!*"

Leon came in a little late, beating his hands on the table. It sounded familiar, now that they were singing it. "How do you remember this stuff? You were just teenagers at the time."

"Teenagers watch a lot of television," Al said.

"And anyway, we were probably a big part of the target audience," Kevin put in.

"Not you," I said.

"I had girlfriends and sisters," he said a little defensively. "The boyfriends came later."

After they all left, I ate a sandwich and settled down to work. Music floated up between the cracks in the floorboards. I could make out brass, a keyboard, drums, and maybe a bass fiddle. The drums were softer than they had been on Sunday, restrained and not intrusive. That was good because I was making phone calls.

First, I ended my game of phone tag with Dr. Suresh when I reached him at home. He sounded congenial, eager to be helpful, but doubtful that he had much to offer.

"I don't remember the young lady as well now as I did twenty years ago," he said. "I probably told your colleague Mr. Hitchens things that I wouldn't remember now. This memory is very vague for me."

"We'd still like to come and talk to you, Dr. Suresh."

"Of course, I want to help, but I'm afraid it will be a wasted trip. My wife teases me all the time about what a bad memory I have."

So, I made the proposal that Moses had told me to make, anticipating offended rejection. But he surprised me.

"Hypnosis?" I could hear the interest in his voice. "I've read about this. A person can recall things he couldn't other-wise recall. I believe there is some controversy, some question of accuracy, but of course you wouldn't rely on my memories in court, and I wouldn't expect you to. You would need to investigate my statements, isn't that right?"

I didn't have to use any of the arguments Moses had given me. The good doctor was selling himself. He sounded quite eager to make the attempt. We made a tentative appointment for Sunday afternoon and I promised to call him back to confirm.

* * *

As soon as I hung up the phone, it rang. The caller identified herself as Katie Perle.

"I heard you wanted to talk to me," she said, as if it were a challenge, not an invitation.

"I'm sure your siblings have explained that Matt hired my partner, Moses, and me to reinvestigate your sister's disappearance. We'd very much like to hear your perspective and any theories you may have. Can we meet sometime at your convenience?" I grabbed a pen and notepad.

"No. It's not convenient for me to meet with anybody investigating Leila's probable murder, not after the cops and that other private dick botched everything so badly."

"Well, wouldn't you like to meet with us to tell us what they got wrong?"

"No, I wouldn't. I have no interest in that. If Matt wants to waste his money, that's his business."

"You said Leila was murdered. Why do you think so?"

"Uh-uh, no, I'm not playing that game. A teenage girl goes missing and never comes home. Why do you think I think she was murdered?"

"But you didn't think so at the time, did you?"

"Not right away," she admitted. "But six months out? Of course, she was dead."

"Where did you think she had gone at the time?"

Silence. That was okay with me, silence was preferable to the sound of a hang-up.

"Katie, do you have a suspect in Leila's death?"

"I have my suspicions."

"I'm listening."

"I'm not telling you. Isn't that what Matt is paying you for — to come up with some suspects in my sister's death?

Or does he really think she's living on the beach in Florida somewhere?"

I took a deep breath. I had spent years dealing with a fractious teenager, I told myself; I could do this. But this one couldn't be threatened or grounded. Later, I would realize how odd it was that I thought of Katie as a fractious teenager, not a fractious adult, but that's how she came across to me.

"I think you spent some time that summer hanging out at Northside Park and the Aquarius like Leila did, didn't you? You must have met some of Leila's friends."

"That was after, not so much before. We were doing our own thing."

Translation: Leila didn't want her little sister tagging along.

"But you did meet her friends, right? What were they like?"

"They were okay."

"Did you get the impression that any of them were worried about Leila?"

"They didn't think about her much, once she was gone."

"Where did they think she had gone?"

"Oh, they all thought she went to Woodstock and met up with some guy, but that's bullshit."

"How come?"

"Because she would've told me, that's how come."

"You mean, before she left? Or afterward?"

A slight pause, then, "Afterward for sure."

"So, you didn't know she was trying to get to Woodstock?"

"Of course I knew." Her voice dripped sarcasm. "She was trying to get the money together. So, when she announced this choir trip, I figured she was trying to make up for Woodstock — for not being able to go, I mean. Although I did wonder if it was just a scheme to get money out of Mom and Dad for the Woodstock trip. But then she never told me she was going to Woodstock, and she would have told me that."

"So, it came as a shock when you heard that she had taken the bus to Columbus, and presumably, to New York?"

92

"That wasn't her!" The shout was loud enough to drown out the music worming its way into my other ear.

"It was somebody else wearing a Leila necklace just like hers?"

"That's right!"

"And you think your sister never left Cincinnati?"

"No. She never left Cincinnati."

"And how could I tell the false Leila on the bus from the real Leila?"

"How should I know? You're the detective. Did she have her guitar with her? Was she listening to her radio?"

"If she had her guitar with her, it was on the overhead rack, or more likely, in the luggage compartment under the bus. The witness didn't mention a transistor radio."

"Which means it wasn't Leila. Look, it was a radio that fit in her hand, a little red one, a Sony. She would've had it with her because she always had it with her." Suddenly, she almost seemed eager to help.

"Okay," I said, "we can ask the witness when we talk to him again."

"When will that be?" The note of challenge was back in her voice.

"This weekend. Look, I know you're all in a hurry for us to finish because of your mother, but—"

"Because of our mother? Is that what he told you?"

An alarm went off in my head. "Your mother's health is failing, isn't it?"

"Yeah, sure, it is."

"Matt told us—"

"Yeah, okay, I get it. So, you're supposed to hurry up and pretend that you're checking what's-his-name's work so we can all feel good about ourselves."

I was about to lose her altogether, I could feel it. I cut across her tirade. "You must have met some of the band members Leila had been hanging out with at the Park. These would

93

have been older guys, for the most part. What can you tell me about them?"

"Well, if you're asking me if they were sleeping with my sister, then yeah, probably they were. They were all assholes."

"How many are we talking about? And are we just talking about Wildfire or others as well?"

"Wildfire for sure, especially that pig Adam Glass and his mate Jimmy Shoe."

"Jimmy Shoe?"

"Jimmy Shoemaker, the other guitar player."

"And you know this because—?"

"You hear things. Those bastards like to brag about their exploits. They're not the only ones. All those guys, especially if they're front men, have egos as big as hot air balloons."

"Sounds like a lot of it could be just that — hot air. I imagine there's a lot of pressure to keep up their reputations as studs."

"Okay, you want to know how I know they screwed Leila? Because they screwed me when she wasn't around anymore, that's how."

I took a minute to process this information and formulate a response. Prickly as she was, I didn't think sympathy would be welcome. Eventually, I said, "What did you think of the Wileys, Chaz and Vicki, who owned the club? I guess she was Vicki Saylor then."

"She was cool. She told me she was sorry my sister was missing. I never talked to him."

"But you talked to other friends of Leila's who hung out there, and I'm guessing they'd be more forthcoming with you than with a male detective. What did they tell you?"

"Nothing. She went off to Woodstock and someday she'd walk through that door again and they'd hear all about it. That's what they thought. Or at least, that's what they told me."

"Did you ever meet any of her coworkers from the Aquarius?"

94

"I met some of them a couple of times when I went in there. That was while Leila was still working there. Afterward, I went in once and talked to the older one, Helen, but she couldn't tell me anything. She was nice, though."

"You were closer to Leila than any of your siblings. You shared a room with her."

"For twelve years."

"Right. Leila's friend Mary Grace says that she changed that last summer. Can you explain how she changed, if you think she did?"

"She didn't change, she just, you know, got older. She'd always been crazy about music, and when the Park opened, she finally had a place to go to hear it and hang out with other people who were musical. That wasn't me. I mean, I took piano lessons as a kid, we all did, and there was a brief time I thought maybe I could play keyboard in a band, but I didn't have Leila's ambition, you know?"

"Mary Grace said that Leila got in with an older crowd and that changed her."

"Mary Grace is a dope," she said, and I could hear the fourteen-year-old in her voice. "Yeah, a lot of the kids at the Park were a little older because they had to be able to get there, but there were a lot of kids Leila's age. The club didn't serve alcohol, so anybody could get in. Just the musicians were older. Mary Grace was probably thinking more about the coffeehouse. That drew an older crowd. And god, the cigarette smoke! Leila came home reeking of it, so of course, our bedroom reeked of it, too, which is probably why I never became a smoker. At the Park, you had to go outside to smoke."

"Did Leila smoke?"

"I think she smoked a little. She wasn't addicted or anything."

At least, I thought, Katie's version of Leila wasn't.

I looked down. I was running out of paper on my notepad.

"Katie, we have some pictures to show you. And I'd like my partner to meet you."

95

"So he can tell you how crazy I am?"

"He might have some questions to ask that I haven't thought of."

"He's another ex-cop, right?"

"That's right. He spent most of his career in Juvie helping kids."

She snorted. "I wonder if the kids would see it that way."

"I've met some who do." I tried to keep the snippiness out of my voice, but I knew I hadn't succeeded. This was one of my great drawbacks as a detective — I wasn't good at keeping my emotions in check. I had been better at it in the old days of motherhood, but as soon as my kids moved out of the house, I stopped trying. That happened at about the same time I took up swearing.

"Well, I'm not sitting down with you for a nice cozy chat. This was it — all you're getting from me. And it's more than I planned to give you, but it will have to be enough."

"I have pictures—"

"Yeah, I heard about them. And I'm pretty sure you don't need me to identify the guys in the pictures. You'll find other people to do that."

"But you know who they are from the descriptions?"

"I'm hanging up now. Have a nice life."

The line went dead.

Beneath my feet, someone was playing a horn solo.

CHAPTER 11

The Aquarius Coffeehouse looked even more like a Smithsonian exhibit than Leila's bedroom had, if Smithsonian exhibits preserved all the original dirt, stains, dents, and other signs of their history. I don't mean to say that it was filthy, only that it had been hard-used by generations of caffeine addicts and boasted all its original decor and furnishings, down to the wobbly tables propped up by folded napkins and desiccated sugar packets. Okay, maybe it was filthy; best not to look too closely. Or inhale too deeply.

The owner, Martin Yeager, fit right in. He'd lost most of his hair, and I was willing to bet that we'd find it accumulated in corners or gumming up the machinery in the vintage espresso machine occupying pride of place behind the bar. He wore a pair of thick horn-rimmed glasses, a bulky stained sweatshirt over baggy khakis, and sneakers that appeared to be on their last lap. He was shorter than Moses and a little older, I guess, with a face made for irony. He had the husky voice of a smoker, which helped explain the bouquet of cigarette smoke that permeated his establishment.

We did not expect him to have been Leila's lover or confidant. We hoped he might lead us to them.

There had been five recorded interviews with the wait staff at the Aquarius and I had listened to them all the night before, after my conversation with Katie. They had been discouragingly brief. If any of these witnesses had been Leila's confidant, they weren't admitting it. One of them, Helen Margolies, had been older than the others and seemed, on the tape at least, more forthcoming and willing to be helpful than the others. But her age had probably excluded her from confidences, as she acknowledged. I had also found Detective Walt Hitchens's notes from the sixth interview, a phone interview with Gigi Beck, and had agreed with his assessment that it hadn't seemed worth following up with a trip to Columbus for an in-person interview. But that was then and this was now. We needed a few more straws to clutch at.

I ordered hot chocolate with whipped cream and was gratified to discover that it was as old-fashioned as my surroundings.

Yeager released a puff of air and shook his head. "Leila Perle? You're asking me to go way back — back to a time when I had hair." He brushed a palm over his slick head. "I barely remember that. That must have been — now, let me see. That must've been 1969, right?"

"If you remember the year," I said, "you're doing all right."

"No, now, there's a reason for that. It's not what you think. Reason I remember, this detective came around, looking for Leila. And afterward I heard she ran off to Woodstock and never called home. Do you mean to tell me she's still missing to this day?" He pressed a finger to the table for emphasis.

"The family's never heard from her," Moses said over his coffee cup.

"That is bad news. Very bad news. I hate to think of that girl dead, but I guess it looks that way, doesn't it? And they sent you two to find the body?"

I said, "Mr. Yeager—"

"Sweetheart," he cut in, "nobody's called me 'Mr. Yeager' since Methuselah wore short pants. Everybody calls me Marty."

"What does Leon call you?"

"Oh, Leon." He waved a hand. "Leon calls me whatever the hell he wants to. I don't interfere. He's got his own system. He calls me 'Mr. Marty.'"

I nodded.

Moses said, "Tell us about Leila."

"Well, like I said, I hardly ever remember the girls after they're gone. It's only because of the detective that Leila became kind of fixed in my mind, you know? Girls come and go all the time."

"No boys?" I asked.

"Boys, too, sometimes. Makes no difference to me, long as they're willing to work. Now Leila, she had a real pretty voice, I remember that. She sang here sometimes." His gesture took in a microphone and stool sitting in the corner.

Moses resumed the questioning. "When she left here, did she tell you she was going to Woodstock?"

"No, she told me she was going on a trip with her church choir. We had to cover her shifts. But it was a crazy time of year anyway, always is, when the girls go back to school. If they're local, sometimes they continue part-time."

"So, you didn't know she was going to Woodstock?"

He shrugged. "Not me. If the rest of 'em knew where she was, they didn't tell me."

"By 'the rest of them,' you mean Joyce Ridgeway, Helen Margolies, Pam Goering, Gigi Beck, Sally Hunt, and Linda Monniter?" Moses was reading from my notes.

He shrugged again. "If you say so. I couldn't tell you who was here at the time."

I leaned forward. "So, you couldn't tell us which of the girls Leila was closest to? I mean, did she have a particular friend among her coworkers?"

"I wouldn't know."

There was clearly no point in asking him whose shifts most often overlapped with Leila's. So, instead, I asked, "Would you know where we can find any of these women?

Have any of them sent you Christmas cards? Or have you seen them around the neighborhood?"

"Now, the only one who ever sent me a card was Helen."

"Helen Margolies."

"That's right. She was a regular, worked here for years before she retired and moved to Florida."

Hope rose and I poised my pen to note down a location. "Do you have contact information for her?"

"My wife does. We visited Helen in Tampa once. She and her husband had a condo right on the beach. You can call Barb — that's my wife — and she can get it for you."

"Weren't any of the others regulars?" Moses asked.

He nodded. "Gigi worked here off and on for a few years. She still comes in from time to time. Pam worked here — oh, maybe five years or so? She was in school at UC. Then she moved out west and I never heard from her again."

"Any idea where out west?" But I was already disheartened and had clicked my pen closed.

He closed one eye. "No, can't say that I do. Montana maybe? Wyoming? One of those cowboy states." He adjusted his glasses as if to improve his hindsight. "Now, the Hunts — that's Sally's family — they used to live around the corner on Knowlton. Don't know if they still do. She worked for me — oh, maybe a year or two off and on and then got some kind of factory job. 'Course, she's probably married with five kids by now, unless she's divorced and moved back home."

Something to hope for, I thought.

"Who else did you say?"

"Joyce Ridgeway and Linda Monniter."

"Joyce Ridgeway. Now, let me think. I don't remember her very well, so she might've been in college when she worked for me that summer. Don't think I'd recognize her if I saw her again. Linda was here longer, maybe a year or two? Seems like she was a teacher, but don't hold me to that. Might've been a nurse. Or maybe it was Joyce who was the nurse. Seems like she left because she had to do some kind of on-the-job training."

"Do you have any employment records from 1969?" Moses asked. "Anything with addresses?"

I didn't blame Walt for failing to record addresses for all his witnesses. After all, why would you expect to need them down the road? But I was hoping they might show up in the CPD case file, if we ever got our hands on that, since police detectives seemed more obsessive about those kinds of details than the average private dick.

Marty was shaking his head. "I used to keep a bunch of that stuff in boxes down in the basement, but then the basement flooded in '81 and I threw a lot of it out. Don't know why I was keeping it, anyway. My wife used to complain that it was a fire hazard. Ha! Fat chance! You couldn't get that stuff to burn if you threw gasoline on it, it was so damp down there. I got a sump pump now."

I wrote it all down:

Helen Margolies — Tampa. Ask Barb Yeager. Pam Goering — out west. Sally Hunt — Knowlton. Gigi Beck — local?

I tried to damp the embers of optimism. One woman might lead us to others.

CHAPTER 12

We thanked Marty for his help and headed up the street to Crazy Ladies Bookstore for our little Woodstock reunion. The sun was out and the snow of the previous weekend had melted into muddy ponds and small mountain ranges of slush. We watched as a car parked on top of a brown ice flow tried to gain enough traction to pull forward without slamming into the car in front of it.

"That's us," I said to Moses, "spinning our wheels. What are the chances that we're ever going to find any of these coworkers of Leila's?"

"Now, Cat, you know if you wanted an easy job, you could always go work as a Walmart greeter."

"Rap's getting us a copy of the CPD case file, right?"

"He's working on it. I reckon it's in storage in another building. We may have to go down there again."

We had put in time at the CPD storage facility during another case we'd worked. It was not my favorite hangout.

"But won't this be mostly case notes? I guess they might have a diary or date book that belonged to Leila, but those can be photocopied. It's not like they have her radio or guitar."

"I don't know what they have. We'll have to see."

"The worst of it is that I can't help thinking that one of these women from the Aquarius might know something, if we could only find them. They were the last people to talk to her, as far as we know. And we've still got that gap of more than twenty-four hours to account for. She must have spent the night with someone."

A small motorcycle zipped past the struggling car and slid into the curb. A petite black-clad figure dismounted, raised black-gloved hands to remove the helmet, and shook out medium-length wavy gray hair.

"Well," Moses said, "we got our secret weapon."

Mildred turned her head, saw us, and smiled. She had traded her sensible skirt for black jeans, a motorcycle jacket, and black boots. I couldn't tell whether she had kept the floral-print blouse with the Peter Pan collar.

"Aren't you cold?" I asked, shivering.

At the same time, Moses said, "Nice bike!"

"It's pretty chilly," she admitted to me, "but I'm well insulated. And it's such a nice day."

I reserved "nice" for days above seventy.

Mildred, meanwhile, was giving Moses a tour of the bike. Although he drove a Fairlane, he was as susceptible as every other man I knew to sporty, speedy vehicles.

"Nice red," I said.

"Can we talk after?" she said. "I have a few things to report."

In the meeting room upstairs, we found Kevin, Al, and Mel organizing the refreshments table. Maureen, the bookstore manager, had also set up a record player and a woman's voice sang plaintively to the accompaniment of an acoustic guitar. Scattered around it were worn album covers, some of which I recognized from my daughter's teenaged years. At a second table Franny herself was laying out some photographs, and I recognized with nostalgia an old scrapbook she had kept as a preteen and teenager. The faded yellow cover was plastered with flower stamps, rainbows, and peace symbols. She opened the book to a two-page spread of clippings about Woodstock.

"This is going to be great, Mom!" she enthused.

I tried to match her mood, but truthfully, I couldn't imagine who would turn out for an event like this one on a sunny Saturday afternoon, and on short notice. Franny, Mel, and Kevin had taken care of most of the publicity.

Happily, I was wrong.

The first to arrive were a pair of women wearing braids and long skirts that matched Franny's. Behind them came Franny's boyfriend Garf, laden with more records that he set next to the record player. Then came a couple wearing overalls and matching short haircuts, and behind them a trio with permed and frosted hair wearing pantsuits. One couple brought four kids but, to my relief Maureen, a veteran of these occasions, had supplied children's books, crayons, and paper. A woman in a power suit was talking to Al and a man wearing jeans and a familiar T-shirt that read "War Is Not Healthy for Children and Other Living Things." In fact, there was a colorful array of T-shirts on display, from the ever-popular "Make Love, Not War" to "It's Ten O'clock. Do you know where your Marines are?" and featuring icons from Nelson Mandela and Bob Marley to The Who. I counted twenty-seven people in the room, and they were still coming in. Many of the faces looked familiar. I guessed that I had seen these people in the company of Franny or Mel and Al.

There was a symphony of herbal odors, the strongest of which I recognized as patchouli. What I didn't smell was Heaven Sent, which reminded me that in this, as in other things, Leila was a rebel. Then I smelled a stronger, viler odor that I couldn't identify until I saw Maureen hurrying over to a man with sparse hair gathered into a long ponytail who was smoking a skinny, obviously hand-rolled cigarette. From their gestures, I gathered that she was telling him to put it out and he was complying, palms down, fingers spread, in a calming gesture. That was just what we needed, I thought: a drug bust.

Kevin materialized at my elbow, eyes glistening with excitement. "I can't believe they all came. Your daughter is a wonder."

The daughter in question spoke from my other side. "I told you, they're meeting attenders. Give them a meeting to attend and they'll come, as long as it doesn't conflict with another meeting."

"Fran, who's the tall, skinny Black guy over there, the one with the Afro and glasses? Do I know him? He looks familiar."

Franny followed my gaze. "That's Dave Haas. I don't think you know him but he's got up to look like—"

A burst of laughter drowned her out.

"I know what Sly Stallone looks like, Franny, and he doesn't look like that."

She raised her voice. "*Stone*, Mom, not Stallone. Sly Stone, as in Sly and the Family Stone. I had their poster on my wall for a while — that's probably why he looks familiar."

Now, you might think that having lived through the '60s in a house with three teenagers, I'd be well versed in '60s culture and counterculture. But like Mrs. Perle, Leila's mother, I had been preoccupied with the war on the home front between my pigheaded conservative husband and my pigheaded radical daughter, not to mention the constant drama generated by the fluctuating hormones of two other teenagers in the house. Like I've said before, it was a major life achievement to get Franny to attend her father's funeral in tears rather than picketing it in Birkies. But if you're waiting for me to condemn Theresa Perle for resorting to tranquilizers, you'll have a long wait. It never occurred to me that I could take drugs to insulate me from the emotional storms raging all around me. Had I but known, I would have turned on and tuned out faster than you can say "psychedelic."

I was gratified to see that the photograph table was filling up. I was making my way over when Moses caught my eye and gave me the high sign.

I'm not big on public speaking, but we'd decided that it had to be me, not the ex-cop.

My daughter Franny caught the look of panic on my face and took me by the arm. "Come on, Mom, I'll help you." I was grateful. Chances were good that I would need, if not a translator, at least an interpreter.

Maureen gave a whistle, and all eyes were on me. Some people found seats in folding chairs, while others remained standing. A few settled cross-legged on the floor.

I cleared my throat, swallowed, cleared my throat again.

"Hi, everybody," my daughter said, "we're, like, so psyched that you're here and we hope you're having a good time at this little reunion." She was interrupted by applause and whistles and beamed back at the audience. "I'm Franny, but I guess you all know that. Wow, it's so great to see you all. Special kudos to those of you who, like, dressed the part. Doug, you're wearing one of my all-time favorite T-shirts, man."

A blond man standing in the back with a ponytail and an earring spread his arms to show off his shirt.

"And EJ — another classic. I used to own one of those shirts."

"You did," said a redheaded woman down front sporting bellbottoms, a neck tattoo, and a single braid halfway down her back. "This is your shirt. You loaned it to me on the way to Washington in '73 and I never gave it back."

When the laughter subsided, Franny resumed. "Special thanks go to Kevin O'Neill, who provided most of the baked goods." More applause and whistles, louder this time. She pointed at the refreshments table. "And to whoever brought Diana Trout's special magic brownies—"

A fist pumped in the back.

"Jonas, I should have known it would be you. Far out! Thanks for the memories, man."

The fist pumper was receiving congratulatory pats on the back and handshakes.

"Anyway, you may know there's also, like, a more serious purpose to this reunion today. This is my mom, Cat. And over there by the record player is her partner, Moses."

We each raised a hand in salute.

"They've been hired to find out what happened to a girl who went missing back in 1969."

Someone raised a voice to say, "Man, I don't hardly remember 1969. I think I was stoned the whole time."

"The girl's name was Leila Perle and we're passing around her picture."

Al, Mel, and Kevin were passing out flyers with multiple pictures of Leila. The volume rose as people passed them around and commented on them.

"She was last seen on a bus headed for New York and Woodstock. So, Cat and Moses are, like, trying to figure out whether she made it to Woodstock or not because her family never heard from her again and her mom's dying and wants to know what happened to her. Isn't that right, Mom?"

"Yes, that's right, Fran," I said, stepping forward a little. In the back, Moses raised a hand to his ear, so I bumped up the volume. "That's right, Fran. Some of you may have known Leila Perle from Northside Park or the Aquarius, and if you did, you may know something about her plans when she left. Or maybe you know where she stayed the night before she got on the bus. But even if you didn't know her, we're hoping you might recognize her from these pictures. Maybe you remember seeing her at Woodstock."

The noise level of the crowd was rising. There were small patches of laughter and a lot of headshaking. Someone said, "You know how many people were at Woodstock?"

"I wouldn't recognize myself at Woodstock," someone observed.

"No kidding," someone else said.

"We do know," I continued, giving them a rueful smile. "We know it's a long shot. But we haven't found anyone who saw Leila after the Columbus Greyhound station."

A middle-aged woman with a child balanced on one hip raised a hand and her neighbors started shushing everybody. "Was this girl rich or something?"

107

I was surprised by the question. "Her family had money, but we understand that she was scraping together her trip money, just like the rest of you. Maybe she hit up one of you for a loan."

This provoked an upswelling of laughter and more chatter.

"Well, I mean, like, why was she riding the bus?"

I could just hear the question. "Why do you ask?"

The crowd quieted a little to hear the answer. "Well, I mean, the bus costs a lot of money. I don't know many people who could afford it. Like, how many of you rode the bus to Woodstock?" She looked around. Nobody raised a hand, and her gaze returned to me.

"See what I mean?"

"She's right," a dark-haired woman put in. "If you wanted to go to Woodstock, you first had to find the ticket money somewhere. If you were going for all three days, that was eighteen bucks in advance, more than eighteen at the gate. Well, after the crowds knocked all the fences down, they stopped charging admission and most people got in for free, but nobody knew that in advance." She began to count on her fingers. "So, you needed ticket money, and food money, and—"

"Weed money," several people chorused.

"'Less you were growing your own," someone put in.

She grinned and continued her enumeration. "—And gas money. So that's the reason why everybody carpooled. Too expensive to take a car by yourself, even if you had one."

"And even if you could rely on it not to crap out on the Pennsylvania Turnpike," someone added.

"Yeah, don't forget the turnpike tolls," someone else said.

A petite woman wearing oversized overalls liberally studded with protest buttons stood up. "Listen, I knew Leila. Several of us knew her from the Park." Her gaze swept the faces around her. "She wasn't rich. She freaked out about money just like the rest of us did. Okay, maybe she had more than some of us because she worked at the Aquarius. But that didn't pay any better than the kind of crappy jobs most of us had. And she was desperate to get to Woodstock."

Chaz's account of the robbery at the Park flashed through my mind. Was that where this was going?

"Are you saying that Leila wasn't the girl on the bus? Are you saying the witness got it wrong?"

"I'm saying that anything could have happened after she was seen on the bus in Columbus. I'm saying she could have figured that once she was on I-70, she could hitchhike the rest of the way. All she'd have to do would be to stand on the entrance ramp and target VW vans with flowers and peace symbols painted on them."

I flashed on an image of Leila standing by a highway entrance ramp in the middle of the night, her guitar case in one hand and her thumb out.

"But why not find a ride in Cincinnati?" said the woman who had first raised the question, now speaking over her child's loud humming. "Couldn't she find one at the Park? I didn't go there much, but it seems like she'd know people there who were going."

"You'd think so," Overalls acknowledged. "I knew one or two people myself. But the crowd at the Park was pretty young, so they weren't well supplied with cars that could handle a road trip."

"Not to mention parental permission to drive hundreds of miles to a rock festival," someone else put in.

"Most kids found rides through WEBN, the radio station," said a voice of authority wearing a mustache and full beard. "Kids used to listen to Michael Xanadu's show, Jelly Pudding."

"Yeah?" My interest quickened. "How did that work?"

"I guess they kept a ride board at the station," he said. "Drivers would register, and then if you called in for a ride, they gave you a driver's phone number." He looked around. "Where's Angie? Angie, isn't that how it worked?"

"Pretty much," a brown-haired woman answered.

"So how many of you found rides or riders through WEBN?" I asked, looking around.

More than a dozen hands went up — almost half of the attendees.

"Okay, thanks. That's good information. Well, I don't want to hold up the festivities. But I'd like you all to take a good look at the pictures we have on the table there and let me know if you spot Leila in any of them or in any you might have at home. We'd like to talk to any of you who knew Leila or who might know somebody who knew Leila. You can talk to me or Moses or Mildred over there, the one in the motorcycle jacket." I turned in Moses's direction. "Anything to add?"

He shook his head but added anyway. "We're just trying to help out a grieving family. I guess most of you can imagine what it would be like if your daughter or one of your siblings disappeared into thin air. We can understand why you maybe held back something you knew at the time, out of loyalty to Leila. But that was almost twenty years ago and you might feel differently now, especially if you have kids of your own. We just want to find out what happened. So, if you know something — anything — that you didn't tell the detectives at the time, please tell us now, even if you don't think it's significant. Let us figure out if it's significant or not." He paused for a minute, then added, "That's all. Thanks for your help."

I was making my way to the photograph table when someone touched me on the arm.

"Ms. Caliban? Cat?" An attractive woman with Asian eyes and long, black hair stepped forward. "It's just that you said you wanted to talk to anybody who knew Leila, and I did. I didn't see her at Woodstock and I don't know how she got there. I never even talked to her about it, so I don't know what I can tell you that would be helpful."

She introduced herself as Maya Zeng.

"How did you know her?"

"A friend took me to Northside Park that summer — in June, that would have been. I got into the Wildfire crowd — you know who they were, right?"

I nodded.

"So, I met her that way, but I didn't know her well. And then she kind of left the group and so I'd see her at the Park but not really to talk to."

"Do you know why she left the group?"

She looked down. "Well, yeah, I do. I guess she left because she'd been having this thing with Adam Glass. Do you know who he was? Lead guitarist for the band?"

I nodded again.

"Yeah, so, I guess she was having this thing with him and then he lost interest. There was a time in there when she started seeing Jimmy Shoe — Jimmy Shoemaker, the bass guitarist. But I think she was really hung up on Adam, so the thing with Jimmy didn't last. Maybe she thought she could make Adam jealous, I don't know."

"So, she was obsessed with Adam Glass, that's what you're saying? And you could tell because—?"

"Well, I guess because I replaced her with Adam." She glanced at me to see how I was receiving this piece of information. "I mean, I didn't set out to replace her, and honestly, that makes Glass sound like a serial monogamist, which he definitely wasn't. I don't even know how long they had been involved before I showed up. But he told me it was over with her." She gave a short laugh. "Of course, he told me that. Leila was young, she was looking for a thrill, no way she could measure up to a mature woman like me." Her singsong tone told me that she was recapping Adam Glass's seduction spiel.

"I get the picture," I said, rolling my eyes.

She grinned at me. "I'm sure he told the next girl that I was too old for him. At nineteen, I thought I was quite mature and sophisticated. I was on the pill and that made me a woman of the world. I attended Wellesley, after all, and that was supposed to make me smart. But it took another six or seven years for the feminists to get through to me and make me realize who was paying for the sexual revolution."

"But you went to Woodstock? How did you get there?"

"One of my classmates from Louisville picked me up on her way and then we went on to Wellesley when the festival was over."

"And you didn't see Leila at the festival?"

"No, I didn't, but there were thousands of people and I probably didn't lay eyes on half of them." She gestured at the photograph table. "I'll take a look at the pictures, but you should realize that even if Leila doesn't show up in any of them, and even if nobody remembers seeing her, it doesn't mean she wasn't there."

"Can you give me the names of other girls at the Park who knew Leila and spent time with her?" I had my notebook out and my pen poised.

But just then, a crash behind me made me turn. I caught a glimpse of Moses just before a fist connected with his face and he went down.

In the confusion of voices that followed, I heard a male voice say, "Coots and Kramer. Shoulda known. Shoulda made 'em both eat magic brownies as soon as they got here."

CHAPTER 13

As I made my way to Moses, I saw Kevin putting one man in a headlock and Mel with an arm bar on another. Moses was sitting on a folding chair when I reached him and Maureen was already handing him a Crazy Ladies T-shirt filled with ice, which he pressed to his cheekbone. A motherly sort sat next to him with a hand on his back.

"There was bound to be trouble and we should have stopped it before it started," she admitted. "I'm so sorry you got in the way." She looked up at me. "Those two have been at it ever since Sunny Gillespie went to Woodstock with one of them and left with the other." She shook her head. "It wasn't all peace and love at Woodstock, I'm sorry to say, and not everybody joined the free love bandwagon."

Since I wasn't the maternal type, I moved away when Moses waved me off and approached a group near the photograph table who were scrutinizing a crowd shot. The two combatants had been shown the door. I hoped that they had been shown separate doors.

"Which one did you say?" somebody said.

"This one right here," said the woman who was holding the photograph and pointing.

"Oh, man, I don't know," said a tall man who was looking over her shoulder. "Hard to tell."

"Show it to Terry," someone said. "She the one knew this Leila chick."

The photograph got passed to a woman with wild auburn hair, who fumbled in her bag for reading glasses and put them on before rendering an opinion.

"Nah, don't think so." She lifted her chin and then lowered it to get the best angle. "She looks older than Leila, and heavier."

This was what I had been afraid of: that soon people would see Leila in every fuzzy, long-distance shot of a blonde teenager. I feared it because I had that tendency myself.

Mildred caught my attention and waved me over, then introduced me to a slender woman named Annie, who had a head full of dreadlocks and was wearing a fashionable pantsuit with a tie-dyed scarf. "Annie has a story to tell about the night she left for Woodstock."

"I hadn't thought of it for a long time and I don't know if it's relevant at all to this missing girl," Annie began apologetically. She used her long, thin fingers expressively as she talked. "But I got my ride through WEBN, like they were saying before. They hooked me up with this guy named Sam who was driving a Chevy Impala. We met up with him in a UC parking lot. We met him at ten at night and loaded up the car — this was on the Thursday, the day before the festival started. Then we stood around for twenty minutes waiting for the last rider, but she never showed. The thing is, her name might've been Leila. I just don't quite remember, but that sounds familiar. If you could track down Sam, he could tell you."

"Did he say anything about this missing rider? Did he know her?"

"No, he said she'd found him through WEBN, like the rest of us had. But he said she'd been kind of dissatisfied and told him she might try to find another ride."

"Why was she dissatisfied? Did he say?"

"I guess she was hoping to leave earlier. She was afraid of missing some of the festival. But we didn't, of course. We made it in plenty of time, so I don't know what her problem was, unless she wanted to help set up the soundstage. But I guess a bigger problem was her guitar. Sam told her we didn't have room for it in the car, not with five people and their bags and some camping equipment. She was going to keep looking around for a ride, but she was supposed to let him know if she wasn't coming and she didn't. So, we waited around until about 10:30 and then took off. Sam was pretty annoyed."

"Do you have a last name for Sam?"

"I don't remember it, but he worked for the radio station. He's really the one you should talk to, because I'm giving you all of this secondhand and I don't really remember it very well. I'm not even sure about the name, it could have been Lisa or Liza or even Martha."

I glanced at Mildred. She tapped a little black notebook she was holding and nodded at me. I moved on.

I felt a hand on my arm and turned to see a tall, hefty man with stringy red hair and a scraggly red beard. He wore a Doors T-shirt, jeans, and an earring in one ear.

"I think I saw her," he said. "Leila, I mean. I think I saw her at Woodstock."

The noise in the room was escalating, so I waved in the direction of the door. "Let's step outside. I'm having trouble hearing over the din."

He followed me out into the hall, talking the whole time. "Yeah, so, like, I came in at the end of your speech and then somebody handed me a picture, and it was, like" — he raised his hands to his head and made a small explosive sound, which I took to refer to his mind exploding — "and I thought, 'Whoa, this is *Leila* she's talking about. She wants to know if anybody saw Leila at Woodstock.'"

"Sorry," I said. "What's your name?"

He put a hand on his chest. "Gary Livingston. But I go by Stoner."

I froze my smile on my face and shook hands. "Did you know Leila?"

"Well, yeah, I knew her. I mean, we weren't good friends or anything. But I used to see her around at the Park and the Aquarius."

"And you knew she meant to go to Woodstock?"

"Well, she was trying to go — everybody knew that."

"You mean she was trying to raise money or she was trying to find a ride?"

"I know she was trying to find a ride, but she might've been trying to raise money, too. I wouldn't know about that."

"And you didn't offer her a ride?"

He drew his eyebrows together and turned down his mouth in an exaggerated expression of regret.

"I couldn't. I was driving with my cousin in his VW Bug. We barely had room for our camping gear."

"So, tell me about this sighting. Where did you see Leila?"

"Oh, I needed to take a piss this one time and I was headed for the latrines when I thought I saw her. And I thought, you know, she must have made it after all."

"How far away was she?"

He put his chin in one hand to think, so I prompted, "From here to the door?"

"Oh, no, not that close. It would've been more like from here to the windows." He gestured toward the room we'd just left. "That's why I couldn't be sure it was her."

"You didn't speak to her?"

He shook his head. "She was in some heavy conversation with this dude. And to tell the truth, I was kind of in a hurry."

"What was she wearing?"

He thought again. "I think it was just a skirt and T-shirt."

"Could you see any of her jewelry, by any chance?"

He shook his head again. "I was too far away."

"By 'heavy conversation,' you mean—?"

"Well, she was frowning and, like" — he waved his arms around — "the reason I remember is 'cause, like, it was kind of a downer, you know? At Woodstock, the whole vibe was totally mellow. You didn't see many arguments. Everybody was just there to groove to the music together, you know? It was all about, like, peace and harmony."

Clearly, he hadn't crossed paths with Coots and Kramer.

"Can you describe the guy she was with?"

"Nah, he had his back to me. Older than she was, though, I think. Kind of—" he raised and lowered his shoulders — "skinny, you know? Bony. He wasn't wearing a shirt."

"Hair?"

"Long. Dark."

I gave him an assessing look. Friendly as a puppy, eager to help, sincere.

"Had you by any chance been smoking dope or dropping acid before you saw her?"

"Oh, yeah!" he enthused. "I had some of this primo weed that these dudes from Iowa gave me." He stopped and his face fell, uncertain. "Unless it was the hydroponic hash from Florida."

I thanked him for the information, took down his phone number, and steered him back toward the room. "You see that lady over there wearing a motorcycle jacket? Could you do me a big favor and go repeat your story to her?"

He lumbered off in Mildred's direction and I sighed.

Kevin was watching the little kids dance to the music. He raised his eyebrows at me and said, "Groovy."

I asked Kevin how the fight broke out and he repeated the story I'd been told about the romantic rivalry.

"This Coots guy, Randy, and Sunny Gillespie, who I gather was quite a free spirit — they were an item when they left for Woodstock. The other guy, Benny Kramer, was the driver. Over the course of the three days of the festival, I gather that Ms. Gillespie transferred her affections to Kramer. Or, depending on who's telling it, she just got caught up in the spirit of the thing and shared her affections more widely. The two men came to blows in the middle of a Crosby, Stills

117

& Nash set, making them unpopular with just about everybody. Coots found another ride home, and the mutual enmity outlasted both romances by nineteen years."

Kevin's eyes glittered; there was nothing he liked better than a good piece of gossip. "Now, ask me which blonde-haired sixteen-year-old of interest to us has also been romantically connected to Randy Coots."

I wrinkled my forehead. "Leila? Damn, how many boyfriends did she have that summer?"

"I don't think the thing with Coots lasted long, Mrs. C. You know how these romances of opportunity go — here today and gone tomorrow. But you might want to add that to your list of standard interrogation questions for the men you talk to — were you then or had you ever been romantically involved with Leila?"

"I'm not sure why Coots would attend an event celebrating the time when his girlfriend ditched him, unless he was hoping to go another round with Kramer. When people talk about this situation, do you get the impression that both men are equally at fault? Do they both have tempers? Are they both considered violent?"

"Well, Coots was the original loser, so he threw the first punch, both then and now. Everybody agrees on that. I get the impression that Kramer isn't the jealous type, but he's more than willing to finish what somebody else starts."

"I don't suppose you got his phone number?"

He produced a paper napkin with a phone number scrawled on it. "He wasn't disposed to give it to me when I threw him out, but I got it from one of his friends."

I did some more circulating after that, but I didn't find anyone who had been close to Leila. I talked to three people who recognized her from the Aquarius and one additional person who recognized her from the Park. None of these people had anything significant to tell me, although one said she might have spotted Leila standing in line to use the phone at Woodstock. But this sighting seemed even more tenuous than Stoner's, so I didn't give it too much credence. It crossed my mind to wonder who she would have been calling, since nobody had so far admitted to receiving a phone call from her.

I asked several people if I could borrow their photographs or albums. There were definitely a few images I wanted to look at under a magnifying glass.

The crowd thinned out to a few diehards who were enjoying the opportunity to reminisce with old friends they hadn't seen for years. Al, Mel, Kevin, and Franny were clearing up the refreshments. Moses, Mildred, and I put some distance between us and the stereo and sat down in folding chairs, drawing together so that our knees touched. I was still trying to assimilate this version of Mildred, in black jeans and a black sweater under a black motorcycle jacket, to the Mildred of skirt and blouse, but at least the sweater had pink roses on it and she was still wearing bifocals.

Mildred wanted to report, so we let her go first. She had tracked down five of the original bus station witnesses who had responded to the Missing posters, scattered between here and New York, and found nothing worth following up on. Although two of them mentioned a necklace, neither could describe it, and none of the witnesses mentioned any of the other items we were hoping for: a friendship ring, a transistor radio, or a guitar. In none of the cases did the date and time of the prospective sighting match the date and time of our most credible sighting.

Using Walt's original case notes and Chaz's annotated mailing list for the Park, she had also tracked down four people who had known Leila from the club. One, Jeremy Fox, had been romantically linked to Leila right before she disappeared, according to Walt. But Fox had claimed that the relationship was in its early days, and that corresponded with what I remembered of Walt's notes.

"He thought she'd put her life on hold until after Woodstock," Mildred said. "He said she'd seemed interested in him but didn't seem willing to make any kind of commitments. I have to say I found him credible. Everything we've heard suggests that Leila expected Woodstock to be some kind of defining or transformative experience for her."

"You ask him about any other boyfriends who might still have been hanging around? Or ex-boyfriends?"

"He'd heard about Leila and the Wildfire boys but said he didn't see much of them. A couple of other people corroborate that — it seems the band was getting popular and they were on the road a lot in July and August. He said he didn't know who her other boyfriends were."

Moses shook his head. "Not yet. I agree we need to cover the ground here in Cincinnati, but it may all be irrelevant. What it tells us was that Leila was connected. Makes it less likely that she went off and never contacted any of these folks again."

"And more likely that whatever happened to her happened between Columbus and Bethel, New York, which also makes it way less likely that we'll ever figure out what that was." I sighed. The euphoria engendered by the few new scraps of information we'd gleaned, especially the possibility that she had arranged for a ride and then skipped out for whatever reason, was deflating. And not even an ex-boyfriend with violent tendencies could prevent that.

"Cat, you learn anything?" Moses asked, ice pressed to his cheek.

"The good news is that somebody who actually knew Leila thinks he saw her at Woodstock arguing with a man, or 'dude,' to be precise. The bad news is that he was too far away to be sure it was Leila and he goes by the name 'Stoner.' Did you talk to him, Mildred?"

She nodded. "Questionable at best, in my opinion," she said, "unless we get corroboration."

"You and Walt ever talk to him?"

She shook her head. "So that's something this little get-together accomplished, Cat. It brought a few more people out of the woodwork. Might be more to come, too, when these folks talk to their friends."

I thought she was being generous, but I appreciated the compliment.

"One more piece of information, for what it's worth." Mildred was thumbing through her notebook. "Yes, here it is. Leila was likely on birth control pills."

"Who told you that?"

"Somebody who got into her handbag. Leila had one of those woven handbags from Mexico or Guatemala or someplace. You know the kind — just a big rectangular sack made from two pieces of woven cloth sewn together. At one point, this girl Bev — well, she's not a girl now, but you know what I mean — needed a pen and somebody suggested she look in Leila's bag because Leila always had a pen. She did, and one of the things she saw was a small, round zipper bag, woven like the purse. Bev said a lot of girls bought them at a head shop on Ludlow because they were the perfect size for a birth control pill container. She didn't look inside to confirm the contents, she just assumed that she knew what they were." She looked up from her notes. "I have her number if you'd like to talk to her."

She wrote something down and handed me a slip of paper.

"That's all I have to report," she said. "I picked up a few more leads today on the Northside Park crowd, but not as many as I'd hoped, so if you have any for me to follow up on, just pass them along."

Moses shook his head. "I didn't get much even before I got my lights punched out." He dabbed at his cheek with a forefinger and winced.

"I've got three names," I said, "but I'm pretty sure they're already on the Park mailing list and I didn't get any updated addresses or phone numbers. I guess what surprises me is how little overlap there was between the Woodstock attendees and the Park regulars."

"Gotta be an age thing," Moses said. "Northside Park was really intended for teenagers, so it's like we've been hearing: younger kids had a harder time getting to the festival than older ones."

"Yeah," I agreed, "and not every kid had a convenient, ready-made permission slip to cover for a few days' absence, even if they could find the price of admission and a way to get there."

"What next?" Mildred asked.

"I've got about a dozen photographs to look at under the magnifying glass," I said, "to see if any of the blurry, groovy blonde girls is Leila. And okay, I know the odds are against me in a crowd of four hundred thousand plus, but I have to admit that the longer we go without finding a single sighting of her, the less I believe that she actually made it to the festival."

I gave Mildred my notes from our conversation with Marty Yeager. "We still have to account for the missing hours between Leila's last shift at work and the 10:30 p.m. bus to Columbus the next night. Whoever she stayed with might know more about Leila's plans. I'm going to try and track down this Woodstock driver named Sam who waited for a girl that never showed up. I doubt that WEBN has an archive containing old ride boards, but if he worked for the station, maybe somebody will remember him."

We promised to let Mildred know what happened the next day, when we were going to Columbus to interview Dr. Suresh with the help of a hypnotist.

"Coulda used the hypnotist today," Moses observed. "Shoulda plied 'em with magic brownies, then turned the hypnotist loose on 'em. Mighta shaken something loose." The inflamed purple mouse on his right cheek was well on its way to swallowing his eye.

As we left, The Beatles were singing, in a downward spiral like a dirge, "She's Leaving Home."

CHAPTER 14

Reluctantly, I spent some time that night on my taxes and concluded that I should have sampled the magic brownies myself. My previous calculations could most charitably be described as exercises in fantasy. I wondered whether I could gain some notoriety and remuneration if I made it to the *Guinness Book of World Records* for the highest number of consecutive erroneous mathematical calculations. This was an appealing thought because no matter how I figured my income, it seemed hardly enough to purchase a year's worth of greeting cards from Leon. There might be an arithmetically challenged chimpanzee somewhere who could beat my record, but I doubted it. The only chimpanzee among my personal acquaintance could calculate rings around me.

I finally went to bed, only to dream of giant animated numbers and long-forgotten math teachers wearing expressions of dismay, disbelief, displeasure, and disgust. This put me in a crabby mood for the car trip to Columbus on Sunday.

I was also grumpy because we were driving two hours to see a psychiatrist. Don't ask me why it never occurred to me that any hypnotist not working in a circus sideshow would be a practicing psychiatrist, but it didn't. I had all the common prejudices against the breed, especially the belief that they were all nuts. The fact that my daughter Franny, the perpetual college student, had majored in psychology three times at three separate institutions just confirmed that belief. Of course, I realized that there was a wide gulf between the average undergraduate psych major, whose numbers are legion, and the psychiatrist who has survived med school and specialized training. But that smaller group was probably not only smarter but more consistently nuts than the larger one.

I also feared that this psychiatrist would take one look at me and read in my eyes the whole story of my long and checkered career as a wife and mother. Nor did I need him to interpret my dreams for me. IRS auditors were not father figures with sexual designs on me, they were just what they seemed to be: powerful CPAs who could expose my incompetence and saddle me with a shitload of fines and back taxes.

Moses, who had slept the sleep of those confident that they could start working on their taxes in mid-March and finish well before the April 15th deadline, was chipper. He had never witnessed a hypnosis session before and was looking forward to it. He didn't seem much bothered by the purple swelling on his right cheek that had spread to his eye. He seemed to think it gave him a tough-guy look. I thought it gave him the look of a not-so-tough guy who had lost the fight, but I wasn't going to say so.

"You can see okay out of that eye, right?"

He turned his head to look at me, but he turned it pretty far.

"How many fingers am I holding up?"

He turned back to look at the road without answering.

"So, tell me about this guy we're going to see," I said as we whizzed along and the landscape blurred outside the car windows. At this speed, my own vision wasn't anything to write home about.

"Dr. Charley Evert. I heard him at a seminar a few years back. He has a practice in Bexley and a lot of experience working with police departments."

"And he's agreed to hypnotize Suresh for us. What's he charging?"

"He won't be doing the actual hypnosis. He's called a 'hypnosis coordinator.' He's the one who listens to all the details of the case and decides whether hypnosis might be useful or not. Then he recruits someone else for the hypnosis."

"Sounds like a scam to me," I grumbled. "Why can't he do the hypnosis?"

"Has to do with professional standards and protocols. He also prepares a brief for the hypnotist based on what she needs to know about the case."

I knew Perley's pockets were deep, but I was offended on his behalf. "Why can't we prepare the brief? I know I'm busy with my taxes and you're working on your horn solo, but we know more about the case than anybody at this point."

"I guess the hypnotist isn't supposed to know too much about the case. I guess we need to be careful not to bias her so she can't bias the subject."

"I still don't see why he can't just take a Magic Marker to our brief, the way the Fibbies do it." I had seen an FBI file before, and I knew this system worked perfectly well for them.

"We have to keep in mind that hypnosis is controversial," he warned me. "Some experts believe that all results you get with hypnosis — what they call 'refreshed memories' — are unreliable. Folks 'remember' things that never really happened. In some states, testimony under hypnosis is inadmissible in court. In other states, it's admissible but likely to be challenged."

"But we're not using it for court evidence," I said.

"No, we're just using it to generate leads. No matter what we hear from Suresh, we have to keep investigating to find corroboration. And it's important to use a board-certified hypnotist, somebody who knows how to ask questions without leading the witness."

"So, the hypnotist can't ask if he noticed a friendship ring, for example. Because — what? He'd start to think he saw it, whether he did or not. I guess that makes sense. If somebody asks me whether I put the clothes in the dryer or not, I swear I can visualize doing it, even if I haven't."

"That's right. I'm not sure where they draw the line, but maybe they can ask him to describe the girl's right hand, for instance."

"Can't we just use a sketch artist to develop a sketch as Suresh describes the girl he saw?"

"I asked about that, but Charley didn't think it was a good idea. He said that Suresh had seen Leila's picture on the Missing flyer, so it was already a part of his memory and could influence his memory of the encounter."

"Huh. I hadn't thought about that, but I can see what he means. Once you'd seen the picture and gotten it into your head that this was the girl you saw, it would be hard to recover the original memory without shaping it to fit the picture, even if unintentionally."

"Right. And he's trying to be helpful, remember. That means he wants it to have been Leila."

"They do realize, these hypnotists, that Suresh is a witness, not a suspect?"

"How do you know?"

I opened my mouth to protest, then closed it when the implications sunk in. "Oh."

Moses glanced at me, smiling ruefully. "Cat, I said the same thing, and that was his response."

We didn't have to discuss why a murderer might call attention to himself by responding to a Missing poster. There were too many possible answers. I sighed. "He's a pediatric cancer specialist, for chrissakes. It can't be him, can it?"

"Let's hope not."

"But if it is him, he might lie to us. He might go out of his way now to convince us that it wasn't Leila he saw."

"Also true."

"I don't suppose the professional whatchacallits allow hypnosis subjects to be hooked up to a lie detector."

"Don't reckon they do."

We met Dr. Charley Evert in his office on the top floor of a three-story office building in Bexley on the outskirts of downtown Columbus. The building was old but freshly painted to conform with the old-fashioned charm of the neighborhood. The carpets and tastefully expensive decor inside betrayed that we were in the high-rent district. Dr. Charley himself was also tastefully furnished in *GQ* casual dockers and a pullover sweater. He had brown bushy hair clipped short, a mustache, and a full beard. The air was lightly scented with pipe tobacco and, looking around, I spotted the pipe on his desk. So far, he had done nothing to dispel my stereotype of psychiatrists.

Dr. Alicia Alvarez, who would perform the hypnosis, was another matter. She was a petite woman, shorter and plumper than me, with laugh creases around her eyes and glossy black hair pulled back into an elaborate bun. Her comfortable jersey pants ensemble could have been hanging in my closet, if my wardrobe ran to ensembles.

"We're using my office because I have the video equipment all set up in the next room," Evert explained. He gestured at a door into an adjoining office. "Alicia and Dr. Suresh will be in there, and we'll be watching on the closed-circuit monitor in here."

"Assuming that Dr. Suresh gives his permission," Alvarez put in. "We record all hypnosis sessions to protect both doctor and client, but it's up to him to decide whether anybody can watch or not."

Evert turned to me. "Cat, I assume that Moses told you something about what to expect, and also about the potential pitfalls of hypnosis. I've briefed Alicia on the case, but I've only told her what I thought she needed to know. We won't be communicating with her during the session."

"You're going to hear three accounts of the encounter on the bus," Alvarez added. "The first will be an account based on what he remembers now, the second will be the account he provides under hypnosis, and the third will be an account based on what he remembers after hypnosis."

This could take hours, I thought, and determined to keep myself awake. On the upside, with any luck, we'd miss today's drum lesson back at the Catatonia Arms Academy of Music.

Shortly afterward, Dr. Nandil Suresh arrived. He was an energetic man with a thin face, a beak of a nose surmounting a mustache, and deep creases on either side of his mouth. He wore khaki pants, a polo shirt, and a sweater. His pronunciation and inflections reflected his Indian origins. He shook our hands enthusiastically.

"Everyone calls me Nandi," he said.

He kept hold of Moses's hand while he peered at the black eye. The two psychiatrists had no doubt been too concerned about distressing Moses to comment, but Suresh had no similar compunction. "Oh, my goodness," he said, brow furrowed in concern. "I hope the other fellow looks worse."

"He doesn't," Moses acknowledged ruefully. "I got between the two combatants."

Suresh nodded. "No good deed goes unpunished, my mother always said."

From his general air of interest and quick smile, I guessed that he was popular with his young cancer patients. But psychopaths are always described as charming, I reminded myself.

Dr. Alvarez took her time with the preliminaries — explanations and permission forms, including one that allowed us to watch from the adjoining room. She explained that he was under no obligation to consent to our presence, but he seemed happy, even eager, to have us watch. She settled him into a recliner in the adjoining room, which appeared to be comfortable, understated in its furnishings, and windowless.

We settled onto a couch to watch the monitor as if gathered for family movie night. I gratefully accepted an offer of coffee and settled my notebook on my knee.

There were more preliminaries. Evert explained that Alvarez was assessing Suresh's suitability for hypnosis. If at this point she found him unsuitable, I would go home crabbier than ever. Then there were more explanations and instructions. Suresh could stop the proceedings at any time, he shouldn't feel bad about what he couldn't remember, he should be as honest as he could be about his memories and not attempt to fill in the gaps, et cetera, et cetera. I was almost asleep before he began his narrative for the first time and Moses gave me an elbow jab to wake me up.

The first account he gave of his encounter with Leila, before the hypnosis started, was substantially the same as the one recorded by Walt at the time. It was less detailed, as might be expected, and several times he apologized for things that he couldn't remember. He didn't mention the dropped pen, for example; he couldn't remember how the conversation had started. He mentioned the necklace but not the rings, and Alvarez didn't prompt him to describe the girl's hands. In fact, Alvarez rarely interrupted with questions. She was more apt to let the silence stretch than to prompt him with a quiet, "Go on." Her questions asked him to clarify what he could see from his vantage point.

She appeared to take a no-frills approach to hypnotic induction — no swinging pocket watch or pendulum, just a suggestion that he focus all his attention on an object in his line of vision. Then she had him raise and lower his right arm a few times. She had a soothing voice that was pleasant to listen to. I was in danger of going under myself.

As she asked Suresh to describe his experience as a young intern, living in Columbus and commuting to Cincinnati, Evert commented, "This is a bit of age regression. She wants to take him back to that time in his life — what his life was like when he met the girl on the bus."

Then he got up, brought the coffee pot, and offered me a refill. This was not the result of any trained perceptiveness on his part. I had nodded off, let the pen slip from my fingers, and scored a direct hit on his Italian loafers.

Moses frowned at me. His look said, *Pay attention. Don't embarrass me.*

My look said, *If you offered to do my taxes for me, I could be the keen, alert, razor-sharp investigator you want me to be.*

Suresh's eyes were closed, but otherwise he was no different for this iteration of his story than the first time around. Finally, we got to the bus station and onto the bus.

"I had been rushing to make the last bus out that night, so I was a little out of breath and relieved to have made it. I could see that the bus was crowded, so I just wanted a seat."

"Were the lights on in the bus?" Alvarez asked.

"They were on at first, but the driver turned them off just as I sat down. The first empty seat was next to a woman with a crying toddler. I knew that kind of crying. It told me the child was tired and cranky and might well keep up that annoying sound — that 'aaa, aaa, aaa' — all the way to Columbus just to annoy her mother. So, I chose a seat in another row — maybe the fourth or fifth? — next to a hippie girl because I thought I would have peace and quiet to read my articles."

"Why do you call her a 'hippie girl'?"

"Oh, I don't know if she was, but she seemed so to me. She had long blonde hair and" — here he swiped an index finger across his chest — "she was wearing a low-cut blouse or dress, I couldn't tell which. She was the right age for a hippie girl." He was smiling a little ruefully, it seemed, as if amused by his own assumptions. "She didn't have flowers in her hair or anything."

"How old was she, did you think?"

"I would say in her late teens, but I'm not a very good judge of that. She was wearing makeup. Certainly, this young lady was under thirty. That's the age when young people stop trusting you, isn't it?"

"Go on."

"She smelled like a hippie."

"What do hippies smell like?"

He wrinkled his nose. "They have that musty smell, don't they? I don't know how to describe it. I used to think that they all wore old clothes from someone's attic and never washed them, but my wife told me that it's a particular scent, something herbal, that they all like. She says they burn incense made out of it. I forget what she called it."

I sat forward.

Suddenly, I was all of the things that I wanted to be: alert and focused.

CHAPTER 15

Suresh's description triggered my own flashback. I had wondered myself why hippie types always smelled so musty and had assumed that it was an inadvertent result of wearing unwashed clothing until my own daughter started to smell that way. As the person who did the laundry, I was in a position to know that all the clothing she bought at secondhand clothing stores ought to smell like Tide. When I asked her about it, she'd assumed the expression of exasperated superiority that she relied on so heavily in those days and said, "It's patchouli, Mother. It's a plant from India."

"Well, how did a plant from India get all over your clothes?"

She gave me an exasperated look. "Oh, Mo-o-m! Everybody I hang out with smells like that."

She had strategically omitted any mention of incense, which she wasn't allowed to burn in her room — further evidence that she was living in a prison camp. She'd decided to focus instead on the political point. "We're not interested in supporting the military-industrial complex that exploits nature and adds chemicals to create artificial scents we're supposed to prefer to natural ones."

Everyone had said that Leila smelled like Heaven Sent cologne and cigarette smoke. Nobody had said that she smelled like patchouli. Was it possible that she had spent the missing night in a Hindu temple or a hippie commune? Possible, but the likelier conclusion was that the hippie girl hadn't been Leila at all.

I tuned back in as Suresh turned on his reading light and opened his *Journal of Clinical Oncology* and began to read.

"What was the girl doing? Could you see?"

"I wasn't paying attention. I was making a point of not paying attention. When you sit that close to a stranger, you know, you make a point of not intruding — at least, I do."

Alvarez didn't say anything, and after a minute, he added, "She wasn't reading because her reading light was off and the bus was dark. It was dark outside the window. I suppose she wasn't writing because if she had been, I would have wondered why she didn't turn the light on and I might even have offered to turn it on for her, in case it was too far for her to reach. So, I suppose she was just thinking or trying to sleep."

"Then what happened?"

"Oh, I had a pen in my hand for making notes — just a Bic, you know — and I dropped it on the floor near her foot. I felt embarrassed, because she was wearing sandals and I might have made a mark on her foot."

I felt a blush rise up my face like a smoke signal. I would have to check the Italian loafers later to see if I had left a mark.

"We both looked down, and she said, 'I'll get it.' And she bent over and picked up the pen and handed it to me."

"So now you are looking at her. Can you describe what you see when you look at her?"

"She is still in shadow, her face is not well lit. I can see that she's blonde, with hair down to here." He used his hand to indicate a place just below his shoulder. "I think her eyes must've been blue, but I'm not sure about that. I can see that she's wearing a necklace, a silver one, with the name 'Leila' in script and a small stone in place of the dot over the *i*. It

133

catches the light, that stone, but I can't see well enough to know whether it's a diamond or a rhinestone."

He paused so long that Alvarez finally said, "Go on. What else?"

He raised his right hand as if holding something between his thumb and fingers. "Her hand is in the light and she is wearing two rings, both silver. One has a round stone, bluish green, I think. It reminds me of my sisters' mood rings, but I don't know if that's what it is. The other—"

He raised his two hands, palms toward his chest, fingers flat and touching at the first two fingertips, thumbs up. My scalp tingled as every hair on my head stood at attention. An Irish friendship ring. Like the ring Mary Grace had given to Leila.

"I think I have seen this ring before also, but I don't know what it's called. It has two hands and a heart between them."

After another pause, Alvarez asked, "Does Leila say anything to you?"

"Oh, I think she says something like, 'Here you go.' I am embarrassed and say something stupid like, 'You wouldn't think a surgeon would be so clumsy with his hands. But I promise I am not so clumsy in the operating room.' Then I ask her if her foot is okay and she says that it's fine. Then she asks me if I work at a hospital in Cincinnati, Columbus, or Cleveland, and I tell her that I work as an intern at Children's Hospital in Cincinnati but I live in Columbus. I ask her if she lives in Cincinnati."

I was feeling a little frustrated by the transition away from direct quotation and wondered whether Alvarez would do anything to get him back to that. I wanted to hear Leila's voice, her words.

"And what does she say?"

"She says yes. So, I ask her if she's going back to school, and she says, 'No, I'm headed for New York, for the Woodstock Music Festival. Have you heard of it?' I tell her that I think I have heard of it. I ask if it's a big music concert.

"She tells me that it will be the biggest music concert that has ever happened. She says that it will last for three days and celebrate the Age of Aquarius. All the famous rock bands will be there, she says. I don't know anything about rock bands, but I want to say something, so I say, 'How about The Beatles? Will they be there?' And she says, 'Definitely. All the famous bands will be there.' 'And The Rolling Stones also,' I ask, 'will they be there?' 'Probably,' she says. Suresh is nodding his head now. 'Everybody will be there.' Now I have exhausted my knowledge of rock bands, so I point to her necklace, and say, 'And what about you? I confess that I do not know of a famous rock singer named Leila, but I do not know much about rock 'n' roll. Are you a famous singer also?'"

I was wide awake now, transported to the past by his account and riveted.

His smile was wide. "'I play the guitar and sing, but I am not a famous rock singer, just a fan,' she says. And I say, 'Oh, but someday you may be. And you will sing and play at a concert bigger than Woodstock. And even I will hear of you and remember you as the girl on the bus.'"

I had crossed my arms across my chest and was shivering. I had abandoned my notebook. I wasn't sure what I had done with the pen. I exchanged a look with Moses, who raised his eyebrows at me. This was definitely worth the price of admission, I had to admit.

"Go on," Alvarez prompted.

"She laughed. It was a very happy laugh. I could tell that I had pleased her. But after that I went back to reading my article. I don't know what she was doing, but she wasn't moving around, so maybe she went to sleep. When we got to Columbus, I put the journal away in my briefcase, retrieved my bag from the overhead rack, and told her that I hoped she would enjoy her concert. She smiled at me and said, 'I will.' Then I got off the bus and that was the last I saw of her."

Alvarez asked him how he came to see the Missing poster and identify that girl with the girl on the bus. He said that he had been killing time one morning in Columbus, drinking coffee and waiting for his bus, when he saw the bulletin board of flyers and posters. It was the name "Leila" that first caught his attention, and he thought the girl in the poster resembled the girl he had seen. The girl in the picture was not wearing the distinctive Leila necklace, but he'd decided to call and report his encounter. He had worried a bit at the time he met Leila that she was going such a long distance alone. He had daughters himself and he would not have wanted them to make such a trip. Now he worried that something had happened to the girl on the bus.

Alvarez ended the hypnosis session with a suggestion that he would remember everything that had taken place while he was under hypnosis. He opened his eyes, blinked several times, and consulted his watch, apparently surprised how much time had elapsed. Alvarez gave him a cup of tea and then settled in for the third retelling.

This account was substantially the same as the one he had given us under hypnosis. This time, he referred to the girl's sandals as "those Indian sandals the kids were all wearing" and didn't seem aware that he hadn't provided this detail previously. But otherwise, he provided no new information.

At this point, I was buzzed on coffee and eager to talk to Moses about what we'd learned. But once Suresh had left, apparently pleased by his participation in the experiment and eager to pursue the use of hypnosis in his medical practice, there was more debriefing to be got through. Both psychiatrists seemed eager to undermine our faith in the accuracy of what he had reported.

"Whenever he reported uncertainty, such as with regard to eye color, we should take him at his word," Alvarez cautioned us. "He thinks the girl he saw had blue eyes, but he could have taken that detail from the image and description on the Missing poster. I'm not saying that he deliberately misled us — after all, he did say he wasn't sure. I am saying that subsequent information might now be influencing his memory."

"What about the sandals?" I asked.

"Yes, that was interesting, wasn't it?" Evert said. "But Alicia is right. It's probable that the girl he saw wore sandals, and he remembered it because he dropped the pen and looked down to see bare feet. But his identification of her as a hippie might have influenced his memory the third time around and caused him to substitute 'sandals' for 'Indian sandals.'"

"Like if I said that Dr. Evert was wearing Guccis on his feet," I said. "Or even if I said 'Italian leather,' I might not be accurate. For all I know, they could be Gucci knockoffs."

The space widened between the mustache on his upper lip and the beard on his lower lip and I presumed he was smiling. "That's right, Cat," he said.

"But what about the rings?" Moses asked. "We can assume, can't we, that the girl was wearing at least two rings like the ones he described?"

"Yes, because there was no mention of rings in the descriptions circulated," Evert said.

"One ring reminded him of rings that his sisters had, though," Alvarez said. "It may not have been a mood ring like theirs, and his familiarity with theirs might have influenced his memory once he made the association."

"So, the stone might have been orange, not blue-green," I said.

"Yes, that's possible," she said. "But it probably was blue-green."

"And the patchouli?" Moses asked. "Isn't smell the sense most connected to memory? Does that make it more reliable?"

"I think we can trust that memory," Alvarez said, nodding. "He could describe it without knowing what it was called, and his wife's later information didn't register strongly enough for him to remember the name."

"What about something he didn't mention, like the transistor radio?" I asked. "Does it seem likely that he wouldn't have noticed it if she was wearing earphones?"

"I suppose it's possible, since she did have long hair," Evert said.

"He wouldn't have noticed the wires?" I said skeptically.

"Remember, Cat, this was 1969," Moses said. "I'm thinking back to my first transistor radio. I used to listen to the ballgame on it while I was building shelves in the garage or waxing the car or raking leaves. Seems to me it only had one earplug, not two, like today. Anybody else remember that?"

"Now that you mention it, I think you're right," Evert said. "Just one plug you stuck in your ear. So, if she was wearing it in her left ear, he'd be less likely to notice."

"Yeah, I guess," I conceded. "And the plug never fell out of your ear?"

"All the time," Moses said. "But then, I wasn't sitting still on a bus."

Later, in the car on the way home, I said to Moses, "There are just too many anomalies. I don't think it was her, but how can we be certain?"

"The problem is, all the anomalies can be explained away," Moses said, "even the scent."

"You mean if she spent the night in a hippie commune."

"Wouldn't have to be that. Could have spent the night in a hippie's bedroom."

"And you think that would be enough to overpower the smell of cigarettes and perfume?"

"I wouldn't think so, no. But it might be. And we knew going into the session that we would have to corroborate everything."

"Are you volunteering to douse yourself with Heaven Sent perfume after poker night and go sleep on Franny's couch?"

"No, I'm just saying we need to keep an open mind. 'Sides, Franny don't smell that bad."

"A person could get lost wandering around inside an open mind," I grumbled. "Anyway, while I'm being open-minded, I keep bumping into a possibility I don't like. What if the necklace and ring really were Leila's, but it wasn't Leila who was wearing them?"

He nodded. "I don't like that possibility, either. It could mean that Leila gave someone else the jewelry to impersonate her on the bus, so that if her choir trip cover was blown and her father sent someone looking for her, they'd be thrown off the scent and Leila could make it all the way to Woodstock without being stopped. The choir trip permission slip indicates that Leila was a planner, and she might have expected her mother to have found her out sooner rather than later and made a backup plan."

"That's my preferred scenario," I conceded. "Because the alternative is that someone else gave someone the jewelry to impersonate her on the bus, and they could do that because—"

"Leila wouldn't be wearing it anymore."

CHAPTER 16

After a minute, I asked, "Why would Leila tell Suresh that The Beatles and Stones would be at Woodstock? I keep coming back to that. She kept up with music news, that's what Chaz said. If she knew about an obscure band from California that was about to hit it big, she probably knew more about Woodstock than any other teenager in the Midwest. She knew The Beatles and Stones wouldn't be there."

"Maybe it's like you said before — she was trying to impress him," Moses offered. "And she could tell how little he knew about rock music, so she knew there wasn't any point in mentioning Jimi Hendrix, Jefferson Airplane, and The Who."

I looked at him in surprise. "Somebody's been boning up." I meant to sound impressed, but I might have sounded a little resentful that he knew so much about Woodstock.

"I got encyclopedias. Be happy to loan you the *W*."

"I got rid of mine when I moved into an apartment. Anyway, I'm pretty sure mine never heard of Woodstock. I'm not even sure they'd heard of Stevie Wonder, much less Stevie Nicks."

Moses grunted. "I've heard of him."

I wasn't sure if he was kidding, but I was showing off a little, seeing his encyclopedia and raising him with a poster from Franny's wall.

"The thing that impressed me yesterday was how surprised they all were that anybody would take the bus," he said. "First, she's scrambling for money like everybody else. Then, she buys a bus ticket when there were rides available. That don't seem right. Yeah, okay, she could take her guitar on the bus and nobody would complain. But there was no way she could beat that carpool to Woodstock on the bus."

"Well, we don't know how far she was going on the bus. It's still possible she was planning to hitchhike most of the way."

Moses frowned. "Standing on the interstate with her thumb out and a guitar case at her feet?"

I shrugged. "I'll bet a lot of kids did it. And I'll bet a lot of kids got picked up by VW vans covered in flower stickers and rainbows. But I agree that what we've heard so far about Leila doesn't make her seem the type to leave so much to chance."

"So, what do we know that we didn't know before we talked to Suresh? We've got more suspicions, but no more facts."

"We know that the girl on the bus wore two pieces of jewelry that Leila wore."

"If there was a girl on the bus," Moses said unhappily.

I was startled. "You think he made her up? You think that was a performance for our benefit?"

"No, I don't, but—"

"I know, I know, open mind. But Moses, you also believe in trusting your instincts, and my instincts tell me that Suresh is a nice guy, completely honest and eager to help."

"Mine, too."

"Good. I'm glad we agree on that. Do we also agree that the second piece of jewelry in Suresh's latest accounts more than doubles the unlikelihood that we're dealing with coincidence?"

He nodded. "If the girl wasn't Leila, it looks like intent to deceive. Whose intent we can't be sure."

"Yet."

"Yet."

"I'll call Mary and ask about the mood ring, the Indian sandals, and the patchouli — whether any of these things has a known association with Leila. In the meantime—"

"I'll call Mildred and ask her to prioritize Leila's coworkers and her friends from the Park. Seems less important right now to go looking for someone who might have seen her at Woodstock."

I stared through the windshield. "Y'know, Moses, if this whole trip to Woodstock is a red herring, then we're back to basics. You're a cop. If someone told you that a girl had gone missing and was presumed dead, who'd you be looking at first?"

"That's easy. The boyfriend."

"Exactly. And in Leila's case, we have several to choose from that we know of."

I snoozed a little after that, which is my preferred way to travel when Moses is at the wheel: unconscious.

But if I was half-asleep when I got out of the car and crossed the parking lot to the back door of the Catatonia Arms, it didn't last. Even before we opened the door, we were assaulted by a series of drumbeats, loud and chaotic. You could not call them "syncopated," because that would suggest that they had some kind of rhythm. The back door handle vibrated under my fingers. Inside, the hall was bathed in a reddish glow. Little red fairy lights glimmered along the banister leading upstairs and someone had hung a disco ball from the overhead light, with a 3D foldout tissue paper heart below that. An unknown soprano was singing an aria in Kevin's apartment, and she appeared to be attempting to shatter all the glass in the building. Rolling down the stairs from Mel and Al's apartment was a juggernaut of rock music.

Home sweet home.

Kevin met us in the hall, a short glass of amber liquid in one hand. He couldn't possibly have heard us come in over all that racket, so he must've been relying on his sixth sense.

"He's driving me to drink," he shouted at us. "It's been going on like this for hours. Who's going to tell him that he's terrible?"

"I imagine it's up to his teacher to do that," I said, and had to repeat it in a louder voice. "It's up to Hope."

He clapped a hand over his ear. "Mrs. C, if you'd been here for the last two hours, you wouldn't say that. You'd have no hope left."

"No, I mean his teacher," I shouted. "Hope Smith is the one to evaluate his progress."

"I can evaluate his progress. He's gotten louder."

"Where are the animals?" Moses put in, scowling.

Kevin shrugged and took a swig of his drink. "Who knows? Winnie's probably sitting on a foot pedal and Sidney is perched on a cymbal."

Moses headed upstairs to check on the animals. In a lull from downstairs, Kevin said, "He didn't even mention the decorations. I hope he appreciates all the lights."

We heard Moses stumble and curse.

"Maybe not," I said.

Kevin wanted to hear about the hypnosis session, so I led the way into my apartment, plucking a Valentine card from under the doormat and another one from the jamb. In an effort to use up the valentines we purchased from Leon every year, Kevin had taken to hiding them, like Easter eggs, around the building and we'd followed his lead. Since everybody had keys to all the apartments, you could find them anywhere. Well, not anywhere; the rules specified that you could not stash them in such a way as to cause a fire hazard or present a risk to working machinery: no valentines taped to the furnace filters or even the underside of the toilet tank lid, no valentines in the ovens. Kevin intended to keep a meticulous list of his locations (his follow-through was imperfect at best and the resulting lists he lost, more often than not) and gleefully taunted us when we failed to find them. The rest of us took a more spontaneous approach, and since my own memory had always been lousy and not improved with my advancing years, I often forgot where I'd hidden mine. It wasn't unusual to encounter an unseasonal Valentine curled inside the fire-starting chimney the first time we barbecued in May or folded inside a lawn chair brought up from the basement for the Fourth of July. Of course, the cats and Winnie found their share and made confetti out of them.

After dinner, I refreshed my Happy Hour drink and sat down to make some phone calls. The main reason that noir detective stories are so noir is that most of the world is at work during the day and not available to be interviewed or spied on or followed. We detectives need to take advantage of prime time if we want to reach anybody.

Leila's sister Mary could neither confirm nor repudiate the details that Suresh had recalled. She did know about the Irish friendship ring from Mary Grace, but couldn't recall any other rings in Leila's repertoire. She didn't think that Leila had ever smelled of patchouli, but she couldn't rule out the possibility of an incense-burning friend or two that Leila might have had. She did think that Leila had smelled of pot a few times that summer and had worried that her mother could smell it as well but doubted that her mother would be able to identify the odor. She didn't remember whether Leila had owned a pair of Indian sandals but considered it unlikely if the sandals were unattractive. She would ask Katie.

After I hung up, I thought about the reference to pot-smoking and felt a little foolish that I hadn't considered it before. Still, my impression was that marijuana had been widely available in the '60s and the claim that it served as a gateway drug for narcotics and a short, miserable life as a dope fiend had derived largely from the imaginations of right-wing extremists who felt threatened by the counterculture. I thought the scenario in which an ordinary middle-class teenager found themselves entrapped by and in thrall to a dope-dealing gang member with prison tattoos and a Saturday Night Special tucked into his waistband was a product more of my times than Leila's. Still, I made a note in my notebook.

I used a number Mildred had provided and reached Mary Grace O'Shaughnessy Hardy, with whom I made an appointment for the following afternoon. She seemed eager to help if puzzled by the reopening of the case. I asked her to bring her address book and a school yearbook, if she had one. I wanted to get a squint at some of Leila's boyfriends.

Moses came in then to tell me that Rap had arranged for us to see the original case file the next morning at the CPD storage facility we'd visited before.

"They've got a new Xerox machine down there, he says. Or rather, they've got a used machine that used to be in Purchasing before it got replaced. He says it works okay and he gave me his code. Then he said—"

"'Don't make me sorry,'" I guessed. "Or was it, 'You owe me'?"

He grinned. "Both. You know him too well."

I peered at his eye. "That eye looks like it didn't get its nap today."

"Matt left a message on my answering machine," he said, turning and bending down to get a look at his reflection in the glass door of the microwave. He raised his bifocals on that side. "He wanted a progress report."

"You call him back?"

He nodded. "I told him we were getting on, tracking down old leads and following a few new ones."

"Did that satisfy him?"

He shrugged. "Don't know. Seemed to. He's an ex-cop, so he'd probably be surprised if I told him more than that. Seemed tired."

"You didn't tell him anything about the Suresh interview."

"'F I did that, he'd reach the same conclusion we did, maybe faster. No point in giving him nightmares before we have to."

"Did you tell him about your Army reunion this week?"

He nodded. "I told him I'd be out of town from Thursday to Saturday. I assured him that you and Mildred were working hard, and I told him to get in touch with you if he had any questions before I got back."

The phone rang and I answered it.

"She hated patchouli," a voice said.

It took me a few seconds to process this statement. Then I raised an index finger in Moses's direction.

"Katie?"

"She couldn't understand the attraction. 'You'd smell better if you just rolled around in the hay,' she said. She wouldn't have been caught dead wearing it, especially not if she was going on a trip to Woodstock."

It seemed to me plausible that she'd wear it to Woodstock so that she'd fit in.

"And she didn't like Indian sandals, either, if you mean those really flat tan leather ones with toe rings. She thought they were ugly."

"She didn't wear sandals?" I was deliberately baiting her. Just because the family was willing to treat her with kid gloves didn't mean I had to.

"Of course, she wore sandals!" The exasperation in her voice reminded me again of teenaged Franny's favorite register. "She just didn't wear that kind. She associated them with unshaved legs."

"I see. She was a fashion-conscious hippie." A thought struck me, and a quick scan of my mental files drew a blank. "Did she ever paint her nails?"

"Sometimes. But before you ask, no, I don't think her nails were painted the last time I saw her."

"Did you ever see her wearing a mood ring or a silver ring with a smooth blue-green stone?"

"She thought mood rings were stupid. 'I don't need a ring to tell me what mood I'm in,' she said."

"Sounds like a girl after my own heart," I said mildly.

"She wasn't," she said venomously. "Don't go thinking you can understand her 'cause she's 'just like' you. She was nothing like you. She was sixteen, for Christ's sake. You probably don't remember that far back."

She wasn't wrong about that, so I didn't bother to respond. "Any other rings with blue-green stones?"

"I don't remember any," she said, grumpily, and added, "and you'd think I would if she wore one."

I let the implication go unchallenged, saying only, "I'm trying to find out whether somebody gave her a ring between her last shift at the Aquarius and the bus to Columbus."

"There was no bus to Columbus!" Katie shouted. "That wasn't Leila."

I sighed. The temptation was great to tell her that I agreed with her, to try and establish some trust. But Moses was standing there watching me, and anyway, I knew it was too soon to voice our suspicions along those lines.

So, instead, I said, "We have to keep an open mind, Katie, because that's what detectives do." I rolled my eyes at Moses. "The girl on the bus might have been Leila or might not have been Leila. We're exploring both possibilities. Right now, we're interested in contacting her friends and boyfriends, and you could probably help us out a lot with that."

I knew if I gave her a task to do, like making a list, she'd probably hang up on me, and I had to keep her talking. Moses signaled me and pointed to the bedroom. I nodded and he disappeared.

"You told me before that Leila was a free spirit, but she must have had particular boyfriends. Can't you tell me about Leila's last boyfriend?"

When Moses shouted "okay" from the bedroom, I knocked a pan off the kitchen counter and cursed as it clattered to the floor.

Into the phone, I said, "Sorry. One of the cats knocked a pan off the counter." The cat in question, who had been curled up in a bread bowl and snoozing peacefully before her rude awakening, now stood in the bowl, limbs rigid, ears up, bristling like a bottle brush. I gave her a slow blink in apology but she turned her back on me to settle down again.

"I didn't know the new one," Katie said, apparently oblivious to the third set of ears on the line. "He was just some guy she met at the Park, Jason or Joshua or Jeremy, something like that. I don't remember now. But I already told you that if you're looking for boyfriends who could have harmed Leila, you should be looking at the Wildfire guys and any other older rock musicians she hung out with. Those bastards were animals."

"This would be Adam Glass and Jimmy Shoemaker?"

"That's right, and Wingfield. And that's all I'm going to say. You've got everything you need now to find out what happened to my sister."

"But, Katie, it would be really helpful if we could meet in person to talk with you."

"No, that's not happening. I've told you everything. I'm hanging up now."

"But, Katie—"

I heard a click, and then after a short pause, another one. Moses came in from the bedroom and looked at me.

"Well, now we know that Leila hated patchouli."

He started to speak, but I held up a hand and continued. "I know, I know, she could have stayed with friends who liked it. Just don't tell me that the girl on the bus was Leila disguised as a hippie girl to throw trackers off the scent."

"No, I was going to suggest that you wear a mask tomorrow. You know how dusty that place is, and you might need to smell something before we're through there."

CHAPTER 17

The CPD storage facility had not improved in the brief time we'd been away — same butt-breaking stools, same wobbly tables, same economy lighting, same musty smell of moldering paper. There was another smell, too, much fainter and fouler and unidentifiable, an odor that leaked through the plastic bags intended to contain it. It reminded us, if we needed reminding, to pull on our plastic gloves.

We'd known enough to bring our own coffee and not to trust our cups to the tilty tabletops. I'd also brought along a copy of Walt Hitchens's report, in case we wanted to compare it to the police report.

First, we made a quick survey of the contents of the box we'd been left to examine.

"Damn!" I said, disappointed but not surprised. "No phone book."

"Must've taken it with her," Moses said. "Here's a list of other things the family identified as missing — not just her guitar and radio, but her toothbrush and hairbrush. Looks like she was planning to be gone a few days."

"She was last seen wearing a flowered skirt, peasant blouse, and sandals," I mused. "No description of the sandals."

"And her necklace."

"That's what the Beck girl told Walt, but I wonder. That hypnosis session has me thinking about memory and how it works."

"You wondering whether the Beck girl really saw the necklace or just remembered it from other times? Yeah, you could be right."

I wobbled on my stool and grabbed onto the table to steady myself. The box began sliding toward us and we both reached out to stop it.

"Any chance Leila sold her jewelry for trip money?"

"To another girl named 'Leila'? Or to a girl who told Suresh she was Leila and she was going to Woodstock? It don't add up, Cat."

"That's true." I took a deep breath. "No, you're right, Moses. If that girl wasn't Leila, she seems to have intended to impersonate Leila, and whoever set up the impersonation had to know that Leila was trying to get to Woodstock."

"Be a good idea to check Missing Persons reports for the week Leila disappeared."

"Oh, right, what a good idea! We need to find out whether any other long-haired blonde teenagers went missing at about the same time."

We made a copy of the detective's report, courtesy of our friendly local police lieutenant, and settled in to read it.

After a while, I said, "Seems like he was pretty thorough, doesn't it? I guess I didn't expect that. I mean, he must've had other cases he was working at the same time, right? I'll bet missing teenagers were a dime a dozen and not that easy to investigate."

Moses grunted. "Easier these days when all you have to do is sit back and wait for the kids to use their parents' credit cards, but it wasn't like that then."

"Yeah. And that made it riskier for the kids. You don't like to think about all those kids running away from home without a dime in their pocket."

"Girls probably had one in their shoe, if they listened to their mothers."

"If they'd listened to their mothers, they wouldn't have run away to begin with."

He shrugged. "Lot of times, it's just a bid for attention. Either that, or they're trying to appeal some decision they didn't like."

"Like no lipstick before you're fourteen."

"No phone calls after nine o'clock."

"No family car so you can take your friends to a Who concert in Dayton."

"No tattoos, not even little peace symbols."

"No skirts more than an inch above your knee."

"No 'fros."

"No loud music, especially if it had explicit lyrics about sex."

We grinned at each other.

"No wonder they wanted to run away," I said. "We were tyrannical."

"Damn straight. And our kids lived to tell the tale to their therapists."

"That's what this police detective, Rausch, thinks, isn't it? That Leila ran away and got herself into trouble."

"Maybe. But he's bothered by the amount of planning she put into it — the choir trip permission slip, for example. That bothered him because it didn't fit the typical pattern. Most kids just take off. Planning for them amounts to stealing a little cash."

"That's why he's inclined to think she went to Woodstock and was planning to come back."

"But he's got his suspicions about the men in her life, too. It's clear he interviewed some of them several times, hoping to trip them up."

"He even checked their alibis for the first twenty-four hours." I lifted a sheet of paper.

"Yeah, the only one in the clear was the Fox kid. He was on a family vacation that week. The other alibis were full of holes."

"So, where does that leave us?" I asked. "Are we going to track them all down and interview them again?"

"Not yet, but soon."

"He clearly didn't like the Wildfire band members, especially Adam Glass and Jimmy Shoemaker."

"Yeah," he agreed, "he probably was itching to get them on a statutory rape charge."

"So, why didn't he?"

Moses shrugged. "He didn't have enough evidence in hand and didn't have time to go looking for more."

"You think we should go after them?"

"We don't have any more evidence than he had. I'd like to know more about them when we do. Anyway, looks like they weren't the only candidates for the statutory rape charge."

"No, there are a few other names here, too. All of them are older guys attached to bands."

"Which makes the last one, the Fox kid, an anomaly. Wonder if he was a cover."

"You mean for another inappropriate relationship with an older man?" I thought about that. "Wouldn't be the first time and we know that Leila was a planner. But you're not suggesting, are you, that the trip to Woodstock was also a cover for a romantic getaway with her boyfriend?"

"If you're asking me do I think she went to Cancún or Barbados or the Riviera instead of to Woodstock, then no, I don't think that. Leila was all about music. Everybody says so. For her, the romantic getaway would have to be to Bethel, New York."

"I'll go along with that."

"But if that was Leila on the bus, she was alone on the bus, and we're back to speculating about what happened to her after that. What we need is a major assist from the patron saint of wayward girls, who so far has done shit to help us with this case."

CHAPTER 18

"Knock, knock."

"Boo."

"Boo who?"

"I'm vewwy sowwy you so sad."

The curly-headed urchin in the tutu and Strawberry Shortcake T-shirt milked the punchline for all it was worth, pursing her lips and turning down the corners of her mouth in an exaggerated frown of sympathy. But like many amateur comedians, she couldn't hold it; she was too tickled by her own joke to repress the laughter that bubbled up inside her. She sported a slash of something neon pink across one cheek and a sprinkling of glitter in her hair as if costumed and made up for a bit part as a fairy in *The Nutcracker*. A true performer, she was standing in the booth looking down on her audience.

Moses, who was always a good sport where kids were concerned, shook his head ruefully. "You got me that time," he said, rubbing a palm on his knee. He opened his mouth to say more but she beat him to it.

"Knock, knock."

"Who's there?"

"Tank."

"Tank who?"

"You wewcome." This time she could barely get the punchline past her giggle.

"Okay, Pigpen, knock it off," her mother said, but with an indulgent smile. "The grown-ups have to talk. Sit down and drink your juice."

The juice in question was a Shirley Temple to which the waitress had added five cherries on a toothpick. We were meeting Leila's best friend from childhood, Mary Grace O'Shaughnessy Hardy, at an IHOP in Oakley, strategically positioned between Mary Grace's interior design studio and her daughter's daycare center. Myself, I wouldn't have chosen to eat pancakes at two in the afternoon, especially unaccompanied by alcohol, but my preferences were moot.

Mary Grace had the Irish coloring that her maiden name promised — red hair and freckles against a creamy complexion. Her daughter had the same curly red hair but dark eyes that suggested a more southern ethnicity — Mediterranean or even Indian.

"Is that your name — Pigpen?" Moses asked.

"My name is Penny," she said with dignity. "Onwy my mom says 'Pigpen.'"

I found myself wondering if there was a Saint Penelope, and if so, what she was patron saint of. Probably knock-knock jokes. If she had earned her sainthood by being tortured by somebody, I'll bet she had tortured them right back.

Penny bent over to scrutinize Moses's face, then pointed at his eye. "What's wong with you eye?"

"Oh, I had a little accident." Then, seeing that this explanation would not suffice, he leaned in and added confidentially, "I was wrestling with a bear."

Her eyes widened. "Why was you westwing with a beaw?"

I didn't hear the explanation because Mary Grace had turned to me and said, "I can't believe you're looking into Leila's disappearance again after all these years, but I'm glad somebody is. I still think about her, you know, and wonder

154

what happened, and wonder if, you know, I could have done something for her."

Her eyes teared up and I laid an impulsive hand over hers. "Oh, Mary Grace, I doubt that very much. We don't know what happened to her, but it's clear she was following her own path. I doubt that anybody could have dissuaded her."

Mary Grace disengaged her hand to root around in her purse for a tissue, then dabbed at her eyes.

"Is Mommy cwying?" The girl in the tutu was looking to Moses, her new best friend, for an explanation.

I didn't hear it because Mary Grace said, "I know, but I think I could have tried harder. I often think that."

I considered suggesting that she cheer herself up with a few slices of bacon, since I often find that food with a high fat content does wonders for a funk, but I thought my suggestion might not be appreciated, practical though it was, so I didn't say anything right away.

Then I said, "Tell me about the last time you saw her."

"It was on my birthday, August 6th. We had this tradition, you know? Since before we were teenagers. We'd take the bus downtown and eat lunch at Woolworth's. We'd eat burgers and fries and ice cream sundaes — really pig out, you know? It was a big deal."

"So, you went to Woolworth's as usual," I prompted. I was aware of childish chatter in the background and wondered how much of this Moses was getting.

Mary Grace nodded. "I hadn't seen much of her all summer. She had a job at this coffeehouse and I was working at the Dairy Queen. But that wasn't the only reason. She had started hanging out at the Northside Park, listening to the music and making new friends there. She didn't seem to have much time left over to hang out with me."

"Who initiated the birthday lunch? Did you call her or did she call you?"

"She called me, and I was kind of surprised to hear from her, but also, it made me feel good because she'd remembered.

She just said, kind of casual-like, 'Are we on for Woolworth's next week?'"

"You took the bus together downtown?"

"Yeah, just like usual. And we ordered hamburgers, just like usual, but she hardly touched hers. She just said she wasn't very hungry. And then she lit up a cigarette, so I said that smoking was killing her appetite, but she just laughed and said that she could afford to lose a few pounds. But she couldn't, not really. She was pretty skinny. I mean, some girls think they're fat no matter how skinny they are, and it doesn't matter how often you tell them they're not, they don't believe it."

"Did you think she might have an eating disorder? Or do you think so now? I'm not sure anybody talked about them in 1969."

"I don't think they did," she said shaking her head. "I mean, I didn't know anybody who had an eating disorder, not back then. And honestly, I don't really think Leila had one, either. I really think it was the smoking, but it also could have been the job at the coffeehouse, you know? I kind of lost my appetite, just from working at the Dairy Queen, but it was worse later when I had other waitressing jobs and served food. I didn't know back then that being around food at your job all day kind of killed your appetite."

"So, what did you talk about, you and Leila, that last time you saw her?"

"Oh, I don't know, just stupid stuff, mostly. I can't remember all that well. I talked about a boy I liked who came into the Dairy Queen and she talked about a boy she liked at the Park."

"Would that have been Jeremy Fox, do you know?"

She shook her head. "I don't think she said his name. She just said he was good-looking and sweet."

"But you talked about Woodstock, is that right?"

The tutued comedian was trying to get her attention, and she broke off to listen to a newsflash about some kid at daycare whose teddy bear had gone on vacation. Mary Grace got her daughter settled in the seat with a bribe about dessert. Given that the little girl's pancakes were swimming in some bright red liquid and covered in strawberries and whipped cream, I didn't see what the promise of dessert had to offer, but it seemed to work temporarily.

Turning back to me, Mary Grace said, "Woodstock, yes. Leila was very keen to go — well, determined, really. She said she'd find a way."

"Was she talking about raising money or was she talking about finding a ride?"

She took a minute to gaze off across the dining room. "I guess I thought she meant finding a ride, but that would involve money, too. I can't remember now if she made that clear or if I just assumed it." She sighed. "It was a long time ago. I remember it better than a lot of things because of what happened afterward, but I still wouldn't say that I remember it well."

"And she didn't mention to you that she was using the choir trip as an excuse?"

Her eyebrows shot up. "No, god, no! I was floored when her mom called to ask me about it. I mean, I guess she didn't think it would make any difference because she'd be back when she said she would. But god, it was a huge risk! I could have run into Mrs. Perle at any time, and so could my mom. Maybe she thought I would cover for her — you know, come up with some excuse. But I'd told her before that I couldn't do it anymore and she seemed to be okay with that."

"Would you say that Leila was normally a risk-taker?"

She frowned. "Well, I guess I'd say that she was more of a risk-taker than I was. But if you're asking if she did things like experiment with drugs, then no, I don't think so. At least, not before that summer. I mean, she was taking a risk to smoke because her dad didn't allow it, even though he was a smoker himself."

"But you said she'd asked you to cover for her. What was that about?"

"Oh, it was usually a party or a concert she wanted to go to that her dad wouldn't have approved of."

I nodded at the three books that she'd placed on the table when she came in. The top one was called *The Amaranth*. "I see you brought yearbooks."

"Oh, yeah, I did. And since you were interested in Leila's boyfriends, I brought my brother's yearbook, too." She lifted the top two books to show the third book, which was called *The Troubadour*.

I felt the heat rising in my cheeks. I glanced at Moses, hoping that "The Itsy-bitsy Spider" was distracting him from my mistake, but he gave me a little smile and arched an eyebrow at me. Okay, so I thought I had been smart to ask her to bring yearbooks. But Leila had come from a prominent Catholic family, which meant she had gone to Catholic schools, which meant that I could look through her high school yearbook till the cows came home without spotting a single potential boyfriend. For that, I would need not the yearbook from Our Lady of Angels, but the one from Roger Bacon, the boys' school next door.

I felt the color glowing in my cheeks, then noticed five sticky little fingers in an even brighter red clutching at the sleeve of Moses's cream-colored birthday sweater, the one his girlfriend had given him, and I felt better. These were uncharitable thoughts, I admitted. There's something about hanging around with Catholics that fosters self-examination, and I resolved to do less of it in the future, always excepting Kevin O'Neill, who was a lapsed Catholic.

"Let's start with the boyfriends," I proposed, pulling the Roger Bacon yearbook toward me.

Mary Grace took me on a guided tour of Leila's boyfriends — or at least the ones she knew about and could produce pictures of. There were five of them, some her age and some older but none younger. As she recounted their accomplishments and exploits, I began to notice a pattern. Leila may have been a good girl, but all her boyfriends were bad boys — or as bad as it got in a Catholic school. They all had a certain glint in their eyes or tilt to their heads or spikes in their hair. Three were smiling and two wore deadpan expressions, but there was no way to tell by looking at them whether they had a jealous streak or a tendency to violence. Mary Grace's report on their criminal records ran mostly to teenaged hijinks, although she noted that one had been suspended for fighting and another had been nailed for an unauthorized borrowing of Sister Anna Josephine's Woody for a trip to Dayton to see a girl he liked.

"And you never met her last boyfriend, Jeremy Fox, right?"

She shook her head.

"But she said he was sweet?"

"That's what she said."

In that case, he hardly seemed to be Leila's type. But maybe he just hadn't been arrested yet — a scary thought.

I started to thank her, but she interrupted me. "Don't you want to see her girlfriends?"

I didn't really see the point, but then she said, "I even found a picture of one of the girls she worked with at the Aquarius."

She flipped through the pages of girls dressed in pleated skirts, some dark and some plaid, and knee socks, then turned the book around to face me again. "Here she is."

And there she was: dark hair in thick waves cut off at her ears, dark eyes, a knowing smile. It was Gigi Beck, Leila's best friend from work.

I angled the page in Moses's direction, trying to keep it out of reach from his sticky-fingered companion. He leaned in and studied it.

"Would you have an address for her or a phone number? We'd really like to talk to her," he said.

I snatched the book back as Penny made a dive for it.

"I don't, but I could probably find it somehow through my connections," Mary Grace said. "She was three years ahead of us in school, so she'd already graduated and started college

159

when we were sophomores. I did notice that Leila mentioned her a couple of times during that last lunch, so I guessed that they'd become closer since they were working together. I think Leila was kind of in awe of her because she was already in college."

She took our numbers and promised to call when she had more information. When she was gone and we stood up, I surveyed Moses from head to foot.

"You look like you played straight man in a comedy skit involving cherry pies to the kisser."

He looked down at himself ruefully. "Charisse gonna kill me," he acknowledged.

"Your best bet would be to dye it red." Actually, his best bet would be to ditch Charisse, his snooty girlfriend, but I wasn't allowed to say so. "How much of that did you get?" I asked as we put on our coats.

He closed his bad eye altogether. "Any of it have to do with a spider?"

"No."

"Then I didn't get much. You can tell me in the car."

I couldn't help feeling excited that we had come so close to tracking down the Beck girl, even though Moses warned me not to be overly optimistic, based on the interviews conducted by the two previous detectives on the case. According to their notes, Beck had gone back to school the day after Leila had disappeared. *Had that been a coincidence?* I wondered now. She had claimed not to know Leila all that well, but she had known that Leila was headed to Woodstock and not on a choir trip, and I now knew that she had attended the same school as Leila, if not at the same time. She had claimed to know none of the details of Leila's trip.

Time for a little good cop, bad cop.

CHAPTER 19

Kevin came in before work that afternoon and handed me an old record album. "For your case," he said.

The cover showed a forest ablaze, with four small figures in the foreground, almost hidden by the smoke and flames: two guitar players, a keyboardist, and a drummer. Blazoned across the top in letters that appeared to have burned a hole in the image was the word "Wildfire."

"Their first album," Kevin explained. "Their most famous song — the one somebody you talked to thinks they stole from Leila — is the third track. It's called 'Magdalena.'"

I handed it back to him and he took it over to the stereo. I followed.

"Did you listen to it? What's it about?"

He blew on the record. "It's about a girl trapped between childhood and adulthood. She has adult feelings but no control over her life, no power."

At first, all I could hear was noise — the kind of loud, not very melodious noise that I associated with rock music, or at least the kind that Franny listened to. Someone was singing in one of those stylized voices that are intended to sound soulful and sincere, but I couldn't make out the lyrics. On the

161

fourth time through the chorus, all the instruments dropped out except one guitar and I could hear the lyrics:

Magdalena,
I can see ya
Singin' your blues.
Magdalena,
So hard to be ya,
'Cause you're too old for innocence
and too young to choose.

I felt my face grimacing when the song was over, but instead of saying the kind of curmudgeonly, old-fart thing I would normally say, I asked, "What do you think?"

Kevin was leaning back against the bookcase, arms folded. "I think that if a straight male wrote that song, I'm Mick Jagger's long-lost love child."

Kevin's prone to exaggeration and prone, too, to think that gay people have more smarts and creativity than straight people. I frowned, but he held up a hand. "I'm serious, Mrs. C. If a straight white male rocker wrote that song, I'll eat my Bette Midler autograph."

I was becoming intrigued. "Because—?"

"Because it's a sensitive and soul-wrenching portrayal of what it's like to be a teenage girl, exploited by everyone, commanded by everyone, expected to fulfill everyone's expectations and have none of her own. And everything she tries to do to gain some control over her own life and her own destiny turns to dust — *every alliance an act of defiance*, she sings, *but they're all in the soul-crushing game.* How many young men do you know would understand that, much less choose to write about it? And we're not even talking about the average young man, we're talking about an aspiring rock star with an ego to go with it. There's no way Adam Glass wrote that song."

"You could make out the lyrics?" I was temporarily distracted from the main point by a flash of anxiety over hearing loss.

He cocked a thumb in the direction of his apartment. "I have them in a guitar book. But there's something else, too. This song is the weirdest mismatch of lyrics and music. The reason you can't hear the lyrics is that the style is so flashy — guitars, keyboard, drums all crashing around and fighting to be heard. This song is about a girl who feels very alone because nobody is listening to her or consulting her on important decisions about her life. But you literally can't listen to her because she's drowned out by the instruments. I'm telling you, Mrs. C. it's weird. It's like these guys don't have a clue what they're singing about."

He turned back to the record player and lifted the needle. "See if you can hear the end."

I strained to make out more of the lyrics, but again, except for the chorus, I was only catching a word here and there. I shook my head at Kevin.

He raised his hands as if to explain. "Okay, here's what it says: *Magdalena, let me free ya. Don't you know that's what love's for? Just let me love ya and take care of ya — you don't have to run anymore.*"

"Jesus."

He nodded, eyes closed. "I rest my case."

"I don't guess you think he's being ironic? You know, revealing to the audience in a creepy way that he's exactly what she ought to be running away from?"

"I've listened to some of their songs now. I don't think irony is their strong suit."

"So, thick-headedness, not irony. God, that's depressing. Especially if she had some kind of romantic relationship with this jerk. Well, I have to agree with you, based on what little I know or can understand of the lyrics. Except for the ending, this song doesn't sound much like Adam Glass. That doesn't mean he got it from Leila, but given Vic's confidence that it's the same song she sang at the Park, it seems likely."

"What can you do about it?"

"That's a good question," I said. "Probably nothing unless I can find the original in Leila's handwriting."

"But if she was hanging out with him, won't he just say she copied it from him?"

"Probably. Our best bet would be to find some of the people who were in the audience the night she sang it. Even better if she played it to somebody while she was working on it."

"The little sister?"

I frowned. "I doubt she has enough credibility to pull off a court appearance. But I think there was a music producer in the audience that night. Maybe if we can track him down—"

Kevin wished me luck and headed off to work. Upstairs, Moses was getting in a little last-minute practice before his band members showed up.

Mildred called with a few more phone numbers for Leila's friends at the Park and Mary Grace called with phone numbers for three of the boyfriends, as well as the Holy Grail: a local phone number for Gigi Beck, Leila's best friend at work. I also had a phone number to try for coworker Helen Margolies from Marty Yeager's wife.

I sat down at the table across from Sophie in her bread bowl. Ever curious, Sidney jumped up to see what I was doing. I scratched him behind the ears and said, "We're living the life, eh, Sid? Action-packed, a thrill a minute. Filled with danger and intrigue. Sam Spade's got nothing on us." Then I pulled the phone toward me.

Beck was a reluctant witness. She hadn't known Leila all that well or all that long, she'd never heard from her after that summer, and she had a hard time remembering things that had happened last week. When she didn't manage to shake me off, she tried to get me to interview her over the phone, but I wanted her back at the scene of Leila's disappearance. I wasn't qualified to hypnotize her, of course, but having watched the hypnotist at work, I saw the advantage of reminding witnesses about context. She finally gave in and agreed to meet us after work the next day at the Aquarius.

Helen Margolies, who must have been in her seventies or eighties, seemed more eager to help. There was no question of flying to Tampa to interview her. She must have known generations of waitresses over the course of her long career at the Aquarius, most of them temporary employees, so I wasn't sure that she'd remember Leila, but she did.

"Well, I worried about her, especially after that detective came around, asking questions."

"Why were you worried about her?"

"Well, to tell you the truth, I worried about all of them. They all seemed so vulnerable, you know? I always thought I would like to have had a daughter, but they might have been too much for me. Do you have daughters, Mrs. Caliban?"

"Two."

"And are they worth it?"

"Most of the time."

"I'm glad to hear it. Anyway, that one — Leila — had an idea that she was going all the way to New York for this music festival. I was worried that she was going to hitchhike to get there. I guess in the end she didn't, she took a bus, they said. But I wouldn't have put it past her. And you say she's still missing, so I guess I was right to worry about her."

"Did you see her on that last day she was there? That would have been a Wednesday, August 13th."

"Yes, now I got there late for my morning shift, I can't remember why. But I was there. And we were training a new girl that day, Linda somebody. Leila had been working that early morning shift, and she left around two, I think. I mean, that's when she would have left at the end of her shift, so I assume it was the same that day."

"Can you think of anything else unusual about that day? Was there anyone around talking to Leila? A customer she liked or one she didn't?"

"I really thought about it after that detective talked to me. But all the days run together, don't they? There was one boy who came around a lot in those days, I think because he was sweet on Leila. He always figured out which station was hers and sat there. I can't remember if he was there that morning, though."

"Do you remember his name?"

"Gerald? Albert? Richard? I think it was Richard. It was one of those names you might think would turn into a nickname but it didn't. I don't know his last name, though."

"Can you describe him?"

"Gosh, it's going to sound unkind, but he really wasn't much to look at. His hair was kind of a dirty blond and stringy, like he didn't wash it as often as he could've. And he had bad acne and kind of pale blue eyes. He always looked like he was trying to grow a mustache and never quite succeeded."

"Tall? Short?"

"Tall and skinny. Pathetically shy. He lit up whenever Leila went to his table. She tried to be nice to him, at least at first, but I told her not to encourage him."

"What did you mean by that?"

"I meant that she shouldn't smile at him so much. She should try to be businesslike with him, take his order and leave. She was a kind person, and she felt sorry for him, so it was hard for her. But I honestly thought he was the type that might follow her home like a little puppy dog."

"Did he live in the neighborhood, do you know?"

"I don't know where he lived. All the girls tried to help out, like they always did if somebody attracted an admirer they didn't want. You know, like one of them would say, 'So-and-so, your boyfriend called. He wants you to call him back.' Or even, 'He wants you to call him back at the gym.' Or sometimes, 'Your fiancé called to say he'd be here as soon as his karate class lets out.'"

"But you don't remember if he was there that day? Anybody else notable that you can remember?"

"Honestly, I just don't remember. I'm sorry."

"That's okay, I understand. Can you remember your last conversation with Leila — what she said to you and what you said to her?"

"Oh, it was probably something like, 'Number twelve wants a refill' or 'No more donuts.' I didn't see her when she left, I was probably in the kitchen."

"But you knew she was going on a trip, and you thought it was a choir trip?"

"Well, that's what I was supposed to think."

"But you knew that she wanted to go to Woodstock?"

"Sure, everybody knew that. So, I had my suspicions about that choir trip. But honestly, Woodstock wasn't on my radar. I didn't have any idea when it was happening."

I nodded. "Can you remember if she was wearing her necklace, the one with her name on it, the last time you saw her?"

"That's right! She did have a necklace like that, didn't she? But I can't remember whether she was wearing it that day. Sorry!"

"That's okay. It was a long time ago." I made a note, then said, "I've arranged to meet with Gigi Beck tomorrow. Based on the case notes I've read, she was the coworker closest to Leila that summer. Would you agree?"

"Yes, that's right. I think there was a little hero worship going on, maybe because she'd graduated from Leila's high school. But are you talking to the others as well?"

"I think we found a phone number for Sally Hunt, now Sally Stillwater. We might have found an address in Wyoming for Pam Goering, which means we'll be able to find a phone number. We're still working on Joyce Ridgeway and Linda Monniter. Do you have any contact information for them? Or do you know what their surnames are now? We could really use some help because Leila's mother's health is failing and they'd like to have some answers for her before she dies."

"I'm sorry to hear that — about Leila's mom. I can't imagine what it would be like to have your child disappear one day, can you? But I don't have any more information about those girls. If you're going to talk to Gigi, ask her. She might know. I wouldn't bother with Linda, though, because she only overlapped with Leila for a few hours and didn't know her at all."

"I will ask Gigi. And thanks for the tip about Monniter."

There was hesitation in her voice the next time she spoke. "You know, I think you should really try to find Joyce Ridgeway. She wasn't as close to Leila as Gigi was, but there was something going on between them in the week before Leila disappeared. The two of them would whisper together and then look around to make sure they weren't overheard, you know? I don't know what it was about, but if I were in your shoes, I'd want to get hold of Joyce and ask her."

CHAPTER 20

Gigi Beck wasn't wearing a wedding ring, which probably explained why Mildred had found her relatively quickly. She was taller than average height, wearing an outfit that made her look European: a dark pencil skirt to midcalf and a tunic belted at the waist. She had thick, dark, wavy hair cut short, dark eyes, and flawless makeup. If Moses had devoted some time to practicing his knock-knock jokes, it was time wasted. I could see why Beck's sophistication would have appealed to Leila.

When we entered, she was sitting at a table having a long-distance battle of wills with Marty at the bar over smoking. She was waving a cigarette in long, slender fingers.

"Come on, Marty, I know you smoke in here all the time."

"Not when there are customers, I don't. There's anti-smoking narcs go around looking for violations to report. There's probably a few in here right now."

A guy at a nearby table who was following the conversation raised his hand. He was grungy, with long hair and a baseball cap. "Yeah, that's me, Marty. How'd you rumble me, man?"

We introduced ourselves and sat down as she put the cigarette away. I turned on my small tape recorder and we began by asking the kinds of easy questions that were intended to relax her and encourage her confidence in us — what she had studied at Ohio State (architecture), what she was doing now (architect), and eventually, what it was like to work at the Aquarius in the summer of 1969.

Her eyes circled the room and she gave us an ironic smile. "Well, the place hasn't changed much, as you can imagine. Marty was never big on ambience, or on cleaning, either, as I'm sure you can tell. That was Barb's department — Marty's wife. Every once in a while, she'd come in and pitch a fit, and then we'd clean a few things that hadn't been cleaned in recent memory. Let's face it, there's enough secondary smoke in here to be declared a toxic site by the EPA."

"A lot of it dates back to your time here," Moses observed.

"That's right, I contributed my share."

"Was Leila already working here when you started?" Moses asked.

"Yes, but I had worked here part-time during the Christmas break, so I wasn't really new."

"Did all the coworkers get along pretty well?" I asked.

"Oh, sure. They were all fun to work with and they all pulled their weight. I probably didn't appreciate that then as much as I should have. But also, Marty was pretty easy to work for. You didn't feel like he was watching you all the time, waiting for you to make a mistake."

"Helen was the oldest, right?" I said.

"Yes, and Leila was the youngest, but she was pretty mature for her age."

"We understand that you and Leila were pretty close that summer," Moses said.

"Well, I think it was the whole Catholic connection — OLA and all that."

"OLA?"

"Our Lady of Angels. She was still in school, but I had already graduated and gone on to Ohio State. Still, it gave us a shared context, I guess. But like I said, everybody got along, especially with Leila, since she was the youngest."

I leaned forward. "Helen said that she worried about Leila in particular. Did you worry about her?"

She looked genuinely surprised. "About Leila? No, why would I worry about her? You mean because of her boyfriend troubles?"

"What can you tell us about those?" I asked.

She shrugged. "Just that she was always falling for the wrong kinds of guys, especially musicians, mostly older than she was."

"Are you talking about the guys from Wildfire?"

She shrugged. "Among others. I didn't keep up, to tell you the truth."

"Did she ever say anything to suggest that any of these guys got physical with her? I mean, were any of them violent?"

She shook her head. "She never mentioned anything like that. If she had, we all probably would've trooped down to the Park en masse and punched the guy's lights out."

"Could be why she didn't tell you," Moses observed.

"Could be," she conceded.

Marty came by to refill coffee cups, and I waited until he was gone to speak again. "Helen mentioned a guy that used to come into the coffee shop who was kind of obsessed with Leila. Do you remember him?"

She put a hand to her forehead. "Oh, god! Richard. I haven't thought about him in years. Yeah, he started with Joyce, but she never took any crap off of anyone, so he gave up and moved on to Leila, who was way nicer to him than Joyce was. But he was harmless."

I pressed her. "So, you don't think this Richard was anyone to be concerned about?"

"A puppy dog, that's all he was. But, anyway, he didn't follow her to Woodstock, and we know that's where she went, right?"

"Did you know that's where she was planning to go?" Moses asked.

"Sure. She'd been scheming to get there all summer."

"You knew that the choir trip was just a blind?"

"Sure. I'm pretty sure we all knew."

I didn't bother to contradict her, but I found it interesting that she assumed that Helen, the oldest waitress, had known everything that the rest of them did.

"Can you tell us about that last day?" I asked. "Helen said that she arrived late that morning."

She shrugged. "There was nothing special about the day, really, except that it turned out to be my last shift before I went back to school. I went in early to cover for Helen and because we had a new girl to train, so I worked a double shift. The espresso machine was giving me fits all day, so I wasn't in a great mood. Leila said it was probably a short and she'd take a look at it later, but she didn't have time then."

"What did she mean by 'later'?"

"I don't know. The next day was supposed to be my last, but after the day I'd had that Wednesday, and because I'd worked a double shift and all, Marty told me I didn't have to come in. So, I don't know if it got fixed or not. I sure didn't turn up to find out."

"Leila was a skilled electrician?" Moses said.

"Sure, I guess so. She fixed things around the coffeehouse sometimes."

"Who else was working that day?" I asked. "Do you remember?" I was covering ground that Hitchens had covered at the time. But we were getting some details that he either hadn't gotten or hadn't recorded, so I thought we needed to go over everything.

"Leila worked the early morning shift with me and the new girl, Linda. And then Joyce came in for the late morning rush. Maybe that's when Helen came. I think Tami got there just as Leila was leaving."

"Can you remember your last conversation with Leila? What did she say and what did you say?" I tried not to look as eager as I felt.

172

"It wasn't a conversation. I was fighting with the espresso machine, which was driving me nuts, and Leila told me she was leaving and I said okay."

"Can you show us where you were standing when you had this conversation?" I asked. I might as well put to use some of what I've learned from the hypnotists.

She huffed a little in exasperation but pointed to the espresso machine. "I was standing in front of the espresso machine — not this one, but the old machine. Well, I guess this one is old by now."

"And what was Leila wearing?"

"I don't know. Probably a flowered skirt and a peasant blouse."

"Still wearing her apron?"

"No, she'd already taken that off."

"What about her Leila necklace?"

"I can't remember. Probably. She wore it all the time."

"Can you quote the conversation exactly?"

She closed her eyes and seemed to make an effort. "She said, 'I'm off, Geeg. I left some stuff downstairs and I'll pick it up later.' And I said, 'Okay.'"

There it was. She'd just given my spine a little tap with a tuning fork. I felt Moses shift next to me.

He kept his voice casual. "What did she mean when she said she'd left some stuff downstairs?"

"I don't know. I didn't really think about it."

"If you thought about it now, what would you assume?"

"Well, downstairs would have to be the basement, so I'd assume she meant that she'd left something on one of the shelves down there or maybe on top of the washing machine."

"What kind of stuff? Do you know?"

She shook her head. "No idea."

"Did you girls do that often? Stash things in the basement?"

The word "stash" conjured up images of drugs — baggies of grass or reefers or matchboxes of little pills. I supposed it could mean a pouch of cocaine, but I didn't think that was very common back in the '60s. I really, really hoped that this whole case wouldn't turn out to be about drugs.

"Not that I know of. The basement was damp and gross. I didn't even like to go down there, so I can't imagine leaving anything there."

"When do you think she was planning to come back for her stuff?"

"I don't know, but like I said, you wouldn't want to leave anything down there for long. It would get damp and moldy and start to rot."

"And did she come to pick it up?"

Gigi shrugged. "I guess so. I wasn't here. But if she took the bus to Woodstock, I assume she had it with her."

Moses's eyes met mine. We stood up. "Let's take a look," he said.

We asked Marty to show us the basement. We were familiar enough with Northside basements to have low expectations, and we weren't disappointed. The smell was a bouquet of mold, dead rodents, and mouse droppings. A few flecks of moldy paint still clung to the rough stone and cement block walls, in some places more than others, but for the most part, they were dark with mold and mildew and streaked with evidence of bygone inundations. Bare bulbs with pull chains studded the floor joists overhead and had to be turned on one by one to provide what weak illumination was available. At the bottom of the stairs was a small island that comprised a washer and dryer on a patch of linoleum. In the dim light beyond, past festoons of cobwebs hanging like Spanish moss, we could make out shelves filled with boxes and a few cabinets against the far wall. These latter appeared to have been constructed by Noah's least competent son. Against another wall, an espresso machine, Gigi's old nemesis, barely recognizable under its discolored and rusted exterior, sat propped on a pallet like an aged diva who has earned her rest and now quietly molders away. A humming sound started up, drawing attention to a sump pump embedded in the concrete floor across from the laundry island.

The furnace was huge and ancient, its exterior covered in duct tape and hand-printed instructions. It came on now with a dull roar of flames igniting and instinctively, I stepped back.

Marty scratched his chin and said, "Damn dehumidifier is on the fritz again."

I followed his gaze to a small box sitting next to the washing machine, likely exhausted from its attempt to make headway against the dampness.

Moses's attention was focused on the wall of cabinets and shelves on the far end of the room. He crossed the floor, produced a small flashlight from his pocket, and began opening doors. Hinges were old and rusty and the wood so rotted that I thought it might come off in his hands. Marty stood behind us wearing an expression of curiosity that suggested he would be as surprised as we would by anything we found in these cupboards. Gigi stood behind him wearing an expression of revulsion, a lit cigarette in one hand.

Moses made his way methodically down the bank of cabinets, poking and prodding their contents. These included everything from chipped ceramic mugs, encrusted ashtrays, and milk-glass vases to cartons of paper placemats, bags of stained napkins, and dusty Christmas decorations. The care he took to examine small items and penetrate to the backs of the cabinets indicated that he was thinking the same thing I was thinking and searching for a stash of drugs. Of course, even if we found them, the drugs wouldn't have to be Leila's, as I knew from a close encounter with the Marysville women's prison, which was heavily populated with women convicted for holding their boyfriends' drugs.

When he reached the tall corner cabinet at the end, he had to move aside a rickety stool and microphone stand. He unlatched the crude wooden latch, opened the door, and stepped back.

Inside were three items. One was barely identifiable as a canvas backpack, its original color a khaki now furred and stained with mold. Two rusty buckles remained, holding fragments of straps that might have been leather. A third buckle lay on the floor. Another item appeared to be a bedroll, strips of rotten cloth hanging off of it like wispy ghosts — the ghosts of Leila's Woodstock dreams. The third was a guitar case, its furry mildewed cover peeling off, its hinges hanging dark and useless.

I probably imagined the scent of cologne.

We had caught up with Leila at last and overtaken her.

CHAPTER 21

After that, we spent a lot of time sitting on our butts and drinking coffee and hot chocolate, waiting for a homicide detective to arrive and then for his forensic team. Moses hadn't taken any chances; his first call hadn't been to 911, it had been to Rap. The first officer on the scene, though, was a young beat cop named Magnuson, who looked a little disappointed by the crime scene he'd been asked to secure.

"It's not really a crime scene," Moses told him, one hand on his shoulder. "It's key evidence in a potential homicide case."

He didn't tell Magnuson that the chances anyone would wander down here and start opening cabinets to look for a lightbulb were nil because he wanted the rookie to feel important.

Lieutenant Rap Arpad was the next to arrive. Having Rap on the case made our job much easier. We didn't have to explain why Leila's stash mattered. A teenaged girl had disappeared, leaving behind some of her most cherished possessions. That raised the probability of foul play to an almost certainty. And it helped that Rap was already familiar with the case, having been talked into giving us access to the old case file. Matt Perle's connections as a retired police officer had helped with that and distinguished Leila's disappearance from the average cold case.

Although we couldn't help speculating, we didn't waste time on recriminations. Gigi Beck had never reported Leila's last words to her, either because nobody had asked for a direct quotation or because she hadn't remembered them at the time or because she had chosen to withhold some of what she knew from the detectives. By the time they'd caught up with her, she had left behind her summer life and immersed herself in college life; the Aquarius had probably seemed very far away to her then. Anyway, Leila had obviously run off to Woodstock — even the detectives thought that — so if she had met somebody there and was shacked up with her new boyfriend, it was none of her father's business.

Gigi's own version, in a conversation with us, was that she hadn't remembered and hadn't tried very hard to remember because she didn't think it was important. When pressed for any other buried memories that might be relevant to Leila's disappearance, she claimed not to have any, although we got our best account so far of Leila's love life that last summer. Leila had fallen hard for Adam Glass, Gigi claimed, in spite of efforts by some of the girls to talk her out of it.

"Not all the girls were opposed," she told us. "Pam, who was always something of a free spirit, said they should leave her alone and let her have fun. I thought it was a bad idea, but I didn't say much, one way or the other, because I figured Glass would dump her soon enough, which he did. I got the blow-by-blow once things fell apart. Then there was the thing with Jimmy Shoe, which wasn't nearly so intense and lasted even less time. And for about two weeks in there somewhere, she was seeing this kid from a local band."

"Would that be Leapin' Leopold?" I asked.

"That sounds right. This guy was a drummer and younger, at least, than Glass and Shoe. I think she may have dated a few other guys, including one who used to come into the coffeehouse."

"Not Richard."

"God, no, not Richard. I don't remember his name, but one of the other girls might."

Moses was wearing his serious cop face when he said, "Gigi, you know we're now looking at a likely homicide. It looks like somebody killed Leila before she was able to leave town."

"But I thought she'd been seen on a bus to Columbus," Gigi objected.

"We think that was a false report — either somebody who happened to look a lot like Leila or somebody who was deliberately impersonating Leila. So, we need you to think hard about your conversations with Leila. We need to hear if anybody ever raised a hand to her or threatened her, or if she was afraid of anybody."

Gigi stared at us. "Listen, if anybody had raised a hand to Leila or even threatened her, we would've gotten it out of her and we would've put a stop to it. She was the youngest of us Aquarians, kind of like everybody's kid sister. The very least the guy could've expected was rat turds in his espresso, and that's if we didn't empty the pot over his head and then bean him with it. That's the treatment Glass and his buddies would have gotten if they'd ever set foot in the place, but like I said, they didn't."

"What about drugs?" Moses asked.

"What about them?" Her defensiveness suggested to me that she'd had a passing acquaintance with drugs herself. She made an effort to tamp it down. "Look, everybody smoked a little pot in those days, and Leila was no different. But Cincinnati was hardly South Central and buying a few reefers didn't put you in the middle of a gang war." She frowned at the unlit cigarette she was holding. "Well, I guess South Central wasn't South Central either in those days, if you know what I mean. The sixties were pretty innocent."

"What about LSD? Did she drop acid?"

Moses knew more than I did about the possible consequences of a bad trip, but even I knew that people could die — could throw themselves off tall buildings or cliffs either because they thought they could fly or to escape some imagined menace. Leila's body had never been found, but it could have been well hidden by friends who had been there when she died and didn't want to be questioned about it.

"I doubt it. You have to understand, Leila was basically a good Catholic girl who was engaged in some standard teenage rebellion, that's all."

We sent her home with an admonition to think things over and let us know if she remembered anything, however small, that might help with the investigation, as well as a reminder that we wanted to talk with the rest of her coworkers. I told her I'd be calling her to ask her questions about them that might help us locate them.

I drove the Fairlane home while Moses and Rap went to talk to Matt Perle. I fed Winnie upstairs and the cats downstairs before making myself a drink and settling down on the couch. But I was in no mood for Happy Hour. The cats settled in next to me and I helped Winnie onto my lap. Then I began to cry.

I was sobbing into Sophie's fur when the doorbell rang. "Go away," I said under my breath as I heaved myself to my feet, disarranging all the animals. But the voice on the intercom was Mildred's, and it spoke the magic password: "I've got pizza."

She came through the door holding the pizza boxes in front of her like an offering and saying apologetically, "Moses called and asked me to come over and pick up pizza on the way."

She took one look at me, set the pizza boxes down on the coffee table, and put her arms around me.

"I didn't even know Leila," I burbled into her shoulder. "And it's not as if I expected we'd find her raising kids in Poughkeepsie or anything like that. I guess I always knew she was dead. But still, I felt like I was just getting to know her and like her and now this."

She patted my back. "I know just what you mean." And from the tears in her voice, I knew that she did and reminded myself that she'd been looking for Leila even longer than I had.

When we broke the embrace, she pulled out a handkerchief and wiped her eyes and her glasses. We put the pizza in the oven to keep warm and I poured us both a glass of wine, then we settled on the couch so that I could recount the day's activities. Sidney clambered into Mildred's lab and gave her a good sniffing.

I had almost finished filling Mildred in when Moses and Rap walked in. They were both blinking and Rap was holding up a small red, heart-shaped card.

"Found this tucked behind the light switch," Rap said.

"While he was trying to turn up the light in the foyer," Moses put in.

"It's only for a few more days," I said. "Then it's back to normal until St. Patrick's Day."

We introduced Rap to Mildred.

"How did he take it?" I asked as soon as introductions were over. "Was it just Matt or were any of the other family members there?"

"Mary was there," Moses said. "I think they knew what I was coming to tell them. At least, they knew it was bad news. They might have thought that we'd found a body. We emphasized that we hadn't, but they both understood the implications of what we did find."

Rap nodded. "They were both pretty devastated. Mary had started crying before we got there, and Perley cried a little before we left. I agree with you, Cat, by the way. Perley looks like hell."

"He says he's got a bad cold he can't shake, but I'm beginning to think you're right, too, Cat," Moses said. "He don't look good."

"Is he living at the house on Mitchell?"

"He says he's got an apartment somewhere close by, but he's spending most of his time there to help out with his mother. Mary lives in Blue Ash, but I get the impression she spends most of her time at the Mitchell house as well."

"We told them that we might make more progress now that we had a narrower window of time to focus on," Rap said.

"Yeah," Moses said, shaking his head, "but Perley's still a cop, and he knows as well as we do what our chances are of solving this thing after all this time."

Rap clapped him on the back. "Yeah, but look here, Foggy. When you and Cat started on this case, I didn't give you a snowball's chance in hell of getting anywhere with it and look what you've accomplished. I'ma have to recalculate my odds."

I was surprised myself that we'd made any progress. I had to give Mildred most of the credit for tracking Beck down and said so.

We sat around the living room then, eating pizza and discussing our next moves.

"Y'all do know that I've got a full plate right now — two homicides and an armed robbery to work. I requested this case to help you out, but I don't have a lot of time to give it. It's still a cold case." Rap checked his watch to make his point, then rubbed a smear of pizza sauce off it with his thumb.

"Coroner's office is going to start looking at Leila's stash tomorrow morning, Cat," Moses told me. "Bony says we can come watch."

Bony Brissard was one of the forensic pathologists who worked at the coroner's office and a particular pal of mine. Bony loved to explain things and I was a good listener. But since he specialized in bodies, I doubted that he'd be the one examining Leila's things. I also suspected that we'd earned brownie points for not examining the items ourselves, the way an eager but less experienced pair of detectives might have done. Or a pair of detectives that weren't concerned about their relationship to the police.

"So, what's your game plan?" Rap asked. He lifted Sidney onto his lap, but not before Sid had left his shoelaces in a slobbery tangle.

"It's more important than ever that we speak to Leila's coworkers and anybody she was close to at the Northside Park those last weeks," I said. "That's Mildred's department."

Mildred pulled a folded paper from her breast pocket and handed it to me. Winnie, who had her head in Mildred's lap, snuffled and turned her belly up without opening her eyes, one paw twitching. "Here are Sally Stillwater and Monniter. I had a talk with Helen Margolies yesterday and she gave me some useful information. I'm hopeful that I can find Ridgeway through Bowling Green. I've found a phone number for Goering, but I haven't gotten hold of her yet." She pointed at the paper. "You've also got two of Leila's girlfriends from the Park and two boys connected with her, including Jeremy Fox, who might or might not have been the last boyfriend."

I beamed at her. "Great! And Chaz and Vic have given us old addresses for four local band members, two from Wildfire and two from Leapin' Leopold. They're probably no good now, but it's a place to start. When you come up with current addresses, we'll want to talk to them, especially the ex-boy-friend, Adam Glass. That affair supposedly ended more than a month before Leila disappeared, but he's the oldest suspect on the list, I think."

"What we need from you," Moses said to Rap, "is a list of girls who fit Leila's general description who went missing around the same time she did."

"And access to their case files, I assume," Rap said. He stopped petting Sidney long enough to make a note in a small notebook, but he had to wrestle Sidney for the pen. "You think one of them might have been impersonating Leila on the bus to Columbus?"

"It's beginning to look like that," Moses said.

We spent the rest of our time speculating on various possible scenarios for what had happened to Leila. These included a double bluff (Rap's contribution) in which Leila ran away from home and confused her pursuers with a false Leila on the bus and a cabinet of her possessions left behind. Kevin, a fan of the baroquely absurd, would have appreciated this suggestion if he had been there, but it was too elaborate for my taste. No way Leila would have left her guitar behind.

"There's always a chance that the truth will turn out to be less sinister than we think," Moses acknowledged after we'd conjured a spate of jealous boyfriends.

Rap nodded and voiced one of my own theories. "Coulda been she was experimenting with the wrong drugs in the wrong crowd. If she OD'd, her friends could have panicked and hidden the body someplace we couldn't find it and might never find it." He looked at Moses and me. "How's your good cop, bad cop routine?"

"It's pretty good," I said, "but we're running out of time. Moses leaves for his Army reunion on Thursday morning."

Moses gestured at Mildred. "You can take Mildred if I'm not available." To her, he said, "How's your bad cop routine?"

She smiled at him and her glasses glinted in the light. "You'd be surprised."

CHAPTER 22

"I told you so."

The voice on the line was so garbled, I wasn't sure I'd heard it correctly, but this was what I thought it had said. And when I figured out who was calling, I thought I had it right.

"I know you did, Katie, and we did take you seriously. I'm so sorry that we confirmed your suspicions. But before we go any further, could you tell me if Leila's guitar case was distinctive in any way? I mean, was it decorated?"

"Decorated?" She sounded puzzled, which was an improvement on belligerent. "Are you talking about the stickers? There was a peace symbol and a rainbow, if that's what you're talking about."

I nodded to myself, then waited to see if there was more she wanted to get off her chest, but all I heard were faint snuffling sounds that suggested she was crying.

"Katie, you know how important it is for us to track Leila's movements from the time she left work on the Wednesday she disappeared. We're going to be looking for anybody who caught sight of her in the following twenty-four hours. We'd really appreciate your help. Anything you can tell us about her favorite hangouts would be useful. You know, was there a place she liked to go for a snack in the afternoon, like an ice cream shop or a burger joint? Where did she go to buy records and music? Were there other stores she went to often? Somebody mentioned a small woven bag she had like ones sold at a head shop. Where would she have gone to get that?"

I couldn't tell whether the lengthy silence that followed meant that she was too choked up to speak or that she was thinking about the answers or reluctant to tell me that she didn't know the answers.

Finally, she said, "She used to go to Wizard Records in Corryville, but sometimes she went downtown to Willis on West 4th Street because they sold sheet music as well as records. She used to go to The Cabinet, too, in Corryville. Do you know what that is?"

I tried to quell my first, entirely maternal, reaction. The Cabinet was notorious. To call it a head shop would be selling it short because along with drug paraphernalia and hippie stickers, it sold sex toys — a line of merchandise that had drawn the wrath of Hamilton County's crusading prosecutor Simon Leis. Once Leis had succeeded in prosecuting *Hustler* publisher Larry Flynt for obscenity, he had turned his attention to The Cabinet, resulting in dozens of charges against Cabinet owners in recent years.

"Yes, I know what it is," I said neutrally.

"Well, Leila used to go there, probably mostly as an act of rebellion and because my parents would've grounded her for life if they'd known."

"Okay, let me put it this way. If Leila was planning a trip to Woodstock for a few days, where might she go beforehand?" She started to speak, but I cut her off. "I accept that she would have gone looking for you to tell you where she was going, but where else? For example, if I was going on a trip for a few days, I might get my hair cut or I might stock up on something I needed if I wasn't sure I could get it where I was going. Would she have wanted to stock up on guitar strings, for example?"

Franny broke a guitar string sometimes, I knew. But that could have been because her technique was so rigorous, not to say brutal. Did the average guitar player keep an emergency string in her hip pocket?

"She'd be more likely to be stocking up on cigarettes or rolling papers."

"At The Cabinet?"

"It's just a guess."

I felt that I was losing her. "Katie, can you tell me if Leila was wearing her necklace — the one with her name on it — the last time you saw her?"

"Of course. Why wouldn't she be?" Then, abruptly, "Look, I gotta go."

Startled, I said, "Would you be willing to meet with us now?"

"No." No apology, no explanation.

And she hung up. I sat staring at the phone. I knew there was no point trying to call her back. I didn't have a handle on Katie at all, but I couldn't help thinking that she had vital information for us and wondering why we were forced to squeeze it out of her, drop by drop, when her siblings seemed to be in such a hurry to find closure. Still, I had a few new places to look for traces of Leila.

The examination of Leila's possessions the next morning proved to be a relatively casual affair. I thought we'd be wearing moon suits, masks, and shower caps on our heads, but the only concession to contamination prevention was the pair of gloves that the technician was wearing. Similarly, the high-tech equipment I was expecting was nowhere in sight. Leila's stash was laid out on a high table under bright lights. The only pieces of equipment I could see were a pair of scissors and a magnifying glass.

The technician was a relatively tall woman named Stella Fu, who, far from resenting our presence, seemed to welcome our company, even though the three of us — Moses, Mildred, and I — made the room crowded. Fu had a sidekick, a wiry photographer named Rodney, whose function appeared to be to set up the camera and push the Record button.

"Based on the information we have," she said, "there's no reason to believe that these items are directly connected to a crime scene. The missing teenager, Leila Perle, is believed to have deposited these items in a storage cabinet before she disappeared, isn't that right?" When we nodded, she went on. "So, while we might find something useful, we're not going to find a murder weapon. We wouldn't expect to find blood spatter or much in the way of body fluids unrelated to normal use, so there's no real call to try and detect them." She leaned closer and sniffed. "Maybe just as well, since I can detect the odor of cigarette smoke. Must've been strong to begin with for it to still be detectable."

The only odor I could detect was mold. I had brought along my little jar of Vicks VapoRub, but since we didn't have a date with a corpse, I had left it in my pocket. Now, I was glad; I hadn't embarrassed myself by compromising the olfactory evidence with the overpowering scent of camphor.

"What's the connection between body fluids and cigarette smoke?" Mildred asked.

I was glad to have someone else along to help me ask the stupid questions.

"Luminol reacts to cigarette smoke as well as blood, and a few other things as well, like bleach. So, it's not ideal if you have a background heavily infused with cigarette smoke."

She was unrolling the sleeping bag now, turning it until she found a manufacturer's label. "Coleman. Popular brand." She laid it aside.

She pulled the guitar case to her and opened the buckles. The case was brown and decorated with peeling, curling stickers, one a rainbow and one a peace symbol. "Pretty standard case, well-used, and the mold isn't doing it any favors. No significant dents to suggest that she clobbered anyone over the head with it." She flashed us a quick smile. She raised the lid, lifted out the guitar, and held it up. "Gibson acoustic. Probably warped from the damp. Shame."

To my surprise, she handed it to me, and I took the hand-off awkwardly, feeling a bit queasy to be holding what may have been Leila's most prized possession. I quickly passed it on to Moses, who at least knew what to do with a musical instrument.

He ran his hands over it and then scrutinized the doohickey where the strings were attached at the bottom. He shook his head. "Yeah, and the glue's loosened up as well. I doubt it can be restored, shape it's in."

He passed it to Mildred, who also seemed to examine it with an experienced eye. She shook her head as well. "Shame."

Fu was now opening the small storage box inside the case. This would be a good time for a helpful piece of evidence to appear — a note of assignation, say, or a threatening letter or even a contract signed by a music producer.

"Anything?" I asked, leaning over to look.

"A capo and three picks." She opened her palm to show us.

As she re-closed the case and set it aside, I said, "I don't guess you're going to take fingerprints, then, or samples of the mold to compare with — anything."

She looked at me in surprise. "Compare it with what? All the other mold samples in that basement? Do you have any reason to believe that the killer stole this stuff from Leila, stored it in his own basement long enough to get covered in a different kind of mold, and then sneaked it back inside the basement at the Aquarius?"

"No." I was just dejected, I knew that. I wanted these objects to tell us more of Leila's story than they did.

My eyes followed her hands as she began unpacking the backpack and laying its contents out on the table. "She was supposed to be headed to Woodstock, right? How many days would that have been?"

"The festival ran from Friday to Sunday," Moses said.

"She had showed her mother a permission slip for a choir trip from Thursday to Monday," I put in. "So, I think we can assume she expected to leave on Thursday and return on Monday — four nights."

Fu laid out six pairs of nylon bikini underpants with lace waistbands; three sleeveless T-shirts — one that had once been white and two tie-dyed; one cotton skirt in a bright floral print; and a pair of bell-bottom jeans. "Either she didn't need a change of bra, or she didn't expect to need a bra at all once she got to Woodstock," Fu commented. To this collection she added a hairbrush, a toothbrush and travel-size toothpaste, and a small plastic bottle. Fu uncapped this last item and sniffed at it. "Probably shampoo."

Next, she extracted an Instamatic camera.

She handed the camera to Moses. "Maybe that will give you something. There should be four pictures to develop."

"I can't remember the last time I traveled that light," I said. "Not sure I ever did."

"You and me both," Mildred said.

Fu now brought out a spiral notebook and flipped through it. "Was your girl a composer as well as a guitar player?"

She handed the notebook to Moses, and Mildred and I crowded around on either side of him to see. On the cover was a faded "Make Love, Not War" sticker. Inside, the pages were brittle and brown at the edges, which were ragged. I didn't know if I'd understand what I saw, but it was pretty obvious, even to me. These were Leila's song compositions. Some were messy, even manic, as if written on a runaway bus, while others were extraordinarily neat. Some were studded with cross-outs and erasures. There were extra pages shoved in between the bound pages, and these usually just contained lyrics and some superscripts I took to be guitar chords. Living with a wannabe guitar player in my living room had taught me that much.

"There must be dozens," I said, a little awestruck.

Moses turned back to the front. On the inside cover was an old-fashioned bookplate featuring a cat holding a shield in its paws. On the shield were printed the words: *Leila Perle. Her Book.*

Her book, her songs. I ran my fingers over the words and wondered whether the notebook contained further evidence that one of Leila's songs had been stolen.

"And this." She held up a metal canister about the size of a salad plate.

I gasped.

"Handwritten label just says '7/4/69' to '8/10/69.' That mean anything to you?"

"We hope it covers Leila's only public performance of an original song at the Northside Park. If so, it could provide evidence of plagiarism." I glanced at Moses and he nodded.

"Evidence in a murder case?" she asked, waggling the canister. "Evidence of motive?"

"Doubtful," Moses said. When he saw my face, he continued, "Cat, Wildfire didn't record the song until the following year. Be hard to convince a jury that any of them killed Leila in the summer after hearing the song for the first time just so they could steal it and record it more than six months later."

"Yeah, you're right." I tried to quash my disappointment.

"If it's evidence in a plagiarism case, you can keep it," Fu said. "If it's evidence in a homicide case, it gets locked up in a storage unit, at least until the body is found."

Fu handed the canister to me.

Fu was examining the backpack with the magnifying glass now and I wondered if she was some kind of mold expert after all, but then she slid her hand inside the lining and gave a grunt of satisfaction. She extracted a small baggie containing three reefers that were better preserved than anything else on the table.

"You wouldn't think three joints would be enough for three days of peace and music," Fu observed, "but she probably figured she'd find more once she got there."

She upended the backpack and shook it. A nickel and two tampons fell out. She picked up the tampons and looked at them thoughtfully, then spoke to Mildred and me. "So, what do you think? Emergency stash? Again, if she was menstruating when she disappeared, two tampons wouldn't be enough and she'd hardly expect to find a tampon dispenser at Yasgur's farm."

"Can I see them?" I took them from her and examined them, then passed them to Mildred. "Hard to tell if they were fresh out of the box when she packed the backpack. They look like they've been lying around at the bottom of a bag for a long time, but then, they have been lying around at the bottom of a bag for a long time now."

She turned to Rodney. "Got everything?"

He nodded and pushed a button on the video camera.

"Sorry, boys and girls, that's all there is. Wish we could have found a wallet or an address book, but those were probably in her purse. Do you know that she carried a purse?"

I nodded. "She had one of those woven bags that all the hippie girls used to carry. It certainly would've been big enough. I imagine she had it with her."

She repacked the backpack, minus Leila's songbook, which I found I was holding. She handed the backpack to Moses and gestured at the guitar case and sleeping bag. "You can see that this stuff gets back to her family, right? And give the camera to Rap along with anything else you think he might want to keep. If he wants other tests run, tell him to give me a call."

"That's it?" I said. "Aren't you going to keep it in storage?"

Fu grinned. "You have an exaggerated sense of our storage space, Cat. We don't keep anything we don't need to. And like I said at the beginning, we don't have any reason to believe that any of these things can help solve Leila's disappearance, or her murder, if that's what it turns out to be."

I felt deflated as we walked out of the building.

"Don't look so gloomy, Cat," Moses said. "We've still got some photos to develop."

I heaved a sigh. I would not get my hopes up again, I told myself.

"And you've got Leila's songbook," Mildred said. "And maybe one of her songs in her own voice."

"Fingers crossed," I said.

CHAPTER 23

"Listen to this.

> Rock-a-bye baby,
> I like to think maybe
> that cow could jump over the moon.
> Little dogs too can blow
> over the rainbow,
> and you will come back to me soon."

I had brought Leila's notebook into Arnold's with me and somehow, I couldn't put it down. Reading her words in her own handwriting made me feel closer to her than I had ever felt.

"Girl had talent," Mildred said. "I'd like to meet her English teacher." She was dressed today not in her motorcycle leathers but in a cream-colored pantsuit that was probably the latest in morgue wear for the fashionable detective. I was wearing jeans with a VapoRub bulge in my pocket covered by a pullover liberally decorated with cat-claw snags. Moses was wearing what he called his "retirement uniform" — khakis and a long sleeve polo shirt.

We had introduced Mildred to Al and Mel, a study in contrasts. Al, a brunette with carefully styled hair, was wearing what Mel called her "lawsuit," which she saved for days when she was facing a particularly contentious judge. Mel, whose dark blonde hair was tipped in dried clay, was wearing overalls over a flannel shirt, both liberally splattered with clay and glaze.

"Too bad Kevin's not here," Mel observed.

"Yeah," Al said, nodding at the notebook in my hands, "if you turn him loose with that, he'll come up with a dozen theories for what happened to Leila."

"Might not be a bad thing," Moses said.

"Yeah," I agreed, "we're not short on scenarios, but without any evidence for any of them, we don't want to overlook anything."

In fact, our lunchtime speculations lacked a certain level of kinky but entertaining weirdness that brainstorming sessions with Kevin always achieved.

"What are you planning to do with the tape?" Mildred asked.

"First thing we'll do is make copies," Moses said. "But we'll need to find someone with a reel to reel that can handle a tape this size."

"Not Chaz," Mildred and I said in unison.

"Not Chaz," Moses agreed. "Our main goal is to preserve the tape, and we don't know how friendly Chaz is with the Wildfire boys. He could make it disappear."

"He could argue that it's his property," I pointed out. "Could even be his handwriting on the label."

"Right. That's why we're not going to tell him about it until we've made copies."

When lunch was over, Mildred and I made arrangements for a telephone blitz that evening while Moses was hosting his weekly poker game. Then Moses and I headed for WEBN radio station in Hyde Park.

The first person we encountered was a young woman with a sleek, short hairstyle and oversized glasses, who seemed friendly and eager to help as we told her that we were looking for the identity of a young man named Sam, a former employee, who had provided a ride to Woodstock through the radio station's ride board. We explained that we were trying to trace the movements of a teenager we believed had intended to ride with him but instead had disappeared. A young man at the next desk who had clearly taken time and care to tousle his short bleached-blond hair made a point of listening in.

"1969? I'll bet he was a friend of Miles's."

"Pay no attention to him," the young woman told us.

"No, but I bet he was, though. Miles knew everybody."

She rolled her eyes, then pointed to a framed photograph on the wall. It had been a poor-quality photo to begin with, badly framed and poorly focused, and the years had not been kind to its color. It showed a young person, long-haired and of indeterminate gender, in bell-bottom jeans and a plain white T-shirt standing next to a cocker spaniel with a ball in its mouth.

"Miles Duffy was the station's first program manager," the young woman said.

Dutifully, we leaned in for a look.

"That's him there, the one with the ball in his mouth."

"He knew everybody," the young man reiterated.

"He was dead by 1967." She had a hand to her head and wore an expression of long-suffering exasperation. "They had him stuffed and set in a barbershop chair on the porch at the original WEBN studio."

In an attempt to get things back on track, I said, "Does the station have an archive?"

"Nothing you could call an archive. What we've got is a broom closet crammed with boxes of crap."

"Could we take a look?" This, after all, was why we had come. We hadn't supposed that the ride board was an actual board and it might have been no more than a scribbled list of names and telephone numbers, but because of its connection to Woodstock, somebody might have considered it worth preserving. We didn't hold out much hope that something so ephemeral had survived the move from the station's previous location in Price Hill to Hyde Park, but it was worth a try to confirm Leila's intentions during the hours following her last shift at the Aquarius.

"You'd be better off calling Bo," the young man put in. He tapped his forehead. "He's got it all up here."

They were misunderstanding me. "I understood that people could call in and offer rides to places like Woodstock. We're trying to find out if a particular teenager, who went missing at the time, had signed up for a ride with this Sam."

The young man shrugged. "I'd still start with Bo. You know who he was, right?" When we shook our heads, he sat up straighter, then leaned across the desk and spoke enthusiastically. "Bo — that's Frank Wood, Jr. — He was the one that hosted the progressive rock show that all the kids listened to, Jelly Pudding."

"He went by the name Michael Xanadu as a disk jockey," the young woman added.

"He was, like, this incredible creative genius," the young man said. "He had a hand in all the stunts, the fake commercials, the Fool's Parade, the frogs on the city council ballot — you name it, if it was wacko enough to be WEBN, Bo had a hand in it."

"Couldn't hurt to ask him, I guess," the young woman said with a shrug. "He does have an encyclopedic knowledge of all things WEBN. Want me to give him a call?"

We thanked her and waited while she dialed. She made a good job of explaining what we wanted and why we wanted it.

She looked up at us. "What was he driving? Do you know?"

"A Chevy Impala, we think," Moses said.

She listened for a while and then hung up. "He'll call back, or Sam will. Sam was one of our sound engineers."

Moses drifted over to look at more of the framed photographs on the wall and I followed him. The young man joined us, looking over my shoulder.

He pointed. "That's the Fool's Day Parade. Ever see it?"

We were looking at a high angle shot of Hyde Park Square, probably taken from the third-floor window of this office. It showed the square on a sunny spring day, with a small crowd of people lining the streets, some of them sitting in lawn chairs or folding chairs, facing the square. The streets were empty, except for casual pedestrians.

We shook our heads.

"Too bad. We really put on a show — every year on March 32nd. And every year it got bigger and better."

I started to correct him, but he was pointing at another photograph, a closer shot a little above eye level, showing a small group sitting in lawn chairs. One of them was pointing at the empty street in front of them and the rest wore expressions of amazement and delight. The man who was pointing wore a WEBN baseball cap featuring a cartoon frog. He grinned into the camera.

I got it then. An un-parade, on March 32nd. These guys must be a barrel of laughs to hang out with.

"There's a real crowd-pleaser," our informant said. "The Our Lady of Perpetual Motion Marching Band started marching in 1968, joined our first parade, and haven't stopped yet. Of course, we've had our share of glitches, like the dark horses that fell off the presidential primary bandwagon that year. But we haven't let it crush our spirit, you know?"

Moses and I exchanged a glance. Maybe this wasn't the place to come for truth.

On the other hand, I tended to believe that imagination was an activity sorely lacking in the world today, especially in the political arena, and I found myself smiling.

The next photo showed people and kids wearing costumes of various kinds and pushing lawnmowers and baby carriages down the street.

"Sometimes the onlookers joined the parade — in between the official floats, I mean," our interlocutor said.

197

This was something I loved about my job: in the process of detecting something, I always learned about interesting stuff I wasn't detecting at all.

But the phone rang then and the young woman held up the receiver. "For you."

I tried to pass the phone to Moses, but he waved it off and nodded at my notebook, so I answered.

A voice said, "This is Sam Bonaventure. I heard you wanted to talk to me."

I introduced myself, explained that I was looking into the disappearance of Leila Perle in 1969, and asked if he was the Sam who had driven a Chevy Impala full of music lovers to Woodstock.

"That was me," he said, sounding a little cautious.

"And was Leila Perle supposed to be one of your passengers?"

"Well, she was supposed to be — at least, I thought so. But then when she didn't show up, I just thought she'd had a better offer."

"Why? Was she looking for a better offer?"

"Well, she was determined to take her guitar, and I said I doubted that we'd have room for it, unless we strapped it to the roof. I wanted to accommodate her, you know? But she was the fifth passenger, and they all had bags and sleeping bags and shit. She said she'd hold it on her lap, but I said she'd probably have her sleeping bag in her lap. So, she said maybe we could strap it to the roof. I said that would be up to her, I couldn't be responsible for it, you know? Now, I have to laugh at that — I was more worried about being held responsible for damage if the guitar fell off the roof in the middle of the Pennsylvania Turnpike than I was about getting arrested for transporting a minor across state lines. I mean, she seemed a little young, but she said she was eighteen, and what do I know? I didn't ask to see a driver's license or anything. We just didn't think about it much in those days. All we thought about was getting to New York and joining this crowd of

198

people to listen to music and celebrate peace and love. We thought we could change the world in three days, you know?"

"You were expecting Leila to show up at your meeting place on the Thursday night, is that right?"

"Yeah, yeah. She was supposed to call me if she found another ride, and she didn't, so I assumed she'd be there. See, she wanted to start out earlier, too, because she was afraid we'd miss the beginning or we wouldn't get good seats or something, which was a joke, really, because there weren't any seats, just better and worse places to sit on the ground. And we were there in plenty of time for the opening. But when she didn't show, I figured she'd found another ride, which I guess is what she did, right? I heard that she took a bus to New York."

"How long did you wait for her?"

"We waited about twenty minutes, and I kept getting madder and madder, until I just said, 'Fuck it! We're leaving.'"

"But you remember the name — Leila Perle?"

"Hell, I ought to remember her name, I've been pissed off at her for twenty years. I always thought I'd run into her and give her a piece of my mind, you know? But now you're saying she disappeared that night and hasn't been seen since? For real?"

"It looks like something happened to her between the time she left work on Wednesday at three and the time she was supposed to meet up with you the next night at — what time?"

"Ten. You're saying she wasn't on the bus?"

"Right. So, we're talking about a nineteen-hour period."

"And when you say 'something happened to her,' what do you mean?"

"That's what we're trying to find out."

"Oh, man!" There was a beat of silence, and then, more emphatically, "Oh, *man*! That's so heavy. I can't even — I don't know what to say." After another brief pause, he said, "To think I've been mad at her all these years, and all this time, she — I mean—" He really did sound choked up now. "It wasn't even her fault, was it?"

"No, probably not," I agreed. "Not your fault, either, that you didn't know."

"Still. She was just a kid. If she's dead . . . she just wanted to get to Woodstock, like everybody else. Was that what killed her?"

"I wish I knew."

CHAPTER 24

On our way home, we stopped off at the Park to talk to Chaz Wiley. We assumed that he'd already heard about the discovery we'd made at the Aquarius the day before, but we now wanted to emphasize how important it was that we find anyone who had seen Leila on the Wednesday afternoon or Thursday she went missing.

Leon had apparently finished painting the walls in the lobby and there was carpet down, though partly covered by a plastic drop cloth where a young woman was painting with a palette and brush. We went on through into the theater. The first person we spotted was Leon standing center stage with another man and Chaz. Leon gave us a big wave, grinning from ear to ear.

That was the thing about Leon: nobody else in my life was so unfailingly glad to see me.

We made our way onto the stage.

"They t-t-training me to s-set up the microphones, see?" He called our attention to an X drawn on the stage in pencil and labeled with some kind of code. "It's exes all over the s-stage, but they be l-l-labeled so I can tell them apart. Like, this one here s-say 'AB 3.' So that's where I put m-m-microphone 3 before the Allman B-brothers c-comes on."

Chaz looked on with an avuncular smile as Leon gave us a tour of all the microphone placements and decoded their labels, but I felt some trepidation. Looking around the stage floor, I spotted a small drawing in the general shape of an oval, which I took to be a drawing of the electrical circuit to which all the various outlets were attached. It confirmed my sense of the complexity of stage logistics and to tell the truth, I wasn't sure that Leon was up to it. "Not playing to his strengths" was how I put it to myself. Surely, Chaz was smart enough to check Leon's work afterward.

Meanwhile, Moses was expressing enough interest and enthusiasm for both of us. And I figured it counted more, coming from him, because he was a musician.

We took Chaz aside for a conversation and learned, as we expected, that he had heard of our discovery at the Aquarius.

"This makes it extremely important for us to speak to anybody who might have seen Leila on the day she disappeared," I said.

"Sure, sure, I get that," he said earnestly. "I can ask around. But it's a hard thing to pinpoint, you know? If you saw somebody on a particular date nineteen years ago."

"We understand," I said. "We'll talk to anybody who thinks they saw her around the time that she disappeared."

"You remember the last time you saw Leila?" Moses asked.

He shook his head. "But it was right before Woodstock. Woodstock started on a Friday, so I assume that means she disappeared sometime in the middle of the week? You probably told me, but I forget."

"We haven't found anyone who saw her after she left the Aquarius on Wednesday afternoon," Moses told him.

"So I probably saw her last on that Saturday night before the Wednesday, if she was here, and she usually was. We were open on Friday and Saturday nights."

We thanked him for his help. I reminded myself that he was still a suspect in Leila's disappearance, and that if he had caused that disappearance, he wouldn't be the first perpetrator to help with the investigation.

We went home — Moses to set up for his Wednesday night poker game and me to prepare for a fun-filled evening on the telephone. The best thing that can be said about cold-calling witnesses to ask them about something that happened almost two decades ago is that it beats working on your income taxes.

Anyway, I had help. Mildred showed up at 7:30 p.m. wearing a fashionable sweatsuit that was the next best thing to pajamas. I had invited her to wear pajamas, but she had demurred, and I'd assured her that I'd make popcorn anyway. We divided our list of names and phone numbers and I set her up in Kevin's apartment. She found a Valentine under the telephone and, to my surprise, replaced it with one of her own. That Mildred — she knew how to blend in when she wanted to.

Two hours of calling netted us very little new information. None of Leila's friends from school at Our Lady of Angels had seen much of Leila that summer, though some had heard rumors about what she was getting up to in that music club and coffeehouse.

The only provocative new information we gleaned came from Mildred's conversation with Linda Monniter, the newest waitress at the coffeehouse at the time of Leila's disappearance. Pressed for detail about the scene, Linda reported that Joyce Ridgeway's last words to Leila were "Good luck!". They had been delivered so softly that Gigi, who had been fighting with the espresso machine at the time, couldn't have heard them, but Linda herself happened to be looking at Joyce at the time. Linda couldn't even guess what they referred to.

Mildred and I sat side-by-side on the couch, a bowl of popcorn between us and two glasses of wine within easy reach, and pondered this exchange.

"Good luck with what?" I said, frowning. "Was it 'good luck with the trip to Woodstock'? She might say that if Leila was planning to hitchhike, but—"

"Leila had already arranged a ride in Sam's Chevy."

"Right."

"Good luck getting out of town without arousing her parents' suspicions?" Mildred adjusted her glasses and looked down at her notes as if searching for a clue there that she had missed.

"I guess you could say it to anyone going on a long trip," I conceded doubtfully.

"But given what happened next . . ." Mildred looked at me speculatively over her wine glass.

I nodded. "The darker possibilities certainly seem relevant. Could she have been saying, 'Good luck confronting Glass about the song he'd stolen and getting him to cough up money for the rights?'"

"Except he hadn't stolen it yet. It wasn't released until the next spring on Wildfire's next album, according to Kevin."

"She could have seen a copy of the lyrics lying around. Or she could have heard them practicing it."

"True." I leaned over and refilled my glass.

"All we know for sure," Mildred said, holding out her own glass for a refill, "is that whatever happened to Leila next, it wasn't good luck."

CHAPTER 25

"Don't do anything stupid, Cat. And if you do, take Mildred." This had been Moses's final admonition to me before he left for his Army reunion.

I had discovered the night before that Mildred had another superpower I could make use of in a sticky situation: she could correct my grammar.

On our third glass of wine and second bowl of popcorn, I had asked her what she had done before she went to work for Walt. She'd told me that she had been a high school English teacher in New Jersey before her husband had been hired as a reporter for the *Cincinnati Herald*, the city's most prominent Black newspaper. After ten years of teaching, she had wanted a change and thought private investigation had sounded interesting. For some years, especially when Walt's partner had still been around, her job had been confined to clerical work, but the content and context had kept her interested. When a major heart attack had forced the partner into early retirement, Mildred had gradually transitioned into a more active role.

Over our fourth glass of wine, she had confessed that she possessed three handguns and was something of a phenomenon at the gun range. I thought of my little Diane, nestled in its shoebox, and tried to crush the feelings of envy that were rising in my throat. I reminded myself that there was a place for incompetent shooters in the business and that the smart criminals were more afraid of us than the other kind. Our aim was unreliable and therefore dangerous.

When Mildred and I had parted company at midnight, around the same time that the poker game was breaking up, she had assured me that she had not given up on tracing Joyce Ridgeway.

But for most of the day on Thursday, I was on my own while Moses reuned and Mildred volunteered at a local early childhood Montessori and then babysat her youngest grand-child for a few hours, only confirming my conviction that the woman had nerves of steel. My options were limited by Moses's exhortation to avoid stupidity as much as by our lim-ited information. So, while I was waiting for Mildred to come up with Ridgeway's contact information and for Rap to come up with a list of girls who had gone missing in August 1969, I decided to pay a visit to Leila's Corryville haunts, Wizard Records and The Cabinet. Corryville was a neighborhood on the east side of the UC campus.

First, I dropped off the Northside Park tape — the one we hoped covered Leila's performance — at an address in North College Hill that Moses had given me. The man who answered the door accepted the handoff and said, "Two copies and two cassettes, right?"

"Whatever Moses said," I responded and he just nodded. "Do you know when they'll be ready?"

"I should have 'em tomorrow," he said. "I'll call Moses."

"He'll be out of town," I said. "Call me." And I gave him my number.

Once I reached the Corryville neighborhood, I chose the easy option first, building up my courage for the infamous Cabinet. I knew that my chances of finding somebody who had been around in the late '60s were slim to none. And that proved to be the case: the young man behind the counter at Wizard Records had surely been in diapers when Leila had last visited the store. He didn't know of anyone on the staff ancient enough to recognize Leila from her picture. There was little point in asking about security cameras in the late '60s, but I asked anyway. No soap.

That left The Cabinet, what passed for a den of iniquity in the Queen City if our prosecutor could be believed. I knew that Leila had bought her rolling papers here, but had she succumbed to any of the risqué merchandise the store was notorious for? I paused in front of the display windows to study the Valentine's Day display, a red and pink extravaganza featuring everything from UC Bearcat boxers, briefs, and onesies to barely-there unmentionables, from balloons to snow globes, from spiraling red glass objects to heart-themed rolling papers. There were other unmentionables as well, which I can't mention because I don't know what they were, except that they seemed anatomical and erotic. Standing on a copy of the *Kama Sutra* were Barbie and Ken, locked in a stiff-armed embrace of sorts. Barbie wore a ruffled apron covered in red hearts and nothing more. Ken was in the buff. Dangling from a string above them was a Troll doll got up like Cupid, dressed in a miniature leopard skin and wielding a small pink bow and arrow.

I froze my face, pushed open the door, and went in. It took my breath away. It was a more psychedelic, naughtier version of Bill's Hardware in Northside in its riotous abundance of merchandise. It was like Bill's, too, in that objects hanging from the ceiling gave it the look of an impenetrable jungle. It was unlike Bill's in featuring at the entrance a monitory sign warning that the store would refuse service to any customer using drug-related words and phrases, including "weed" and "bong," and adding the helpful advice, "If you don't know what to say, point."

When my breath returned, I inhaled a snootful of patchouli.

My resident trivia expert Kevin had once mentioned that The Cabinet had started life as a five-and-dime store, and it still showed vestiges of that history in its glass display counters. I edged past one filled with jewelry and covered in racks of beads. Although I was moving slowly and cautiously to avoid knocking anything down from its perch, my movement caused air currents that set a whole succession of mobiles, sun catchers, beaded curtains, and windchimes trembling and bobbing. I passed a display of party games on my left and stopped short at a display of blown glass objects. They looked too big to be incense burners, so maybe they were what is commonly referred to as "drug paraphernalia." I studied a particularly curvaceous one in a shape that, though familiar, I couldn't identify.

"Are you looking for something in particular?" said a voice behind me.

I felt the telltale blood rush up my neck and flash across my cheeks. Although I didn't know what I was looking at, I was pretty sure it was X-rated.

I can take a hint. I pointed. "What is it?"

I turned to see a middle-aged woman with a blonde braid and disconcertingly intense, light-brown eyes. She was dressed in jeans and an oversized tie-dye sweatshirt with the store logo emblazoned on it. I was heartened by her wrinkles. This woman might actually remember the '60s, depending upon what she had been smoking at the time.

She followed my finger and studied the object herself. "Some might describe it as 'vulval,' I suppose."

This required some translation on my part as the blood glowed brighter in my cheeks.

"Kind of like a Judy Chicago painting?" I said.

She gave me a look of surprised approval. "Exactly. Are you a fan of her work?"

I understood that the average old lady of my ilk didn't know Judy Chicago from the Chicago Transit Authority or Judy Blume or "Hey, Jude" But Franny had added an art history major one spring at Antioch and spent her spring break writing a paper on Judy Chicago, so I knew more than

I wanted to know about her. (Me: "Are you sure your professor won't mind reading a paper three times longer than the assignment asks for?" Franny: "It'll show her that I'm passionate about my subject." Me: "Do people really hang that on their walls?" Franny: "Mo-om!")

"Not really." Since I didn't want to get thrown out of the store before I had asked the questions I had come to ask, I repressed my follow-up question: *what's it used for?* Instead, I plunged into my spiel about a girl gone missing in August 1969.

"I wonder if you knew her." I proffered my photograph.

After a minute, she said slowly, "Yes, I might recognize her. If I'm thinking of the right one, she used to come in in the afternoons. Sometimes she carried a guitar case. But I don't remember her name, if I ever knew it."

"Her name was Leila and she wore a necklace with her name on it."

She shook her head. "That doesn't ring a bell. But then, I've waited on hundreds if not thousands of customers between then and now. And in those days, lots of them had long blonde hair, so I can't even be sure I'm remembering the right girl."

"So, I don't suppose you can tell me whether she came in on the afternoon of August 13th or 14th, 1969? This would have been just a day or two before Woodstock and she planned to attend the festival. She might have mentioned that."

"No, sorry."

"And I don't suppose you have any sales records that would tell us if Leila bought anything that day? Or footage from a security camera?"

She kept shaking her head. "Nothing that old, sorry."

"Are you the owner?"

"Carolyn Loehmann. My brother and I own the store, yes." She offered me a hand and I shook it.

"I understand it used to be a dime store."

"Yes, that's right. Over the years, especially with the new Walgreens opening in University Plaza, we found that we needed to diversify."

I nodded, trying to disguise my thoughts, which had conjured up the first shipment of bongs or dildoes to arrive on their doorstep. Nor would I say what she had undoubtedly heard many times before, "You don't look like a purveyor of porn."

Instead, I gave her a rueful smile and said, "What I really need is an old-fashioned beat cop who spent time watching the people on the street. Or even better, I suppose, would be a panhandler who camped out on your doorstep."

She laughed. "What you need is an eye seller."

"An eye seller?"

"They saw everything that happened on the street."

Now I did wonder what she had been smoking. "Because of their eyes?" I ventured.

"The *Independent Eye* was an alternative newspaper. It was an important part of the counterculture. I don't remember when they stopped publishing, but I'm sure they were around in '69. You could buy a subscription, but most people just picked it up on the streets. The sellers, who were often quite colorful characters, had their own territories. They made a percentage of every paper they sold. Ours was named Ernie, and he was usually camped out in front of the store in the afternoons. He was pretty unusual, even for an *Eye* salesman. I guess today we'd call him an 'autistic savant.' In some respects, he was a genius."

I felt my interest quickening. "What do you mean?" I didn't need persuading that clinical labels were rarely adequate to represent a human being. I knew Leon, after all. But I wanted to know what kind of a genius Ernie was.

"Well, he had an amazing head for numbers, for example. If you told him you wanted to buy, say, fifty-seven papers at a quarter each, he'd give you the cost without missing a beat and he could tell you immediately what he was going to earn on the sale."

I had read about people like this, and I held my breath as I asked, "How was his memory?"

"Phenomenal. I'll give you an example. His parents had been taking him to see *The Nutcracker* every year since he was five and he had all the cast lists committed to memory. If a dancer lost a shoe or a prop fell down, he'd remember it, and if you asked him about it later, he'd say, 'Oh, that happened in 1972, when so-and-so played Clara.' In fact, the more I think about it, the more I think Ernie's your man, if you can find him."

"But you don't know his surname?"

"I doubt I ever heard it. But maybe you could track down some of the people involved in publishing the newspaper and they might remember him. They used to have offices on East McMillan, but of course, those are long gone. Somebody must still be around, though."

Back in the car, I turned up the heat, glanced at the clock, and considered my options. I was on my own for several hours yet. Ernie the newspaper vendor was worth checking out, although my initial exhilaration had ebbed. Ernie's spectacular memory would only be helpful if he'd happened to cross paths with Leila during a fairly short span of time nineteen years ago and what were the chances of that? On the other hand, the discovery of Leila's stash at the Aquarius might have been a sign that our luck was changing.

My first impulse was to drive to the library downtown. My first impulse was always to drive to a library. But was that the best or fastest way to get the information I needed? Alternative newspapers were fairly ephemeral for the collection of a large city library. And what would the masthead of a counterculture paper, assuming it even had a masthead, tell me about one of its vendors? I could spend a lot of time tracking down the original publisher, but could that person tell me where to find a guy named Ernie today? What other resources did I have?

As often happened, my thoughts went to Leon. In Northside, Leon knew everyone and everyone knew Leon. But how far outside of Northside did Leon's magic circle extend?

This was a promising path to explore, but Leon was still in school. So, I went to see Leon's countercultural counterpart: Franny.

Franny worked at a health food store in Clifton, purveyor of many foods my daughter thought I should eat. Even the smell of the place bothered me, it was so macrobiotic. I found Franny on her knees, stacking packages of tofu in one of the refrigerators.

"Ernie? Ernie Iles? You're looking for Ernie Iles? Sure, I know him. I met him years ago when he used to sell the *Eye*. He's a savant." She stood up. Her light-brown hair was pulled back in a messy ponytail and she tucked a wayward strand behind her ear. "He did used to sell outside The Cabinet, and the Aquarius, as well. If he sold outside the Park on Friday and Saturday nights, I wouldn't know because *some*body wouldn't let me go there."

I raised my palms. "Not me." Then I added, "Oh! Maybe you mean the Ohio legislature, since they were in charge of the driving age." But I didn't want to be distracted by this old battle. So instead of pursuing it, I asked, "Do you know what became of him? Do you know where he is now?"

"He's around. Patty hires him sometimes to help with inventory here. I heard that he was bagging groceries at a Kroger somewhere — Hyde Park, maybe? Want me to ask for his contact information?"

She returned with a slip of paper and a report. "I was right — it is Hyde Park. Apparently, the work satisfies his desire to count things and add them up and calculate."

The Hyde Park Kroger is the flagship store in Kroger's hometown. In no time, I was sitting in the employee break room across from a man in his late thirties with curly blond hair and luminous eyes that were a color between green and hazel. His grin exposed two rows of teeth like matched pearls. He had the look of a mischievous angel who had lost his halo, which made him seem younger than he was. But he was dressed rather formally in a button-down shirt and tie under an apron, and I wondered if he missed the wild days of his youth, when he sold countercultural newspapers on the streets.

I introduced myself and offered him something from the vending machines.

"I like potato chips," he said.

Once we were well supplied with sodas and snacks, I said, "I think you know my daughter Franny, Franny Caliban."

"I like Franny," he said.

"Franny likes you, too. She told me you were good with numbers."

He nodded with satisfaction and spoke through a potato chip. "I am good with numbers."

"I also heard that you have a very good memory."

"I do have a very good memory."

It's a wise man who knows his own strength, I thought.

"That's good, because I want to find out if you remember something that happened a long time ago. Do you remember when you used to sell newspapers on the street?"

He nodded enthusiastically. "Ten cents."

"The newspapers cost ten cents?"

His head swung in the other direction. "No. The newspapers cost twenty-five cents. Ten cents to me."

"You earned ten cents for every paper you sold? That's pretty good. I'll bet you were rich."

"I was rich," he affirmed. "I bought a bicycle."

"I want to show you a picture of someone and ask if you remember her. Is that okay?"

He nodded.

I laid the headshot of Leila on the table and slid it toward him. He looked down and pointed with a potato chip.

"That's Leila."

"It is Leila. What can you tell me about her? Was she a friend of yours?"

"She was a friend of mine. I liked her. She gave me candy and sometimes stickers. She sang pretty songs. But then she went away and didn't come back." He raised his eyes to me. "Where did Leila go?"

"That's what I'm trying to find out," I said, meeting his gaze.

His eyes returned to the photograph. "She waved at me and then she got in the car and went away. And I never saw her again."

"When was this, when she got in the car?" I was holding my breath.

He barely paused. "August 13th, 1969."

"About what time?"

He thought. "Between five o'clock and five-thirty. I can't tell time on a watch with hands."

"Did Leila look happy?"

He shrugged. He seemed to struggle with this question and I thought he might have difficulty reading emotions. "She smiled at me."

"Do you remember if she was wearing her silver necklace with her name on it?"

"She was wearing her necklace. It said 'Leila.'"

All of the ambient sound died away and I felt a little dizzy. Finally, I croaked, "Do you remember what the car looked like? Was it dark or light, big or little?"

"It was a yellow Ford Thunderbird hardtop. Maybe a 1958, 1959 or 1960."

I was stunned. "Do you know a lot about cars?"

He nodded. "I like cars." After a pause, he added, "Thunderbirds didn't have a backseat before 1958. Leila got in the backseat and waved at me again through the window."

"What did the driver look like? Were there other people in the car?"

"I couldn't see the driver very well. I couldn't see anyone else in the car and I couldn't see if there was anybody in the backseat. The driver was a Black guy, but I couldn't see his face."

"A Black guy?" I croaked. I felt the ground shifting under my feet. Why would she sit in the backseat?

214

"775TK."

"What's that?" I scribbled the numbers in my notebook under a note that read "1958-60 yellow T-Bird."

"License plate."

"You remember the license plate number? Are you sure?" He nodded. "Sure."

He wadded up his empty potato chip package and I slid mine across to him. He took a potato chip and said nonchalantly, "I saw that car again, four times: Short Vine, September 25th, 1969; Hamilton Avenue, October 12th, 1969; McMillan Street, May 5th, 1972; Vine Street, June 10th, 1972." He bobbed his head for emphasis with each sighting.

"Did you ever see the driver?"

"I didn't see him up close. Not ever. But he was a Black guy."

"Every time you saw the car, a Black guy was driving?"

He nodded.

"I want Leila to come back," he said. "I always looked for her."

"I know, but I don't think she's coming back."

I wanted to talk to someone, but no one was available. It was too late to find Mel or Al at Arnold's, and Kevin had a lunch date, I knew. Mildred was playing with the hyperactive three-year-old and Moses was probably in a bar swapping war stories. So, I went home and opened a can of tomato soup.

There was no point in castigating the previous two detectives for not finding Ernie Iles nineteen years ago. The police detective hadn't had the time that I did to follow leads as skimpy as the one I had followed: a store where Leila liked to shop. Had he visited The Cabinet, he might or might not have encountered a newspaper seller there and recognized the kid's value. Walt Hitchens probably hadn't gotten that far before he found a witness who put Leila on the bus to Columbus and drew the conclusion he was supposed to draw, that whatever had happened to Leila had happened after she left the city. It all came back to that damn necklace. Somebody had gone out of their way to misdirect investigators.

I had been keen to get the list of missing girls from Rap but, as usual, I was second-guessing myself. It was always possible that the Leila impersonator, having reached Columbus and established her false identity with a witness, had turned right around and come back to Cincinnati. That would make the list of missing girls useless since she had never really gone missing. Now I called Rap with the license plate number I wanted him to trace, but I was forced to leave a message.

I spent a few hours cleaning my apartment and avoiding my taxes. At around five, Moses called. I could hear crowd noises and music in the background. I had just started my own Happy Hour celebration and sat down at the kitchen table.

"Say, Cat, you know that silk scarf Charisse gave me for Christmas? I think I left it hanging on the back of the kitchen chair. Would you go up and put it away before Winnie finds it?"

I turned my head and followed a drunken trail of shredded cat and dog toys to where two bodies lay inert on the living room rug — a little black cat and a beagle.

"Bad news, there, Moses. I can see it from where I'm sitting."

"Damn."

"Sidney and Winnie are sleeping on it. But I'll be glad to put it away as soon as I can get it out from under them."

We had an unofficial policy at the Catatonia Arms to let sleeping dogs and cats lie. In my part of the building, this policy extended to other critters as well. I figured that spiders had their own contribution to make to the universe, so I let them get on with it.

I silently resolved to assess the condition of the scarf and ensure that it had received the full treatment before I put it away. If Sidney and Winnie hadn't yet played tug-of-war with it, I would make that suggestion. Kevin would be proud of me. Moses's girlfriend Charisse was determined to transform him into the kind of *GQ* model she would like to have on her arm at an NAACP banquet or an Urban League dance and we'd been waging a covert campaign against her for several years now. This included the animals; Winnie had once puked all over a smoking jacket — a smoking jacket! — that Charisse had given Moses. We had been trying to train Winnie to puke in Charisse's lap, but so far without success.

"What've you been up to?" Moses asked now. "Any progress on the case?"

"How much time do you have?"

There was a brief silence and then I heard the frown in his voice when he said, "You haven't done anything stupid, have you?"

"No. But I talked to a witness who says that on the afternoon she disappeared, Leila got into a car on Short Vine Street and was driven away by a Black guy."

"Credible?" As a former cop, Moses always played it cool, but I could hear the tinge of excitement in his voice.

"He's an autistic savant. His specialty is memory."

"Where in the world did you find him?"

"He used to sell the alternative newspaper, the *Independent Eye*, in front of The Cabinet on Short Vine — a favorite place of Leila's, according to Katie."

"Cat, that's great. I'm impressed. Maybe I should leave you alone more often. You get a description of the car?"

"It was a yellow T-Bird, about ten years old, according to my witness. But I can do better than that. Moses, he gave me a license plate number. I left a message for Rap to track it down, but I don't know how long it will take for him to pick up the message and get back to me."

There was a brief pause on the other end of the line, filled with a burst of background laughter. Then he said, "You don't need Rap to track it down, Cat. That yellow T-Bird belonged to a former juvenile offender name of Tyrone Weeks. Couldn't have been two cars like that in the city, and most cops on the force and all the cops in Juvie would say the same."

"What did he have on his rap sheet?"

"Drug dealing, theft, burglary, and assault."

"No kidnapping?"

"Not until now."

CHAPTER 26

"So, what's your first thought on this, Moses?" I asked. "Drug deal? Tyrone Weeks drove Leila around the block while they traded money for weed? She went to The Cabinet for rolling papers and met her dealer outside? One-stop shopping? I thought drug dealers hung out in playgrounds."

"Doesn't usually work that way," he agreed. "And to do your dealing in a car that distinctive with your license plate in full view? Naw, that ain't right. 'Course, nobody ever accused Tyrone of being the sharpest knife in the drawer. If we track him down and ask him, he's liable to say that he took the car because he was late for supper."

"I was considering the boyfriend angle," I mused aloud. "Leila was drawn to bad boys, we know that. But she got in the backseat. So, unless there was another guy in the car, it doesn't seem likely, does it?"

"I'm going to have to think on this. Tyrone had a running buddy name of Zackery Lloyd, spelled with a *c-k-e*, who usually partnered with him in his various criminal enterprises. So, Zack could have been in the car. But where would Leila have met either of them?"

"Were they into music?"

"Zack had a boombox that he toted around on his shoulder, probably more for street cred than a love of music."

"Still, it could've started a conversation. Where did they hang out?"

"They grew up in the projects off Ezzard Charles. If they were driving around Clifton and Corryville, it was because they had customers there."

"College students."

"Wouldn't have to be the students, Cat."

"Could they have had any connection to the Wildfire band members? The Wildfire guys lived in a house in Clifton, so not far from The Cabinet. Maybe Weeks and Lloyd were friends of theirs."

"Or their dealers, more likely." I heard someone calling his name in the background. "Cat, I got to go. Let me think on this."

"Just one more thing, Moses. Do you think you could find Weeks and Lloyd now?"

"If they're still alive, I reckon I can. Be a miracle if they're not inside."

"And if Matt calls for a progress report tonight?"

"Just tell him we're following up on a new eyewitness lead, trying to confirm the details. That's all you need to tell him."

At seven I picked up Mildred and we headed out. She had found an address for Adam Glass and we wanted to catch him unaware for a little talk about Leila. Of all the boyfriends mentioned by our informants, he was the one she'd been most serious about, according to them. So far, we had no way of knowing whether he'd ever been serious about her.

I filled Mildred in on the day's activities, and I could tell she was chagrined that Walt hadn't found Ernie Iles nineteen years ago.

"Somebody went to a lot of trouble to make Walt think that Leila had skipped town," I said. "You can get your revenge when we find out who that somebody was."

"Yeah, but there was still that gap of more than twenty-four hours between the time she left work and the time she was seen on the bus. He should have tried harder to account for that gap."

I couldn't argue with that, so I didn't.

She told me that she had traced coworker Joyce Ridgeway's place of employment through a nurse's registry, but the hospital where she worked, Bethesda North, wouldn't give out a phone number or even tell her what shift Ridgeway was working.

"We can go tomorrow and see if we can track her down," I said.

It was fully dark now and I was driving in alien territory. Indian Hill was an opulent northern suburb studded with oversized manor houses that could have been mistaken for minor royal palaces if they had been set down in rural England. Mildred was my navigator, but we had to stop several times to consult a map. I felt out of place and conspicuous in my little blue Rabbit.

"Damn, Mildred!" I said. "I didn't think Adam Glass had been this successful."

I was pretty sure that what I was doing counted as the "something stupid" Moses had warned me against. But I had a sidekick — two, if you counted the little Diane, fully loaded and stashed in my purse. I was a murder mystery enthusiast, and nothing annoyed me more than an investigator who walked into danger as if oblivious and wholly unprepared. These people clearly had more confidence in their guardian angels than I had in mine, who was inclined to go on break at inopportune moments.

But was Glass my number one suspect in Leila's disappearance? After all, we had no way of knowing how much time Leila had spent in Tyrone's car after she'd waved goodbye to Ernie Iles. She might have ridden around the block and departed with a baggie of weed. Or she might have taken the weed to Adam Glass as a love offering. On the other hand, by all accounts her relationship with Glass had ended almost two months before she disappeared.

In any case, we had two crimes to investigate here, as I reminded Mildred.

"I'm curious to see what he'll say when we question him about the plagiarism accusation. To tell you the truth, now that I've seen his neighborhood, I'm beginning to appreciate how much money could be involved."

But what would it take to prove the plagiarism to a jury? I had checked Leila's notebook for the original lyrics and confirmed that they were there. The page wasn't dated, although if we could prove that Leila had died before Glass supposedly composed the song, that would help. If, as we suspected, we had a tape of Leila's performance in the summer of '69, that would seem conclusive to me. Certainly, other people had heard that performance. But recent experience had taught me the unreliability of memory, and sadly, Ernie Iles had not been in the audience that night. So, we really needed the tape.

I had been afraid that we'd have to talk our way past a gate and into the front door, but when we found the address, the gate was standing open. The parking area in front of the house had space for four or five cars, but there was only one in evidence. I don't know shit about cars, but even I could recognize the hood ornament: the trisected circle of Mercedes-Benz. The house was difficult to make out in the dark, but I had the impression of a large building that extended some distance on either side of the front door. I rang the bell and rehearsed my spiel. It would have to be good to get us an interview with Glass on a Friday night. I had a business card that identified me as an investigator with Fogg and Caliban, and I was holding it when the door opened.

I was surprised to be confronting the great man himself, or at least the man who had once been a minor celebrity. I recognized him from the photograph of Leila sitting on his lap. He appeared to have shed his youthful good looks along with the celebrity, although you could see their vestiges in his rumpled long dark hair, now thinning at the temples, dark eyes, and rugged jawline, less conspicuous with the fuller face of age. He wore jeans and a baggy, stained sweatshirt that failed to conceal a paunch. He wore white socks and a tatty pair of bedroom slippers on his feet.

"Mr. Glass, my name is Cat Caliban and this is—"

That's as far as I got. He wasn't listening, he was talking. "Took you long enough."

He turned his back on us and walked away.

"Place is a mess, and my first house guest arrives tomorrow. You should have been here yesterday."

Mildred and I exchanged a look, and then she stepped across the threshold and followed him and I followed her, closing the door behind me.

"Now you'll have to stay till it's done." He kept up a litany of complaints in a querulous voice. I couldn't make out everything he said, but the tone never changed. He had told our boss he needed service ASAP. He had asked for a team of cleaners, and what had he got? Just us. He hoped there were more coming, because if not, he was going to have to have words with our boss. And he had other things on his mind. He was a creative artist with a goddamn performance to get ready for. He couldn't be bothered with petty shit.

The word conspicuous in its absence before "performance" was "comeback."

We followed him from the foyer across a large sunken living room and through a kitchen as big as my apartment but messier, which is saying something. At least I didn't leave open food containers and pizza boxes on the counter. His voice was partially drowned out by loud rock music. He opened the door off the kitchen and led us into a large storage area full of cleaning supplies. It smelled of bleach and pine replicated in a laboratory.

He gestured at the room's contents. "Everything's here. If you can't find something, don't ask me, I can't help you. I never come in here." I thought of the state of the kitchen and I believed him.

"Guest bedrooms are upstairs." He made another gesture. "Studio's outside. Take the door at the end of the main hall. Better get busy."

He took a last look around. "Don't bother me for anything less than a dead body in the fucking bathtub. I'm working."

Then he was gone.

Mildred and I exchanged a glance.

As if I'd spoken, she said, "But what would we be looking for?"

I shrugged and started unbuttoning my coat. "Anything that belongs to Leila. I know he was living in a different house in Clifton at the time, but you never know. Maybe we'll find her transistor radio. Or maybe she wrote him a threatening note. Or maybe we can find another copy of the lyrics to 'Angelina' — one that's dated. Or anything that we could use to get him to talk when we question him."

"You mean when Moses questions him," she said. "We're just the cleaners."

She put a hand on my arm as I was taking off my coat. "Better keep our coats and purses with us for a quick getaway."

"Good thinking. Why don't you take the main house and look for a home office — the place where he keeps his papers?" I wouldn't insult her by making further suggestions. "I'll take the studio, wherever that is. Maybe he's got an archive of lyrics and song ideas."

I had picked up a bucket and was rummaging among the cleaning supplies. I found a bottle of floor cleaner and dropped it in the bucket, but Mildred retrieved it and replaced it with a large bottle of vinegar, which was covered with dust. When I raised my eyebrows at her, she said, "We should take pride in our work."

She picked up a vacuum cleaner and draped the hose around her neck. She had unbuttoned her coat.

I looked at her and then down at my own clothing. We were both dressed in nice corduroy pants, blouses, and jackets.

"Is this really what the well-dressed cleaner wears to work these days?"

"Men like him don't notice what old ladies are wearing."

"His mistake." I armed myself with a mop and set off.

"I'll come looking for you in half an hour," Mildred called after me.

The studio turned out to be a separate small building reached by a breezeway connecting it to the main house. The lights were on. It was a large open space with a high ceiling and no windows. The carpet was on the walls instead of the floors, which were some kind of blond natural wood, probably expensive. There were folding chairs scattered around, along with several easy chairs and headphones like beached squid trailing cords like harpoon lines. There were perhaps a dozen guitars in evidence, as well as a drum set in one corner and a keyboard. There was a large control panel with dials and levers and more headphones. There were speakers of various kinds, some upright and some stacked against the wall. But my eyes were drawn to a small old-fashioned desk flanked by a file cabinet on one side and a four-drawer wooden cabinet on the other that was too battered to be called "antique."

I spotted a large misshapen stain on one wall and my eyes followed it down to a pile of moldy towels on the floor. The odor of mold was not strong enough to mask the odor of marijuana, but it was perceptible. I reviewed my tour of the house so far and recalled other signs of deferred maintenance — some chipped tiles and a stretch of missing baseboard in the entry hall, signs of wear including a burn mark on the kitchen linoleum, a water stain on the ceiling in the storage room. Was this the kind of "shit" that creative geniuses couldn't be bothered with or was it an indication that the homeowner had experienced a financial reversal since he had bought this very expensive house?

I decided to start on the file cabinet, gratified to discover that it contained contracts and professional correspondence.

"Who are you?"

Startled, I looked up. Peering at me from around the back of an easy chair was an inquisitive young face, large dark eyes under heavy dark brows.

"I'm a cleaner," I said, belatedly finding my bucket and putting an explanatory hand on top of it.

The eyes gleamed over a broad smile. "And I'm Pippi Longstocking. Cleaners don't dress like that. Nice try."

She turned until she was kneeling in the chair and I saw that she had a book in one hand.

"Want to try again?" she asked, not hostile but friendly.

"Okay, you caught me. I'm an IRS agent conducting an investigation. My name's Cat."

Her eyes widened. "Cool! Can I see your badge?"

She climbed out of the chair, abandoning the book, and approached. She was a kid — a preteen, I'd say — dressed in red print pajama pants and an oversized sweatshirt that emphasized her small stature.

"We're not allowed to carry them when we're under-cover," I told her. "That would risk compromising the entire operation." I could feel the sweat tickling the backs of my ears and trickling down my neck. Of all the agencies I could have chosen to work for, why had I picked the goddamn IRS? Sure, she was too young to have filed a tax return and so unlikely to quiz me about 1040s, but what if she tested my math skills or asked for help with her homework?

I went on the offensive. "And you are?"

"Oh, don't worry. I'm not one of his sweet young things. I'm his daughter."

"That's a relief."

She made a face. "I know! It's so embarrassing the way he goes after girls. He can't keep it in his pants — that's what my mom says. I don't even like to bring my friends here. I'm afraid he'll, like, hit on them."

I made a face of my own. "Gross!" A better word for the teeny bopper set than "appalling" or "criminal" or any of the other words that leapt to mind.

"I kno-o-ow!" She offered me a hand. "Izzy."

Before I shook, I made a point of wiping my hand on my pants as if I had actually been cleaning something. "Cat."

Her gaze shifted to the filing cabinet. "So, are you, like, going after my dad for income tax evasion? 'Cause my mom would be totally on board with that. She says he's so tight his pockets squeak. She says he's loaded, but every time the child support or school tuition comes due, he pretends to be poor."

"You don't live here with your dad?"

"God, no! That would be a disaster! No, I'm just visiting for a few days while my mom lives it up on a cruise with her new boyfriend."

"But you don't like it here? That is so unfair."

"I know! It is, isn't it? Although to be honest, when I'm here I get to eat anything I want, it doesn't have to be healthy. In fact, I don't think he'd notice if I ate nothing but Twinkies all day. Anyway, I doubt there's any healthy food on the premises, except what my mom brought."

"So, have you ever had your friends over?"

"One time I did. That was enough. You're not really a police officer with the vice squad, are you? I mean, I wouldn't mind seeing him punished for some of the stuff he does, but it would be totally embarrassing if they locked him up in the slammer for hitting on underage girls."

"I'm just the IRS. If I see evidence of another crime, I can contact a colleague in the police department or FBI, but that's not what I'm here for. I'm just here to collect what he owes the government."

"Well, good luck with that, as my mom would say."

She perched on an edge of the desk, and I could see that I would have a hard time getting rid of her. But I was warming up to her, and also to her mother.

"Anyway," she said, "the really important stuff that you want isn't here, it's in his office. This is just the music stuff."

"I have a colleague who's searching the office. But you'd be surprised how much I can learn about his income from looking at these music contracts. For example, does your mom know how much he earns every time somebody plays 'Magdalena' on the radio?"

She leaned forward with keen interest and shook her head. "A bundle, I bet."

"More than that. A shitload." When her eyes widened, I handed her the file I had in my hand. "You might want to take a look at this."

After that, I found enough files to keep her occupied while I continued my search. I suspected she was right, though. I was betting that all the really juicy financial stuff was in the office. And meanwhile, I hadn't found anything in Leila's handwriting, nor had I found the original lyrics that Glass had written for "Magdalena."

For a change of pace, I started in on the little four-drawer cabinet. Here I found a treasure trove of old knickknacks, mementos, keepsakes, and souvenirs that had been shoved in a drawer and forgotten. There were ashtrays and napkins and match books from various music venues around the country, along with a scattering of business cards soft with age, rolling papers brittle with age, two pairs of silky undies and a lacy push-up bra.

Then I turned a Northside Park napkin over and caught my breath. On the reverse was a drawing of a much younger Glass. It was beautifully executed. I was sure that the artist had been Katie Perle.

I had known that Katie had met Adam Glass. But there was something intimate about this drawing, familiar and even romantic, that made my skin crawl. I would have to think about what that meant.

But the biggest surprise was waiting in the bottom drawer. A shock of long, cottony white hair standing straight up. A semicircular grin under a wide pug nose. Luminous large round eyes. Arms spread. "Surprise!"

And I was surprised. Flabbergasted, even. Not, as he seemed to expect, because he was naked as a jaybird. It was because the only thing this little Troll doll was wearing was a silver necklace wrapped around his neck. The pendant, which was dull and spotted with tarnish, said "Leila" in an elegant script.

CHAPTER 27

I stared, transfixed. My hand reached out to touch the necklace, but I caught myself in time and drew back. I couldn't touch the necklace, couldn't pick up the little guy and examine him in better light, couldn't slip him into my pocket. In case he turned out to be evidence in a homicide case, I had to leave him where he was. Nor could I risk spoiling any existing fingerprints by handling him, not even with gloves.

But was he evidence in a homicide case? The only logical conclusion I could draw at the moment was that he connected the girl on the bus to Adam Glass — that Glass had masterminded her impersonation of Leila. At some point, the imposter had returned to Cincinnati and returned the necklace to Glass, with or without the Troll attached. Having no further use for the necklace, Glass had tossed it in a drawer and forgotten about it. But was he really that stupid? Anyone with half a brain and a moderate sense of self-preservation would have gotten rid of the necklace — the sooner, the better. Why hadn't he done that? Surely not because he had really loved Leila and treasured the keepsake; it was not keeping company with other valuables. And Glass's own daughter did not give him high marks for loyal devotion.

But maybe I was letting my own prejudices blind me. The simpler explanation was that the girl on the bus had been acting on her own initiative. She herself could have been Leila's killer, whether out of sexual jealousy or a motive that I hadn't yet imagined. She could even have been acting on Glass's behalf without his knowledge or consent. Or, wait — here was another idea. Perhaps she had wanted revenge against both Leila and Glass, so she had killed Leila and left the Troll doll in the drawer to implicate Glass. Had he never even looked there? Not even when he'd moved out of the Clifton House and into this Indian Hill mansion? My head hurt with possibilities.

Someone cleared their throat behind me and I jumped, turning to see Mildred standing in the doorway, toting her vacuum, her coat, and her purse. Her eyes slid in Izzy's direction.

"Oh, Mildred, there you are. That's Izzy, and she figured out that I was no housecleaner, so I had to tell her about the IRS investigation. But she's cool with it. Apparently, her dad owes a lot of back child support as well."

"Hello," Izzy said.

"Have you found anything we can use?" Mildred said guardedly.

While Izzy was studying Mildred, I nodded my head. "Not much. Come and take a look."

Mildred played it cool. She ambled over and glanced in the drawer. If I hadn't been watching for it, I wouldn't have noticed how her eyes focused.

She slid a small camera, no bigger than her palm, out of her purse and knelt beside me. It made a Lilliputian click every time she pushed the button. Still, I kept talking to cover the sound.

"The papers in these files out here" — I nodded in the direction of the files — "these are mostly about music contracts and copyright registration and things like that. Izzy says that most of the financial papers are in the home office. Still, you can tell that he should be raking it in by the number and terms of these contracts. What about you? Find anything we can use?"

At this point, we were startled by the introduction of a new voice in the mix.

"What's going on out here?" said Adam Glass. When I spun around, I caught him looking from us to Izzy and back again.

Mildred turned more slowly, and between the two of us, we managed to get the bottom drawer closed, screening this maneuver with our bodies.

Glass strode toward us and stopped. He was a big man accustomed to looming over inferiors and he was good at it.

This was a sticky situation. With my arthritic knees, it would take some time and effort for me to regain my feet so that I could look up at him from a more advantageous height. I edged my purse closer, reached in and fumbled with its contents until I found the comfortable solidity of the little Diane. "We were just—"

But Mildred cut me off. She was running a hand over the floor. "Mr. Glass," she said in a surprisingly assertive voice, "what in the world has someone been putting on these floors? And who was that someone? Don't tell me it was somebody from our company because I won't believe it. You haven't been cleaning them yourself, have you?" She made the last sentence sound like an accusation of criminal wrongdoing.

Easily distracted, he went on the defensive. "No, of course I haven't been cleaning the floors. I usually have another company, but they couldn't come out on such short notice. Why? What's wrong with them? They look okay to me."

"Everything looks okay if you stand far enough away," she chided him. "But you get down here close and take a look, you'll see what I mean. Cat knows what I'm talking about."

Startled, I picked up my cue and began running a hand over the floor and shaking my head. To tell the truth, all I felt was a dirty floor — a subject on which I am an expert. But I wasn't about to queer Mildred's pitch. "It's pretty bad."

"I'll bet they gave you instructions when they installed this floor and you never read them, did you?" She favored him with a censorious frown.

Wrongfooted, he tried to bluster. "How the hell should I know if they gave me instructions? Floors don't come with directions."

Izzy decided to stick her oar in. "When I heard them talking about it, Dad, I thought the same thing: what's wrong with the floor? But then I looked again and I could see what they were talking about."

Mildred nodded in satisfaction. "Once you see it, it's obvious."

"See what?" he bellowed.

She crooked a finger at him. To my amazement, he rolled his eyes but then got down on his knees. Izzy gave me an elaborate wink and a thumbs-up when his back was turned. Mildred grasped his wrist and slid his palm over the floor.

"Rich and famous people like you get taken advantage of all the time," she told him. "You pay top dollar for services, and you expect top quality. You buy a certain brand of floor cleaner because the company told you to or because it's a brand you've heard of. You don't even realize what's happening until you try to sell the house a few years down the line and your realtor tells you that the floors will need to be replaced before you can put the house on the market."

He actually blanched. If he was planning to sell this house anytime soon, it was going to need a lot of work. The floors might be its best feature. But that bad news could wait for another time, after we were long gone.

"You can see it now, can't you?" she asked him, and the expression on his face told her he could.

"Yeah, yeah, it's kind of—"

"Exactly. And even if you couldn't see it, you could feel it, right?"

He frowned. "It feels kind of like—"

"You've got it now."

"But what brand should I buy?"

Glass was following the script now, and she rewarded him with the smile of a TV pitchwoman as she reached into my bucket and extracted a bottle like a rabbit from a hat.

"That's the best part. It isn't about brands at all."

"But you said—" Then he focused on the bottle she was holding. "Wait, vinegar?"

"That's the secret. Doesn't matter which brand. The cheapest brand works just as well as the most expensive. Now you can see why the big corporations don't want you to know about it. They spend a fortune concocting pine and lemon scents in the lab and charge you an arm and a leg for the results. What they don't want you to know is what all those harsh chemicals are doing to your floors." She kept her gaze steady on his face and her glasses made her look smart.

He sat back on his heels. "Huh. I should sue somebody."

"I know how you feel," she said. "But most cleaning companies use the same products, and most people who do their own floors use them, too. Jurors won't want to hear that they've been tricked."

I flashed on an image of myself sitting in the witness box, testifying. All the defense attorney would have to do to undermine my credibility would be to take one look at my own floors. "This woman is no cleaner," he'd tell them, and he'd be right.

"I know you've got important things to do," Mildred told Glass. "Why don't you go back to doing them and let us work on this floor?"

She got to her feet and hauled me up. He stood up as well and left us to it.

We also got rid of Izzy, who went off to watch *Bewitched* after making a point of locking her lips and throwing away the key.

I breathed a sigh of relief. Glass had never noticed the file folders I'd piled on his desk. Now I showed Mildred some of the contracts I had pulled.

"We should be able to match them up with the statements I photographed and get some idea how much he's earned from the plagiarism. While I photograph these, why don't you vacuum and put some water in this bucket?"

"We're actually cleaning it?"

"It will make him less suspicious if we do. Once I photographed the documents I wanted, I vacuumed the office, straightened it up a little, and dusted. I did the same in the master bedroom. That leaves about five bedrooms to vacuum and dust, four bathrooms to clean and the kitchen. It shouldn't take too long. You got something better to do tonight?"

"Anything."

"Look, Cat, we don't want him to get suspicious. We don't want it even to cross his mind that we might not be cleaners after all and start wondering what we might have seen when we were sitting on the floor in front of that chest of drawers. We want to make sure that the Troll is still there when the cops open that drawer. He probably hasn't thought of the Troll in years. We don't want him to think about it now, right?"

"I guess. But I can't remember when my own floors got this much attention," I grumbled. *Probably never*, I added to myself. I didn't want Mildred to think I was a slob, though she'd already seen my apartment and knew the worst.

Mildred was fast, I'll say that for her. For the next hour and a half, we vacuumed, dusted, straightened, washed counters, cleaned floors, even threw stuff away. "He'll never miss it," Mildred would declare as she dropped a pile of junk mail or a moldy loaf of bread into the trash can. We even collected all of the trash bags and left clean ones behind.

We chased Izzy out of the living room; she cheerfully retired to her room to finish watching her TV show. Glass kept out of our way, and Mildred speculated that he had gone back to the studio to admire his clean floor.

When we were finished, we made our way cautiously through the house, taking care not to distract Izzy from her television show, left the cleaning equipment in the closet, and slipped out the front door.

"What are you going to do about the Troll?" she asked as we were driving away.

"Tell Moses. He'll know what to do."

"Do you think we have enough evidence for the plagiarism case now? Or does it depend on what you find on the tape you recovered from Leila's backpack?"

"Well, I found the lyrics in Leila's notebook, but they're not dated. There were certainly people in the audience that night who heard her sing the song, but my recent experience has taught me how unreliable memory can be."

"Unless you're a savant, like Ernie."

"Yeah, unless that." Something flickered at the edge of my consciousness, then flitted away before I could catch it.

Moses called again later when I was reading in the recliner with a cat on either side and one in my lap. Since the cat in my lap objected to being a book rest, I had been forced to hold the book awkwardly, but I figured I was exercising my biceps and triceps in the process. If you added the lifts of a G&T glass, I was burning quite a few calories. With all the cleaning, I already felt like I'd run a marathon that day.

"Cat, I had another thought about Tyrone Weeks. It could have been a drug deal, just like you said — Leila got in the car, traded cash for weed, and got out a few blocks up the road. That's probably the most likely. But here's another thought. Was a time I heard that Tyrone and Zackery were working for an abortion doctor — you know, back when abortions were illegal. The way it worked, according to some of the girls I talked to, was you called a number. Sometimes there was a meet-up with a woman who talked about the procedure and collected a down payment, and probably checked you out to see if you were a police informant, sometimes not. You were then told to wait on a street corner somewhere. A car picked you up and you were told to lie down in the back seat, maybe put a blanket over you, to make sure you didn't know where they were taking you. Afterward, you'd be dropped off on another street corner, usually near a bus stop. If you were lucky, it would be in your neighborhood and you could walk home. Otherwise, you would have to take the bus. I think Tyrone and Zackery were working as drivers."

I closed my eyes and thought of a teenage girl — Franny, say — woozy from anesthetic and painkillers and loss of blood, alone on a street corner at night in a strange neighborhood, and I shuddered.

Moses was still talking. "Those two had the criminal contacts and street cred, and they might have seen the job as a way to attract new customers. Maybe they sold weed to the girls on the way home. Of course, I'm sure they weren't supposed to use the yellow T-Bird for pickups, but like I said before, Tyrone was never the sharpest knife in the drawer. Anyway, it's worth considering." He took a breath. "Do you think it's possible Leila could've been pregnant?"

I nodded slowly, even though I knew he couldn't see me. "Sure, it's possible. Seems unlikely she would have arranged for an abortion on the eve of her trip to Woodstock, but on the other hand, she was a teenager and teenagers don't always make the best decisions."

"Also means she would've needed money for the abortion as well as the trip," he said.

"Yeah," I agreed. "But, Moses, the yellow T-Bird may be moot." And I told him about the little Troll wearing Leila's necklace.

"So, you think the girl on the bus was connected to Glass somehow. You think she might have colluded with him to cover up Leila's death."

"Either that, or she tried to frame him by planting the necklace in his studio. Glass is a guy who leaves a lot of resentment in his wake. I've only met him once and I already resent him."

"Yeah, but Cat, when the cops didn't arrest Glass, why didn't she call them with a tip? If she had, they would have gotten a search warrant and found the Troll."

"Maybe she got cold feet."

"So, in this scenario, the girl on the bus killed Leila?"

"I'm keeping an open mind on that score. She could have killed Leila out of jealousy, sure. Or Leila could have overdosed or taken bad drugs. That's still a possibility. So, what should I do about the Troll?"

"Tell Rap if you see him. Otherwise, I'll talk to him when I get home. Get your pictures developed. Speaking of cold feet, has Perley called?"

"Not a peep. Maybe he only wants to talk to you."

"Or maybe he's finding the truth too painful."

"I know just how he feels."

CHAPTER 28

Bethesda North Hospital was a daunting place to look for a single nurse. We had her married name, Joyce Hardcastle, from the nurses' registry, and a nineteen-year-old physical description from her coworker at the Aquarius, Linda Monniter.

As we faced the massive multi-level Lego construction that was the hospital complex, I said, "We should have tried to find a picture of her."

"How many people have pictures of their coworkers?" Mildred said. "I don't have any of Walt. If you have any of Moses, it's probably because you live with him."

We decided not to split up on the principle that two old ladies were two times less intimidating than one. Our story was that nurse Joyce Hardcastle had encountered Mildred in the parking lot when she was wrestling with a baby, two toddlers, and a baby stroller and had managed to get the stroller open and functional, for which we wanted to thank her again in person. We had no idea how credible the story was, since, as Mildred pointed out, the staff probably parked in a different lot from the public one. But we decided to give it a shot.

The first seven people we encountered were sympathetic but ultimately unhelpful. The majority seemed to think that our best bet would be the hospital's personnel office, which we thought likely to be less sympathetic than our random selection of non-informants. The eighth person we asked knew of two nurses named Joyce, one in Radiology and one in Emergency — unless the one in Emergency was named Joy.

After that, we met Joyce Killebrew in Radiology, Joy Culpepper in Emergency, Joyce Yarrow in Orthopedics, and Jo Marvin in the Fertility Center, before arriving at the NICU to be told that Joyce Hardcastle wouldn't be on duty until 4:15.

"But don't come looking for her then," our informant told us, "she'll be too busy to talk. Best give her an hour to catch up."

Given our cover story, we didn't think we were in any position to ask for a home address or phone number, so we left.

Mildred looked at her watch. It wasn't even lunchtime yet, and I'd run my second marathon in two days. "What now?"

"I have to pick up the list of missing girls from Rap. Let's see if he's there so we can tell him about the Troll."

Someone had called that morning to tell me that Lieutenant Arpad had left an envelope at the desk for me. I needed to pick it up, even though given recent developments, I doubted that a list of girls who had gone missing about the same time as Leila would be much use to us. We now knew that the Leila necklace, and presumably the girl who had worn it, had returned to Cincinnati at some point after being seen on the bus. That expanded our list of suspects to include all blonde teenagers between, say, fifteen and eighteen who had lived in Cincinnati at the time.

Rap was in, so I asked to see him. When we reached his cubicle, Rap said, "Did you get your list? I know you were in a hurry."

"Yes, thanks." I wasn't about to tell him that we probably didn't need it now. "We have something else to tell you. Got a minute?"

He found an extra folding chair and we sat down in his office and described the previous night's adventures.

When we finished our account, he leaned back in his chair and steepled his fingers. "So, this Troll wearing the necklace was just tossed in a drawer with a bunch of other junk?"

"Yes."

"Doesn't look like he took any trouble to conceal it, right?"

"Right."

"And we can't be sure that she was wearing it on the day she disappeared?"

"Oh, I forgot that part. We have an eyewitness who says that she was wearing it." And I told him about Ernie.

"So this guy is never wrong about the stuff he remembers?"

"Far as I know. He told me that Leila got into the back seat of a yellow Thunderbird and waved at him as the car drove off. He gave me that license plate number — the one I asked you to look up. But then Moses recognized the car from its description."

"Belonged to Tyrone Weeks, that what he said?"

I nodded. "Do you think we can find him? Or his buddy Zackery Lloyd?"

"Oh, we can find Weeks all right. He's doing eight to ten for burglary with a firearms specification at Lebanon. Lloyd's out, far as I know, but I don't know where he's staying. Maybe at his sister's."

"I don't suppose you can get a search warrant for Glass's house?" I asked.

"On the basis of what we've got now? Not likely. Best I could do would be to pull Glass in for a talk, which would put him on his guard. That what you want?"

"No," I admitted.

"'Course, you can go talk to him anytime you want. Or maybe Foggy should be the one to talk to him, considering you got into the house under false pretenses."

"He's got no room to complain," Mildred said. "We left that house cleaner than it's been in years."

Rap cocked a dubious eyebrow at me, but I nodded. He knows the state of my apartment.

He stood up. "Well, when you get more evidence, come back."

Next, we picked up the photographs from Leila's camera. There were only six, and four of them were shots of bands performing at the Park. The fifth and sixth were medium-close shots of a good-looking boy. He had a full Afro, clear brown skin, long eyelashes over mischievous eyes, and a lazy smile. He was what we used to call a "dreamboat." Neither of us recognized him.

"Another new boyfriend?" Mildred speculated.

"Well, she's not sitting on his lap and she doesn't have her arm around his neck, so he could be just a friend. But I'll bet teenage girls went weak in the knees whenever he looked at them like that."

"There's something about the eyes, don't you think? He's just the kind of bad boy Leila was attracted to."

I agreed. "We'll show these around, for what it's worth. The ones of the new boy are five and six on the roll, so if we want to narrow down the date, we can find out who the bands are and when they played the Park."

Then, we went to North College Hill to pick up the tapes. The audio man handed me three canisters, the original and two copies, and piled two boxes like bricks on top.

"What's all this?" I asked. "We only wanted two copies on cassette."

He nodded at the boxes. "That's what you've got. Takes a lot of cassettes for a reel of tape. It's a lot of recording hours."

I looked at the boxes in dismay and wondered how long it would take me to determine if Leila's public performance of "Angelina" was on any of them.

I had a sudden thought — the one that had escaped me earlier. I looked at my watch and said to Mildred, "Want to meet Ernie Iles?"

I had no idea what Ernie's hours were, but my luck was still holding and soon we were in the Kroger break room, plying him with Coke and potato chips.

"First, I just wanted to make sure that I understood you. I asked if Leila was wearing a necklace the last time you saw her."

"August 13th, 1969."

"Yes, that day, when she got into the yellow T-Bird. Was she wearing her necklace that day?"

"Yes, she was wearing her necklace that day."

I smiled. "She was?"

He nodded emphatically. "She was wearing her necklace."

"Let me ask you about something else. You said that Leila sang pretty songs. Where did you hear her songs?"

"Sometimes, when she was carrying her guitar, she would take it out of the box and sing to me."

"Was this outside The Cabinet?"

"Outside The Cabinet and outside the Aquarius."

"Did she ever sing you a song called 'Angelina'?"

He nodded. "She sang it outside The Cabinet on Saturday, July 20th. That was the day after the astronauts landed on the moon."

"Well, you do have a good memory." Mildred was impressed.

"Yes, I do have a good memory."

"Do you remember any of the lyrics? That is, what the song said?"

"Yes, I do remember what the song said."

"Can you sing some of it for us?"

"I don't have a good voice."

"That's okay, we're not picky. Just do your best."

He raised his eyes to the ceiling, as if the lyrics were printed there. His voice was high-pitched and breathy, little more than a whisper.

"*An-gelina,*
I can see ya,
singing your blues.
An-gelina,
It's so hard to be ya,

243

'Cause you're too old for in-cense,
And too young to choose."

I managed to stifle my laughter. When you spent your days selling newspapers outside of a head shop, I supposed that it stood to reason that you were more likely to hear "incense" than "innocence." It didn't matter; the lyrics were close enough to support a plagiarism suit.

We applauded enthusiastically as he broke off and said again, "I don't have a good voice. But Leila liked my ears." He put a hand to one ear and fingered it, frowning as if in bewilderment.

"Leila told you you had a good ear?" Mildred asked. "That means you knew a pretty song when you heard one."

We killed time at a Skyline Chili after that and got to know each other better over a five-way and a chili dog. Mildred's husband had died five years before Fred, and neither of us was inclined to remarry — in her case because the first time around had been so good that she couldn't imagine matching it on a second go-round, and in my case because I had been underwhelmed by the experience and saw nothing in it worth repeating.

"Well, you've got the best of both worlds anyway at the Catatonia Arms, as Moses calls it. You have your own space, but you're surrounded by friends you can socialize with whenever you want to." She laughed. "I was going to say that you have your own private space, but I thought better of it when I remembered the valentines."

"Just one example of how sharing your house with others requires some give-and-take. Anyway, Valentine's Day is in two days, and then the decorations will come down and the foyer will be fully lit again and I won't have to listen to Moses complain until St. Patrick's Day."

She had raised four kids — two sons and two daughters, one of them adopted. The adopted daughter had been a late arrival, offspring of a cousin who had died unexpectedly. This information only increased my opinion of Mildred's fortitude. I had counted the days until Franny turned twenty-one and couldn't imagine taking on a five-year-old late in that count.

At four o'clock, we moved two doors down to a bar and nursed a drink apiece until it was time to go back to Bethesda North to look for Joyce Hardcastle.

When we found her, we had to wait another half hour in the hospital cafeteria until she could take a break and join us. She had seemed astonished to hear Leila Perle's name, but not alarmed.

Now she sat across from us, sipping coffee from a cardboard cup and looking at us expectantly. She had dark hair in a chin-length bob and wore a lot of eye makeup. I wondered if she knew how severe her penciled and heavily tweezed brows made her look, though her tiny patients in the NICU probably couldn't see her all that well.

"I haven't thought about Leila for years," she admitted. "That was such a crazy time! I knew other kids at BGSU who dropped out after Woodstock. It's like they just disappeared into the counterculture."

"You were at BGSU at the time. So, you were only working at the Aquarius for the summer, is that right?" I wasn't ready yet to disabuse her of her assumptions about Leila.

"I worked for Marty two summers. He must've hired dozens of girls over the years. So, you might not think he'd remember me, and I doubt he could come up with my name. But I've been in there once or twice, and he recognizes me." She shook her head, smiling. "The good ol' Aquarius. Amazing that it's still going. You been there?"

"I have," I said. "Mildred hasn't been yet."

"But looking forward to it," Mildred said.

"You should definitely go. The coffee's a hundred times better than this stuff." She frowned down at her cup. Our cups were untouched, but I took her word for it.

"What did you want to ask me about Leila?"

I leaned forward. "When you talked about kids disappearing into the counterculture, is that what you think happened to Leila?"

She looked surprised. "Well, sure. She went off to Woodstock and didn't come home. Didn't she? Or, wait — are you telling me that nobody ever heard from her? I mean, her family — they never heard from her?"

"Now it looks as if Leila never left Cincinnati." I gave her a moment to take this in.

"Never left Cincinnati? How is that possible? Everybody said she went to Woodstock."

"We don't think she made it, Joyce," Mildred said.

"So, we'd like to hear about the last time you saw her." The color was slowly draining from her face.

"I saw her at the end of her shift that day — I mean, the day before she was leaving. I thought — actually, I thought she was coming over later to spend the night, but she never showed up. I thought maybe she'd found a better offer, you know? We weren't really all that close." She was speaking slowly, as if feeling her way.

"If you weren't really close, why was she spending the night with you?" After a pause, I added, "Was it because you knew something that other people didn't?" I was leading her like a skittish horse, slowly and cautiously, afraid she would bolt.

"Yes." Almost a whisper.

I thought about Moses's speculations and decided to take the risk. Of the available options, I picked the one that seemed to me most likely. "Was it because you knew about the abortion?"

She nodded and I stopped holding my breath. I could see she was working things out in her head.

"Are you telling me that something went wrong during the procedure?"

"We really don't know. According to Linda Monniter, you wished her luck when you said goodbye to her that day. Was she supposed to have an abortion later in the day?"

"Yes, I think they were picking her up around five."

"Do you know who was picking her up?"

She shook her head. "She didn't know who. I mean, you didn't, when you were having the procedure back then. It was illegal, you know, so the whole business was very hush-hush. Mostly, it was just a voice on the other end of the phone. In Leila's case, she actually met a nurse at a coffee shop somewhere — I don't know where."

"Did Leila mention the nurse's name?"

"If she did, I don't remember. God, it was such a long time ago, and we were all young, dumb, and naive. I was a little older than Leila, but I didn't know anything about abortion, not then. Even now, some girls think they can 'take care of it'" — here she made air quotes — "themselves, and of course, it doesn't work and we see their babies in the NICU. And sometimes the doctors performing illegal abortions were slipshod and incompetent, and those girls ended up in the ER. But the doctor Leila was seeing had a pretty good reputation. I knew several other girls who had been to him."

She said this last so earnestly that I knew she'd been the source of Leila's referral.

"Do you remember his name?" Mildred's pen was poised over her notepad.

"God, nobody knew his name," Joyce said. "You didn't even see him before the surgery, or so people claim. And if you saw him afterwards, you were pretty much out of it and he was wearing a surgical mask, so there was no way you could rat him out to the authorities. He was super careful."

"So, the plan was for Leila to have the procedure and then make her way to your place to spend the night."

"I was subletting from a girl who was gone for the summer. I had two roommates, but one of them was never there and the other had been to this doctor herself, so she was cool with it."

"And Leila thought that she would have this procedure and then she would be fine to catch a ride to Woodstock the following night?" Mildred asked.

Joyce shrugged. "That was the plan. I tried to talk her out of it. I tried to tell her that something could go wrong or she could be in a lot of pain from the procedure. But she just said everything would be okay. She told me that the doctor would just kind of vacuum it out — that's what she'd heard, anyway — and she'd have more than twenty-four hours to recover."

Mildred and I exchanged a glance. Teenagers.

"So, you never heard from her after she left the Aquarius. Didn't you think that was odd?"

"Well, I thought it was kind of rude, seeing as how I'd agreed to put her up and all. But like I said, I thought she might have gotten a better offer."

"A better offer," I repeated. "Did Leila ever tell you who the father was?"

She shook her head. "If she knew, she didn't tell me. But then, we weren't especially close, Leila and me."

"Did you have any reason to suspect that she might have gone to visit the father after the abortion procedure?"

She shrugged. "Sure. I guess it was a possibility. Or maybe she went to see her current boyfriend, whoever that was. I can't say I gave it much thought."

"I've heard that Leila's closest friend at the Aquarius was Gigi Beck. So why were you the one helping her out with this crisis instead of Gigi? Didn't Gigi know about it?"

She shifted in her chair, perhaps eager to share the burden of guilt. "No, that's the thing. Gigi didn't know about it, and Leila didn't want her to find out because she was too embarrassed. She looked up to Gigi, and she didn't want Gigi to know that she had messed up so badly."

"So, how did you know?"

"I just happened to walk into the bathroom one day and find her sitting on the floor, sobbing. She'd just found out she was pregnant, and she'd just thrown up, and she felt like crap. And the first thing she said was, 'Don't tell Gigi.' I mean, don't get me wrong. We weren't especially close, but I liked her well enough and we got along fine. So, when I found her in the bathroom, I did what anyone would do — I cleaned her up and got her to stop crying and told her it wasn't the end of the world. And after that, I was her confidant."

"Did you give her a number to call? For the abortion, I mean."

"Well, yes, but she could have gotten it from other girls. Lots of girls knew about it."

"We're wondering if you could put us in touch with some of those other girls," Mildred said gently. "We really need to find out what happened that night and give her family some closure."

Tears leaked from her eyes and formed little black rivulets down her cheeks.

"You think she died during the procedure, don't you?"

She was a nurse, and so on more intimate terms with death than I was.

"Do you?"

CHAPTER 29

"How do you feel about a return trip to Indian Hill to talk to Glass?" I asked Mildred when we were back in the car. "We have Rap's blessing."

"But not Moses's." She glanced at her wristwatch. "Okay, if you're willing, I'm willing."

This time it was Izzy who answered the door. She was wearing flannel pajama bottoms and a long-sleeved jersey shirt cut short enough to show her navel. She was barefoot.

Her eyes widened in surprise and apparent delight. "Are you going to arrest him? Did you bring your handcuffs?"

"We just want to talk to him," Mildred said.

"In private," I added.

She looked disappointed, but not too disappointed, which made me predict that she'd be listening at the door when she showed us to the music studio.

"Some people to see you, Dad," she said, and after giving us a knowing look and a wink, made a point to close the door until the latch clicked.

Glass was slumped in one of the easy chairs, wearing faded jeans, a stained and ratty Northside Park T-shirt, and headphones that tethered him to a large tape deck. The sound of the door closing was what made him look up, and he frowned at us as he pulled off the headphones.

He surprised me by recognizing us. "You're the cleaners. What do you want? I'm really busy here."

"That's right, Mr. Glass. Last night we were the cleaners. Tonight, we're visiting you in a different capacity as investigators looking into the disappearance of Leila Perle in August of 1969." I handed him a business card.

He stared at it. "Investigators? What the hell are you talking about?"

"About the disappearance of sixteen-year-old Leila Perle in the summer of 1969, Mr. Glass." Mildred sounded calm, unflappable. "You met Leila at Northside Park that summer."

She held out a photo, but he didn't even glance at it.

"Listen, lady, I met a lot of chicks at the Park that summer, and I don't remember any of 'em." He pulled up short, looked from Mildred to me and back again, raised a hand and grinned. "Wait! Did Chaz Wiley put you up to this?"

"Nobody put us up to it, Mr. Glass," I said, probably too sternly, like a schoolteacher scolding a class cutup. "The Perle family hired us to find out what happened to Leila when she disappeared."

He raised his palms. "Well, that's got nothing to do with me, lady, and I don't know why you think it would. I don't even remember this Leila chick."

"That's surprising, because she was a singer-songwriter who wrote a song called 'Angelina,' which you stole and recorded as 'Magdalena' in 1970."

"Whoa! Now, stop right there!" A flush of anger flooded his cheeks, but I hadn't missed the flash of fear in his eyes. "Who the hell do you think you are, coming in here and accusing me of shit like that?"

"If you could tell us where you were on August 13th and 14th, 1969, Mr. Glass, that would be extremely helpful to our investigation." Mildred was clinging to her good-cop role.

"I don't have to tell you shit!" he thundered, on his feet now and making the most of his height to tower over us.

"Or you could tell us whether Leila ever mentioned her pregnancy to you," I said. "That would also be helpful."

He took a menacing step toward us and pointed toward the door. "Out! Get out!"

Mildred didn't even flinch. "If you don't answer these questions now, Mr. Glass, you may find yourself answering them in a police interrogation room in the future."

He advanced on us, incoherent with rage, and we retreated.

Back in the car, we looked at each other.

"That went well," Mildred said complacently.

"I suppose so," I said, unconvinced. "Do you think we would have gotten more out of him if I hadn't accused him right off the bat?"

She shrugged. "I doubt it. We weren't expecting a confession."

"No," I conceded. "And I'd swear he was alarmed when we mentioned the plagiarism."

She nodded. "More alarmed than when we mentioned the pregnancy, I thought."

"I guess we learned one thing."

She nodded again. "He's certainly capable of losing control and, I imagine, committing violence."

I gazed at the house reflectively as I started the car. "He had two of us to deal with, and his daughter as a witness."

"But what would he do to a defiant sixteen-year-old who came alone with her accusations?"

CHAPTER 30

When I got home Friday night, I stayed home, successfully fending off Mel and Al's attempts to get me to go ice skating at Fountain Square with them. I had been running around in the cold all day, so all I wanted was to sit still in a warm house. Besides, the last time I had "gone ice skating," Leon had towed me around the rink like a Zamboni towing a trailer. Without Leon, I would've ended up in the emergency room; as it was, I had barely been able to walk the next day.

So, I sat at the kitchen table and started on Rap's list of missing girls. Now that Leila's necklace had turned up at Adam Glass's house, I doubted that this list could shed light on what had happened to Leila and who had been involved. It was looking more likely that something had gone wrong with Leila's abortion, but what had happened next? Had she gone to Glass for help or confrontation? In that case, he might or might not have been culpable in her death, although if he had refused to take her to the emergency room, he shared some responsibility for that outcome. Or maybe he hadn't realized how badly injured she was. Or maybe nothing had gone wrong with the procedure and she had simply wanted to confront him, emboldened by the painkillers she had been given, and the confrontation had ended in her death.

That was a lot of maybes. And here was another: maybe one or more of the missing girls on Rap's list had visited the same doctor that Leila had.

Rap had been unwilling to hand over the files, but he had tasked some underling with the compilation of an annotated list. At my request, he had included girls whose cases had been closed because they had returned home or been found. He had cautioned me, though, that these cases had been buried for years, and that it was always possible that some of the girls still designated as missing had returned home eventually and never been reported by their families as found.

There were six girls on the list — who knew so many teenagers could go missing in such a short space of time? Two had returned within two weeks of the initial missing report. One girl had been found dead of a drug overdose three months after she had been reported missing. That left three, although any of these could have been found dead long after she was reported missing or returned home years later.

Moses called before I got started and I gave him an update. He said he would make a few phone calls and try to locate Zackery Lloyd.

"You might call Rap first," I told him. "He might have come up with an address."

"At least we know where Tyrone Weeks is, and he's not going anywhere. If we can't find Zackery, we'll try to get into the prison at Lebanon to see Tyrone on Sunday."

"It's not going to be easy, though, is it? One or both of them could be implicated in Leila's death. They won't be eager to talk."

"No, they won't. But if the necklace ended up at Glass's house, he's got to be our chief suspect. If Weeks and Lloyd were working as drivers for this doctor, they might be willing to tell us what shape Leila was in when they dropped her off that night after the procedure and where they dropped her off. Now that abortion is legal, I doubt that the prosecutor would want to prosecute the boys for their involvement in abortions nineteen years ago."

"I hope you're right."

"Have you heard from Perley?"

"No, and I checked your answering machine. He hasn't called."

"Maybe his mother is dying, or maybe she's already passed. We don't have any way of knowing."

"I doubt he'd want to share with her any of the information we've found so far. Maybe that's why he's lost his sense of urgency."

I was playing the first cassette in the background, trying to keep the volume low, but now there was a burst of sound and I lunged for the volume control.

"You playing music?" I could hear the smile in his voice.

"The first cassette from Northside Park, summer of '69. Moses, there are hours of tapes."

"Good you're getting started then. Just remember, we weren't hired to provide evidence for plagiarism, so don't sweat it. Be a nice bonus, though, 'specially if the lawyers don't think Ernie will fly in the courtroom."

I heard another voice. "I got to go," he said. "How's my girl?"

"She likes to listen to your voice on the answering machine. She makes little beagle sounds, like huffs and snuffles. She likes it so much when you call and talk to her that she's contemplating doing something really naughty so you'll call up and scold her. I think Sidney is putting her up to it."

When Moses hung up, I started my calls. I first called Mr. and Mrs. Trent Jackson, whose daughter Toni had gone missing on Monday, August 11th, 1969, two days before Leila. The number was no longer in service. My compiler had helpfully included phone numbers for her best friend and boyfriend, but these seemed even less likely to be operational, so I moved on.

On my second call, I reached Mrs. Jerome Mecklenburg, now widowed, whose daughter Maggie had gone missing on Wednesday, August 13th, 1969, the same day Leila had disappeared. I told her that I was trying to trace another girl who had gone missing that day. Mrs. Mecklenburg was eager to talk to me, and I soon felt guilty that I had no new information to give her.

"Mrs. Mecklenburg, did you have any suspicions at the time about what had happened to your daughter?"

"No, nothing. Maggie had always been a good girl, not like one of these hippie girls you read about. She had a summer job at the Dairy Mart and a steady boyfriend. She was making plans for college. I suppose she used to squabble with her father, but what girl doesn't at that age? It was about hem lengths and makeup, you know — the usual stuff. Nothing important. She was just a typical girl." Tears thickened her voice.

I couldn't bring myself to ask whether her daughter could have been pregnant.

"This other girl, what did you say her name was?"

"Leila Perle." I felt a flash of hope that the two girls had known each other. I should ask if Maggie hung out at Northside Park.

"Yes, I read about her at the time. I even thought maybe I'd call her mother and, you know, commiserate. But I just couldn't get up the energy to do it, you know?"

She asked whether she could hire me to look for Maggie. I said that I was busy with Leila now, but I gave her Walt Hitchens's name and my phone number, in case she wanted to get in touch with me later.

On my third call, I reached Mr. Lawrence Grossman, whose daughter Cassandra had gone missing on Thursday, August 14th, 1969, the day after Leila disappeared.

"Oh, yes, that's right, she did run away, but then she came home early that next summer. I don't guess I ever told the police. Is that a crime?"

256

"I don't think so. But I'm not a police officer, I'm a private investigator."

"You're like that Jessica Fletcher on television, is that it?"

"Well, sort of." I didn't point out that Cincinnati was a little bigger than Cabot Cove. "Mr. Grossman, did your daughter tell you where she had gone when she ran away?"

I doubted he would tell me if the story involved an abortion, but I asked anyway.

"Cassie was always a hippie," he said. "She was a hippie before hippies were invented. And she had a hippie boyfriend with hair longer than hers, and a beard and an earring. So pretty soon, they get it in their heads that they want to go to California, to Haight-Ashburger, and hang out with other hippies. The boyfriend went first, and I guess it took her a little while to save up the money for the ticket. Don't ask me where she got the money. She sure didn't get it from me! But she got it, all right!"

Nothing promising here.

"So off she goes! All she left was a note saying, 'Don't worry.' Don't worry! As if we could do anything else!"

I heard another voice now, and his voice turned away from the phone and became muffled, but I thought he said something about a "lady detective" and "Jessica Fletcher."

He was back. "So anyway, about a week later, we got a letter. She said she was in San Francisco with Johnny — that's the boyfriend — and all the other flower children, and she was having a great time, and having amazing talks with people about philosophy and world peace and I don't know what all, and we shouldn't worry."

"How old was she at the time?" I asked.

"She was seventeen, going on eighteen. Her birthday was later that month. So, some of the people we talked to told us to let her be, she'd contact us as soon as the money ran out. Well, we didn't like the idea of leaving it alone, not knowing where she was living or how she was living, but we have four other kids and detectives are expensive, if you don't mind me

257

saying so. And I guess some states considered her an adult. Johnny always seemed like a nice enough kid — polite, you know, and we never heard a cross word between them. So, we let it ride."

"That must've been hard."

"We got letters from time to time, and I thought they sounded really happy, but after a while, Thelma — that's my wife — said no, there was trouble in paradise. And I guess she was right because in early June, she wrote and asked us to send money for a bus ticket home, and we did. She walked back in the house one day like she'd just been on a trip to the IGA. I was so relieved, and at the same time, so angry. I just wanted to hug her and strangle her, all at the same time. You ever feel that way toward your kids?"

"All the time."

He offered me her phone number and I wrote it down.

"She lives on a farm out in Clermont Country. Not with Johnny, he's long gone, but she has another one name of Amos, and he seems nice enough. They raise sheep and vegetables and flowers, though Lord knows how they pay the rent. Seem happy."

I thanked him, hung up the phone, and dialed the number. I'd like to tell you that I did it out of instinct, but to tell you the truth, I wasn't expecting to learn anything from Cassie that would help me with Leila.

The voice on the other end was a little breathy, a little indistinct, and I wondered what she had been smoking.

I explained that I was a private detective re-examining the case of Leila Perle and hoping to talk to her.

There was more to my spiel, but she broke in, sounding more alert now. "Leila? You're calling about Leila? Boy, do I need to talk to you!"

"You do?"

"Yeah. I've been trying to return her necklace for years!"

CHAPTER 31

When I turned in under a hand-painted rainbow and a sign that said "Rainbow Acres," I hoped that it was a good omen. I had squelched my curiosity the night before to arrange an in-person meeting because I had wanted to judge for myself the trustworthiness of my informant. But I am not a patient woman and was by now a thoroughly confused one, which meant that I hadn't gotten much sleep the night before. As if to ensure that I wouldn't nod off, a handful of dogs surrounded the car in the farmyard, gleefully making as much racket as possible. They could probably generate enough electricity among them to power a generator hooked up to their wagging tails. Oh boy, a visitor!

They were hard to take in at a glance, but there seemed to be five of them — among them some kind of German Shepherd mix, a large hound, and one of the most enormous dogs I had ever seen in person. I hoped he was the kind with a flask of brandy in his hip pocket because I didn't see anything attached to his collar. The other two dogs were smaller, probably average size when surrounded by average dogs.

A woman — presumably Cassandra Grossman — entered stage right from one of the barns. She wore her long blonde

259

hair in braids like Heidi. She also appeared to be wearing a pair of overalls under her barn jacket. The day was brisk but the sun was out. As she approached, calling each dog by name like Santa in his sleigh, I studied her for signs of resemblance to Leila and conceded that the likeness was close enough for a darkened bus. She had a nice smile and the dogs clearly adored her — two points in her favor.

"Don't worry, they're friendly," she said as I climbed out of the car and waded into the pack. One of the smaller dogs, feeling crowded out by his larger companions, stood on his hind legs and pawed at my elbow. "Just a little too friendly, I'm afraid." To the dog, she said, "Get down, Marley. You'll have your turn."

That sounded ominous. Maybe I should have waited for Moses after all.

As we shook hands, two kids appeared from the direction of the house, both of them towheads in their preteens, looking for their father, who was reported to be mending a fence in the north field.

The whole gang moved toward the house and I was shown to a seat at the dining table, a homemade solid-wood affair flanked by long benches. My seat put me pretty much nose to nose with the biggest dog, who seized the opportunity to give me a few kisses before being warned off. From where I was sitting, the large open space showed me a kitchen of well-used appliances and a living room of comfortable furniture in front of a fireplace ablaze. The boys were given a plate of cookies and a handful of dog biscuits and sent off to argue about the best way to tend the fire. The dogs went with them to kibitz. I could feel my suspicions eroding.

If this woman had spent her youth colluding with a killer, there was no sign of it.

She set two mugs of coffee down on the table. Between them were a plate of cookies and a small box. She picked up the small box now and handed it to me.

Inside were an Irish friendship ring and a "Leila" necklace.

I hadn't given anything away the night before after she mentioned the necklace. I'd wanted to assess for myself what she knew and didn't know. I had mentioned Leila in the context of a case, but I had soon wondered whether she'd heard me or not. She confirmed it now.

Nodding at the necklace, she said, "You know Leila, right? And you can give those back to her? Please tell her that I never meant to keep them so long, it's just — I didn't know where to find her, and I couldn't find the other person, either. I should've gotten an address, but I wasn't thinking too clearly at the time, and then when I was, I didn't have anything to go on — just the phone number, and it had been disconnected. And then years later, when I saw her on the street one day — the other person, I mean — she said it wasn't her, though I'm pretty sure it was. But she wouldn't talk to me, which was a bummer, but what could I do?"

She tapped the little box with a fingernail cut short and showing a little dirt. "So, you'll tell her, won't you? Tell Leila, I mean. That I kept them all these years, 'cause I just knew somehow that our paths would cross again someday. Isn't that weird? It was just this feeling I had — like, cosmic, you know?" A gesture sent one overall strap over the edge and she unconsciously retrieved it and pulled it back over her shoulder. "And now here you are — a person who knows Leila."

She beamed at me as if I were a celestial messenger sent down to walk among the mortals and eat her ginger cookies. But as anyone who knows me will tell you, it's a mistake to confuse me with a celestial messenger. An instrument of justice, maybe. But if a higher power were choosing instruments, I was pretty sure he wouldn't choose me. Unless, as Kevin would likely add, the Almighty wanted to play a joke on someone.

"I didn't say I knew Leila," I said cautiously. "I said I was working on a case that involved Leila."

I saw suspicion dawn in her eyes, though it was no more than a faint rosy glow. She was a person constitutionally more inclined to see rainbows than thunderstorms. "What do you mean, a case?"

"A missing persons case."

She was frowning now, but she hadn't yet worked it out. "Who's missing?"

"Leila."

"Last I heard, she was going to Woodstock with her boyfriend. But that was a long time ago."

"She's been missing a long time. How do you know she was going to Woodstock with her boyfriend? Did she tell you?"

"Well, no, this other person told me. But . . ." She was still working it out, and I didn't interrupt. "I thought you meant she was missing now. Are you telling me that she went missing then and nobody ever heard from her again? That can't be right. I mean, I knew that she was totally miserable at home, but—"

"How did you know that she was totally miserable at home? Did she tell you?"

"No, this other person did. Gee, if she's been hiding out from her family all these years — I mean, I don't know if I should help you catch her. But anyway, I probably couldn't help you even if I wanted to. I don't know where she is. Like I told you, I've been kind of looking for her myself." The injection of this moral dilemma into the situation made her tug on her braids.

"Cassie," I said gently, "we have evidence that Leila never left the city."

"Never left the city? What do you mean?"

"I mean that something happened to her before she ever left town. Which could be why somebody wanted you to impersonate her on the bus from Cincinnati to Columbus that Thursday night in 1969."

She stared at me. Then her eyes flooded. "What do you mean, 'something happened'? Are you—? You're not saying she's dead, are you?"

"We think so."

"It can't be true. Not Leila."

The big hound padded in from the other room and came to stand next to her, leaning in. One by one, the others followed. She stretched her arms out to embrace them and buried her head in the German Shepherd's fur. The two boys were in the next room watching television, oblivious. I gave her a moment.

"You knew Leila?"

"I never met her. But all these years, I've felt connected to her, you know? I mean, we were in similar situations and we helped each other out — that's what I thought. That's why I saved the jewelry. I thought one day I'd run into her and give it back."

"Who told you about Leila's situation? Who gave you her jewelry? Who was this 'other person'?"

She sighed. "Well, I guess it doesn't matter if I tell you now. The nurse did. I never knew her name. You didn't know anybody's name — they were careful about that."

The nurse. Not Adam Glass.

"Can you describe her, this nurse?"

"She was just average-looking. She was probably in her forties, but I'm not a good judge of age. Taller than you and shorter than me, maybe five-six? Light-brown, medium-length hair, kind of frizzy. She wore eyeliner and eyeshadow. But that's all I can tell you, honest."

"Any moles, birthmarks, or scars that you could see?" I thought of asking about jewelry, but I already had more jewelry in this case than I could handle.

"No, nothing like that."

"Cassie, I think it's time you told me exactly what happened in the summer of 1969."

She nodded. She reached for a kitchen towel that was hanging from the oven door and began mopping her face and blowing her nose.

"The way it happened was this. I found out I was pregnant, and so I asked around and got this number to call. This was before *Roe v. Wade*, you know? Back when abortion was illegal. Anyway, I called this number and then I met this woman — she said she was a nurse — at a coffee shop downtown. I was supposed to bring a down payment and I was really nervous because I was twenty dollars short of the two hundred they charged. And I kept expecting her to ask for the money, but instead she asked me questions about myself and my family. Then she asked me about my boyfriend, and I told her that he had gone to San Francisco and I was going to meet him there as soon as I could raise the bus fare. But, of course, the operation meant that it would take that much longer.

"So, then she starts talking about this other girl named Leila, who looks a lot like me and who's in a similar situation, except that Leila is desperate to go to Woodstock, but her parents are really controlling and everything and they'll never let her go. But Leila comes from a rich family, so she has money and she has a ride to Woodstock, so she's going to go anyway. And Leila has this plan. If I'd be willing to leave that night and take the bus as far as Cleveland, Leila would pay for my bus fare and for my abortion once I got to San Francisco. She'd give me some of her jewelry to wear and I should pretend like I was going to Woodstock. So, I said yes, because why not? I didn't see any harm in it. She'd be back home the next week. And in the meantime, if her father came after her, he'd follow me instead — except, of course, he wouldn't get very far because I'd take the jewelry off in Cleveland and put my hair up."

"How did Leila give you the money and the jewelry?"

"The nurse met me at the bus station that night and handed me a ticket and an envelope full of cash. She called me after we met and told me what time to be there. She gave me the necklace and ring, too."

She blew her nose. "I know you'll think I was dumb. I mean, I never even met Leila, but I felt like I knew her after this nurse told me her situation. I just wanted to get to California so I could be with Johnny — that was my boyfriend. It was kind of fun, pretending to be somebody else."

"And somebody sat next to you on the bus."

"Yeah, he was this really nice intern from Columbus. I felt kind of guilty misleading him, but I didn't really see any harm in it. And I never actually told him my name was Leila, he just assumed it because of the necklace. So, then I walked around a little at the bus station in Columbus and again in Cleveland, and I bought a candy bar and a bag of potato chips, but there was nobody sitting next to me between Columbus and Cleveland. So, in Cleveland I took the jewelry off and went on to San Francisco. I didn't think about returning the jewelry until after."

"And then you came back to Cincinnati the following summer, is that right?"

She nodded. "The whole Haight-Ashbury scene had gotten kind of old by then. Johnny and I broke up in May, and finally in June I wrote and asked my parents for bus fare home."

"You mentioned seeing the 'other person' on the street later. Was that the nurse?"

"Oh, my god, yes!" She scooted forward on her chair. "I was waiting for a bus downtown at Fountain Square when I spotted this woman carrying a shopping bag. She was wearing a nurse's uniform, and maybe that's what caught my attention. Her hair was different and she'd put on weight, but I recognized her all the same. So, I ran over and told her who I was and said I wanted to give Leila's jewelry back to her, because even if she'd said at the time that she didn't want it, she could have changed her mind, you know? But this nurse pretended not to know what I was talking about and said I must have her confused with somebody else. Well, she was a little heavier, like I said, but I still think it was her. I thought it was odd at the time, but then I figured maybe she was working someplace really respectable and didn't want them to know about her past." She shrugged. "Well, that was okay. I had a past myself, and if she didn't want anybody to know about it, I understood."

She pushed her coffee mug around in a little circle, gazing at it. "I'm not sorry I did it, you know? The Haight-Ashbury thing. It was an important part of my whole, you know, like, maturation process. That experience is part of who I am, you know?"

I nodded solemnly. It was a response I had resorted to often when listening to my daughter Franny's self-analysis.

"It's like, I don't know, I had to make mistakes so I could learn from them. I had a chance to correct my mistakes." The tears were back now, and her voice wavered. "But Leila never got that chance, did she? You think something went wrong during the procedure, don't you?"

Based on what I knew now, I imagined Leila lying on an operating table — maybe no more than a kitchen table — eager to correct the mistake of her pregnancy and get on with her life, excited to go to Woodstock and immerse herself in the countercultural music scene. But maybe she never woke up.

That image was enough to make my own eyes tear.

CHAPTER 32

I was in the kitchen around two o'clock baking cookies when Winnie, who was sacked out in her new favorite sleeping spot with Sidney, made a little noise in her throat, rolled to her feet, and went to the door, where she sat down.

"He on his way?" I crossed the living room, tumbling Sidney out of Charisse's silk scarf and scooping it up on my way. I crouched next to Winnie. "Might as well take it home." I wrapped it around her neck a few times and then knotted it at its now-bedraggled fringe so that it hung under her chin like a mangy beard. I regarded the results. "Still looks cuter on you than on him."

In winter the downstairs hall was colder than the apartment, and Winnie was content to stand sentry just inside the door. About twenty minutes later, she gave a single bark. I opened the door and let her out into the hall. Soon I heard the crunch of tires on gravel that heralded Moses's arrival, and shortly after that, a frenzy of barking and baying, accompanied by a deep voice.

I went back to my cookie baking.

For the record, I am not one of those doting grandmas who keeps a jar of fresh-baked cookies on hand for her grandchildren. I bake cookies because I like to eat cookies. I am more likely to hide them from my grandkids than hand them out. I share them with my grandkids occasionally, but not often enough to make them crave regular visits to Grandma's.

Moses showed up as I was pulling the last cookie sheet from the oven. As he helped himself to a cookie from the warming rack, I nodded at the small box next to the cookies. "Open the box."

He regarded its contents in silence for several seconds. Then, frowning, he said, "You went back out to the Glass place?" I could tell he was working up his lecture on stupidity and danger.

To postpone the lecture, I avoided the question. "That came from one of the missing girls, a Cassandra Grossman. She was the girl on the bus."

He sat down slowly. "I'm listening."

I told him Cassie's story. "I believed her. I didn't expect to, but I did." I got two beers out of the refrigerator and passed one to Moses. We liked beer and we liked chocolate chip cookies, so it stood to reason that we liked them together. I handed him a Valentine to use as a coaster and sat down across from him. "I suppose that it's a less violent and traumatic scenario than anything else I've imagined — that Leila just went to sleep and didn't wake up."

"Coulda happened that way, sure."

He didn't bother to say that it could have been much scarier than that. He didn't bother to say that Leila could have realized she was dying.

"How come we got two necklaces in this case? The Troll necklace Glass has came from another Leila?"

I shook my head. "I called Gigi Beck this morning and she confirmed my suspicions. Leila gave the necklace to Glass as a love token and was too embarrassed to demand it back when he stopped seeing her. She was really upset that she'd lost it, and Gigi told her she should just order another one

— told her Matt would never know the difference. So, she did. Gigi claims she'd forgotten all about it. We asked her if Leila was wearing the necklace the last time Gigi saw her, but she didn't have any reason to mention that Leila had owned two identical necklaces."

I took a breath and pushed the cookies closer. "Have another. We did go back to talk to Glass, Mildred and me. He threw us out and told us we could talk to his lawyer."

I could see the effort it caused him to repress the lecture and focus on the more important matter. "What did he have to say about Leila?"

"Claims he doesn't remember her. Claims there were so many 'chicks' chasing his sorry ass in those days, he can't be expected to remember a single girl."

"He steal songs from all these chicks?"

I snorted. "I doubt it. If he did, he should have his emotions under better control by now. The plagiarism charge really pushed his buttons. Mildred thinks he was angrier about that than the question about Leila's pregnancy."

Moses shook his head. "Y'all didn't hold back, did you?"

"There were two of us, and his daughter on the other side of the door. We didn't think he'd assault us under those circumstances."

Moses was still shaking his head. "You didn't think." He helped himself to another cookie. "So, our main priority now is to track down this doctor, which won't be easy," he said. "We need to talk to Zackery and Tyrone to see if they know anything about him. Your original theory could still be right. What your eyewitness saw — did you say his name was Ernie? What Ernie saw could have been a drug deal, pure and simple. Let's hope it wasn't."

"Long odds," I said glumly.

He nodded. "Good thing we got cookies."

He said that Rap had given him an address for Zackery and we might as well go try it. He'd try to arrange a visit with Tyrone at the Lebanon prison the next day.

"Tomorrow's the 14th."

"Yeah?" He paused in the doorway.

"Valentine's Day."

"Yeah? You got a hot date in the afternoon?"

"Not me."

"Okay then."

"I expect there'll be a drum lesson, though."

"Good reason to plan another road trip."

An hour later, while we sat in the car waiting for it to warm up, Moses asked me if I had heard from Matt.

"Still not a word. No new messages on the answering machine?"

"Nope, nothing. Seems strange."

"Could be what you said — he doesn't want to tell his mother what we've learned, so the investigation isn't as urgent as it was. But do you really think he expected us to find Leila alive after all these years and eager to reunite with her family? He's a cop, after all."

"Cat, ain't no predicting what folks will believe when they want to believe it, even cops." He put the car in gear and screwed around to look behind us. "I'll call tonight, and if I can't get him, I'll try the other siblings."

"If you call the motherhouse and don't raise anybody, it might mean something's happened. They never leave her alone. So, if nobody's there, they could all be at the hospital."

Zackery Lloyd lived in a tall Italianate brick house in the West End. It must have been beautiful once, with its tall, elegant windows and decorative cornice. But the cornice and lintels had been painted so long ago that they had forgotten what color they were supposed to be. The brick had been painted a golden yellow but was now peeling badly to show its original red beneath. A massive vine, brown now in February, was crawling up the side of the house, pooling around its base, and surging up the steps as if intent on getting in. Past the vine on the south side of the house I could see a fire escape silhouetted against the sky. One of the upstairs windows was boarded up.

"He doesn't live there alone, does he?" I asked as we sat across the street surveying the house. "It's a lot of house for one guy."

"I doubt it."

"Tell me about Zackery." A few light snowflakes danced across the windshield. The car was warm enough now to make the prospect of getting out again unappealing.

"The reason Tyrone is inside and Zackery isn't? It's not because Zackery is smarter, it's because he's less ambitious. Got no ambitions to be a drug lord, he's happy to be a foot soldier."

"So, he's never been inside?"

"I didn't say that. He did a couple of stretches at Twenty-Twenty before he turned eighteen. Done some time in Lebanon, too, but he never gets put away for long. Judges and DAs know he's small fry. Cops don't like to arrest him 'less he's done something so stupid they can't ignore it. On the other hand, he's good at what he does. He's found his niche."

"You figure he uses those two front windows as a drive-through?"

"Let's go ask."

He pounded on the door and then stood back, hands on his hips, staring at the peephole. We waited.

"Maybe he's not home."

"You think he's out doing his Saturday grocery shopping? Naw, he's home. These are peak business hours."

"Maybe he's not going to open the door because it's you and because you're glaring at him."

"He'll open."

Eventually, we heard the snick of a lock and the door opened.

Zackery Lloyd stood a few inches taller than Moses. On his head he wore an orange knit Bengals hat with a pom-pom. He sported a washed-out blond mustache against pale skin and a motheaten blond goatee that accentuated the thin bone structure of his face. He wore a tracksuit, several gold chains, and a scowl that didn't let up the whole time we were there.

"Aw, man, what you doin' here?" His eyes flicked up and down the street, but whether he was searching for our backup or his, I couldn't tell.

"Nice to see you, too, Zackery. Need to have a little talk."

"Aw, man, what you want to talk about? I ain't got nothin' to say to you."

"Got some questions for you about a former employer."

"You supposed to be retired, what I heard. What you want to come around here for, asking questions? If you ain't no cop no more, I don't have to answer none of your questions. Ain't that right?"

I avoided Moses's eyes. Any criminal who would ask a cop for legal advice was no candidate for master criminal. On the other hand, it might've said something about Moses's integrity that a perp he'd once arrested would ask. And from what I'd gathered, when Moses was in his heyday, if they'd taken a poll at Twenty-Twenty, the Hamilton County juvenile lockup, he would have been voted Most Popular Arresting Officer.

"No, that's right, you can leave me and Cat out here on the stoop to talk to your customers." He turned around and surveyed the neighborhood as if hoping to spot some.

I really hoped he wasn't serious about this because I was freezing my butt off.

After another glance up and down the street, Zackery opened the door wider and let us come in. We stood in the hall. Zackery made no move to break out the hot cocoa and cookies.

"Let's sit down," Moses said and waved me into an adjoining room, the living room, which featured some kind of fake Naugahyde overstuffed furniture. I was relieved that there were no lines of cocaine across the coffee table and no reefers in the overflowing ashtray. The place smelled more like cigarette smoke than marijuana.

Zackery trailed us in like a recalcitrant teenager, sat sulkily in a chair across from us, and lit a cigarette. Moses introduced us, which earned me my share of the scowls.

272

"What you need a partner for? You ain't no cop no more."

"Cat and me's private. Got some questions for you."

"What you mean, you want to talk about my former employer? Don't know why you picking on me."

"It's your memory, Zack. That's all I'm interested in. See, something came up the other day, and I thought, 'Where'm I going to find someone remembers that far back?' And then I thought of you and Tyrone, because you were there."

"What kind of something? You know my memory ain't so good after I got hit in the head with that baseball bat."

To me, Moses said, "Was a store owner didn't take kindly to getting robbed, Cat."

"Fucker nearly killed me."

Moses ignored him. "It's about that abortion doctor y'all used to work for. What was his name?" He raised his eyes as if the name might be written on the ceiling. "You know the one I mean."

"Dr. D?" Zackery said, then thought better of it. "I ain't saying we worked for him."

"Yeah, but you did, though. Picked up the ladies and took 'em home afterwards, what I heard." This was a more genteel version of the truth, but I wasn't about to contradict him.

"I ain't saying we did that."

Moses shrugged. "Nothing wrong with it. Just like a taxi service or medical transportation. Wasn't illegal."

That was probably true. I doubted that you could get arrested for transporting someone to an illegal procedure.

"Anyway, I know y'all did it because I got a witness says you did."

"Who?"

"Doesn't matter. All I'm interested in is the doctor's name."

A phone rang. It was sitting on the coffee table so the noise was loud and obnoxious.

Moses nodded at it. "Go ahead."

"I'll call 'em back." Belatedly, Zackery seemed to notice a small notebook open next to the phone. Like an incompetent magician, he snaked out a hand to cover it, closed it, and slid it into his back pocket.

"So this 'Dr. D,' what was his real name?"

"Man, I don't know that. He just go by 'Dr. D.' That's what everybody calls him."

"You don't know what the 'D' stands for?"

"Sometime he goes by 'Dr. Dave.' But that's it. That's all I know." He made an emphatic gesture with his cigarette hand.

"You never saw a letter addressed to him?" I pressed. "You never saw him write a check and sign it?" I knew there was no point in asking if he'd signed their paychecks. As employees of a criminal enterprise, they would have been paid in cash.

"That's what I'm saying. I ain't never seen no checks and no letters — nothing."

"Can you describe him? What did he look like?"

"I don't know. He a white dude, look kind of Italian." He pronounced this "eye-talian." "Got black wavy hair, kinda greasy, got dandruff. Wear glasses."

"Tall or short? Fat or skinny? How old?"

"Not too tall, not six feet. Not fat or skinny, but kinda pudgy, like he don't work out."

"How old?"

"Man, I don't know. Old."

"Older than you are now?"

He hesitated as he realized that to his younger self, he was now old. "Yeah, maybe some. Hard to tell with old white dudes."

"Okay, that's cool," Moses said. "Maybe I can find him through his nurses. What were their names?"

"Oh, man, what you want to ask me that for? It was a long time ago, and I had that head injury, like I told you." He rubbed a spot on the back of his head as if feeling for a permanent dent there. "I can't remember that."

"Try."

"No, man, I'm telling you. I can't remember that far back. Me and Tyrone, we didn't work for him all that long. We didn't have nothing to do with the nurses."

"Was it Mary? Or Jane? Or Joan? Or Kathy? Maybe one of them was named Kathy," I said. "Eloise? Maybelle? Cynthia? Dora?"

"See, Zack, Cat's trying to be helpful. I bet if she keeps mentioning names, you'll hit on it eventually."

"Barbara? Kate? Esmeralda? Virginia? Sarah?"

The phone interrupted my catalog and we all looked at it. There was a moment of silence after it stopped ringing, and I drew breath to continue my list.

"It was Annie and Wanda," Zack said sulkily. "They was the two nurses." He stubbed out his cigarette in defeat.

"Which one had frizzy, light-brown hair?" I asked.

"That was Wanda. Annie was Black, and she was younger. Wanda was kinda . . ." He searched for the word. "Strict. But she treated me okay, don't deserve no trouble from you. 'Specially not now, when it ain't even illegal."

"No, that's right. The procedure isn't even illegal anymore. But supposing some day somebody — a teenage girl, say — showed up for the procedure and then nobody ever saw her again. There could be something illegal about that."

He was reaching for another cigarette, but he froze, arm outstretched.

"I got to take a piss," he said, stood, and bolted from the room.

Moses and I looked at each other. I stood up and went to the door to look down the hall, but he was nowhere in sight.

"No point in chasing after him, Cat," Moses said placidly. "We wouldn't catch him and don't have any legal right to detain him if we did."

"But he knows what happened, Moses," I said. "He knew who you were talking about."

"Probably so. Which makes him an accessory, though we don't yet know what he was an accessory to. We have more information than we had when we came, so we'd best be satisfied with that. We'll go see Tyrone tomorrow, see what he has to say. Zackery can always get picked up later if he's needed to testify."

275

As we sat waiting for the car to warm up again, I said, "David, Ann, and Wanda. You think Mildred can make anything out of those names?"

"We can ask her."

I couldn't stop my teeth from chattering.

Moses grinned at me. "Look at it this way, Cat. We're getting warmer."

CHAPTER 33

Our client, meanwhile, had also gone AWOL. Moses's attempts to reach him on Saturday night elicited from older brother Frank the unhelpful information that Matt sometimes went off by himself. Frank had refused to speculate on possible causes or triggers for this behavior, except to say that it probably had something to do with his Vietnam experience. Moses read this vagueness as a masculine reluctance to discuss emotional issues, so I called his sister Mary to see if I could get further enlightenment.

"No, that's right, sometimes he just has to be by himself," she said. "We never know where he's gone. He's got a cabin somewhere, not too far away, and I think he goes there. It's possible he's told Katie something, especially now that Mother is so sick."

"Katie?"

"Yes, they're pretty close. Maybe because they've both experienced so much trauma in their lifetimes. Well, the rest of us experienced it, too, but none of us had a breakdown."

"It's just that he was calling regularly for updates, and now we haven't heard from him for days."

"If there's something in particular you want to tell him, you can tell me and I'll pass it along as soon as I hear from him."

277

"I really appreciate the offer, Mary, but since he's our client, we need to tell him directly and let him decide what he wants to share with you. I'm sorry."

"No, no, I understand."

"I will say that our last communication with him might have upset him, and that's one reason why we are eager to talk to him. Did he mention his talk with Moses and Lieutenant Arpad on Monday night?"

"Yes, he said that you found some of Leila's possessions at the Aquarius. It seems like you're making progress."

From her casual tone, I assumed that Matt's account to his siblings had been vague enough to avoid setting off alarms. Mary had not recognized the significance of Leila's stash at the Aquarius.

"And your mother is doing okay?"

"As well as can be expected at this point."

"It's just that Matt originally emphasized the urgency of this investigation because of your mother's precarious health. So, when we didn't hear from him, we thought perhaps he didn't consider the matter so urgent anymore."

"Oh, I'm sure he does. You shouldn't read anything into his — well, his sudden absence. We've learned not to do that. He's probably just working something out for himself. And he may be feeling a bit under the weather, too. But I'll tell him you called."

"Tell Katie as well, please."

Late Sunday morning, we drove to the Lebanon Correctional Institution, with Rap riding shotgun and me in the back. Moses didn't think we'd get anything out of Tyrone Weeks unless we were prepared to bargain. Rap had the authority to do that, we didn't. Tyrone wouldn't be able to bolt the way his buddy Zackery had, but he didn't have to open his mouth, either. The boys talked college basketball and I did crossword puzzles, which distracted me from the blur outside the window and the speedometer. The sun was out again, glinting off the thin blanket of snow that had accumulated overnight.

The room where we met Tyrone Weeks was very like the Kroger break room where I had interviewed Ernie Iles — same nondescript paint on the walls, same scuffed linoleum on the floor, same cheap plastic chairs and wonky table. Introductions were made, and although he clearly knew Moses, his expression remained neutral.

He was a little shorter than Zackery but broader and more muscular. His skin was dark and his shaved head gleamed. He had a habit of letting his eyelids droop over sharp eyes as if to conceal his thoughts. He leaned back in his chair, legs spread wide, arms crossed against his chest. He wore a faded blue-green uniform that would have made him look like a nurse if it weren't for his prisoner number printed on the pocket. The muscles of his arms and chest pressed against his shirt.

Rap was taking the lead in this interview. He made no attempt at the casual tone that Moses had taken with Zackery the day before. He said that we were investigating the disappearance of a teenager, Leila Perle, in the summer of 1969. He said that the last confirmed sighting of Leila put her in his yellow Thunderbird, Ohio license plate 775TK.

Rap paused to let that sink in, but Weeks showed no reaction.

"Care to comment?" Rap asked.

Weeks remained impassive.

Rap laid a photograph of Leila on the table. "Was she a customer of yours?"

Weeks continued to regard him from under lidded eyes. He didn't look at the photograph.

Moses sat forward and put his elbows on the table. "We talked to Zackery yesterday, Tyrone, so we know that you were working for an abortion doctor at the time. Take a look at the photograph. Was she a patient of the doctor's?"

"What's in it for me?" he said finally, his voice deep.

"Immunity from prosecution, as long as you didn't kill her," Rap said.

His mouth split in a wide grin, showing a gold incisor. "That's a good one, copper. You come here to see me in stir and tell me you ain't gonna put me in prison if I answer your questions." He shook his head. "And that license plate is bullshit. 'F you could arrest my ass for that, I already be talking to my lawyer and you wouldn't be here talking to me about no immunity."

Rap raised his eyebrows and shrugged. "Yeah, you be doin' time now, but you could do more time or less time — up to you." He leaned back now and crossed his own arms.

"What's that magic word parole boards like to hear?" Moses asked. "Cooperation — I b'lieve that's it."

I had a dog in this fight but no experience in dogfighting so I kept my hands in my lap and maintained a neutral expression.

The silence lengthened.

Finally, Weeks said, "That immunity you offering — that go for Zackery, too?"

Okay, I gave him points for negotiating on behalf of a pal not smart enough to do his own negotiating — especially since he was doing time and the pal wasn't.

Rap nodded.

"In writing?"

Rap pulled an envelope out of his coat pocket.

"Give it here."

We sat and watched while he read it. Nobody interrupted him. Nobody insulted his intelligence by offering to explain it to him. Finally, he sat back again, folded his arms, and nodded.

"Can we tape this part?" Rap asked.

Weeks shrugged. "Go ahead."

This was my cue. I fished the tape recorder out of my shoulder bag, set it on the table, and pushed record.

"First off, we ain't kill nobody. Ain't nobody kill nobody. The girl die. Sometime it happen that way."

"Is that what the doctor told you — sometimes it happens that way?"

"Yeah. It's like when they give birth to a baby — sometime something go wrong and the woman die." He said this earnestly, as if it would be new information to us. Then his eyes landed on me and darted away. He was embarrassed. Women learned this kind of stuff from their mothers and grandmothers and aunties, so I probably didn't need him to tell me.

"So, you picked up Leila in Corryville and took her to the doctor's surgery. About what time was this?"

"'Bout five."

"You were driving your own car, the yellow T-Bird," Moses put in. "Is that what you usually drove to pick up patients?"

"Nah, but I was late — didn't have time to go pick up the doctor's car." After a pause, he added, "We supposed to make 'em lay down under the blanket so they couldn't see where they was going, but I didn't have no blanket in the T-Bird, so she just laid down."

"Zackery wasn't in the car with you?"

He shook his head. "Just me."

"And you took her to the surgery. Where was that?"

"Doc rented a house in Westwood off Montana Avenue. I don't remember the street."

"Were you there when the girl died?" Rap asked.

"Nah, uh-uh. Me and Zackery had some business to attend to. When we went back to pick her up, the doc told us she was dead. He was all like, 'We got us a problem here. I got her all wrapped up and you boys need to take her up to Mount Airy and bury her.'"

"Mount Airy Forest?"

He nodded. "He say, 'I got her in the Belvedere,' and take us out and show us inside the trunk. He got the body all wrapped up in a blanket and two shovels look like he just bought from the hardware store."

"So you never saw the body before it was wrapped up? How do you know it was Leila? Was she the only patient that night?"

281

"No, it was another lady, but she was big. Couldn't have been her."

"This other lady — was she still there when you got back to the Westwood house to pick up Leila?"

"Nah, Wanda had ran her home."

"That was the doctor's nurse, right? What was her last name?"

"I don't know. I ain't never heard it."

"How about the doctor's last name?" I put in. "Ever hear that?"

"Naw, ain't never heard nothin' but 'Dr. D' or 'Dr. Dave.'"

"Can you describe him?"

"Medium-height, pasty-faced, soft middle-aged white dude with black hair. Got hair in his ears, too."

"So, you and Zackery drove to Mt. Airy Forest," Moses said. "Why did he tell you to take her there?"

"I don't know, man. 'Cause it was close and big and dark and you could lose all kind of shit in there."

"So, you found a spot and buried her?"

"No, no. That ain't what happened." He sat forward and brought up his hands for purposes of illustration and emphasis. "See, we went up there like he told us to. He say, 'Turn your headlights off so can't nobody see you.' And we driving in the dark. It's midnight, kind of cloudy, ain't no moon, and that place is blacker than a witch's tit. And Zackery start talking 'bout all the things go on up there, how it's devil worshipers up there, sacrificing cats and shit like that. How we might get snatched and sacrificed ourselves and wouldn't nobody never find us."

I shivered. I lived close enough to the forest to have heard the stories myself. They were probably urban legend, but I wouldn't have wanted to wander around there some dark night to find out. And I made sure to bring the cats in at night.

"And Zack was right. We was supposed to be driving people around, not burying 'em. Doc wasn't paying us enough to be messing with no dead bodies. What if the cops be driving around up there, looking for satanic rites and missing cats and shit, and they find us instead, with a dead body in the trunk? And if the devils and the cops don't get us, the forest will, 'cause I can't see where the hell I'm driving, can't see the fucking road and it's trees and bushes and shit all over the place, so I turn on the low beams, and damn!"

He turned his palms out for emphasis and I flinched. He was really getting into his story and gratified to have a captive audience.

"Two big eyes was staring at us — biggest fucking eyes I ever seen, and bright, like a neon sign! Devil's eyes and hungry! Zack screamed and I cut the lights and then we heard two thumps, one in front and one behind. And Zack, he say it come from the trunk, and I don't know what to think. But I say, 'Fuck this shit!' And I turn on the lights all the way to bright and turn the car around and we haul ass out of there. We take the car back to the house and tell the doc we quit. We collect what he owe us and we go. Don't know what he did with the dead girl."

He sat back. "That's it. That's all I know."

Moses pushed a carton of cigarettes across the table to him, and when he reached out, his hand was trembling.

"You never saw the doctor again?" Rap asked.

He shook his head. "Ain't never seen him and don't want to."

Rap surprised all of us by turning to me. "Cat, you got any questions?"

I shifted in my chair a little to break the spell of Weeks's story. "After Leila got in your T-Bird that day, on the ride to Westwood, did she talk to you?"

He didn't answer and at first I thought he wouldn't recognize my right to ask questions. But he was looking away and I decided that he was just trying to recover the memory. Then he spoke, his voice hoarse. "I had a tape in the tape deck. She recognize the band."

"What band?" Moses asked.

"Sly and the Family Stone." Now I realized that he was trying to repress an emotion.

"She tell you that she was hoping to see them at Woodstock?" Moses's voice was compassionate.

Weeks's hands were in his lap now and he looked down at them. "Yeah."

He had wanted to see Leila as just another knocked-up white chick in need of his boss's services. But Leila had been Leila — friendly, unique, and unforgettable.

CHAPTER 34

"How much of that do you believe?" Rap asked as we climbed back into the Fairlane.

I let Moses speak first. I didn't want them to think I was naive.

Moses turned the key and dialed the fan up to high. "I guess I believe most of it. I believe he wasn't directly involved in Leila's death. Not sure whether he saw the body afterward or not."

"I believe most of it," I said cautiously.

"Not sure I believe that he doesn't remember the street name."

"Yeah, could be he just want an outing with his dawg Zackery," Rap agreed.

They had a point. On the other hand, I couldn't name the street my dentist's office was on, and I'd been going to him for twenty-five years.

"We'd better hope he's telling the truth about not burying the body in Mount Airy Forest," Rap added.

"Yeah, and we'd better hope the doctor didn't turn around and take her back up there," Moses said, "'cause if he buried her there—"

"We'll never find her," I finished. "How big is that place?"

"More than a thousand acres," Rap said.

Moses put the car in gear and backed out of the parking space. "And even if we can track down Dr. Dave, anything he remembers about the site from nineteen years ago won't do us much good now. Some trees have grown, some trees have died, and some have gotten hidden behind newer trees. The ground has shifted, low spots could have been filled in by floods, high spots could have collapsed into a burrow or been torn up by tree roots, and nothing will look the same."

"So, we're hoping he buried her in the backyard?" I asked.

"That's what I'm hoping," Rap said. "We find the place, I can get a cadaver dog to look for her."

"A cadaver dog? I think I've heard of them."

Rap turned in his seat to face me. "Yeah, yeah, they're trained to find dead bodies, even when the bodies are buried pretty deep. It's because dogs have such sensitive noses, you know? I read an article about it. There was a man who was a dog handler in Vietnam, and when he came home, he started training dogs to use their noses for all kinds of things. About a year ago, there was this case in Connecticut where a flight attendant disappeared and the cops suspected the husband but didn't have a body. They brought in a German Shepherd to a certain area where a witness had seen a wood chipper, and the dog found minuscule fragments of bone and tissue, so the forensic team searched and found a couple of teeth and a fingernail — enough to convict the husband of killing her."

Moses was skeptical. "Yeah, but they didn't wait nineteen years before they asked the dog to search, did they?"

"No, but there's other cases where dogs have found a corpse that has been buried for years. I don't know enough about it to know what the time limit is."

"Let's hope it's more than twenty," I said. I felt a frown coming on. "And cadaver dogs are different from sniffer dogs?"

"I think there's other names for them, but yeah, they're trained differently from ordinary sniffer dogs. I wouldn't mind seeing one in action."

"Me, neither," I said. "When do you think you can arrange to get Weeks out to look for the house? And once you find it, will you need a search warrant to look for the body?"

I still felt a little flutter every time I called Leila "the body." I didn't like to think of her that way.

"It'll take a few days. I'll try to set things up to expedite the search warrant as soon as we find the property." After a short pause, he added, "You know, Cat, I can't take you with me on an official search? This is an active case, now."

"That's okay," I said. "We have our own car. We can take ourselves. Just tell us where and when to show up so that we can follow you."

He gave me a stern look and opened his mouth as if to remonstrate, then suddenly grinned and shrugged. "Nothin' I can do about that."

"If the crime scene is in Westwood," Moses said, "you'll need somebody from District 3 involved."

"Yeah, and there'll probably be a sheriff's deputy along for the ride."

I stared out the window while they swapped gossip about various personnel who might or might not show up for the search. When the conversation flagged, I said, "I believe most of what he said, Tyrone Weeks. And I believe something else that he tried hard not to say: Leila got to him."

Moses glanced up at me in the rearview mirror. "I think you right about that, Cat."

"I like him for it. And I like to think that in her hour of need, when she was frightened and anxious, he distracted her by talking about music. He was probably the last person she had a conversation with. I'm glad it was him and not Zackery. Zackery wouldn't have known what to say to her, and because he was embarrassed, he wouldn't have said anything."

"You right about that, too, Cat."

We dropped Rap off and went home, where the house was quiet and all the drumbeats had faded into the woodwork. It was Valentine's night. Kevin was working, but I knew he had gone to brunch with his current flame. Mel and Al were going out for dinner and a movie. I had a date to spend the evening in the recliner with three kitties and a good book, which is to say that I wasn't doing anything special. I assumed that Moses was taking Charisse out to some hoity-toity restaurant that would serve food so precious he'd come home hungry.

But I met him when I came upstairs from the basement lugging a full laundry basket. My mood had soured because everything had come out of the dryer with little red shards of Valentine clinging to it and because I'd barked my shin on a music stand that hadn't been fully stowed. He was buttoning his coat over his Chef Grandpa apron, a pair of blue slacks, and a Hawaiian shirt.

I watched him stoop at the back door to pick up the bag of charcoal snuggled up to the snow shovel.

"You grilling out tonight?" I asked in surprise.

"Yep."

"What's on the menu?"

"Hot dogs." He picked up the charcoal lighter in the other hand.

"Does Charisse know?"

"She's not invited."

He closed the door behind him as I stared.

A little while later, I was standing at the kitchen counter spooning cat food into three dishes when I heard the clatter of a motorcycle, distant at first and then louder and closer. I looked through the kitchen window to see a black-clad figure dismount, unbuckle the helmet, and extract a six-pack of beer from a storage box mounted on the back.

"Well, dog my cats," I said to the kitties.

The next day I helped Kevin take down the Valentine's decorations — an act of generosity on my part that prevented me from tackling my taxes. Our activities included the hunt for Valentine's cards that hadn't yet been found.

As Kevin paused on the basement stairs and scanned the room, I grumbled, "We do this every year, and every year, we miss some."

"That's part of the fun," he said, opening Moses's toolbox to extract a card.

As he opened the dryer door, I said sourly, "That one's been found. Pieces of it are all over my towels and sheets."

He reached under one of the drums in the drum set and slipped out a card. "Huh. You'd think they'd notice the difference in sound."

"I don't think Leon's ear is that finely tuned. And, by the way, if Mel gets confetti and a trip to the repair shop when she starts the lawnmower in the spring, your life won't be worth a blade of grass."

His eyebrows popped up. "The shed! I forgot about the shed. Thanks for reminding me, Mrs. C. Better go out there now before the next snowstorm."

He paused at the back door to remove a card taped to the back of the snow shovel. "Speaking of valentines, what did His Nibs give the Queen for Valentine's Day?"

I stared at him. "You don't know?"

His brow knit in trepidation. "What?"

I decided to enjoy my superior knowledge a little longer. It wasn't that superior, but I never got to steal a march on Kevin. "Well, if you don't know, I don't know."

"Well, where did he take her for dinner?" We were on the back patio now, and he took a conspicuous sniff. He threw a hand out to quiet me. "No, wait!" He sniffed again. "He grilled out? It was, what, thirty degrees last night and he grilled out?" He strode to the barbecue grill and threw up the lid, wrinkling his nose — Sherlock Holmes on the scent. "Not salmon," he said meditatively. "So, it must have been steak or prime rib." He bent down to examine the grate. Any minute now, he'd whip out his magnifying glass and tweezers.

"It was hot dogs, actually. Some people think they just taste better grilled, whatever the weather, I guess."

He whipped around to face me. "Charisse ate *hot dogs* on Valentine's Day?"

"Did I say that?" I headed past him to the garden shed where we kept our tools, certified organic garden chemicals, and lawn mower.

He hurried to keep up with me. "Charisse wasn't here? Did they have a fight?" He said this hopefully.

"I wouldn't know."

"Well, didn't you have dinner with him? He didn't grill hot dogs in freezing temperatures just to eat by himself, did he?"

"I didn't say that, either. I think Mildred stopped by." I was trying to remain casual, but I had to see his reaction.

"*Mildred?!* You mean — oh my god! You mean Mildred? But that's terrific! I loved Mildred! Not that I got to know her all that well. I mean, anything would be an improvement over Charisse, but Mildred's way better than that." He paused at the open door to the shed, misty-eyed. "Just think — their first date on Valentine's Day."

"I doubt that Moses would call it a 'date' and I don't think he'll be happy if anybody else does."

I had to do most of the searching myself after that. Kevin was too busy planning the wedding.

CHAPTER 35

Matt finally called Moses on Monday night. According to Moses, he apologized for being out of touch and said that the news of Leila's stash at the Aquarius and its implications had hit him harder than he'd expected. He had, as his sister had speculated, gone off to be by himself for a while and to "think things over."

"I told him about our visit to Lebanon and our conversation with Tyrone," Moses said soberly. "I tried to break it to him gently, Cat, but—"

"Yeah, I know." I laid a hand on Moses's shoulder. "There's no good way to tell a story like that."

"Not with that ending, there isn't. He said — well, you can guess what he said: 'After all this time, to have it come down to this — an illegal abortion gone wrong, a damned abortion!'"

"Not much comfort to offer him."

"I couldn't think of anything. I told him we'd let him know when we went looking for the house with Tyrone."

"You don't think he'd come, do you? And watch the cadaver dog at work?"

Moses shrugged and shook his head. "I don't know if he will or not, Cat. Don't know what I'd do in his shoes."

Around eleven, my own phone rang and I knew who it would be.

The voice said, "I heard you think she died from an abortion."

"That's what we think right now, yes. If we can track down the doctor, we may know more."

"What's the doctor's name?"

"We don't know yet, Katie. We only know he went by 'Dr. D.'"

"Dr. D," she echoed.

There was a long pause and I tried to imagine what she was thinking, but I really didn't have a clue.

"Katie?"

"Yeah, yeah. It's just — I heard of him." Her voice faltered on the last sentence.

"Do you know his name?"

"Nobody knew it. He was careful." When I didn't say anything, she added, "That's what people always said, anyway." Then she said, "Matt says you talked to the guy who took her for the abortion."

"That's right."

"What's his name?"

This question made me nervous. I didn't really have the right to release any information to her and I'd probably already said too much. If Matt chose to confide in her, that was his business, but it wasn't mine.

"It doesn't matter. He was just a driver." Then, finding I wanted to give her some comfort, I said, "As far as I can tell, he liked your sister. They talked about music."

"Was he a tall, skinny—?"

Now alarm bells were sounding in my head. It was a pretty generic description, but it fit Zackery Lloyd. "Where'd you hear that?"

"No place in particular. You just hear things."

"Well, that description doesn't match the person we spoke to about the abortion doctor."

"And you haven't found the nurses yet?"

"Katie, the person you should really be asking is your brother. We have to respect client confidentiality."

"He's my brother. He confides in me."

"That's great. He can pass on any information we give him if he wants to. Or you can ask the police detective who's now working on the case, Lieutenant Arpad." This suggestion would not make me popular with Rap. "But I can't report information directly to you."

"Fine." And she hung up on me.

Mildred called to say that if she wanted to find a registered nurse whose first name was Wanda, she would need to go to the Ohio Board of Nursing office in Columbus and search through their registry, but it did not appear that she would find any contact information in the listing, just a license number and any specialties for which the nurse was certified. As far as the doctor was concerned, her idea was to search the state medical board records for a doctor named David whose license had been suspended sometime in the '60s.

"Seems likely that doctors performing illegal procedures would have lost their license at some point," she said. "Again, we might not get contact information, but we might get some names to try to match to the description we have."

I was impressed and said so. "But before you drive to Columbus, let's wait a few days to see what the search turns up. If Weeks and Lloyd can identify the house, we can find the former property owner and then maybe identify the renter from the summer of 1969."

But as it turned out, we didn't have to wait that long. Rap made all the arrangements more quickly than I would have thought possible. On Wednesday morning, we found ourselves bringing up the rear in a parade of cars headed for Westwood. At the head of the parade was a Ford Bronco carrying Rap, Tyrone Weeks and Zackery Lloyd, a prison guard, and a sheriff's deputy. Behind them came a patrol car from District 3, and behind them came a sheriff's car. Then two news vans fell in behind us and we weren't the dragon's tail anymore.

There was no point in asking how the press got wind of the event. It was like asking how Kevin knew the Pope's favorite tipple or the Queen's shoe size.

"If they find human remains, will somebody from the family have to formally identify the body as Leila's?" I asked.

"I doubt it," Moses said. "If they find a wallet or something similar, and it's still recognizable, I reckon they'll ask the family to identify that. Normally, they'd be looking for jewelry."

"We've got too much jewelry in this case already," I said ruefully.

"They'll probably have to use dental records to identify the body."

We made three passes up and down a five-mile stretch of Montana Avenue, turning off four times only to be forced into a six-car U-turn.

"How much longer you think they can keep this up?" I asked.

"Probably not much longer," Moses said. Then, as he made another turn and slowed in front of a house only a block off the main road, he added, "Here we go."

The street was narrow and hadn't been repaved since the Model T had been mothballed. The house wasn't set back far from the road and there were houses on either side, but there were no houses across the street and large side yards buffered the neighboring houses. A profusion of overgrown bushes around the perimeter served as a privacy fence and a reminder how close we were to Mount Airy Forest. There was almost room for four cars on a gravel parking strip that ran the width of the house, and beyond that was mangy grass that was probably indestructible.

The one-story frame house was wide and low and ugly. It seemed to be sporting its original white paint job of maybe thirty years before. There was a middle-aged maple in the front yard whose leaves had not been subjected to the attentions of a rake and a similarly unrestrained conifer between the drive-way and the front porch that should have been surrounded by something other than hard dirt. The garage had been intended for a car the size of a Frigidaire, but the gravel parking area in front of the house flowed into a wide gravel driveway, where an old pickup truck shared space with a rusty Rambler up on blocks and a disassembled motorcycle. I had a queer feeling that I was seeing the house just as Leila had seen it, and that her death had cast a spell over the property and frozen it in time.

Rap and a uniformed officer were knocking on the door when we climbed out of the Fairlane. Eventually someone came to the door and a confab ensued, joined by a sheriff's deputy. Tyrone and Zackery stood off to the side, pretending not to be as interested in the proceedings as the rest of us. The front door group broke up, and Rap went back to the cruiser.

After about ten minutes, Rap came to give us a report.

"We're waiting on the search warrant now, but it shouldn't be long because they just have to fill in the address. Owner's name is Dolan, but his tenant doesn't know how long he's owned the place. Tenants are a father and son — that was the son. Father's an auto mechanic, gone to work. Son's a security guard, works nights. They've lived here about six months. Son doesn't know anything about previous own-ers or tenants. When the warrant comes through, we'll search the place anyway. I'm kind of hoping we'll turn up something in the garage — looks like the Smithsonian in there."

"And the dog?" I asked hopefully.

"Dog's on the way."

I knew from experience that these kinds of situations involved a lot of standing around. The day was overcast and damp, more October than February, but cold when you stood around in it long enough. Moses made the rounds, then came back and sat in the car with me for a while.

"Owner's on his way. Looks like we might get lucky because he got the property from his parents, and they owned

295

maybe a dozen rental properties all over the city. His mother managed them for a while after the father died, but then turned them over to the son. She's got all the old records in her basement, though, and Rap has sent somebody to help her look through them to find the tenant in August of 1969."

"Wow. That easy."

But he was shaking his head. "Don't get your hopes up too high, Cat. Doc might have used a false name on the lease."

Another patrol car showed up and two officers got out. One of them handed Rap a document while the other, a petite young woman wearing a ponytail, pulled on latex gloves. Rap walked them to the open garage and gave them their instructions for the search.

An SUV with the words "Search and Rescue" on the side pulled into the driveway and everyone gravitated toward it. We stood in a semicircle around it as a man opened the back and released a German Shepherd wearing a harness. Tyrone Weeks was the first to approach the dog, though I noticed that his buddy Zackery hung back, an anxious frown on his face. I wasn't sure if we were allowed to engage with the dog, but Weeks crouched down and spoke to it in a gentle voice.

"What's her name?" he asked.

"This is Polly," the man said.

"Are we allowed to touch her?" the prison guard asked.

"Maybe after," the handler said. "Let's let her do her job first. But yeah, she loves pets and she loves to be the center of attention."

"Tyrone's been working with dogs at the prison," Moses told me. "They train dogs to be support animals for wounded veterans. He loves the work. In fact, the guard told me it's one reason why he's not much of a flight risk. You only get to work with the dogs if your conduct record's clean, so he's not likely to do anything to jeopardize that. Plus, he comes up for parole in five months and he could get early release."

I nodded to where Zackery was standing off to one side, with plenty of bodies between him and the dog. "Doesn't look like his buddy Zackery is on board with the whole dog training business."

The handler put some distance between us and Polly. "Okay, Poll, time to go to work. Where's the Napoo?"

I looked at Moses, but he shrugged.

The handler, a middle-aged man wearing a search and rescue cap, grinned at us. "The Brits and Australians used that word, 'Napoo,' in World War I to mean 'dead' or 'all gone,' so a lot of cadaver dog handlers use it. It's just a tradition, I guess."

Polly was already working the yard, nose to the ground like a canine vacuum cleaner.

"Do you want us to stay out of the yard while she works?" I asked.

"Best stay back," the handler said. "She's not going to mistake you for a corpse. On the other hand, if you get in her way, she'll run right over you."

So, we followed at a discreet distance and I found myself walking next to Tyrone Weeks.

He was smiling broadly. "Look at her go!"

"I hear you're a dog trainer, too." I said.

"Yeah, that's right. I already trained two dogs to work with paraplegics. They really special, those dogs. And when they new owner show up on adoption day? That's something to see."

"You planning to work with dogs when you get out?"

His eyes were glued to the dog. "Like to. I think I be good at it, too. Everybody says so."

We heard a shout. "There it is!"

Polly was sitting by a couple of bushes, a miniature thicket of dead branches oddly placed several yards from the perimeter. The handler praised her as the small crowd approached the site. Two cameras were whirring. At some point, the current tenant had joined the fray, clutching a mug of coffee and yawning. The owner had arrived as well.

"Shouldn't we stand back?" I said to Moses. "Won't we contaminate the crime scene?"

He shrugged, and a sheriff's deputy turned around. "Crime scene's probably at least six feet down. There's been a lot of traffic here in nineteen years, so we probably can't do much damage."

The handler released Polly to continue her sweep of the grounds, but to my immense relief, she didn't find anything else worth sitting down for.

Moses asked the question I didn't want to ask. "Do we know if this is an adult body?"

"Burial site is big enough for an adult," the handler said, nodding.

We stood around some more before the crime scene unit showed up and started processing the scene. As we watched a slender but muscular young man attack the bushes with a chainsaw, Moses shook his head and said, "Glad that's not my job."

Somebody else said, "Bastard knew what he was doing. That's bush honeysuckle. It's gonna take them hours to cut that out of there and separate the bones from the roots."

Suddenly, I could smell it: the sweet, heady scent of honeysuckle.

I closed my eyes and breathed deeply. When I opened them, it was gone. Napoo.

CHAPTER 36

Moses was talking to me. "What was that?" I said.

"I asked if you wanted to leave."

I looked up in time to catch a slight nod in our direction from Tyrone Weeks before he climbed back into the Bronco. Polly and her handler had departed. Rap was talking to the homeowner. The two honeysuckle bushes lay on the ground, only their trunks protruding from the rock-hard dirt. The crime scene crew was assembling a canopy over them.

"The deputy was right — it's going to take hours here, maybe days."

"Oh, Moses, we have to stay, don't we? We don't even know yet if she's down there."

"No, we don', but she is, though. Don't you think so?"

What he really meant was couldn't I feel that she was? Didn't my instincts tell me she was there? But he was too much of a cop to traffic in feelings, even though he was more open than most of the cops I knew.

"We have to stay," I repeated, "at least for a while. At least until we know that somebody is down there."

Rap introduced me to a gray-haired man wearing a gray suit under a parka. "Cat, this is Lieutenant Jerry Webster from District 3. He'll be taking over the case."

He shook my hand cordially and nodded to Moses. "Foggy, how've you been? Thought you were retired."

"We lucked out on the rental records," Rap said, handing me a slip of paper. "We already got an ID on the tenant in 1969."

I looked down at the paper. "Wanda Sherman?" I felt my anger rising. "Hell, he rented the house in the nurse's name. What a bastard!"

"Yeah, looks like he was careful," Rap said.

I looked up at the two men. "And you're giving us this information because—"

The two men exchanged a look. "Because I've already got a full caseload, Cat," Webster said, "and I haven't got the manpower to track this person down. In fact, if it had taken more than an hour to find this name, I couldn't have justified helping with the search."

"Jerry knows that the highest charge we're likely to get here is 'negligent homicide,' and even that's not likely. We'll be lucky to get a cause of death determination. Even assuming that Weeks and Lloyd are willing to testify in court, all they can say is that the girl was under the doctor's care and wound up dead. The DA's office might be willing to charge the doc and his nurse with hiding the body, but chances are good that they won't consider it worth their while."

"Even though the doctor and nurse conspired to misdirect the investigation into Leila's disappearance by hiring someone to impersonate her?"

Rap shrugged and Webster said, "Even so, Cat, they'll likely be charged with a misdemeanor at most. Rap is right."

Rap said, "You want my advice? Perley hired you to find out what happened to his little sister. You found out. It won't do the family any good to know the names of the parties involved. If I was you, I'd report back to Perley and close the case."

"Assuming the body is Leila's," Moses said.

"Assuming that," Rap agreed.

"If it is and we get a positive ID," Webster said, "I'll be paying the family an official visit to close the case."

The two of them left and Moses and I sat in the Fairlane.

"I caught that look on your face back there when I called Dr. Dave a bastard. What was that about?" I stared out the front window.

I could hear the shrug in his voice. "I just think we might want to reserve judgment, that's all."

"You mean *I* might want to reserve judgment. Because the doctor was just trying to make an honest living?"

"We don't know how Leila died. The doc bears responsibility for covering up her death and so does his nurse. I'll grant you that. What we don't know is how much responsibility he bears for the death itself, and we may never know. Could be they waited too long to call an ambulance or take her to the hospital. Could be she died so fast they didn't have an opportunity. But I think it's worth remembering that they were providing a service their patients valued at a time when that service was hard to come by."

"A service for which they were well paid," I pointed out.

"True," he acknowledged. "And I don't guess they were providing it to anybody who couldn't pay. But how many doctors do you know who charge on a sliding scale? How many of them waive their fees for indigent patients? For that matter, was two hundred dollars out of line for a surgical procedure in 1969? Most of the girls and women I knew who needed it couldn't really afford it, but most of them managed to scrape together two hundred dollars to get it."

I looked at him. "How?"

He looked down. "That's another story. My point is—"

"Your point is that I have the luxury now, after the Supreme Court made abortion legal in *Roe v Wade*, to condemn somebody who was providing a vital service while that service was still illegal. Your point is that poor women with too many children already and teenagers whose lives were just beginning and victims of rape and incest needed a place to go to solve a very big problem, and Dr. Dave provided it."

"That doesn't make him a saint. We don't know how good he was or how careful, but—"

"He was safer than a coat hanger. Otherwise, Polly would have found more bodies buried in the yard."

"I imagine so. Now" — Moses nodded at the paper — "you want to give that name to Mildred?"

"Yeah, I do. At least if we can trace the nurse, we have a shot at finding out what happened. Then we can decide what to tell Perley. Otherwise, the whole business seems unfinished to me, doesn't it to you?"

He nodded. "If we'd hit a dead end, I'd feel different. But as long as we still got something to investigate, I say we investigate it."

We took a lunch break and Moses called Mildred with the nurse's name.

On the way back to the Westwood house, he cautioned me again not to be too optimistic. "We still might not find the nurse. She could have married, divorced, or remarried, and if any of those things happened outside of Hamilton County, Mildred may not be able to trace her. She could've left the area."

There was no one at the burial site when we returned except for a young District 3 patrolman, who was sitting in his cruiser. We went over to examine the hole and he joined us. At its deepest point, it was almost as deep as I was tall, and you could see roots everywhere.

"Sometimes I think it would be cool to be a crime scene tech," the patrolman admitted. "But then I see what they have to go through and I realize what a pain it is."

"I wouldn't have the patience," Moses said.

"Yeah," the patrolman said. "They've been working — what?" He glanced at his watch. "Almost three hours? And so far the only thing they've found is roots."

Seeing the depth of the hole made me anxious, but I didn't say so. Wouldn't they have found something by now if there was anything to find?

The team returned then, and twenty minutes later, I was glad I had kept my doubts to myself. They uncovered the top of a femur.

Fifteen minutes later, they found a wallet, but it took the better part of an hour to extract it from the tangle of roots intact — or as intact as it could be after nineteen years underground. A technician laid it on a plastic sheet on their work-table and gently pried it open with a gloved finger. The plastic pocket inside was smeared with mud, but when the mud had been wiped away, the smiling face on the driver's license and the name were unmistakable: it was Leila's wallet. Napoo.

CHAPTER 37

We left after that. I had seen dead bodies before, including skeletons, but they had never been people with whom I had the kind of strong personal connection I felt to Leila. I didn't want to see her skeletal remains.

Moses tried to reach Matt later in the afternoon, but without success.

"Don't worry, Cat," he told me. "Because the wallet gives us a tentative ID, I imagine Webster will try to contact the family as soon as he can find the time. Maybe already has. He won't want them to see the story on the six o'clock news."

The six o'clock news story I saw featured footage of Polly doing her job. The story was relatively short and did not indicate that the body had been identified. There was no mention of the word "abortion." The search had been based on a tip, that was all. I wondered if other women watching the newscast would catch a glimpse of a house that stirred memories for them. I caught myself assuming that those memories had been bad, but Moses was right — maybe they hadn't. Maybe what women remembered most was an overwhelming sense of relief when the procedure was over and they could go on with their lives.

In the late afternoon on Thursday, Mildred called and asked us to meet her at Arnold's. When she came in, she had the look of someone who had gone ten rounds with a rabid dust bunny and lost, but her eyes gleamed with victory. Her glasses were smudged and there was a streak of dirt across one cheek. Several cobwebs decorated her hair. When she removed her coat, I could see that the cuffs of her pantsuit jacket were grubby and there was a smear of grime across her breast.

She laid a piece of paper on the table in front of us. On it were two names and addresses and a phone number.

She took a swig of the beer Moses had ordered for her, flipped open a small notebook, and began talking.

"Wanda Elaine Sherman, RN, married David Allen Bryce, MD, in Kenton County, Kentucky, on March 22nd, 1967."

"Kenton County?" I said in mixed admiration and dismay. "You have had a time of it. How many courthouses did you need to visit?" There were several Ohio counties included in the Greater Cincinnati area, and it was easy to forget that there were several more across the river in Kentucky.

"Just four."

"So they were married, the doctor and his nurse," Moses said. "I hadn't thought of that, but I should have. They used her maiden name to rent the house. According to Rap, they rented the house in February of 1969 and left in September."

"Shortly after they buried Leila's body on the premises," I mused.

"According to Tyrone and Zackery, they moved around. When the boys first started working for them, they were working out of a house in Walnut Hills. Then they moved to the Westwood house. By the time they left, the boys weren't working for them anymore."

"They'd had to find new drivers," I said. "I wonder if the other nurse, Ann, was still working for them, and if she knew about Leila."

"Probably never know," Moses said. He tapped the first name and address on the sheet of paper. "So, this name, W. E. Heming, is the name the nurse is using now?"

Mildred nodded. "The second husband's name was Howard C. Heming, but he disappeared from the phone directory in 1979. When Wanda next appears in the directory, she's 'W. E. Heming.' Long story short, I drove out to an apartment in Norwood and checked the mailbox, where the name used is 'Sherman'. It contained an advertising circular for medical uniforms addressed to 'Wanda Elaine Heming' and a letter from an insurance company addressed to 'Wanda E. Sherman Heming.'"

"Wow," I said. Mildred had the tenacity of a cadaver dog.

Moses tapped the other name on the sheet. "And the doctor's name was 'Bryce,' but he's going by 'Bryson,' is that it?"

She nodded. "I think so. The dark features Weeks and Lloyd describe — hair, eyes — those must come from his mother's side of the family."

"Do you need a birth certificate to get a marriage license?" I asked. "I don't remember."

Mildred smiled. "Me, neither. But you probably have to have some kind of official document with your name on it, don't you think?"

"So, if he changed his name, how did you figure it out?"

She grinned at him. "You don't want to know, but I had to use my gumshoes. When he disappeared from the phone directory, it was possible, of course, that he'd left the area. But it was also possible that he'd changed his name, especially if he'd lost his medical license, which is only one reason why he might be practicing medicine under the table. People who change their names usually pick something very like their original name. I found three candidates to check out, and this one, D. A. Bryson, seems to fit the bill.

"Unfortunately, Bryson lives in a condo in Hyde Park with a mail slot in the front door instead of an accessible mailbox. It's also harder to find gossipy neighbors in a condo complex, and especially in the winter, so it took me a couple of hours before I helped a woman with a screaming toddler carry her groceries in. I got a description from her that seemed similar to our doctor."

She took a deep breath and then a deep swallow of her beer.

"So, what I'm saying is that I'm not a hundred percent confident that Bryson is our Dr. Dave. Somebody will need to pay him a visit."

"If it is him," I said, "I for one will want to ask how you go from being a provider of illegal abortions to a Hyde Park condo. Is the abortion business that lucrative? Was he living in a condo in 1973 when the Supreme Court decided *Roe v. Wade*? That should've put him out of business."

"My informant thinks he's a salesman for something medical — medical supplies, maybe? She met him briefly at some condo social event."

"That would explain it," I said.

Moses was looking at his watch. "Want to take a drive, Cat?"

"Isn't it dinnertime?" My eyes and nose were following a plate of onion rings being delivered to the next table.

"Best time to catch folks at home," Moses said, reaching for his coat.

"We're supposed to get a big snowstorm tonight and tomorrow," Mildred said. "Can't tell what it will amount to, but it might be harder to get around the city after tonight."

"Yeah, yeah, all right." I finished my beer and stood up.

"Good day to work on your taxes tomorrow, if it snows," Moses put in.

To my surprise and embarrassment, tears of frustration sprang to my eyes, and I blinked to clear them but not before Mildred had noticed.

"Cat, what's wrong?" she said, looking concerned.

I avoided her eyes. "Nothing. It's just — taxes. They're my nemesis. Starting with the fact that I can't add a long column of figures and get the same total twice."

She frowned and glanced at Moses. "Well, can't Moses help you?"

"I tell her she's got to learn to do it herself," he said. "She's got a computer, and I've been telling her to take a class so that she can learn how to use her computer to do her taxes. I don't know how it works, but I hear that a lot of people are doing them that way. In the meantime, she just has to be persistent. She gives up too easily."

Mildred aimed a deeper frown at him. To me, she said, "I'll help you. I'll help you get them done for this year and then we'll set up something on your computer that will make things easier next year. Sound good?"

I was beyond grateful. "Oh, would you?"

She nodded. "Tomorrow night we'll get started. Me and you, kiddo, we'll figure it out."

Moses had the grace to look discomfited as I put on my coat.

"Want me to come?" Mildred asked, though she was making no move to get up.

Moses shook his head. "You've done enough today. You deserve to go home and put your feet up."

She didn't argue.

The condo where D. A. Bryson lived was one of a block of row houses not far from Hyde Park Square. It was hard to tell in the growing darkness, especially in this fashionably gas-lit neighborhood, but they looked fairly new, and since Hyde Park didn't normally run to row houses, they probably were. The windows showed a light on downstairs and one on the second floor, but all the curtains were pulled so we couldn't see any occupants if there were any. Moses rang the bell.

It had occurred to me that Bryson and Heming might have seen a news story the night before and recognized the house. If so, what would they do? Would they even remember that the lease had been in Heming's maiden name? How long did they think it would take the police to track them down?

Nobody answered the doorbell. There was no sign of movement inside. But I put my ear to the front window and thought I detected sound — a television or radio. Still, the sound was faint and might have emanated from the next house over.

We did all the things you do when you are determined to raise a house's inhabitants — pressed a finger on the doorbell longer and longer, hammered on the door, shouted. Nada.

Moses looked at his watch. "Maybe out to dinner."

Maybe on the lam, I thought but didn't say.

We drove to Norwood, where the address we had led us to an older apartment complex built around an outdoor covered staircase. We found a directory with no Heming listed.

I pointed. "It's 'Sherman,' number four."

We rang the doorbell and the door flew open. We were looking at a woman in her mid-twenties with mouse-brown hair tucked carelessly behind her ears and dark eyes that expressed both disappointment and suspicion. She was short and a little stout, wearing an oversized sweatshirt and leggings.

"Who are you?" she demanded.

Moses was extracting a business card from his wallet, but I'd heard the crackle of a police radio and spotted a uniformed officer standing behind her in the living room and I preempted his introduction. "What's happened?"

"My mother's missing, that's what's happened. Do you know where she is?" She spoke belligerently, as if we'd shown up in person to demand a ransom.

Moses spoke calmly, handing over the card. "We're private investigators. We came to ask your mother about a case we're working on."

The officer had stepped forward. She had intelligent gray eyes behind red-framed glasses that made quite a fashion statement with the uniform. Her hair was hidden under her cap. "Ms. Sherman's mother has disappeared and she's afraid something may have happened to her. Do you know where Mrs. Heming might be?"

She spoke to Moses but I didn't take offense because I assumed that she had made him as a cop as soon as she'd laid eyes on him. Belatedly, she realized her mistake and flicked a glance at me.

"Maybe we'd better come in," Moses said.

He was easing the door shut when a burly middle-aged cop with a ruddy complexion caught it and followed us in. "Car's in the lot," he said to his partner. "Blue Honda Civic."

We all sat down in the small living room — all except Sherman, who preferred pacing to sitting. It hadn't escaped my notice that she was a Sherman, not a Bryce, which probably meant that Bryce wasn't her father.

Moses spoke to Sherman, his voice soft but businesslike. "Yesterday, a body was discovered buried behind a house in Westwood. Maybe you saw something about it on the news? A dog found the body."

She shook her head, but the male cop said, "I heard about that."

"Why would that have anything to do with my mother?" Her voice was now more bewildered than belligerent.

"Your mother's name was on the rental agreement for the property at the time they think the body was buried. She may have lived there."

"Rental agreement?" Sherman said, preparing to work her way back up to belligerence. "I don't know what you're talking about. When was this?"

"Summer of 1969."

"1969? That's bullshit! That doesn't have anything to do with my mother. We were living in Price Hill."

"Can I ask — David Allen Bryce was not your father?"

"No, he was my mother's second husband."

"And Sherman was your mother's first husband?"

"No, that's my mother's maiden name. She went back to it after her first marriage ended and she uses it sometimes. Her kids — we all use it. But I don't see what any of this has to do with where she is now and why she's disappeared."

"You never lived in a one-story frame house in Westwood?"

"No, I told you! I don't understand about this rental agreement and a dead body. That doesn't have anything to do with my mother. She's a nurse."

Moses's gaze swept both cops. "Lieutenant Webster of District 3 is working the case. Maybe you should give him a call."

The younger cop nodded and retreated to the next room, presumably a kitchen. We could hear her voice but not what she was saying.

The elder cop said to us, "Ms. Sherman was supposed to pick up her mother for dinner tonight. But there are signs that her mother left the premises in the middle of dinner last night. So, she seems to have good reason for her concern."

Moses stood up and walked to the kitchen door to survey the room and I followed him. On the kitchen table lay a plate smeared with gravy and something green. The younger cop held a receiver to her ear but didn't seem to be listening. The receiver was tethered to a base mounted on the wall next to the refrigerator. She waved us in and we peered down into a half-empty coffee cup.

In the living room, the older cop was saying to Sherman, "Have you thought of any other places we might call — any other friends or family we might get in touch with to see if they've heard from your mom?"

"No, I've given you everything I can think of," she said petulantly.

"Is your mother employed right now? Is she working as a nurse somewhere?"

"She works at a nursing home in Roselawn. But I don't know how to get in touch with her boss. And I don't remember the name of the nursing home. She hasn't worked there that long."

Using a handkerchief to cover his hand, Moses began pulling out drawers. From the third one, he extracted a small black address book, held it up for the younger cop to see, and laid it on the table. He fished in his jacket pockets for a pair of gloves, put them on, and pawed through the address book awkwardly before closing the cover again.

The cop wrote something down on a pad, hung up, and dialed. After a brief conversation, she held out the phone to Moses. "It's Webster. He wants to talk to you."

As Moses reported to Webster on our evening's activities so far, I went back into the living room.

311

Sherman had sprouted tears like an underground gusher. Like me, she was an ugly crier. "It was just an ordinary Thursday night dinner. That's all it was. And now she's missing, and I don't know where she is or where to look for her or who to ask for anything. I don't know anything. And now you want to talk about this dead body that got buried almost twenty years ago, as if I would know anything about that. Or as if my mom would know anything about that! Well, we don't. She doesn't and I don't and I just want to find her so we can go have a nice quiet goddamn dinner."

To tell you the truth, I'm extrapolating a lot of this because it was hard to catch by the time it emerged from her tear-thickened throat and there were the extraneous noises of blubbering to contend with. But Moses's expression as he re-entered the room seemed to show genuine concern for her, and I know that I often come across as unsympathetic, so I tried to shape my face into a facsimile of concern and caring.

I knew that the wailing that accompanied these waterworks ought to have moved me to pity and I honestly don't know why it didn't, I only knew that I would give half my stash of beer and gin, including my emergency supply, to any genie who could materialize and shut her up. This was why Moses was such a good cop and I would never match him as a detective.

The younger cop re-entered the room at that point to announce that Webster was on his way.

I caught Moses's eye and angled my head toward the exit. He nodded and we made our getaway.

"Back to Hyde Park?" I said in the car. "You told Webster that we went there, right?"

"Yep. I sure hope Dr. Dave is there, but I got a bad feeling about this."

"Did you check the address in her book?"

"Wasn't there, not under 'Bryce' or 'Bryson,' not under 'Dave.' I guess she considered him ancient history."

"Until she saw the news last night. And then what? She ran? We should've found out whether any of her clothes were missing, and her purse."

He grunted. "Should've checked the bedroom."

"Okay, second possibility. She saw the news and called him. She's got the number committed to memory or whatever. They arranged to meet or to run together."

"And the third?"

The snow was picking up and as it melted against the windshield, the oncoming headlights dazzled my eyes.

"He came for her," I said. "He saw the news story and decided to eliminate the only witness to Leila's death."

CHAPTER 38

Except that she wasn't the only witness, as Moses pointed out. There were the two drivers, Tyrone Weeks and Zackery Lloyd. They hadn't witnessed the death, but they had seen the body.

"We'll have to let Zackery know to be on his guard," Moses said. "I doubt that Dr. Dave has the contacts inside to get to Tyrone. I'm still skeptical that he's the type to go bumping off witnesses, but better to be safe than sorry."

The Hyde Park condo looked exactly as we had left it an hour and a half before. The same lights were lit and the same faint sounds of a broadcast were audible. All our efforts to raise somebody inside resulted in the same response: none.

Moses brought out the gloves again and grasped the door handle. The door opened.

A bad sign.

Moses opened the door and walked in. He called out in a loud voice, "Mr. Bryson? Mr. Bryson?"

There was no response. I followed the sound of a television, louder now that we were inside, down the hall and into a small den off what looked to be an enormous living room. I recognized the voice before I saw the face, and then there he was, suit and tie and rumpled hair and all — Dan Rather on *48 Hours*. I pulled my sleeve down to cover my hand and switched off the television. Now the house was utterly silent.

"Are we searching?"

Moses shook his head. "Only for Bryson. Photographs in the living room match the description we have, so it's probably Bryce."

I followed him upstairs, where we checked two bedrooms and a bathroom.

"He seems to be a sales rep for a drug company, like Mildred heard," I said, holding up a printed canvas tote and a fistful of glossy brochures. "That could explain his lifestyle."

"You see any car keys?" Moses asked.

"No."

We went back downstairs and I found a set of car keys in the pocket of a man's overcoat hanging on the coat in the downstairs hall. I held them up for Moses to see. "Porsche."

"So, either he left on foot or he took a cab or—"

"Or somebody picked him up," I finished. "Not Sherman — her car was in the lot."

"I'll talk to Webster again and suggest that he come take a look around this place," Moses said. "But there's nothing else we can do."

So, we went home.

As Mildred had predicted, the snow continued all night and all day Friday. I did a little housekeeping, rewarded myself with a couple of hours of reading, and baked a cake in honor of Mildred's pending arrival and because I figured taxes would go better with cake. The schools must have declared a snow day because all day I heard the sounds of kids outside and occasionally caught a glimpse of them toting large pieces of cardboard or dragging sleds as they headed for the best sledding hill in the neighborhood. I sometimes heard the scraping sounds of snow shovels as a few eager beavers among my neighbors shoveled their walks.

In the late afternoon, Leon and his drum instructor, Hope Smith, surprised me with a visit.

"Happy snow day, M-miz Cat!" Leon said. "I can sh-shovel you walks for you t-t-tomorrow if you w-want me to. Won't be n-no charge, on account of we b-b-been using your b-basement."

"I'll have to ask Mel and Al," I told him. "They like to shovel snow."

I made hot chocolate and cut the cake and we sat in the kitchen, where Hope noticed Leila's notebook sitting open on the kitchen table.

"What's this?" she asked.

So I told her about Leila as she skimmed the pages. I even told her about the likely plagiarism of Leila's song "Angelina" by Wildfire.

"'Magdalena' — yeah, yeah, I know that song. Here it is. And she died at sixteen? God, that's so tragic. And these songs — they're incredible! I mean, they really are, Cat. Some of the lyrics are really haunting. I'd love to try and play them. I mean, if the band saw them, they would flip out! They're so feminist."

I caught my breath. Maybe there was a way to honor Leila's legacy.

"Maybe that can be arranged, Hope. Let me talk to the family."

"Would you do that? That would be so cool, if we could play some of Leila's songs. Too bad we don't have the music, just the chord progressions."

I thought of Ernie Iles, singing in his soft, breathy voice. Still, he'd got the tune right. Leila sang for him sometimes, he'd said. "I might be able to help with the music as well."

"Speaking of music, how are the drum lessons going?" I gave Leon an encouraging smile.

The two of them exchanged a look I couldn't interpret. "Actually, Cat, that's what we wanted to talk to you about," Hope said. She turned to Leon and nodded.

"See, we thinkin' m-maybe it ain't no f-f-future in it. I been tryin', b-b-but I just can't seem to g-get the rhythm right. Hope a real good teacher and all, and I b-been working hard, it ain't that. She say maybe it just ain't m-my, my — what that word, Hope?"

"Forte," Hope said.

"My for-tay," Leon repeated carefully.

"Well, I'm sorry to hear that, Leon," I said. "I know you had your heart set on becoming a drummer. But it's good to know what your strengths are. Everybody has strengths and weaknesses." God, I sounded like a motivational speaker.

"So maybe M-m-mr. Chaz can find s-somebody else want a drum set for free," Leon said magnanimously.

"Yeah, maybe he can."

"I been thinkin' maybe I like to try the t-t-trumpet next. You think M-moses will teach me, M-miz Cat?"

I got caught with my mouth open. Finally, I said, "You can ask him."

He nodded and stood up. "I got to go now. It's a rehearsal t-tonight at the Park."

Leon left and, on an impulse, I asked Hope if she would like to borrow Leila's notebook.

"Just a temporary loan," I said. "I'll need to take it back to the family."

I walked her to the door and praised her generosity in undertaking Leon's drum lessons.

"Oh, it's always fun to hang out with Leon. But it was frustrating, too, because he really did struggle."

"Is there any chance he could learn to play the trumpet? I'd be interested in your opinion."

"Hard to say. I mean, I don't think he realizes that his sense of rhythm is going to handicap him whatever instrument he plays. But who knows? He could have a kind of natural genius."

"At least he's got the Park. I guess this is his big night."

"Yeah, poor guy."

"Why do you say that? You don't think he's up to the job — this microphone placement business?"

"Oh, I think he's up to it, sure. But he says the electricians won't let him do it. One of them told him today that she'd set up the microphones and he shouldn't touch anything once they did. Now he's frustrated because Chaz told him to do it, so he thinks it's his responsibility. I'm sure he's on his way there now, checking to see that they're all in the right places."

"Why would the electricians get involved in microphone placement?" I said.

She shrugged, but my mind was racing ahead. Perle Electrical Contractors. I thought back to our first visit to the Park. A woman electrician with a pencil behind her ear and a pencil sketch on the bare wood of the stage. A name stitched over the pocket: Kathy. Kath. Katie.

"I have to go," I said and ran.

I grabbed my coat and car keys, zipping up the coat as I raced for the back door. I jammed my feet into boots, flung the door open, and stood still, dismayed.

In the dim evening light, the parking lot was an alien landscape of white with three white humps like breaching whales to mark where the cars were parked.

I stepped off the back steps and felt my boot sink.

I would have to run. I could run in the streets, which at least had been plowed. But how long would it take me? And would I slip and break my neck before I got there?

I had to try.

The snow had stopped now and all the kids had gone home to dinner. The neighborhood was quiet under its blanket of snow.

And then I heard the faint rhythmic clatter of a motorcycle. I began wading across the parking lot. I was only a few feet from the street when a slender black-clad alien pulled up to the curb, separated from the lot by a Himalaya of snow: Mildred.

"Leon's in danger!" I shouted to her. "Can you get me to the Northside Park on this thing?"

She nodded and reached out both arms to drag me the last foot and hoist me across the snow dam and onto the bike.

We took off. From what I could see, the side streets were just passable but there was no traffic. I didn't see much because my eyes were closed most of the time. I felt a few skids, but we managed to stay upright.

"Get me as close as you can to the back door," I shouted in her ear.

If Leon had unlocked it, maybe he'd left it open.

Then I was off the bike and pushing toward the back door of the theater, alarmed to see the confusion of footprints that had preceded me. The door slammed against the wall when I wrenched it open. I had already considered and rejected the idea of stealth. Let them think Leon's posse had arrived.

"Leon! Where are you?" I called. "Leon!"

I needed a weapon or shield, preferably both. I picked up a snow shovel by the back door and advanced. I was letting my eyes adjust to the low light as I moved slowly toward light ahead of me. Then I stopped to listen. From somewhere in the building came the sound of a staccato series of thumps.

Leon was here and he was alive. I knew he was alive because he was moving and making noise. I knew it was Leon because there was no rhythm to the thumps.

I stepped cautiously onto the stage, which was lit with a single spotlight.

"Katie!" I called. "Where are you? I know you're here."

"I'm here," a voice said behind me. I turned to see a figure in the shadows. After the glare of the spotlight, she was even harder to make out. "What are you doing here?"

"I'm here to find out what you're doing here. Where's Leon?"

"Oh, he's around. And I work here." I could see her more clearly now, wearing jeans, a T-shirt, and the same oversized shirt she had worn the last time I had seen her. Her hands were visible and empty.

"Leon said that you wouldn't let him touch the microphones. Why was that?"

She shrugged. "We had some last-minute adjustments to make. We wanted to set them up properly, and we didn't want him to screw things up."

"Let me rephrase." I was moving away from the spotlight. "What did you do to the microphones?"

"I don't know what you mean."

"Yes, you do. So, I'll repeat the question: what did you do to the microphones? Are they rigged to electrocute somebody?"

I saw her expression change, but I couldn't interpret the change. "It would be fitting if they were, don't you think? If Glass and his buddies went around seducing and impregnating underage girls, and especially if one of those girls died as a result, shouldn't they be held accountable for that death? Murder is a capital offense, isn't it?"

I had set myself up for an ethical debate I didn't want to have, especially since I agreed with her.

She reached behind her back and brought out a gun, which she aimed at me. She shrugged. "That's what I think, anyway."

I made an effort not to react. "What have you done with Sherman and Bryce?"

She grinned at me. "Wouldn't you like to know?"

"Are they dead?"

She considered a minute, as if choosing her favorite among several possible responses. "Wouldn't you like to know."

"Where's Matt?" I looked around, half expecting him to appear from the shadows with a second gun.

"You haven't worked that out yet? What kind of detective are you?"

The old me would have spoken my thoughts aloud and said, *I'm the detective who found your sister after nineteen years*. The new me — the one who was working on anger management — said nothing, a small victory in my professional development. I didn't know what would set her off, after all, and I didn't know how many players she was planning to take off the board. Plus, I couldn't tell from this distance what caliber pistol she was holding on me. I was holding a snow shovel.

"Matt's in hospice," she said at last, and her voice broke.

"What's wrong with him?"

"Non-Hodgkin's lymphoma. A lot of the helicopter pilots who sprayed Agent Orange in 'Nam got it. He doesn't have long."

"So, the urgency he ascribed to your mother's failing health was really about his."

"Hard to say who'll go first." She gestured with the gun. "Now, if you'll just step this way, Cat, I'll take you to see Leon."

Something flew through the air behind her and crashed stage left. She swung the gun toward the noise and Mildred rushed her, bringing something down on her wrist. I heard the gun hit the floor and dived for it. When I raised my head and the gun simultaneously, Mildred had Katie in a chokehold. Katie was taller than Mildred and must have outweighed her but seemed unable to break Mildred's grip.

"Cat, we need something to tie her with," Mildred said, as if remarking on the weather. "There's a pocketknife in my back pocket. If you'll cut some rope off those curtains and tie her, I'll hold a gun on her."

"Don't touch the microphones," I warned Mildred. "I think she's rigged them somehow."

In point of fact, there were two guns — the one I was holding and the one Mildred pulled out of her back waistband as soon as I approached Katie with a length of cord to tie her wrists.

We got her down from the stage and tied her to one of the few bolted-down theater seats in the audience. I unclipped a set of keys from her belt and handed them to Mildred. "Why don't you go look for Leon and a telephone? He probably knows where one is."

As soon as she was gone, Katie tried to recruit me for her team.

"Come on, Cat," she said. "You know they're all pigs, every last one of them. We don't even know for sure that Glass was the father. It could have been Jimmy Shoe. You want to know how I know? Because both of them screwed me, that's how. I was fourteen years old, and I wanted to live my sister's life. And you want to hear how that turned out? I met with that nurse — Nurse Wanda. And you know what she told me? I was too young for the procedure and too small. She considered me 'high risk' and she turned me down. And I spent the first half of my sophomore year in lockdown at this Catholic institution run by Nazi nuns. They wouldn't even tell me whether I had a girl or a boy."

I was appalled. But I also knew that I was a sucker for a sob story, and this one might not even be true. "I'm really sorry, Katie. I'm sorry for all of it — your sister's death and the impact it had on your life, Matt's condition, your mom's condition. All of it."

"Then let me do it. Let me accomplish this one last thing — for Leila. You can rat me out afterward, I'll even turn myself in. But let me get justice for Leila."

"Katie, your sister loved you. She wouldn't want you to ruin your life by committing murder."

Tears started to her eyes. "My life is already ruined. Let me ruin a few others and I'll die happy."

"Doesn't work that way, kid. I'm sorry, but it doesn't."

I heard Leon's voice, raised in indignation.

I consoled myself with the thought that I was doing what Leila would have wanted me to do.

CHAPTER 39

There was no rehearsal that night at the Northside Park. Chaz showed up shortly after the confrontation with Katie and arranged for another electrician, a friend of Mel's, to examine the microphones and sound equipment. The electrician confirmed that they were wired to electrocute anyone who handled them, although the circuit hadn't yet been closed because the cord that powered it hadn't yet been plugged in. So, the rehearsal could have gone on, but Chaz wasn't willing to do anything until all of the building's circuitry had been examined. Katie emphasized that she didn't hold Chaz responsible for her sister's death, but he wisely chose to proceed with caution.

We all spent time soothing Leon's ruffled feelings, including Moses, when he arrived, but I was grateful to Katie for choosing to lock him up rather than harming him, and told her so.

"Who would hurt Leon?" she said. "Nobody would hurt Leon."

She refused to give us any information on Wanda Sherman and David Bryce, although she didn't deny abducting them.

"But how did you even know about them?"

She shrugged. "You have your sources, I have mine. I'm an electrician with a brother who's an ex-cop."

"But—" I was struggling to put my finger on the source of my uneasiness. She could have found the property owner of the abortion house, but maybe she didn't need that as long as she had the address. Her contacts could probably tell her whose name was on the electric bill for that address in August of 1969 and maybe even current addresses for Sherman and Bryson through their electric bills. But how did she know the address? By following us, yes, but did that mean she had us under surveillance all the time? We hadn't reached Matt to tell him when we were going to look for the Westwood house, and he didn't have an answering machine.

And suddenly, I knew. It was all about electronics.

"You tapped my phone," I said.

She shrugged. "Not hard to do, and you wouldn't talk to me, remember?"

I shook my head. "You tapped my phone before I told you I could only report to Matt."

She shrugged again.

"You were in my apartment?" I felt a frisson of fear as I pictured this crazy woman around the cats.

"Didn't need to be." I could hear the pride in her voice. "Easier to do it from the pole. That way, I could get Moses's phone as well."

I thought about how much important information we had passed back and forth on the phone, especially while Moses had been out of town, and winced.

But if she was eager to impress us with her cleverness and skill, she remained stubbornly silent on the whereabouts of her two abductees. It was Matt who suggested that the police check a small cabin on some property he owned in Brown County when Moses and Lieutenant Webster visited him in hospice later that night. I anticipated a return engagement for Polly the cadaver dog, but the two were found gagged and back-to-back, handcuffed to a support beam. They were in poor condition, but alive. Both had suffered contusions on the backs of their heads that suggested they'd been struck — probably by a pistol butt, Moses and I speculated.

"I reckon she got them as far as the car — or more likely, a Perle Electric van — by holding a gun on them, then knocked them out," Moses said. "That's what I'd do."

"She's got an electrician's muscles," I observed. "I guess she's used to lifting heavy cables."

"And probably used to figuring out how to lift the stuff she doesn't have the strength for."

After they were found, Katie agreed to an interview with me, and only me, down at the jail. She hadn't been granted bail yet, despite the best efforts of the Perle lawyers and the serious health conditions of two family members. There were no lawyers present at our interview. She was wearing a bright orange shirt with "Inmate" on the back and khaki pants. We sat in a bare room with stained and faded walls, a scarred wooden table and two wooden chairs, the last three items bolted to the floor.

"I didn't even think you liked me," I told her.

"I don't. But you did find out what happened to my sister."

"And so you must have known that her death was an accident. Did you ask Sherman and Bryce what happened that night?"

"Oh, sure, they were so eager to explain how they weren't responsible for Leila's death, how she must've had a reaction to the anesthetic, how they couldn't explain it, how fast it all happened." Her voice was growing hoarse and she cleared her throat. Her eyes glinted with tears.

"And even if her death was accidental, you were going to hold them responsible for it?"

"They could've saved her!" she said fiercely. "They could've saved her and they just let her die!"

"You don't know that."

"I know. The only thing they were interested in was saving their own goddamned skins! And then they buried her in a hole in the back yard like a dog."

"So, what was your plan? Were you planning to starve them to death?"

325

She slumped back in her chair. "I hadn't decided. You'd think I'd know, after all that time, right? I'd spent years fantasizing what I would do when I caught up with my sister's killers, and then when it happened, I couldn't make up my mind. There were just so many appealing possibilities."

"But you didn't have the same problem with Wildfire," I pointed out.

She smiled. "No. As soon as I knew what those bastards had done—"

"But not all of them."

"They all stole her song — you found that out. And there was no way to know whether Glass or Shoemaker was responsible for the abortion. I know for sure that Glass landed me in a home for unwed mothers, but they all helped him do it. None of them stopped him. They all had to die. Looking back, I know I should have made them suffer more, but I thought electrocution would be a more fitting tribute to Leila, don't you think?"

"I think a more fitting tribute would be to get Leila recognized as the author of 'Angelina' and to make those bastards pay back royalties."

She huffed. "Yeah, right. What are the chances of that happening?"

"Maybe better than you think."

Afterward, I reported to Moses, who in turn reported on his conversation with Matt.

"He didn't seem surprised when I told him what his sister had been up to," Moses told me, sitting at the kitchen table. "But he might be beyond surprise, Cat, you know what I mean? 'One foot in the grave' is how I'd describe it. But then, they've got him shot full of painkillers, too, so it's hard to tell if he feels anything at this stage. He thanked me, though, for finding out what had happened to Leila and for successfully completing the assignment so quickly. He particularly wanted me to thank you as well. He said he knew how hard you'd worked on the case."

I felt myself tearing up and so focused on stirring the ice in my gin and tonic with a finger and then licking it.

"He's right, Cat. You're a good detective. You worked hard on this case and we wouldn't have solved it without you."

"And Mildred."

He smiled. "And Mildred."

CHAPTER 40

"We didn't kill that girl."

I'd gone to visit Nurse Wanda Sherman in the hospital where she was being treated, mostly for dehydration as well as for other effects of her captivity. Nobody ever looks good in a hospital bed, and she was no exception. Her lips were cracked and her voice was hoarse, but she was sitting up in bed. Whenever she attempted a gesture, she seemed to find her arms too heavy to lift. Now she made an attempt to fluff up her frizzy light-brown hair but the effort seemed too much for her and likely would have failed anyway.

Bryce/Bryson had already lawyered up and refused to speak to us, but Nurse Wanda had agreed to see me on my own, apparently out of gratitude for saving her life.

"We'd done dozens of successful surgeries over a period of maybe three years — I imagine we'd done over a hundred — and we'd never encountered a situation we couldn't handle before. Well, I should say twice we'd had to take a patient to the ER, but do you realize what an amazing record that is? I know surgeons in this hospital who couldn't match it. And then along comes this girl — Leila Perle. And in the middle of the procedure, she stops breathing, her blood pressure drops, her pulse disappears, and she's dead within five minutes."

She made a feeble gesture in the direction of her water glass, and I retrieved it from the bedside table and handed it to her, angling the straw in her direction. I knew that her strength — and more importantly, her voice — could give out at any minute, so I cut her off.

"Why did you decide to bury the body? Why not drop her off somewhere — a hospital parking lot, say — so that she could be identified and her family told?"

"I didn't have anything to do with the burial," she said, choking a little in her eagerness to correct me. "I wanted to do exactly what you said. But we knew who her father was, and David was afraid that there would be an investigation that would eventually lead to us. Perle had the money and the influence to badger the police and fund a huge private investigation if the police didn't satisfy him. We were always very careful, of course, but we were afraid of Perle."

She shifted uncomfortably in the bed and handed back the water glass. Her eyes were starting to droop.

"So you decided to hire another girl to impersonate Leila on the bus."

"I did that, yes. It wasn't something I'd planned, but I had meetings with prospective patients the next day. I couldn't just not show up, David said that we had to behave as normally as possible. And there was this girl who looked so much like Leila, it — well, it gave me the shivers. Maybe that was partly imagination, but—"

She shivered now and closed her eyes. "As she talked about wanting to go to San Francisco, this idea formed in my head. David was so afraid of Perle, what if we gave the police another person to follow? Leila had been planning to go to Woodstock that day. What if we sent her at least part of the way on the bus? And this other girl — I forget her name now — she was happy to do it because she was being well paid." She sighed. "I had to convince David that it was the best thing to do, but I finally brought him around, so I met her at the bus station with a ticket to Cleveland and Leila's jewelry."

"And you walked away," I said, but not accusingly. "You gave up the house in Westwood and moved on."

She nodded.

"But once, some time afterward, the second girl — Cassandra — spoke to you on the street because she recognized you and wanted to return Leila's jewelry."

She nodded again. "She gave me a pretty bad scare. But I just kept saying she was mistaken. She didn't try to follow me when I got on my bus." She sighed. "By then, David and I had split up and I thought the past was behind me. But it never really works like that, does it?" Her voice had dropped to a whisper and a tear trickled down her cheek, though whether out of pity for herself or for Leila, I wasn't sure.

"And then that woman came to the door and held a gun on me and forced me into this van and knocked me out and took me to that cabin. Next thing I know, I'm handcuffed back-to-back with David. It looked like we were finally going to be called to account. She would've killed us, wouldn't she?"

"I think so, yes."

"He kept trying to convince her that it wasn't our fault, but I know crazy when I see it, and he might've saved his breath. But he was always so confident, so—"

Her voice was barely audible and her eyes closed and stayed closed.

I left quietly.

Matt died two days later, and his mother, Mrs. Perle, died the day after that. Katie, who was facing charges of assault and attempted homicide, was finally out on bail with an ankle monitor and attended the joint funeral. The Perles had decided to include Leila in the service as well, even though her remains had not yet been released to them for burial. Moses, Mildred, and I sat in the back. Mildred and I held sopping handkerchiefs to our eyes and tried to blow our noses as quietly as possible.

A week after that, Moses knocked on my door to tell me that Bony Brissard in the coroner's office wanted to see us.

"I wonder if he's going to give us a cause of death after all. Do you think he might? And what would that mean? Do you think he's found signs of trauma on the bones? Or a broken hyoid? That would mean strangulation. Sherman and Bryce told Webster that Leila died on the operating table for no apparent reason, but they could be lying. Moses, what if Leila panicked and became hysterical and one of them strangled her to shut her up?"

"Cat, you know as much as I do," Moses said.

"I know I don't want to see her bones," I said, staring out the windshield. "But I guess I'll have to, after all."

But there were no bones in sight when we were ushered into the office of Buster "Bony" Brissard, Assistant Coroner. Bony looked like a stoop-shouldered Orville Redenbacher and he was normally more energetic than you'd think a coroner could be, but today his face was grave. He found two chairs for us to sit on and then passed us a small box about the size of a shoebox. Moses lifted the lid and we peered inside. We saw a small plastic baggie, ripped and muddy, with some kind of white residue inside.

"That was probably in her pocket," Bony said. "They dressed her in her own clothes before burying her."

"What is it?" I asked.

"Diazepam."

When I looked at Moses, he said, "Valium."

"Oh, shit."

"It was a popular tranquilizer in the '60s," Bony said. "Still is. Mother's little helper. Not used much in abortions, and Bryce said he never used it, for what that's worth. You know anybody in the Perle household who might have had a prescription?"

We nodded in unison.

"Mother still alive?"

"Just died," Moses said.

He nodded, his hands folded in his lap. "Good. Just as well. The official cause of death will still be listed as 'unknown,' you understand. The doctor and nurse both insist that the death was sudden and unexpected — respiratory distress, sudden decline in blood pressure, then cardiac arrest. But if the kid helped herself to some of her mother's Valium shortly before she was sedated for the procedure, cardiac arrest would be one potential outcome."

"But what if they had taken her to an emergency room or called an ambulance?"

He shook his head. "Nothing to do at this point but speculate. We can't even say for sure that she took the Valium. If she did take it, we don't know how much." He nodded at the baggie. "There's maybe three tablets worth of residue in there, but we have no way of knowing how many were there to begin with. The tablets are tiny. Easy to talk yourself into taking more. The doctor and nurse say they performed CPR, and I'm sure they did. We just can't say whether anything would have made a difference."

"You going to tell the family?" Moses asked.

"Not planning to. You know a reason I should?"

"Nope." After a pause, he added, "Webster?"

"You can tell him. He'll call me if he wants more information."

Outside the snow had melted and the sun was shining in a clear blue sky. Lenten roses bloomed next to the parking lot, their subdued pastels camouflaging them against the winter-weary grass.

"Do you think Leila is finally finished with us?" I asked Moses.

"I reckon she is, Cat," he said.

CHAPTER 41

But we weren't quite finished with Leila. One Sunday evening in early April, we attended a special event at Northside Park. The date was April 10th, five days before the income tax filing deadline, but I was serene, my life calm as a limpid pool under a cloudless sky. Thanks to Mildred, I had filed my taxes a month ago.

The event was a tribute to Leila, headlined by Hope's band and featuring three bands and two solo artists singing Leila's music. All the remaining Perles were there, including Katie, who remained out on bail while her case was making its slow way through the legal system. Frank and Mary seemed disconcerted by the seating arrangements, but Tim had shamed them into leaving the scanty theater seats for people who were truly handicapped, and they gave in and sat on the floor. Chaz and Vic insisted that three of the theater seats were being saved for Moses, Mildred, and me, but we declined because Mildred didn't need one and Moses was offended by the idea that he might need one and I was with them and outvoted. At least I was well enough informed to arrive early and snag a coveted space against the wall for back support.

As the place filled up, I noticed that many, if not most, of the celebrants had dressed in full sixties regalia, like the attendees at our Woodstock gathering. Franny arrived wearing one of her customary long skirts and peasant blouses, but she was sporting love beads and a flower in her hair for the occasion. I was glad to see Ernie Iles present, though I hoped that the occasion would be sufficiently memorable to attendees lacking his extraordinary memory skills. Ernie had his own fan club, I saw, and some of them induced him to reprise his cry from his days as a hawker of the *Independent Eye* on the sidewalks of Corryville and Northside. He was quite the showman. Mary Grace introduced me to some of Leila's other school friends. Three of Leila's former coworkers — Gigi Beck, Joyce Hardcastle, and Linda Monniter — came in together, though in short order I saw Gigi leave with Marty Yeager, and I suspected they'd gone outside for a smoke.

There was a strong scent of patchouli in the air that would have annoyed Leila, but if she was among us, she was polite enough not to manifest her disapproval.

Mildred, who had painted flowers on her motorcycle helmet for the occasion, showed me a line in the program: *with special guest appearance by percussionist Leon Jakes.*

I laughed and nodded. "It's a lot of responsibility. He's the only male on the bill."

That meant that the rest of the Jakes clan was here and I soon spotted them, Leon's four brothers towering over most of the crowd and their mother.

Walt Hitchens arrived just as the program was starting. He made eye contact and gave me the thumbs-up, then found a space on the floor and lowered himself awkwardly, grimacing.

The music was beautiful, moving and powerful with lyrics that tugged at your heart. You could tell that all the performers took seriously their responsibility to pay tribute to Leila. The sheer number of songs reminded me how prolific she'd been — how much she had accomplished in her short life. Many of them had been reconstructed from Ernie's memories, but some had required new compositions, and it was a tribute to the composers that you couldn't tell which were which. Even Leon's performance was letter-perfect; at a nod from Hope, he would ring a bell or tap a cymbal or even, in one breathtaking moment, provide a drumroll. I doubted that Leila had imagined any of these effects when she had written her songs, but I suspected that she was pleased with them.

The final song of the evening was "Angelina." Most of the people in the audience knew that the Perles were suing Adam Glass over the rights to this song, and that Glass was threatening a countersuit if they included it on the program tonight. The audience grew quiet as the screen behind the stage lit up with a still image of Leila, playing her guitar and singing, and the room was filled with Leila's beautiful, clear voice.

"An-gelina,
I can see ya,
Singin' your blues.
An-gelina,
It's so hard to be ya,
'Cause you're too old for innocence,
And too young to choose."

The crowd had slowly gotten to its feet. When the tape ended, low lights came up on stage as Hope's band began playing and Hope sang the lead. When she reached the chorus again, a second voice joined in — a woman from one of the other bands, singing harmony. On the third chorus, several other voices joined in and Hope's band was joined by all the musicians who had performed. This ensemble included Leon, who made no contribution until the song had finished. Then he sounded a bell three times, letting each note reverberate through the space before adding a second, then a third.

When the final note died away, there was a profound silence that seemed to stretch on and on. At last, someone started the applause.

THE END

ACKNOWLEDGMENTS

Many, many thanks to my first readers: Carol Blum, Andrea Tuttle Kornbluh, John Kornbluh, Joe Musser, Louise Musser, Sharon Schrader, and Marty Schwartz, as well as my editor, Lauren Dooley, and copyeditor, Sarah Bauer. They make my books better. Thanks also to music consultants Michael Grossinger and Jerry Powell, and to motorcycle consultants Toby Weiss and Doug Johnstone.

THE JOFFE BOOKS STORY

We began in 2014 when Jasper agreed to publish his mum's much-rejected romance novel and it became a bestseller.

Since then we've grown into the largest independent publisher in the UK. We're extremely proud to publish some of the very best writers in the world, including Joy Ellis, Faith Martin, Caro Ramsay, Helen Forrester, Simon Brett and Robert Goddard. Everyone at Joffe Books loves reading and we never forget that it all begins with the magic of an author telling a story.

We are proud to publish talented first-time authors, as well as established writers whose books we love introducing to a new generation of readers.

We won Trade Publisher of the Year at the Independent Publishing Awards in 2023 and Best Publisher Award in 2024 at the People's Book Prize. We have been shortlisted for Independent Publisher of the Year at the British Book Awards for the last five years, and were shortlisted for the Diversity and Inclusivity Award at the 2022 Independent Publishing Awards. In 2023 we were shortlisted for Publisher of the Year at the RNA Industry Awards, and in 2024 we were shortlisted at the CWA Daggers for the Best Crime and Mystery Publisher.

We built this company with your help, and we love to hear from you, so please email us about absolutely anything bookish at feedback@joffebooks.com.

If you want to receive free books every Friday and hear about all our new releases, join our mailing list here: www.joffebooks.com/freebooks.

And when you tell your friends about us, just remember: it's pronounced Joffe as in coffee or toffee!

9 781805 733072